Almasi

Aka
Glock Mommy
By
Dartanya A. Williams Sr.
Second Edition

Copyright © 2019 by Dartanya A. Williams Sr.
All rights reserved. This book or any portion thereof
may not be reproduced or used in any manner whatsoever
without the express written permission of the publisher
except for the use of brief quotations in a book review.
Printed in the United States of America
First Printing, 2019
ISBN
Ni Jamba La Publishing
Philadelphia, PA 19138
www.dartanyaawilliamssr.com

Author's Note: I used Ebonics to heighten the character's speech and tone. Certain words are spelled differently because in the world of Almasi they speak differently.

RIGHT OUT OF THE GUTTER!

Here right now in my darkest hour while I'm in Philadelphia FDC Federal Detention center I'm writing down the story of my life for the very first time. I was inspired by the warden talking shit to me one day. I guess everyone does this once there in the belly of the beast. It looks like I will spend the rest of my life behind bars. I've been really thinking about doing this right after my arraignment. My Son Little Boom is 20 years old now and my man Jay Black was there to support me looking on with sad eyes knowing my fate. Yet, with my lawyer by my side, James Campbell but, I call him Jimmy". I stood strong and put on that I don't give a fuck look on my face while smirking at them devil motherfuckers. Months later the asshole prosecutor with a long funny looking nose that look like Jimmy Durante from them old corny ass movies. Then the gray hair faggot ass judge who looks just like Raymond Burr from the TV show, Iron side. I was looking at an 848 A & 848 B charge I don't know that much about the law" but I know that's a life sentence right from the fucking door!

Some Kingpin status shit everybody in the streets and in the criminal justice system are saying, "you might as well stick a fork in my ass because I'm done!" I'm not going to lie or front like it didn't shake me down to my core at first. I would not give any of them crackers the fucking satisfaction of seeing me crying or looking sad.

After all the shit that went down and how I was dealt a fucked-up hand in life there was no room for tears. The only thing I could do was to play it the best way I know how like the old folks say, “when life gives you lemons you make lemonade with the quickness.” I was not going to hang my head right now I looked them right in the eyes and took it like a porn star getting fucked under the bright lights on the set with no fucking Vaseline. What they don’t know a little birdie just told me that he’s going help me take all of them down. In this cesspool of a system that want to cast judgment down on me when all of them are doing the exact same thing I’m doing. Some of them doing the same shit and even worse than anything there charging me wit. There fucking low lives dragging me out my crib in the middle of the night doing the perpetrator walk with TV cameras rolling for all of white America to be scared out their fucking mines.

What fucks me up is the Warden William Joseph Simmons this bitch made motherfucker with the big ass spooky eyes and gray hair old goat calls me into his office with his eyes on fire yelling at me with spit flying out his rotten yellow teeth mouth giving me that fire and brim stone horse shit. That I’m not special speech because I have 457 requests for interviews for me and he was not going to turn his prison into a celebrity criminal reality show!

“So, the Black God Mommy aka Glock Mommy shit or whatever you fucking called yourself on the streets will fucking end right here and now. He’s denying all media request and I will remain in the hole the whole time while I’m here until my trial starts.”

He said, “I suggest you write a book because you’ll have a lot of fucking time to write it and I will give you plenty of paper and pens to do it. So, you can write down all of the fucked up atrocious things you did in your life.”

He continued, “You’ll be about 50 something when I’m done with it. You will have no outside contact with the rest of the world for a very long time. The only person you can talk to is your lawyer!”

He just didn't know that put a spark under my ass to really write my book about my life. When it is finished, I bet he is not going to like what I'll have in it for sure it's going to surprise and shock the world when I'm done with it! So, after all the big headlines and all the sensationalize drama they were all saying and writing about me and my peoples to sell more papers and magazines. All the bullshit those devils been talking about me and my crew like a dog in heat. Like we were some kind of subhuman or some kind of fucking low life animals. Out here in the concrete jungle they created in the first place. I know my writing is not going to be a New York Times best seller novel like Terry McMillan or any deep poetic heart felt words like Toni Morrison. I will sure enough give it my best fucking shot at it and tell my truth from the depts of my soul.

Sure, nuff tell it my way, raw Dawg without the fucking bag and tell the world or anybody who would really listen. How my life really was like from my point of view right from the gutter. Not none of the horse shit they just made up in the papers portraying me and my friends I call my family. As if we were some kind of soulless trigger-happy niggas and some blood thirsty monsters who let loose on the whole city for no reason. As if we were preying on people selling drugs and killing people for no reason. After two months inside this shithole of a place everyone and their mother becomes a fucking philosopher and a writer of some kind so here it goes.

This is for all you Kingpins dope dealers, real killers and big money-making hoes! I'm starting my story with a tragic event that forced me deeper into the game when I was 17 years old. Its July of 1996, I lived in the heart of the foul ultraviolet chasm known as the ghetto located in Killadelphia Pistolvania aka Philadelphia, Pennsylvania. My hometown I love to this very day. I was born and raised in South Philly.

I was staying inside of a ran down red brick row house in the middle of 1500 block on Ringgold street. I found out later on after rolling with the gang why I was living there in the first place.

Now in 2017, I'm 37 years old. I have seen and done it all but what fucks me up about the whole thing is my entire life was one big fucking lie. I never knew who my father was and the woman who was supposed to be my mother did not know who the fuck he was neither. She was having sex with so many men in all the bars and clubs in South Philly. She could not narrow it down to who it was.

Plus, she stayed so fucked up and high all the time she would not know who my father was from Dick's hat band. What's fucked up about the whole thing is she would not know who my father was if she tripped over his ass in a crowded bar at the first of the month. I will not blame that on the twisted road I took to get where I'm right now. I can live with all the choices I made in this life. I don't have no fucking regrets on what I did and what I had to do to survive in the mean vicious cold streets of Philly.

Most people in my position would have gave up or just folded under the pressure, but not me. I really thrive under any kind of pressure that came my way. I took the bull by the Gawd dam horns and I'd road that bitch like a fucking bucking bronco like I was Sally Star! I beat incredible odds to get where I'm at now. I'd flip the script right quick on all the motherfuckers who counted me out as a poor and uneducated black bitch. To the world I'm just another statistic in the slums of the ghetto, but any who.

The house I lived in had a real funky stench from all the forty bottles scattered along the floor, overfilled ash trays with cigarette butts and old cocaine bags, different colors plastic crack vials and the caps on the floor. Dirty clothing laying around in big funky piles and I had to clean this shit up all the time by myself. Sometimes I could not keep up with my so-called mother fucking the house up after she have her company over getting high. Days of tricking with niggas in the living room almost every night. I'd felt trapped and a shame of the way we were living. I had only a few friends like Shamika, La-Nesa, Big Kim, and Queisha who were my road Dawgs.

I met them outside all the time because only my room was the cleanest place in the whole fucking house. I hated walking through the house to get to my room. After she was done, I had to clean up all her fucking mess she made. She used to say all the time she was doing what she was doing to keep the lights on in the house and a roof over our heads. I knew she was doing all that shit to keep her drug habit flowing and nothing else. I had to do all the cooking to make sure my little sister ate, or we would have not had anything to eat at all. She would spend up all the food stamps for drugs. So, I'd use to hold on to most of them, so we can eat from week to week. She did not fuck wit me after a while knowing I was responsible.

My mother leaned on me a lot to take care of the house and my little sister. I know if it was not for me the system would have been took me and my sister Robin. Then we would both be in the fucked up foster care system for sure. The house we lived in had a dull white paint peeling off the walls and roaches crawling all over the place. You would see one every five minutes running past you like cars running up and down like 95 going North. But once I started making money, I took care of all that shit. I'd sprayed, cleaned and painted the whole the house by myself.

Good thing I did because her social worker came to the house the next week checking out the whole house. The crack head who posed as my mother for so many years Dotty Miller was 32 years old at the time. She's a light skin woman a lot of men found her an attractive woman in spite of her being hooked on drugs. I could not see it she was all right looking to me but all I saw was a Trick Mommy bitch. It was just that niggas like fucking with light skin hoes with a fat ass when they got high. All the drugs she took never affected her looks yet now but she's getting worse as time goes by.

Once I became a teenager my name was changed from Sharonda Miller my government name to the streets calling me Glock Mommy or Almasi which means Diamond in Swahili. Nokey Blaze gave me that name when I was 17 years old and gave me a whole new way of life as well. When I left home for good and I never looked the fuck back. I was selling a little drug just crack but was mostly staying there to be looking out for my baby sister Robin. If I was only thinking of myself, I would have jetted a long time ago. My mother would not have gotten to me like she did.

I was making some good money with my little ruff neck crew. It was Me Shamika, Big Kim, Jagger, Tamika and Little Row-Row. I call my self-looking out for the family buying food and helping with the rent and bills. She knew where the money was coming from. Once I made a little change selling crack, she did not give a fuck just as long as it was helping her sorry ass out. I had to hide and lock my money from this junkie bitch. I never brought drugs home and she knew that too. So, I felt more grown helping out around the house and fixing the place up with the money I was making in the streets. I found out that was one of my biggest mistakes in my life. I had no way out living with this crazy ass drughead bitch. I found out more about Dotty fucked up ass, she suffered from depression and low self-esteem all her life. Her Stepfather Big Frank Miles use to beat the shit out of her almost three or four time a week when he was high. My grandmother Miss Glenda stayed drunk and high all the time.

While Frank was having his way with her doing every sex act under the sun with her. My grandmother was so high off coke she felt powerless to stop him. Big Frank called her all kinds of whores and bitches abusing and raping Dotty every chance he got while my grandmother Glenda was somewhere all fucked up in the dope spot somewhere. What can I say mother like daughter with all her demons coming to haunt her? She took it all out on me all the time driving me fucking crazy.

I should be on drugs by now with all the bullshit she took me through. It was my aunt Lisa who told me about Big Frank abusing my mother. Her mother Glenda knew what was going on the whole time and she never said a Gawd damn word about it. When Dotty found out her mother knew about it while listening to the two of them talk about it outside of her bedroom door one night she was so hurt. Yet, she did that same shit too me with some drug dealing low-life niggas Dotty was getting high with. She ran out of money again smoking up all their product and they did not want to trick wit her anymore. I heard them speaking loudly and they said, "We're tired of her dried-up pussy and she don't suck Dick right once she gets high."

One night I did not know she would stoop so fucking low to put them niggas on me. What kind of mother would do that shit to her daughter that stayed in my mind for a very long time? I can't lie I still have nightmares about what happen to me to this day. I used to feel sorry for that crack head ass bitch of a mother when I found out all about all the shit that happen to her in her life. I have no heart or love for her because she allowed history to repeat itself.

Dotty like me never knew or found out about who her real father was. She found out his name was Nick thinking he abandoned them, but he was killed in a bar fight in North Philly. He beat this guy up really good over some drugs he sold him that was fake. The dude was in a gang from 17th & Jefferson street his name was Black Lou. A crazy ass hood low life drug head killer came back to the bar. At Board & Girard street with his crew of drug attic Thugs niggas. All of the two-bit goons beat Nick to death killing him outside the bar. They stomped him bloody on the curve and they all fled. No one said anything to the police when they arrived on the scene. By Nick never having any ID on him he was a John Doe in the morgue for over six months. Before he was buried in potter's field in an unmarked grave. Her sister's Lisa, Jovita and Arianna ran away from home after Big Frank raped them as well. But two years later Big Frank mysteriously was killed being stabbed all over his body 67 times in the head in a known drug house at 15th and Norris street.

I know my mother did it, but I never said a word about it. I know she had help from the same women he raped, but he had it coming to him. The week before he died, he came to Dotty's house with over 50 vials of crack he stole from some of the corner boys stash in North Philly.

He quickly jumped in his beat up dark blue pickup truck and came to our house showing her the drugs. After she seen how much shit he had on him she let him in the crib. So, she can get her smoke on with him right after they both got all fucked up high. He attacked and he raped her. I was only 13 years old at the time when this happen, he beat and raped my so-called mother so brutally.

He did not come after me. I went in my room and locked the door shaking in deep fear until he was gone from the house. I was shaken up and confused because he was the only grandfather I ever knew. That fucked my head up for a long time. Later on, when I got heavier into the game me and my aunt Lisa linked up doing business together. That's not even related to me I found out later on in my life. But that bitch Dotty kept all this bad shit to herself and she never told a soul about this. She did not report it to the police because of all the drugs she had and sold in the house letting some of the local young thug crack dealers sell out of our house. All the time so she can get high that's why she let Big Frank in the house in the first place, so she would not fuck up some the young boys stash. She had to trick wit them as well when they felt like it, she was sucking a few dicks from time to time for payment on what she fucked up when she smokes too much of their product. But after a while the young dangerous men got tired of tricking with my so-called mother Dotty. She did all the sex act half-hearted on purpose, so they just give up trying to get there shit off on her. It was like fucking somebody dead one of them said. They did not want no dead ass shot of pussy or a bull shit blow job from a crack head whore. She did all the time and she got away wit it, but they all got hip to her game. They wanted some young fresh pussy so one night she let the wild cocky men run up in my room. They bum rush my bedroom and I had my door locked that night my so-called mother used a coat hanger to take the latch off my door to let them into my room. They busted into my bedroom and the four men came in there and rape me and Dotty was the one standing outside of my door watching. They ran inside and jumped on me while I was half sleep. It happened so fast I'd screamed my head off and I'd was fighting them back pushing and kicking them off of me as there jumping on me. I was fighting with all my might when I was fully awaking. I was in the middle of the worse nightmare of my life. They beat me down hard leaving me in a daze. All the blows to my head made me lightheaded. It made my sight really burry too and I was getting tired of fighting so many of them all at the same time. They stuck a sock in my mouth and tried to tape it to my face with the duct tape to muffle the sounds of me yelling and shouting. They could not get the duct tape around my mouth because I kept biting their fingers. I tried to bite them the fuck off their hands for real, so they just held the sock to my mouth holding me down. Hitting me everywhere on my body, face, my stomach, my ribs and my chest. Even with them overpowering me I still was fighting back.

With them holding the sock to my mouth while I was wiggling back and forth and moving my head around. And I was in so much agonizing pain I was crying and the more I cried the more they would beat me. Laughing, giggling and yelling out loud saying, "we got you tonight, bitch!" Yeah were all fucking your fine dark brown ass tonight you are a fucking whore! They kept beating on me and they held my legs open for one another to get on top of me. They turned me over to fuck me from the back. They all were smacking me on my ass really hard yelling, "damn man she got a really nice fat ass too look the way it jiggles when I smack it!" Then they were sticking their fingers in my ass hole shoving it in my ass really hard and inside my pussy with two and three fingers. In and out really clumsy hard and super ruff hurting me like I was a piece of raw meat. Saying look at that deep pink fresh pussy meat we got here boys! I'd never felt pain like this before never in my life I pleaded with them to stop.

I was trying to shout and scream with the sock in my mouth, but they just kept laughing louder smacking me on my ass still finger fucking me and beating me. For their sick twisted enjoyment. I could not take it any more of the pain I'd thought I was going to lose my mind they had me pushed down face down on my own bed. I could not get loose I kept trying really hard, but I could not get out of their tight grip. They had a hold on me as they took turns fucking me hard with three of them holding me down on my bed. The other was one having sex with me ripping my insides up. They all were yelling and cheering each other on like it was a sick twisted football game or something. They were really strong too they turn me over to the front holding my legs open really hard for the next guy to get on top of me. They all were stoking hard with their manhood inside of me the pain was so bad I was thinking my heart would pop out of my fucking chest. They were yelling loud and talking shit to me the whole time violating me saying, "you know you like this shit your black ass bitch!"

All I kept hearing, "Yeah were going to fuck your ass really good before we go!"

The other voice barked, "Yeah were tired of your mother's old dried up pussy and it smells really bad too." They smell like weed and beer. The musky smell from their bodies the smell filled the whole room. It was making me sick with disgust and anger. They were all yelling having their fun with me this just made me more upset. I was thinking to myself if they try to stick their dick in my mouth, I will bite it the fuck off for real. But they did not try that shit I just wanted this to stop there really were hurting me there tearing my inside up ramming their funky ass Dick's into me really hard and fast. Every one of them being so fucking ruff like there fucking wild animals. I was still fighting them every step of the way. I would not give up, but they overpowered me at every fucking turn beating me more. They hurt me bad I was in so much excruciating pain after each one of them penetrating me one by one. I wanted to die right then I ask God to kill me right now! I didn't want to live any more after this.

I was drained but I'd was still trying to fight them back to make them stop abusing me. That just made them more upset beating on me I blacked out a couple times. It seems like it would not end in a sweaty painful blur. They beat on me like I was some kind of fuck doll or something. Like I was not real to them this was all a game to them. They all were laughing loud in my face this was the most humiliating day of my life. I felt so dirty and used up I could never forget their faces as long as I live. I knew one day I was going to get their ass back and I never killed nobody at this point in my life, but right after that I knew I could kill every last one of them motherfuckers!

I would never give it a second thought. I knew deep down inside of me I was going to kill all four of them one day and I would not rest until I made that shit happen. These motherfuckers made so much noise they woke up my baby sister Robin. She was only 8 at the time wondering what's was going on. My lousy ass fake mother Dotty quickly stop her at the door from coming in the room and seeing what they did to me. My sister could tell something had happen to me. She was yelling at the top of her lungs, "where is Sharonda, Mommy!"

For the first time that night the men who raped me got quiet by a little 8-year-old girl. All of them quickly leaving the room then running out of the front door laughing. Their snickering really cut me deep down into my soul. I think right then and there my soul died. I prayed to Gawd for vengeance holding the sock they held up to my mouth in my hand squeezing it hard trying to hold back the tears.

What was really fucked up little Robin seen all of them before they all ran out of the room. She knew something happen she did not know what doe, but she could feel something just was not right. My ass hole bitch for a mother could not hold her any more wiggling out of her hands running into the room towards me. I had to cover myself up with a sheet I took off the bed when she ran to me. When she looked in my face, I was so embarrassed even doe she did not know what happen to me. I put on a painful smile, but it was so hard for me to do it, but I did it for her. I did not want her to lose her childhood so early in her life. Like I had to do in this same house seeing my drug head mother sucking three niggas dicks for four caps of crack. Robin looking up at me with her sweet little soft voice and said, "are you all right, Sharonda?"

She touches my sweaty face looking at me with them deep brown innocent eyes of hers. I looked her right in her eyes "I'm just fine you don't have to worry about me baby girl."

"I'm okay but when I looked up at my crack head unauthentic mother my eyes were on fire, I'm going to get this low-life bitch back tonight."

I was filled with so much rage and anger I wanted to jump up and choke that slut with my bare hands for real.

"Why don't you go back to bed Boo-Boo. I'm just fine all right." She hugged me I wanted to just break down and cry.

I held it all in and she slowly walked back towards that no-good bitch Dotty and she quickly grabbed her hand and they when out of the room. With that crack head whore calling herself my mother looking at me closing the door. I quickly jumped up and locked the door. I'd quickly got some fresh under wear and a towel I open the door peeking out I did not see or hear anybody, and I run into the bathroom. I locked the door behind me, and I take a shower and try to wash off all of that ugly shit that just happen to me. I washed up really good and I went back to my room getting dressed real swift. Soon as I got dressed, I got my phone and I called up Spider Gee. He's the one who got me started in the game, but he always looked out for me from the first time I found a gee pack he tossed when the cops when to lock him up. I found it for him and when the cops let him go after not finding the drugs, I gave it back to him and we've been cool from that day forward.

Then after a week later he put me on in the game. It was on and popping. He picked up after the phone rang three time answering, "Yo, what's up, Sharonda?"

"Yo man do you have a gun?"

"You know I do what you need a gun for, Shorty?"

"My mother just had these niggas she was getting high wit roll up in my room and rape me!"

"What? Look I'm on my way!"

I waited in my room but I'm packing me a bag, so I can get the fuck out of here. It's only 15 minutes later I hear this big bang at my front door. I open up my door just as I'm going to the front door my mother comes to the door yelling, "who the fuck is banging on my door like this?" She opens the door and I'm running up and its Spider Gee with his two goons Xavier we all called him X and Fat Jerome Spider quickly grabbing my mother Dotty up in her collar yelling, "you crack head bitch! What the fuck you do that shit to my girl for? What the fuck is wrong with you?" He quickly put his gun up to her head I came up looking at her and to tell you the truth I wanted him to blow her fucking head off, but I say to him, "don't do it, Spider man! No! No!"

"Sharonda man let me put a hot slug in this no-good bitch head right now then he started hitting her with his pistol Boom! Kook! Plow" As she fell back on the floor falling on her ass. Doom! She's looking up at me yelling.

"you're going to let this nigga kill me?"
"After what you just did to me, I should kill you myself I'd take the gun out of Spider's hand. I point it at her head, but I was thinking about my little sister in the back of my mind a voice kept telling me shoot that bitch right now! Spider repeated, "shoot that bitch so we can get the fuck out of here!" Then my little sister Robin came out of her room screaming, "Mommy! Mommy! Mommy!"

She ran and jumped right into her arms that's the only thing that saved her ass. I really was going to shoot her, but I knew I could not do what I do and take care of my little sister. That is why I gave this bitch any kind of break. I'd just have people from the system on top of her ass until she's a little older than I'll come and get her when I get on my feet so that shit that happen to me don't happen to her. Spider tapped me on my arm and said, "go get your shit you are staying wit me." I run and get my bag but I'm hoping he don't shoot her ass while my little sister holding on to her. I went and grabbed my bag. I look over at my mother whose is bleeding from her head and mouth as well mumbling all kinds of bullshit. I didn't really want to hear any of that shit she had to say at the time. I just wanted to kill her ass, but he fucked her up really good.

Spider looked me in my face and asked, "Are you ready to go? You should have shot that bitch in her motherfucking head. Don't nobody do that kind of shit to their daughter for real!" After he said that from that day forward his words were ringing inside of my head and kept growing from that day. It played over and over again. I was so angry and upset I just wanted to get the fuck up out of there. I should have listened to him after what I found out later on in life about my so-called crack head mother.

So, I went out the door and I'd never looked back, but I did go back and checked on my little sister from time to time. I did come get her to live with me when I got stronger in the gang. Once I had more rank and Juice on the streets, I knew she would be good with me.

It is how I got out of that fucking house. He pointed at her and said, "your one lucky bitch for right now. Oh, and them niggas you got to do that shit there all dead you best believe that shit!"

We walked out and got into Spider's gray BMW he took off down the dark street soon as we pulled off. I was expecting for Spider to hit me with the I told you so shit because he kept telling me to move and get my own spot now that I'm making some good money with his crew. But no, I called myself looking out for my family and all that good shit. I fucked up and I'd knew it after that night. He just kept cussing and carrying on about my mother to me. It seemed like he knew something about her that I didn't, and he did not want to tell me yet. When we arrived at his huge luxury apartment, I'd only seen a place like this in a fucking magazine or on TV.

His place is Sharp. Decorated with a dark brown leather couch set with white carpet, old curtains in the window and crystal ornament all over the place. He had some colorful black art on the walls.

He waves at me for me to follow him I walked behind him, and Spider showed me the room I would be sleeping in. My eyes almost popped out of my head the room had a queen size bed with a nice dark brown bed cover, light brown curtains and light brown carpet, dark brown wood night end tables and a dresser. I can tell they were expensive this shit seems like a fucking dream to me at that moment in time.

I'd felt so much better about myself I was still in a lot of pain, but I'd really felt safe. I began thinking to myself this is how I should have been living like this all my life. I looked at Spider Gee in a whole new light after that for real. Here I am selling crack for this nigga for two years and I never really knew him at all. I got started selling when I was 15 years old and he always told me I was one of his best workers. Spider is a lot older than me, but I could see after looking around his place he was on a whole new level in life. The whole house smelled good he looked at me and said, "are you all right now?"

"I'm still sore but I'll be all right."

"Good that's what I want to hear, baby girl. You got to be strong in this wicked ass world today are you hungry?"

"Yes! Okay then put up some of your things and come into the kitchen I got some pizza for you, okay."

"Thank you for everything Spider!"

"You don't have to thank me, baby girl. I look at you as my family so put up some of your things and come eat, all right. Don't worry about any clothes I'll hook you up and send you shopping tomorrow and make sure you got everything you need, Shorty." That's what he always called me before he knew my name. I'd just giggled and nodded my head yes. As he smiled and walked away, I took a few things out of my backpack and put them in the drawer and then I went into his nice state of the art kitchen. He pointed to the stool at the long counter as he heated up pizza in the microwave with Xavier and Fat Jerome sitting next to me talking about the hood versus hood basketball game last night in the playground. Spider pulls it out and set it on the counter shaking his hand from it being too hot.

He chuckled, "Fat Jerome go get everybody a nice cold beer." I never had Heineken beer before, and he open it with a bottle opener I was trying to open it with my hand they were all laughing at me.

Spider said, "don't feel bad baby girl these same niggas laughing at you was doing the same thing you was doing the first time I gave them a Heineken." They started laughing loud and we all had a really good time, talking shit, laughing and smoking a little weed. Right before I went to bed that night Spider Gee came up to me and said, "after we get all your shit together, you're going to have to Soldier up."

I really did not know what he was talking about I had a real puzzled look on my face. He said, "look after you get some things tomorrow, I'm taking you out for some training that's what I mean by soldier up. You want to get them low life cock suckers who raped you, right?"

"Yeah, I want to kill every last one of them motherfuckers!"

"Well good and the only way you're going to get them back is to learn how to use a gun and machine gun the right way I'll help you get them motherfuckers but you're going to have to put in some work as well. Go get you some rest we have a lot work to do tomorrow. Okay!"

"Now you're on a whole new other level of the game, baby girl you're in school right now nigga go to bed and I'll talk to you in the A.M."

"Alright." He walked away and I went to my bedroom. I was still sore as shit as I closed the door and took off my clothes and went to bed."

SOLDIERING UP

Well after a couple of them Heinekens and a few blunts they put me out cold last night. When I woke up in the morning my whole body was hurting even more from that beating them asshole niggas put on me last night. My private area was in so much throbbing agonizing pain. It felt like it was on fire like someone put three blow torches right down on my pussy and burned it up torturing me to death. I'd got up around 10 A.M. I was moving around real slow. I was stiff as a fucking board too. I'm still a little high I looked up at the clock radio in the room sitting on the really nice light brown nightstand When I hear someone knocking on the door asking, "are you up yet?" I know the voice from anywhere its Xavier saying, "Yo, get up, Sista we have to go get you some new gear and meet Spider Gee at the scrap yard in North Philly."

"Are you decent?"

I yell out to him on the other side of the door,

"No, I'm getting dressed right now."

"Okay, you can use the bathroom right now it should be some fresh wash rags and towels in the top drawer on the left in there. I'll be in the kitchen fixing us something to eat before we roll out, all right."

I yelled, "okay thanks." I get my underwear out of the drawer on the right I put in there last night and just like he said I looked in the drawer on the left and it's a brand-new washrags and towels in there. I quickly grabbed them along with my underwear and went into the bathroom. I walked in there the bathroom and it is off the fucking hook. I'm looking around in this joint and I never seen nothing like this shit in my life. "wow" the bathroom is as big as the room I was sleeping in. Damn and its really nice and super clean, too. It smells really good in here. It was white and blue tile floor with white block tile on the walls. White and blue towels on the racks with a big shower and tub. It also had two sinks and a giant block mirror with lights all around it.

Shit, I can get used to living like this for sure, but I was wondering why this bathroom had two toilets in this bitch. I jumped in the shower and I washed my whole body it is still hurting. I can see all the marks on my legs and arms from them ruffing me up. My coochie was still sore as well so I had to wash carefully in that area. I want to get a gun and kill all of them right now for what they did to me, but I guess he's right if I'm going to get some pay back, I would have to know what I'm doing with a gun. Then to run up on them and get my ass killed not knowing what the fuck I'm doing.

I get dressed and did my hair. I just brushed it back and put it in a ponytail. I go in the kitchen and he said, "your food is right here, Sister." I fixed you a bacon and egg sandwich is that cool?"

"Oh yeah that's good to go, Bro. Thank you X man he just smiled.

"No problem, sis. Are you all right?"

I'd look up at him and said to him looking him right in his eyes, "yeah, I'm going to be all right." He pours me a big glass of orange juice after we bust this grub were going to go get you some new shit and head out to the scrap yard. We use it as a firing range. Spider is going to meet us there. "Where is he at now?"

"He's working he told me to make sure your cool."

"Where you want to go to get you some new shit?"

"I don't have that much money."

"I did not ask you all that, okay. Don't worry about money your family, all right. He told me to take you to get some new shit and don't worry, okay."

"Well I'll go to city blue downtown then we can go to the gallery."

"See now you're talking, sister. Soon as your done eating that what we're going to do!" So soon as we were done eating, we when out the door and we jumped in X's black 95 Cherokee Jeep parked down the street from the apartment. I was playing it off because I never sat inside of a brand-new fly ass whip like this before, but I was really cool about its doe. Then soon as I got inside of his Jeep and put my ass into them really nice leather seats, he started banging the sounds driving down the street and I was loving it. He was playing Nas if I ruled the world with Lauryn Hill. Then some of the Fugees Ready or Not along with Fu-Gee-La, SWV's You're the One, If Your Girl Only Knew by Aaliyah, I love that song. Next, was Jay-Z's Can't Knock the Hustle and we were jamming our ass off all the way downtown to Center city at 11th & Chestnut street. In City Blue I got about six pair of jeans with tops to match, four pair of Nike sneakers to match all of my outfits and some Timberland boots for girls.

We went to the Gallery mall on market street I got two leather jackets, one black and the other one dark blue, a few hats then I went into few of the women stores and got a bunch of brand-new bras, panties and socks. We went to Rite Aid at 10th & Market street and I got all my Dove soap deodorant and female and hair care products I need. He parked on 10th street in the parking lot underground X had to help me carry all the bags I had, and we put all my bags in the back of the Jeep. I just had to ask him why he got two toilets in his bathroom?

"That's not a toilet girl that's a Bo-day that's for you to wash you back side after you take a dump you sit on it and you hit the button on the side and the water squirt up on you ass and wash it all out."

"Oh okay, I did know what the fuck was going on wit that shit for real. I just had to ask." We both laughed but at least he did not make fun of me for asking him that. I'd always knew X was a cool dude he's like the big brother I never had, and we got closer as more time went by and were still close to this very day.

While we were shopping that day, we kicked it for a little bit then after we had lunch at the gallery inside of the food court, he told me while we were walking back to the Jeep in the parking lot that I have to go get checked out by the doctor. After what happen to me last night right then and there let me know that they really care about me not all of the materialistic things they brought me. Just what he said to me about going to the doctor I was really touched and moved by that. He said to me that Spider will take care of it and don't worry about it. I wanted to cry right then and there but I just held it in and said thank you. Holding the tears back he just smiled and said, "I don't want to see no tears out your fucking eyes you're going to fuck up a really good day over here!" We both chuckle and went to his jeep talking about all the good shit I brought. So now we drive out to North Philly to this big ass old red brick warehouse next to this car scrap yard and we parked near this big ass gray steel door. He steps out and said, "come on." I get out and he points his remote to his Jeep Boo-Beep locking it. We both walked up to the door and he bangs on it really hard.

Fat Jerome open it and then bumps fist with him. He said, "what up Sharonda?" He bumped fist wit me too as he walked us inside. When I got in there this place was huge and it smelled like a bunch of old wet clothes inside there. They had two long steel racks with all kinds of guns like machine guns and clips with their home-made targets in the distant on the left.

Then Fat Jerome walked up to me with a jump suit on and said, "here you go put this on, Sharonda."

Spider came up to me and said, "all right soon as you put on the jump suit over your clothes. I'm just going have you shooting today and that's what you're going to be doing for the next two weeks until you're ready to go through the obstacle course with the regular gun and then the machine gun. He points to where I could put on the dark gray jump suit on the left-hand side of this giant warehouse.

I sit down where it's a long line of chairs with hooks on the walls with jump suits hanging up. I slip on the jump suit and zip it up. I was ready to go, and excited to get started. To tell you the truth it is because I wanted to get my pay back on them niggas. I walked back over to where Spider is standing and he hands me a Glock nine announcing, "where going to start with this and then were going to work our way up to a Bravo Company 30-shot mag to a 50-caliber machine gun. When I'm done with your ass, you're going to be one of the best but for right now were going to start with the nine, okay. This is your target he points at them in the distance they had up. I want you to point and hold it with two hands like this." He showed me how he wanted me to hold the gun and I did like he said. He just let me shoot most that day for about three hours. To me that was lot of fun too I really like it. I know I wanted to do this shit and to get good as well.

Then we went back to the spot, ate, talked a lot shit and got high. We did this every day for the next three months by the time September came around and now I'm one bad bitch with all kinds of weapons and machine guns. I'm going through the obstacle course like I was Ram-baleana ripping shit up. Not only did he teach me how to use all of them. I can take them apart. Ruger P345, Heckler& Koch P30/P3OL, Glock 34/35, Beretta M9/92FS/96A1, DPMS machine gun Panther 204 caliber Semi-Reccon, Daniel Defense machine gun M4 Carbines Semi-auto 30-shot mag, Colt LE6920/LE6940 machine gun 5.56 mm with direct gas system now. Spider was right this was school and school for an assassin and I never forgot what he told me too. To stay sharp and you have to be training all the time and I did. I never stop after that and I started learning more and more shit every time. He told me he was going to bring in some of the guys who trained him to show me a whole lot more. I was down he told me the guys who trained him was in the marines and I'm not going to lie I was loving this shit.

This was the first time in my life I found out that I was really good at something other than selling crack to niggas on the street corner. I was thinking about going back to school, but this is what happened and why I didn't go back. It is this guy name Big Steven Gram a drug boss from 28th street in South Philly they could not get next to this motherfucker. He was selling drugs for them at one time then he went out on his own now. He doesn't want Spider and his crew to sell drugs in their territory anymore. He got all the niggas in that area more organize, and they tried to take him out a few times. He wound up killing about four of Spider Gee's men and this pissed him off, so he came up with a master plan to use me to hit this nigga.

He talked it over with his boss Nokey Blaze by this time I'd did not meet Nokey Blaze yet and that was one of my goals to that as well. I really wanted to meet the big man and he told Spider to go ahead and do it, so this is my first hit. I'd got a lot to prove to everybody I know I could get this shit done so I could move up really fast in the crew and plus I wanted to get that loot. So, I can stack up my chips, so I can get my own spot one day. So, Spider told me where he was going to be at on Saturday afternoon, and I told him what I was going to do to get close to his ass. He loved it so everything is all set and I was more than ready to get busy and earn my stripes.

MY FIRST HIT

So, the day of the hit it was a sunny day in the second week of September 1996. Two cars pull up on the corner of Buster's barber shop at 28th & Warton street. on the corner of the block the first car is a new black Nissan Pathfinder and the second car is a black Mercedes-Benz so Big Steven Gram's bodyguards jump out the first car. Two big black Greasy ass niggas they both looked like line backers for the Green Bay Packers or something. They both are posted up by the Barber shop door looking both ways then getting out of the second car is another big ugly light skin dude name Duke. He gets out opening and holding the back door for Big Steven he gets out then Duke closed the door. He walks right beside him strolling and Big Steven is puffing on a cigar walking real slow looking up and down the street checking out everything around him as well. He's wearing a light blue sweat suit with his big fat belly hanging out with white Nike sneakers on by this time.

I'm coming up the street on the right-hand side of the sidewalk and I'm pushing this big dark blue baby carriage switching my hips really hard for all of them to be looking at me. I put on fire engine red lipstick on my thick lips, I wore this tight yellow short skirt outfit, half my boobs out showing a lot of cleavage and I got this long dark brown weave on. I know I look like a super-hot in the ass hoochie mamma whore looking to catch some trick ass niggas with a very big fucking net. When I rolled up and I know for sure they all got their eyes on me. I even made Big Steven to stop and take a peek at me as well once he seen the way I was walking pushing that baby carriage. I didn't know he would stop and take a look at me I'm thinking to myself this is even better for me now that I got all of them off guard with all eyes on me. Switching my hips just a little more and I can see their eyes filled with lust, so I get even closer. I am right in front of him just I got little closer for him to see he smiled at me saying, "hey baby, you really looking good today like a big ray of sunshine making the whole world happy. Can I holler at you right quick?" He's trying to look at my ass when I'm bending over so I give them all a really good look at me. I'd quickly turned around and smiled at him letting him get a really good look at my fat ass. I got on these dark red panties on with little darker red hearts on them and all of them can see them good with my bright yellow tight shorts on.

I acted like I was fixing the baby inside of the carriage and all of them got their eyes glued on my sexy body, so I quickly reach inside, and I pulled out my SIG Sauer 522 with a short black 16 inch barrel Semi-auto 30-shot magazine and I open up on Steven. The big man first he had a real shock expression on his fat ass grill with his mouth open. Katackatak kactacatka katackatacka kactakckakata kactackatackla!

Hitting him in his chest and head with the blood shooting out with his big frame fell sideways to the ground screaming and then the big fat ugly light skin guy named Duke I hit him in the middle of his big ass head and dead center in his chest. I wet his shit up with the blood gushing up to his ugly ass light skin face that nigga was turning red when I was pumping the hot shit up in his ugly ass. Then I quickly turned almost lighting fast getting low and took aim at the two big black ass line backers looking niggas posted up at the doorway both their eyes got wide. Kactacka Katackat kactackata! Katchkatacka!

I sprayed both of them right quick before they could even get their guns out hitting both of them in their chest and in their great big stomachs ripping the flesh from their bodies. All I can see is the blood shooting up on the doorway window with the glass flying everywhere soon as they hit the ground grunting and yelling in deep pain gasping for their last breath. I never even seen them hit the fucking ground bleeding to death because I was gone after I'd smoked both their asses. X came speeding up the block in a dark green pickup truck I jumped in still holding the machine gun and we were fucking ghost.

We went back to Spider's apartment to celebrate and we had a little party it was me, Fat Jerome and Spider Gee. It was the first time I meet Spider Gee's brother Damon.

Now that nigga was crazy for real and a lot of fun too. I got really close to him as well over time, but Spider Gee was really happy and that was the first time I drunk champagne in my life. I became fucked up with all the weed along with it right after that I went to the doctor Spider hooked up for me to go see. Good thing everything was all right with me after he checked me out. I felt good about myself after that hit now I just want to know how much money I was going to get for the job now.

The next day X came to my room knocking on my door and ask, "are you up, sis?' I run to open the door and he hands me a fat envelope, smile and walked away I close the door back. I looked inside of it I went and sat on the bed all excited. Wow after I finish counting it was five-grand. Damn right after that I became hooked just as if I smoked crack for the first time.

Spider put me right back to work a week later this time it was another dude they could not get close too again and they wanted to take over his territory in South West Philly. His name was Black Lou Diamond. All his friends and enemies a like called him Diamond Lou he broke away from the black Mob and started his own thing and at the time in 1996. Nokey Blaze was still working with the La coaster Nostra the Don Big Dominic The Fox Gigante gave the order to take him out because he was not paying the Don any money for selling drugs and was not buying from him anymore. He was in violation from the door, so this time Spider told me that this guy had a tire shop on 56th street and he hung out there with all his men. They are all out there on Fridays drinking and carrying on before they went to his bar on 60th street. This time is I'm in a little dark blue Suzuki side kick Jeep. They were the shit back then with the hatch back so it about4 in the afternoon it's still really nice outside. I came up driving up with all these men sitting outside of the shop drinking and talking real loud to one another when I drove up with a flat tire. I get out the jeep all of them stop talking there all looking me up and down with their mouth wide open.

I'm wearing this tight white mini skirt high heels with a white shear see through blouse on with a yellow bra and thong panties on with little red kissy lips print on them. I'd walked up to the crowd of men asking, "can somebody help me, please?" All nice, soft and sexy in my best sex kitten voice. Standing right in the doorway is Diamond Lou one of his men went to jump up to say something to me but he pushed him back answering, "well, little lady you came to the right place, baby. I know I can help you for sure. What is your name, girl?"

"My name is Cherry." I looked him right in his eyes and smile as he came up on me licking his lips like he was LL Cool J or some shit rubbing his hands together. Looking me up and down with his eyes getting wide and a big trick daddy smile on his fucking face.

I can see all his men sitting along the front of the shop their eyes are popping out their fucking head checking me out I say to him, "I was on my way to the club and I got a flat. I got to go get this money."

"Oh, don't you worry, baby. I'll take care of it right away. So, Cherry what club was you going to, baby?" I was going downtown to the gentleman's club on 13th street to dance. Why? You are thinking about coming to check me out and see me dance baby?"

"Oh, hell yes but how about if you could give me a private lap dance in the back of the shop. I sure would make it worth your while, darling and I'll change your flat for free. How about that, Miss Cherry?" He reaches in his pocket pulling out a big fat bank roll out showing it to me and he sticks it back in his pocket smiling even more.

"Oh, it sounds good to me, baby, but you have to change the tire first, right?" I put my hand on my hip and my pocketbook handbag up under my arm he could not take his eyes off of me. He is watching my every move I make. He said, "Oh yeah I'll do that right now baby where is your spare tire at?"

"It's in the back of my Jeep let me pop my hatch right quick so you can get it." I slowly walked to the back he's standing there near the flat left side tire looking at my ass." I turned around real fast and smile at him. I pop it open and I reach inside pulling out my DPMS Panther machine gun while he's bends over looking at the tire. I let him have it. All he seen was the muzzle flashing. Kactackakat! Kackatckatacka! Kackapackatacka!

He went down fast I hit him in the head, neck and chest with the blood flying up in the air. He fell back on his ass then I quickly turned around with the quickness towards where all his home boys where sitting in front of the shop. I sprayed all six of them niggas like there were roaches on the wall. It was just like shooting fish in a fucking barrow all of them were in shock Kactackata! Kapackatckatack! Katackatapackatacka! I hit most of them center mass in the chest and in the head fucking them up really good. I can see all the blood and their skull fragments flew on the side of the back of the dull white walls of the front of the tire shop. I quickly kick off my high heel shoes and I ran outside of the gate of the tire shop holding the machine gun then X came speeding up 56th street in his green pickup truck. Soon as I jump inside, I reach in my pocketbook getting the remote hitting the button when some of his other men inside of the shop came out shooting at us just missing us, hitting the truck. When X took off down the block and I hit the remote. Kaboom! It rocked the whole block I blow up the Suzuki side kick Jeep. Spider Gee made a bomb with enough C4 to blow up three houses. Soon as he went four of his men came out at us and I know for damn sure we got them all as X made a really hard right turn getting the fuck from out of there. Later on, we all sat around the TV seeing it flashed on the six O clock news cheering and jumping up and down like we just won the big game, like we all had money on the motherfucker. I can't lie I was really feeling myself right about now.

I knew Spider Gee will have more work for me to put in and I was Gawd dam ready for it too! All that week all we did was party then on Sunday while I was chilling laying around the house. When Spider Gee came and knocked on my bedroom door he asked, "Hey baby girl, are you decent?" I'd sit up on my bed and answered, "yeah come on in." He entered with a smile on his face, "hey what up wit you?"

"Chillin. After last night fucking with yawl I have to recuperate." We both chuckled. "Look, I got another job for you but this time you are going have to get up close and personal with this one. I want to see if you can do it?"

"So, I have to go to bed with the mark is what you're saying?" "Well you don't have to fuck him. You just got to let him think he's getting some pussy and you smoke him."

"Yeah, I'm down but how is all this going to work? How do you know he's going want to go to bed with me?"
"Because were setting him up he think he's getting a call girl and he's getting you to blow his brains out."
"Okay so I'm the call girl? Who is my back up to get the hell out of there?"
"Me and X. Good then I don't have shit to worry about then." We both laughed, and he gave me a high five. He said, "That's my girl. Look were getting our groove on you can come join us if you want?"
"No, I'm cool I have to chill out today after last night. I'm good trust me." He burst out laughing," all right I holler at you later." He walks out the room still laughing, and he closes the door. I lay back down thinking about this job and I fell asleep.
All that week Spider Gee gave me the run down on the mark. His name is Deon Young he's the leader of a drug gang called FPC The Fat Paper Clique. He loves call girls and he's at war with BSN, The Black Syndicate Nation who I'm down with now. X put me down on who runs shit in our whole outfit when I first started rolling with their crew. They got someone on the inside of this call girl service and when he calls for a girl there going to send me in to take him out. Spider Gee told me a couple days before the hit he wanted my head clear, so he did not want me to get high for a few days.
After the job is done, I can get high as I wanted to get so, I'd listen to him and I did not smoke, or drink shit the rest of that week.
It's the end of November 1996, they were sitting around waiting on the call and when it comes in, I had to be ready to go. I had to practice with a silencer. This is the first time I seen one up close I only seen that kind of shit in the movies but after a while I got pretty good with it, too. Spider showed me how to break it down and how to put it back together really fast. He showed me how to aim, how to stand and the whole nine. Its Friday night it's 3 O' clock in the fucking morning I was knocked out sleep when X came knocking on my door saying, "come on its time for you to get dolled up." I knew that was the call, so I put on my little hooker outfit Spider hooked up for me and I put on some make up looking like a real ho bitch in the game.

Soon as I came out the door with my big coach bag pocket book with my change of clothing out fit and my silencer inside of it, I'm ready to go soon as I open the door and came out Spider looked at me and said, "good that what we were going for right there. You nailed it, baby girl! You got everything make sure double check." I made sure I had everything I need. I announce, "yeah, I'm good." "Okay, let's go." I walked behind him as he waved at X for him to follow us out. We walked out to Spider's dark blue Range Rover it looks black because it dark outside. I sat up front and X sat in the back with Spider taking off. I ask him "Where is the mark at?" "The Double tree hotel 5th floor room 503.Don't worry we got peoples in there as well were going to be right next-door baby girl. Just put two in his dome and text me a smiley face when it's done. Then you change your shit and text me a basketball when you're ready to bounce and make sure you got the ticket; I gave you so you can drive out separate from us. You got me?"

"Yeah, I got you." We drive to the hotel he rides up into the parking lot on the right-hand side. I get out of the whip and I go right up in the hotel and get on the elevator up to the 5th floor. I get off the elevator I looked up on the wall and see the number signs. I walked to the room and knock on the door and it's this tall dark skin muscular dude who opens the door. He's not too bad looking he looks me up and down with a big smile on his grill and said, "oh yeah what up sweetheart please come in."

I walk in and I put on a little extra with my walk and he can't take his eyes off of me. I smile for the nigga when I walk in. "What's your name baby? Tina so how are you tonight dark and handsome." and what's your name? My name is D" would you like a drink before we get into something? Sure, do you have any Vodka Mister sexy?"

"I sure do Miss Tina. Have a seat and relax while I make our drinks, baby."

"They said they was sending me somebody new, but you look way better then them other girls. I hope you're as good as you look baby." He made the drinks and he hand me one. He sits next to me putting his arm around my neck looking me right in my face and asked, "so Tina where you from, honey?"

"I'm from West Philly 52nd & Market street."

"Oh yeah, I know a few people up that way but he started feeling me up on my breast and kissing me on my neck. At the same time, my hand rubbing his Dick and sipping on my drink giggling like a schoolgirl then he puts his drink down. He has both his hands feeling on me and started loosening up my blouse. He said, "let me see what you're working wit over here sweetheart."

He's looking at my titties then he started feeling on them pulling my bra down. I help him do it to as he is licking on my nipples and reaching down up under my short dress fingering me. I put on a real good act on for him moaning and kissing him back then I get on top of him. He's reaching up feeling on my breast while I'm humping on him grinding on him for a little while. I can feel his Dick getting hard. He's getting really hot and I reach down pulling my panties to the side I'd sit up some more letting him see my smooth box. Standing up over him with my legs open and I reached down pulling his jeans off and I said, "why don't we take this to the bed Mister Big." He releases a big grin looking up at me with his eyes getting wide, "Yeah, let's do this shit." As I'm ready to walk over to the bed he smacked me on my ass. "Damn girl, you got a dunk on you shit!" I smiled looking him right in his face as I'd walked toward the big bed on the right-hand side of the room. I get my pocketbook, high heel shoes and the bottle of Vodka saying, "get the glasses for us, baby." He is nodding his head and I'd walked over to the bed. I set the bottle of Vodka and my pocketbook on the nightstand. He came with the glasses as I stand on the other side of the bed taking off my skirt nice and sexy for him. I know he's watching I have my back turn to him then I turn around, so he can see me, and he moaned, "yeah baby take it all off for me."

I wink and I take off my bra first then I slowly take off my panties then I pointed to him and said, "all right get on the bed and I'll get on top of you. I can't wait to get that big black Dick of yours up in me baby!"

He rubbed his hand together and removed his boxer short and his wife beater while he was doing that. I quickly get my pistol with the silencer on the tip and I cut the lights out holding the gun behind my back and I get on top of him. I said, "just lean back, baby. I'm going to give it too you just like you wanted it. Hot and wet, baby. You're going to love it!" He giggles, "oh yeah, baby give it to me with your sexy ass." I take the pistol and I mashed it to his head Poouuff! Poouuff!

Pooouufff! I'd get up off him and got some of the blood blow back on me. I get my phone out of my pocketbook and I go inside of the bathroom and I text Spider with just a smiley face letting him know it's done. I jump in the shower and I wash off the blood. I go pick up my panties and bra.

I reach in my pocketbook and I pull out a zip lock bag I had inside putting my underwear inside of it along with my high heel shoes. I take out my change of clothing this old lady Moo-Moo dress with this bright flower print and this big pink floppy hat. I put on the dark sunglasses on my face and my flip flops. I'd text Spider before I roll out sending him a basketball letting him know I'm ready to bounce.

I walked out the door and close it real slow. I walked towards the elevator Spider and X came out of the room next door. I pressed the button and after a few minutes the elevator came I got on. Then X and Spider got on we all acted like we did not know one another riding down to the garage. I walked up to the tall skinny dark skin valet dude and go in my bag getting the ticket Spider gave me the other day telling me the whole plan. I give it to him, and the valet pulls up with a white Volvo and hand me the keys. I give him a 20-dollar bill tip. He smiles showing all his yellow crooked teeth and his blood shot red eyes. I jump in the Volvo and I drive off smooth as a baby's ass.

Later on, we all met up at the spot and we had a party. This time Spider pulled out some ice-cold Cristal Champagne I never had it before Spider, X, Fat Jerome and myself Spider gave all of us our glasses and he pops it open. He started pouring everybody some and he made a toast while everyone is holding up their glasses and yelled, "To taking over these streets thanks to our newest member of the BSN Sharonda!"

We all tap glasses cheering loud and I whisper to Spider, "what is BSN?"
He just smiled, and he did not put me out there he pulled me to the side talking low saying, "Black Syndicate Nation that's the gang you're in. I thought the name of the click is named MMMC. Mad Money& Murder Clique. That's the name of our clique but the gang is BSN."
"Oh, I did not know that. So now you know I pull you on the side to tell you that I don't want the boys to be Clowning you."
"So, it's the same thing, right?"
"Yeah, it's the same money, baby girl. I'll break you off soon as were all done getting our groove on, okay."
"So, when am I going to meet the big man?"
"I'll take you to go see him next week if you want?"
"Yeah, I'll like that. What time?"
"In the afternoon if that cool with you plus, he wants to meet you after all the work you been putting in so let get back to the party."
We went back and got real fucked up that night and just like he said he gave me my loot, but I was more excited about meeting the big man for real. I went to bed floating on a cloud after we talked a lot shit getting higher than a motherfucker. That Cristal with some weed is no fucking joke I got twisted and went to bed.

MEETING THE BIG MAN

It's the first week in December 1996, its 10 A.M. When Spider came banging on my door yelling, "get up baby girl and get dressed so we can roll out to the spot."
I yelled back, "all right, I'm getting up.
"I get up and rolled into the bathroom to get washed and dressed. I turned on the TV to check the weather on the weather Channel and its colder than a motherfucker outside.
I put on all my winter gear on my thick black pea coat, some black jeans, thick wool socks, black boots, and black wool skull hat. It is no time to get cute. I go in the living room where Spider is waiting for me and asked, "you ready baby girl?"
"Yeah, I'm ready let's go." Spider get up off the couch, "so what are you going to do with all that money you been making, Sharonda?"
"I was thinking about getting my own spot and a car."
"That's sounds good, baby girl just let me know what you going to do, and I'll help you out with anything you need, all right." We are family for real doe."
"I know you been holding me down from day one, Spider and one day I'm going to show you how much I appreciate everything you done for me."
"Like I said were family for real and when you get on your feet. I know you're going to do the right thing so don't worry about it all right." We jumped in his dark blue Range Rover he sits in the driver seat saying, "you want to drive?"
"Oh, hell yes but I don't know where I'm going doe?"
"Don't fucking worry about it. I'll tell you how to get there okay."

"Sure thing." He got out the driver seat and he got on the other side and he sat back puffing on his Newport, smiling, putting on some banging ass music. I got behind the wheel and I took off. I never drove no fly ass whip like this before man the shit is super smooth. He told me where to go we jump on the expressway. He told me to get off the exit at City Line Avenue. It took us about an hour to get there I never seen houses like this in my life. I only seen shit like this on TV. All I see is big giant beautiful houses with long wide lawns and luxury cars in their driveway. He told me to pull over at the next house over there while he's pointing. I pulled up in this big ass parking lot and the house was on this hill with a long pathway and this lawn is as big as a fucking football field.

He said, "all right we are here. Come get out, baby girl. We get out the car and I said to him, "I have to ask you something, Spider." As were both walking up to the house.

"What's that?"

"How come you never came at me?"

"Look I dig the shit out of you, and I don't get down like that you're like my little sister. Not to say you're not a very pretty woman but I want you to find someone around your age. Have some kids and be happy. I have someone if you want to know that too okay, nigga. I want you to learn more and run shit, okay. Listen to what this man has to say to you and soak all that shit up like a motherfucking sponge. One day when you're on top you're going think of old Spider who put you on. I didn't try to fuck you like all the rest of the niggas you're going to run in to."

I giggled as we went up to the door from the long ass pathway. Then I ask him that night when they rape me you acted like you wanted to tell me something? "Now is not the time. I'll tell you soon enough after you put in some more work." Spider rings the doorbell. Shit the doorbell even looks rich too. The door open and it's this tall muscular ugly ass black dude with scars and tattoos all over his body wearing a wife beater he laughed, "hey, what's up my nigga, Spider!

"What's up with you, Buck Shot?"

"Man, good to see you, nigga?" They hugged one another.

"Come on in here motherfucker. Who you got with you?"

"This is the shorty y'all been hearing about putting in all that work. This is Sharonda"

"Sharonda this is my brother Buck Shot. He's good people we don't say homies were brothers because were all family you understand, baby girl." I'd just nodded my head and smile as I'd went to shake his hand. He said, "we don't shake hands we hug one another and then we bump fist, okay." I'd looked at him and responded, "okay". I hugged him then we bumped fist. He looked me in the face and said, "after we do that then we say it's all love, family. All right?"
"Okay I got you it's all love, family."
"All right now you have to school these niggas to the BSN shit, Spider. Show them all the inside family shit baby boy so everybody knows who is fucking who out there in the streets. You know what I'm saying."
"Where is Nokey?" He's up in the music room come on right this way! He started walking towards the left in this huge ass joint. I'm walking right behind Spider looking around thinking man this place is like a palace. I want to live just like this one day for real. Spider is walking behind this nigga, Buck Shot strolling hard. I can see his two pistols tucked down in his jeans with his boxer shorts hanging out. We went to the back on the left-hand side to this giant ass light brown pretty ass door. Spider knocked on the door and then he walked in this room which was huge. Sitting in this large black office chair behind this big ass board with all of these buttons that are Lit up. The shit looked like a fucking spaceship or something then I looked up and it this dude in this giant ass glass booth.
Soon as Nokey seen us walk in he hits this button talking to the young dude with all these tattoos and said, "take five Mecca while I talk to my peoples black."
He stands up as Spider walked up to him hugging him then they bump fist saying at the same time, "it's All love family!" As the young dude walk up bumping fist with Nokey. "hey, go take a smoke or something for me while I holla at my peoples."
"Okay my nigga and by the way good work nigga this shit is going be fire when were all done." He walks out the huge ass music room soon as the door close.
Spider, is that the nigga?"
"Yeah that nigga is tight too, man. So, who you got with you over here? Yeah this is Shorty I've been telling you about putting in all that work for us. Sharonda this is Nokey."

"So, this is Shorty, damn girl you're really doing your thing. I really appreciate everything you been doing out there so you down with us now."

"Yeah, I'm down for whatever."

"Good to hear do you speak Swahili, baby girl?"

"No, I don't but I'm willing to learn."

"Good, because we have to do something about your name. I'm going to call you Almasi that means Diamond in Swahili because you're a Diamond in the ruff, baby girl. You like that name?"

"Yes, I do now that I'm down can I get the tattoo like everybody else?"

He looks over at Spider and smiled, "that's really up to your Captain over there but what he's been telling me about you. I think you earn a few of your stripes but I have one more thing for you to do and then you can get that tattoo and you can wear it proudly after that.'

"Okay then what is you want me to do?"

"Look first off I want you to learn something here, Almasi is that we do things by protocol. Spider is my Capo and you take all your orders from him. Do you hear me?

"Yeah, I hear you, Sir." That the way shit has to work, baby girl without structure to this whole thing would be fucked up and you're going to find that out once you move up in rank you feel me?"

"Yes, I feel you Mister Nokey." He started laughing at me and said, "just call me Nokey, alright. You're going to be fine once you get everything were teaching you to stay up in that pretty little head of yours. I got some dudes coming in town soon there coming to teach you a whole lot shit their ex-military cats. I want you to learn everything there is to know before you go rain down on them niggas who did you wrong." I'd turn around and looked at Spider.

"Don't turn around and look at him. Yeah, he told me all about it. He tells me everything about my peoples that's his job but your family now. Don't everybody treat you, right?" "Yes, they do."

"See, ain't nobody is trying to fuck you over. You got paid for all them jobs too, right? "Yes, I did."

"You're in now and what you have to do now to stay is learn and grow after a while you're going to be running shit with your own crew of niggas you, hear me?

"Yes sir. I hear you."

"Good now go back to the spot and in a few those people will be coming to town. Spider is going to tell you what you have to do before you go get that tattoo then you can come back here and sit down with me and talk about your future okay. "Yes, sir and thanks for seeing me today. I will not let you down, sir."

"I know you won't Almasi." Then he put out his hand and bump fist with me and said, "all right, nigga let me get back to work with my man. Have a good day, baby girl."

Spider walked next to me and said, "come on Almasi time to roll up out here let's go!"

I just smiled walking out of the large room with Spider and his man Buck shot who said, "now you heard the man you have to learn Swahili. Spider and X is going to work with you on that so you're in very good hands baby girl."

"I think you did, okay but you had a little too much lip with your Capo."

"Here but your young so after a while you're going to be the shit. Working with Spider and his peoples let me walk y'all out front." I felt better now that I just met the big man we get to the front door. Buck shot said to me, "now remember what we told you today and you take care yourself Almasi. okay."

"I will nice meeting you. Goodbye." Spider just looked at me and said, "come on, I need to holla at you while were riding back to the spot." So were walking to the car and he yelled, "don't you ever run your mouth off again unless I'm out of fucking town or fucking dead. Do you hear me, girl? I'm not going to tell you this but one fucking time. And other bull shit Almasi.

"Okay."

"See just like what he told you we have a protocol and a structure in BSN, okay. That why we out last all the other niggas with crews and gangs are shit is tighter than the fucking mafia. You're not a made nigga unless I say you're a made nigga, okay just know that shit. I like you that's why I brought you in don't fuck it up all right because all the people who betrayed me are not around very long on earth." So, we both get in the car saying, "I won't so is he a music producer?"

"Yeah, along with a whole lot of other shit. He does that to show where all the fucking money is coming from to these devils or you're just asking to go to jail. Take me for an example I have a scrap yard and I sell auto parts on the books your going to have to do the same shit with your money. You're going to have to figure out what you want to do you can't have a 70,000-dollar car, a fly ass spot and don't have nothing to show where the fucking money is coming from you know what I mean."

"Yeah that is kind of smart."

"Yeah, it is that what keep us rolling better than any other motherfuckers out here. Now drive the car and don't talk." It was the first time I seen Spider get upset with me but right then and there I had to learn not to just run off at the mouth. On the ride back to the crib it made me think about what I wanted to do. I want to open up some hair & clothing shop, maybe a few laundromats, some cleaners and make it an all-cash business.

BLOODY CHRISTMAS

Its Christmas day Spider been cooking up another job to take out the 11th street crew in North Philly who stop buying coke from Nokey Blaze. They killed all of his powerful allies from Frankfort Avenue called the Black Out Squad. Nokey had an inside snitch nigga down with the 11th street crew that is telling him there every move for some fat ass loot. The 11th street crew was having a Christmas party at their leader's house Fat Rocko in North Philly at 13th & Lehigh Avenue this is one of his houses he's redeveloping. We suppose to hit them before they get to the house. Rocko is riding with his sister Dena and his two of his top Goons Kian and Antoine two real known killers from the hood. We're going to hit them soon after they pick up his sister from the projects on 11th street going to see some of their family.

The day of the hit we gear up for this job this time I have a bullet proof vest. I'm sitting in the back seat dressed in all black with a ZASTAVA PAP AK machine gun four extra clips two in each pocket. X is behind the wheel of a black GMC truck we follow them until they went and picked up Dena. X stayed far enough back so they could not see him, and Damon stayed in front of them in his dark gray Chevy Impala. I don't know how he did it, but this nigga got skills at that. Fat Jerome with his brother Fly Ty following us just in case shit go sideways. X was ready to make our move calling Damon on his phone saying to Damon okay were ready brother. Okay here we go! Damon started slowing down as the dark blue Benz wagon there were driving in is slowing down as well with Damon's car in front of them. X then speeds up 11th street is so wide with no cars in front of him on the left-hand side he drives up beside the Benz Wagon. I opened up on their ass Kactapackatack! Kapacktacka! Kapackpackackat! Kackpackatacka! Glass flying from the Benz wagon, but I hit every last one of them and if there not dead there going to wish they were. X sped off and with Fat Jerome and Fly Ty driving up to check shit out. Soon as he drove passed them, he texts X with a big black thumbs up. X yelled to me as I'm taking off my black mask "Gawd damn, Almasi you got them all sister there all dead! That was the first time X called me my new name that Nokey Blaze gave me."

I was feeling good when we went back to the crib and had our own little Christmas party. All of us getting twisted all night long even Nokey Blaze came to the party with some of his peoples having a good time That's when I met his brother Jasper for the first time, he seems nice when I first met him, and I met Zelda Nokey's wife. She's really nice, pretty and super smart too. Her and I got tight later on over time. I met three more of Spider's peoples Big Nuzzle this nigga is a stone-cold killer, Gilbert super slick smooth and a killer as well. Then its Brenton another true blue thugged out nigga down for whatever but really smart and his girl Dakota one of Nokey Blaze's singing artist on his label Blaze Out records. Dakota and I hit it off right from the door. I like her she's a down ass bitch.

Man we had a fucking big bowls of weed on the tables and the Cristal is flowing X came back with two cases of it he came back with it ice cold too Spider had food catered in from Delilah's Soul food place to the spot and it was delicious while we were all eating at the table with Fat Jerome, Fly Ty, Dakota and X Spider walked up me saying, "you all right?"

"Yeah, I'm good.

"What I wanted to tell you good job today and he bumps fist with me saying what I had to tell you that day was for you to get your mind right you know that right?" Yeah I know Spider man you know me and you is brown as shit **Nahodha** *(Captain)* Spider looked up at me smiling oh good work Askari(Soldier) I see X is been helping you out to learn a little Swahili X just sat up smiling still eating his food then he reach out his fist so we can bump fist saying keep studying you have to learn that shit okay and he winks his eye at X then his phone rang. He looks at it and asked, "y'all keep enjoying yourself. I have to take this excuse me good peoples. He walked away and me and Dakota started chopping it up with her telling me about her girl from South Philly.

"My girlfriend Gwynn hair shop in South Philly on Point Breeze is all that you need to roll through she will hook you up girl."

"Well give me the number so I can make an appointment."

"Sure thing, girl. Give me your phone so I put her number in for you. So, I hand her my phone and I see Spider rolling out of the door and I see X get up from the table and follow behind him with Brenton Fat Jerome, Damon and Fly Ty walking outside. I know something is going on, but I have to be cool and wait until somebody let me know what's up. I notice after a few minutes they all came back in the house all huddled up. I'm still talking with Dakota just kicking it. Then Gilbert came over to the table with a bottle of Champagne and he set a big zip lock bag of weed on the table and said, "so what's up wit you, Shorty?"

"I'm good what's up wit you, brother?"

"I'm good baby girl. So, what's your name again?'

"Almasi and what's yours?"

"My name is Gill Smooth baby. You ready to help me smoke this good shit I got here?"

"Sure, thing Mister Smooth. you got something to roll this shit up with?"

"I just ran out why don't you run to the corner and get us a few Dutch's for us."
"First of all, I don't run to the corner for no nigga and second of all its Christmas nothing is open any way."
"Yes, it is the Chinks don't care about no fucking Christmas so why don't you get up off your fine fat booty of yours and make that run for big daddy Gill?" He did not know that Spider came up on him and he heard everything he was saying. I'd looked at this niggah asking, "Daddy, is this nigga tripping or what?"
Spider yelled, "Yo Gill, don't make me fuck your ass up nigga, Man."
"I was just rapping a little with the fine Shorty."
"Man, you know me. See that the whole thing I know you, nigga but Shorty right here is off limits for you. I'm not going to tell you again and plus I need to holla at her about some business, okay. Yo Almasi I need to talk to you in my office right now." Then he points at Gill, so I get up and walked behind him to the big back room we all called it the office. Spider had the large back room hooked up like a conference room in some type of company X, Fat Jerome, Brenton, Damon Gee, Fly Ty is all sitting around the table. Spider sit at the head of the long wooden table saying take a seat, "baby girl, look we have to go holla at these black bikers tomorrow about some more work. So, don't get to fucked up tonight I need y'all on your toes.
We went back to our little party joking and laughing with one another and eating some more food, but I did not drink or smoke too much. I did just what he asked so my head would be clear to put in some more work.
I went to bed thinking about this next job wondering what it is. We have to do with each job. I grew more confident and wanting to get better. The next day came in blazing fast but we did not roll out until the afternoon. I got washed and dressed and sat in the living room waiting on everybody else. Spider came in the room first, then X and Fat Jerome last, we all rolled out at 11 O'clock on the dot we drive out to the King of Prussia Mall to meet up with the bikers. The Black Demons MC's. it took about an hour to get there we pull up in the parking lot and Spider said," okay we wait they know where we are going to be at, they're going to come find us everybody sit tight.

Check this out gang there hiring us out for a job as a favor to Top-Cat the president of the Black Demons a very powerful man in the black underworld. He's a very good friend to have on our side they can't kill one of their men because they have the DEA all over them and because their peoples are tight with one of the old heads. His name is Pot Belly Paul one of the club members his son Bill Deazy is working with the DEA and they have to take him out without upsetting his whole club. Soon as he said that four black dudes on motorcycles came riding up on us. Spider said, "okay, here we go. Come on." We all get out the Range Rover they get off their bikes and Spider shakes hand with their leader smiling, "What's up, TC?
"I'm good."
"Hey TC. This is Almasi you already know Jerome and X."
"Yes, I do what's up fellas? He shakes hands with both of them smiling. Top-Cat said, "okay Almasi or should I say Miss Diamond?" We all started laughing, "yeah we all speak Swahili fluently. I'm Top-Cat this is my son Dream."
"What's up? Da Da (Sister). This my VP over here this Jo-Jo Outlaw."
"Hey, what's up baby? This is Dr. Jerry."
"Hi, how you doing little Lady?
"This is my sergeant of arms Gee-Gee Thug."
"Hey baby what's shaking."
"Okay, this is the gig my son Dream the guy who set the deal up. Billy one of our members who is working with the DEA and another one of our men Kam is riding with him to meet up with the buyer. Soon as the exchange jumps off at the first parking area on the left-hand side of FDR park, we need for y'all to kill him and the buyer. This is what they look like he pulls out his phone and pulls up the picture and he hand it to Spider. He looks at it and swipes to the next picture then he hands it to X. He looks at both of them then Fat Jerome and then me and I hand the phone back to Spider. Spider give it back to Top-Cat who said, "I'll still send you the pictures. You can give it to your peoples. It will have to go down today in FDR park in South Philly very few cops on duty. Smoke them two and I'll give you 10 large for each one of y'all. Spider nodding his head no and replied, "No, give me 10 for setting it up, 20 each for my men and we got a deal."

Top-Cat looks at Jo-Jo Outlaw nodding his head yes. All right Jo-Jo give me that as he steps up handing Spider a brown paper bag from out of his Cut saying, "this is 40 large you get the rest when the job is done. Okay meet me at my other spot with the money, cool?"
"Yeah, I'll be there my old friend."
"You got three hours to the drop I'm sending you them pictures right now."
Spider looks at his phone and announces, "I got it." He shakes hands with him, and we all walked back to the car and all of them walked to their motorcycles and take off roaring up the road. We pull off jumping on the expressway. Spider said, 'we have to get you guys geared up to put in this work." he drives to this garage under the bridge on 25th street in South Philly. X and Jerome jumped out opening up the gate as Spider drives inside parking on the left near the wall in this big garage. I never been here before X and Jerome quickly shut the gate real fast and came to the back of the garage. It's about four trucks inside of this joint it smelled like oil, gasoline and it is really musty in this motherfucker. I get out of the Range Rover as Spider got to the back of the place and he hits the panel and flips around. It is like six rows of all kinds of machine guns, handguns, hand grenades and bullet proof vests. Spider said to me, "pick one out, baby girl I know Christmas was the other day but you getting you gift today all right." I get myself a vest and I'd put it on right quick then I get a MP-5 and an AK-47. I make sure I get the right clips for each one of the machine guns and I make sure I have extra ones too plus I get about three hand grenades just in case we get in a fucking tight spot.
At the same time X, Fat Jerome gear up as well while Spider pulled up the black GMC truck for us then he waited on us to all get ready. Soon as we were done getting dressed, he waves us all over and said, "look X, you're on the wheel. Almasi you're behind the trigger and you Jerome you're in the switch car in the Acme market parking lot. I'll have Brenton and Damon to come get the truck after y'all is gone okay. Let's go to work."

Me and X jumped in the black GMC truck. Spider and Jerome open the gate and let us out then Jerome went and jumped in the blue work van and drove out with Spider. He gets in his Range Rover, drove out then he stopped, jumped out, ran up closing the gate locking everything up, jumped back in his whip and pulled off. It only takes us 15 minutes to get to FDR park we get there early that's a good thing we park on the far-right hand side of the park and we sit waiting on our target. A half an hour blaze past we can see the DEA guys approaching us.

They pull up in one dark green car and a big blue van there looking around we are ducking down, and they set up the van. We park on the right but we both know there the jump out boys after the shit goes down. Then after about a good 20 minutes later three motorcycles dudes in all black leather came riding up on the left just like they said it was going to go down. Then we see the dude get out the car smiling they ride up and park their bikes. The guy Billy got off his bike as the other two dudes just sit on their bikes not too far from him. I got my mask on and gripping my machine gun in my hand ready to go then X started up the car and said, "here we go, sister. He put his black mask on and pulls off really fast. Soon as the guy Billy came up and shake hands with the dude out of the car. I let loose on their ass Kapackatackat! Kackatackapack! Kapackatackata!

I sprayed both the men hitting both of them center mass as X drove off making a fast-hard right turn outside of the park then I hear X yelling, "we got company, baby girl." I looked back and this blue van and their shooting at us and they're on our ass. I'd reach out the window shooting back at them then I said to him while I'm shooting back at them as the truck is swaying from side to side, "Yo X, slow down man"

"What?"

"Slow down?"

"What the fuck are you crazy, Ma?"

"Just slow down so I get this motherfucker off our ass man trust me!"

"Okay, but if we get caught were both dead you know, that right?" He slows the truck down and soon as they started speeding up on us, I pull the pen and toss the hand grenade right before it hits the windshield Kaboom! Then the van flips over on fire and crashed in a row of cars on the right-hand side. As X sped off with mad skills good thing, I was a Tomboy when I was younger. X drove to the car switch in the Acme parking lot he parks right next to the black van with Jerome behind the wheel. We took our time getting in the van as he pulled off nice and smooth. I pack all both of the machine's guns and the grenade in a duffle bag so I can take this shit home with me.

Later on, were all at the spot chilling in the living room watching a basketball game on ESPN getting our puff on. Then Spider came in the door about an hour later with a big smile on his face and big fat yellow envelopes filled with money in his hand.

He said, "damn, baby girl you're getting better each hit there both dead and one of them that was in the driver side of the van that was chasing y'all. He hands X one of the fat envelopes and he grabs it right quick. Then he hands Fat Jerome his then he hands me mine winking his eye and said to all of us good job, "Top-Cat is really happy he said he might have some more work for us."

I was feeling the biker dude Dream, but I kept it to myself because I don't want Spider jumping on my ass about talking out of turn again. So, I stayed cool about saying what was on my mind now. With this money here is enough for me to get my own spot and I can see anybody I want to see.

"Okay y'all have a good time. I holla at y'all a little later. I have to go talk to a few people and he went back out the door.

I'd got up off the floor and went to my room to count my money. I close the door and sat on the bed and its 20 thousand dollars. My phone started ringing and it's my girl Shamika we talked for a very long time and made plans to hook up to see one another. I told her I need her to go with me while I go look for my own place.

That very next week that's just what I did I'd looked around at about five houses. me, Shamika, Spider and his wife Sheila was a big help. She even helped me find some really nice furniture for my new house. His wife Sheila helped me understand the paperwork for my house too. I brought a three-story house on 22nd & Pine street not too far from Spider's apartment.

GETTING MORE SKILLS FOR THE NEW YEAR

It's the second week in January 1997, I'm in my new house I'm just chilling on the couch watching TV. When Spider told me, he was coming over to take me for some training. The military dude Nokey Blaze had sent him in to give everybody some skills for the new year. So, I get myself together before he comes to the crib. He came and picked me up a half an hour later and when I get in the car, he asks me, "So how is the new place?"

"It's nice I'm need help with the bathroom other than that it's great."

"Good, one thing when you have a house, you're going to find out it always something that needs to be repaired, baby girl but I'm happy for you over here you deserve it. You worked hard to get it."

"Thanks to you and your wife look I've been thinking about going to get my little sister?"

"Yeah, but if you're asking me for some advice about that I'll tell you to wait until you're really on your feet, stack up some more chips for yourself if you're asking me that's what I think."

"Maybe you're right so who are these guys that are training us?"

"There the BMF Black Militia Force. Mister Irving, his son Big Boom and Hugo all of them are soldiers of fortune they were in both wars Iraq and Afghanistan. They're going to train y'all for the next three months or so until y'all got the shit down tight. Don't worry me and my wife will look after the house and the bills for you okay." "Sure, you know I trust y'all were family."

"See that's what I'd want to hear from you, baby girl I have to say you've been on top of your shit after I gave you a little talking too and I want you to stay that way as well you hear me?"

"Yes, I hear you but it's something I want to ask you Spider."

"I know what you want to ask me, but I'll tell you after you come back from training and I'll tell you everything you want to know about your family and when I tell you you're going to wish I never told you."

"Okay that sounds fair soon as I come back you and me will have that sit down. We pull up at the scrap yard in North Philly and it's this big ass van with fucking camouflage on it. Spider looks over at me and said, "well there go your ride and don't worry you can trust them they already know I'll rip their balls off if they fuck with you trust me. They are crazy but they know I'm fucking crazier so you good. You sure? Do you trust me? Yes, I trust you not them. Well you going to have to trust them. Go ahead you're going to be all right. X and Fat man will be there looking out for you for me from the door." He patted me on the shoulder and gave me a sign of safety. He continued,

"So, you're going to be just fine, baby girl."

"You promise your going have that talk with me when I get back."

"Yeah, I am a man of my word. Nokey want this done and this ain't fucking cheap neither so go." I get out the car and I walked up to X and Fat Jerome is there. I bump fist with both of them and Mister Irving came walking up. This guy is a huge black dude this nigga looks like he eats nails for breakfast and shit out bullets. He came up yelling, "okay let's move that fucking ass of yours, cupcake. Right now, let go into the fucking van let's go! Let's go! We all jumped in the van as Spider came up and shake hands with Mister Irving. He just nodded his head and jumped in the van and he drove us up in the fucking mountains somewhere from day one. He worked the shit out of us drilling us. The next day I met Hugo he's one ugly ass motherfucker, but Big Boom is fine. This nigga Big Boom is not giving me no kind of fucking break whatsoever to tell you the truth. I think he was working me a little harder because I was a female, but I was not going to let these motherfuckers break me. The one strange thing doe the more Big Boom worked me that's what made me like him even more.

I learned fast and a whole lot of shit every day. They taught me more about machine guns, handguns, hand grenades and hand to hand combat. The shit was crazy to me how the whole three months went past in a blaze. I tell you right about now nobody can tell me shit. I'm one bad bitch. The day we were all ready to go home I wrote my number down and I handed to Big Boom. He just gave me an evil look with a smirk and acted like he still hated my guts. I was really glad to get home and sleep in my own bed. Just like Spider said they really looked after my house I had a stack of fucking junk mail. I'd seen they paid all the bills and had all the receipts up on my refrigerator. A week later I called my girl Shamika to help me celebrate my birthday she came over and we got our smoke on after being the in the fucking woods for the last three months playing G.I. Fucking Jane and shit. It's about time I went out and have a good time we both agree to going out on Friday night and get twister for real.

"So, where the fuck you been at girl?" While she's puffing up a storm leaning back on my couch. "I was training for the gang."

"What's up are you going to put me on because I'm getting my shit from Duck and the product is fucking weak. I think he's tapping the shit before he's giving it to us. I need to know where yawl from the shit it is bumping." Now shit is slow now that you not hooking us up." "Man, that's bad for business. I'll take care of Duck ass what I need you to get me one of your packs when you first get it and bring it to me. I'll let Spider know about this shit."

"Well good he's getting me my shit tomorrow. I'll sure nuff bring it too you after that. Are you going to hook us up?

"Yeah, I will once you show me what's going on, he'll let me hook y'all up. So, were getting our smoke on for a while when I get the call its Big Boom. "Hey, what's up tough girl?"

"Oh, shit after you work me like a fucking dog and you calling me tough girl. I should call you Mister Slave driver."

"Oh, you got jokes I have to do that it's my job or my father would not let me work with him anymore. I'm sorry about that. I'm feeling you, but I had to do what I had to do, baby."

"Okay, then you are going have to make it up to me then."

"Sure, I'll make it up to you. How about dinner tonight?" "Sure, come pick me up about eight. Is that good."

"I'll be there sweetheart see you that."

Shamika snickered and said, "I thought you was out there training bitch this nigga calls you up for a date and shit." "I was but we could not do shit it was all business that why he called me up for a date plus I have not done shit sense them assholes raped me. That's why I'm glad I went and did it because I'm going to kill every last one of them motherfuckers who did it."

"I hear you girl; I love this spot you got least you're not in the hood. I know it's quiet around here?"

"Yes, it is, and I love it too. I don't miss the hood to keep it real with you."

We both laughed and smoked another blunt, she got up and put on her coat. I'd walked her to the door, and she announced, "don't forget about Friday, bitch was going to paint the town girl!"

"I said you know it." She drove off and I went and got ready for my date. I have not been on a real date in about a year.

So, I did my hair and put on a really nice blue dress, my black three-quarter length leather coat and some sharp black flats. I admire myself in the mirror and I must say I look really nice. I clean up really good. After checking myself out for a little while my phone rings I run and answer its Big Boom.

"Hey beautiful, I'm outside the door right now."

"Okay, I'll be right down to let you in. I looked in the mirror right quick as I primp just a little more. I ran down stair to get the door. I slowed down and I played it real cool. I open the door and he looked a whole lot better in a shirt and some jeans then all that fucking camouflage I seen him in for the last three months. I smiled and said, "please come in." He winked and he has something behind his back. He handed me a bouquet of flowers, "these are for you I hope you like them." He handed me a bouquet of flowers, I'm thinking to myself, so Mister Hard ass have a soft side to him that's a good thing. I smell the flowers and say, "I love them thank you"

"Have a seat while I put these in some water there beautiful, I can't say I'm surprised because I see who you were looking at me while you were so mean to me. But I know you was doing your job, baby there is no hard feelings. I know how it goes, okay."

"Well, I feel better that you know that, baby. Are you ready to go? Yes, I'm am let me go get a few things and I'll be ready to go all right."

"Sure thing, baby. I go get my new handbag and make sure I have everything I need. I check and see if I got my keys and I walk to where he's sitting and announce, "I'm ready to go."

He stands up and said, "good, I'm hungry. what about you?"

"Yes, where are you taking me?"

"Ribbits on Walnut street. I never been there but I heard people talking about it." We both walk out the door and I locked up my house.

Big Boom pointed and said, "my car is right over here it's the dark blue Cadillac Escalade. He opens the door for me, and I hop in and off we go. We had dinner and a great conversation. I must say he's pretty smart not just a good-looking dude. I learned a lot from him in those three months out in the fucking woods and with very little conversation. At dinner as well, we talked for a while before he took me home and walked me to the door. I was thinking to myself I was not going to give it up on the first date, but I did kiss him long and hot and nothing else. I told him after we kiss, we have a lot more to look forward to in the future. He just nodded his head and smile saying, "he understood." I'm thinking to myself he's all right if he willing to wait. I'm feeling this guy out so far so good. It's about time I have a life outside of the gang I'm hoping this thing works out because I really like Big Boom. I go to bed and I have sweet dreams about this dude until I can get with him and find out if he's for real. If we go out two more times, I know after the next time we go out I'm going to give him some by then I'll know more about him.

WERE AT WAR

In the last three weeks I did not talk to Spider now I think it time I holla at him and find out what was really going on with him. I think he's my father and he don't want to tell me. It's about 11 in the afternoon and I call him up he picks right up and said, "hey what's up with you, Shorty?"
"I'm good I think we need to have that talk now?"
"Sure thing, I be over to your spot in about an hour, okay."
"All right, I'll be here, and I hang up, but I think I'm ready to hear what he has to tell me."
So, I sit up on my couch waiting for him to come. Just like he said he came he came and soon as he knocked on the door my heart was racing. I jump up and get the door I peek out the window to see if its him. I open the door, "come on in, please."
"Damn, you really hook this place up really nice, baby girl." I sit on the couch and he sat on the loveseat. He looks up at saying, "okay, you been waiting on this for a very long time so after I tell you this you have to promise me you're not going go after the person who killed your father or you and me are both dead. Do you understand what I'm telling you?"
"Yes, I understand but you have to tell me why?"
"I'm telling you because the person that killed your father you met him, and you know how put the order out for it to get done"
"So, was it you?"
"No, it was not me, but I was there I was just a soldier."
"Was it Nokey?"
"No before Nokey took over it was Giovanni Black. Nokey was just a Capo like me now."
"So where is Giovanni now? He's doing life but he still a shot caller from prison don't get it twisted."
"Okay then I promise not to say anything about it. I'll keep it with us."
"You have to or were both are dead do you hear me; Almasi I'm trusted you with my life here."

"I will never put your life on the line for everything you done for me. Could you tell me what happen, please?"

"Okay like I said we had hit on this big-time drug dealer name Leon Williams, your father he had Giovanni's son killed. His name was Malik, so Giovanni sent the woman you know to be Your mother Dotty to set it up. Leon because he had a thing for her, she left the door unlocked for us to get in we killed the four goons. It was me, Buck Shot and Crazy Tee so he killed your father and your mother."

"What was my real mothers name? Her name was Teja. So, what is my real name did you know?"

"I don't know that, baby. I wish I could have help you with that we just hooked up Dotty some fake birth certificate for her with the name you have Sharonda with Dotty's last name."

"Can I look it and find out on the low? You can and you will see that you as a baby is missing or presumed dead, so I don't want it to freak you out when you see it."

"Okay, do you know anybody who can help me with that kind of shit. I got a guy I got his number I'll call him he's really good. His name is Layne West. He was navy seal he got caught selling drugs overseas after he got kicked out and did his time. He's been putting in work on the street for people like us but he's not cheap, baby girl but it will be no blow back on us. I'll have him call you tonight, all right?"

"Sure thing, now I want to hear the rest of the story."

"So, things go sideways with the hit because Crazy Tee and Buck Shot get into over the baby."

"The baby?"

"Yeah you were the baby then Dotty ran in the room yelling not for them to kill the baby." She said, "you guys did not say anything about killing the baby." Then when I came in the room to see what was going on Crazy Tee said, 'Giovanni want everybody in the house dead and then mean you too bitch.' So, Buck Shot looked at me nodding his head. So, I shot Crazy Tee in the head and Buck Shot got the baby and gave it to Dotty. He told her if she says anything about this shit, he was going to kill her and for her to take care of the baby that you me and Buck Shot was not going to kill a little baby that had nothing to do with the sins of the family. We just told Giovanni that one the goons killed Crazy Tee when we came in the spot and from time to time, I came checking on you since I gave Dotty some money until she got too far gone on crack. So that's why I always looked out for you like you was my own. I wish I was your father but I sure nuff feel like it sometimes. So now you know I did not want to tell you, but I knew one day I had to. Just understand if the story gets out about me and Buck Shot killing Crazy Tee his son who is in the gang as well will have us killed."

"So, what's his son name? His is Gill the one who was trying to talk to you at the Christmas party. So, you see how close this shit is."

"Yeah I do I won't say anything Spider."

"Good, but one other thing you have a brother and a sister out there."

"I do?"

"Yeah, you do your sister lives in Las Vegas her name is De-Wanda she's married with three kids and your brother is here in Philly. He's the head of the **Hadid Ajundi** that means Iron Soldiers. He's one of our friends of the gang. If you want, I hook up a sit down with you and him. He doesn't know I was one of the men who was there to kill his father so that can never come up or we will not be friends anymore."

"So how are you going to tell him that were brother and sister?"

"I just tell him that Dotty took you in after his folks got killed. We just don't tell him the other shit Dotty won't say shit she knows she will get killed too."

"You sure we can trust Dotty junky ass?"

"I don't but if she says anything nobody would believe her anyway. She's so cracked the fuck out but if she does, she's dead. You cool with this?"

"Yeah I'm cool with it if she run her mouth."
"Okay and you better not say shit to her about anything I just told you here today.
"I won't say shit to her. And don't take out on her what happen before only the rape thing not how you got there."
"I hear you, but I was really hoping that you were my father but just like you said you are in a way and thank for telling me the truth about everything."
"Well I really did not want to tell you but it's something I wanted to do for a very long time. Look I'm going to get out of here, I'll stop by the crib tomorrow. I got some shit to run by you too."
"Look, I got something to run by you right now."
Like what? Your boy Duck is tapping the product that's why sale is down in South Philly."
"Oh really, you have some of it so I can test it. I sure do my girl Shamika drop some of it off I'll go get it."
"No, I'll have one of my men come get it I can't ride around with that shit on me."
"I'll send somebody in about half an hour to come get all right."
"Sure, let me walk you to the door and thanks again."
"You don't have to thank me it was something I had to do for you, Shorty. I'll talk to you later." He hugged me and I watch him walked to his car as I'd stood in the door way the shit did not turn out like I thought it was going go but I don't feel bad about what I know now after I'd watch Spider drive off. I wanted to flop back on the couch watching TV and I forgot about him send somebody about the weak crack I hear the doorbell ring I go to the door and its Brenton. I open the door, "Yo what's up, Sis."
Spider sent me to pick up that thing from you. "Okay, come in I'll go get it have a seat, man. I'll be right back."
"Wow you really got a nice spot over here." I went and got the weak crack I put it under my sink, and I came back and handed it to him. He said, "I know I don't know you that good, but I heard from somebody that you Spider's daughter?"
"Who told you that?"
"I just heard it from somebody in the gang that's all."
"And if I was what is it to you?"
"I was just asking, sweetheart. I just have the heart to ask you to your face that all and not talking behind your back like everybody else."

"Well now you know. What are you doing writing a fucking book Nigga?"
"No, I was just asking I won't say shit about it. I'm sorry I didn't mean any harm asking you know what I'm saying?"
"Okay, then you can bounce with the shit."
He Just looked at me and he went out the door fucking ass hole. I went back to watching TV for about an hour or so when Spider called me saying, "hey, I'll have Fat Jerome to come pick you up and take you to the garage were at war right now. I tell you the rest when you get there." I quickly put on my boots, my black velour sweat suit, my black hoodie I get my two Glocks soon as I ran down the steps. I hear a knock at my door I peek out and its Fat Jerome asking, "you ready, sis?"
"Yeah, let's go!"
I jump inside of his green Chevy truck I'd check my guns and make sure I have some extra clips. If we really get deep into the shit, we can blow off a nigga's head and his Dick right quick and scream out loud the BNS click. Fat Jerome he took off down the street and I say, "what the fuck happened? We got hit by Black Lou Diamond brother's Dumar is on the war path they hit five of our spots and they shot up Nokey Blaze brother Jasper house the one you met at the party. He's shot up bad but he's not dead but there saying his son little Jasper might not make it."
"Damn that's fucked up so what are next move? I'm not sure but I think Spider is going to hit Dumar's peoples spot he going to tell us everything at the garage."
The last war we lost about eight people about three years ago, so I hope all that training you did up in the woods help you out because it going to get really bloody, sis. I know you ready."
"How you know I'm ready?"
"Because I can see it in your eyes, I seen it from the first day you came to the gun range you're going to do just fucking fine."

I just smile as we pulled up at the garage then I see X come out the side door and he opened the gate. Fat Jerome drives in and parks on the right-hand side we jump out and go to the back. Spider is standing there he bumps fist with both of us and said, "look gear up I'm waiting for the call from that dude I was telling you about today. He's giving me the location of Dumar's right hand man's hold up spot and his house too. But he's looking for us to hit him, so he'll be ready.

I got my man Layne West to track him down and let us know where he's hiding at until then were going to hit his right-hand man and then his son Kalear's house he doesn't think we know where he lives at. They shot up Nokey's brother and his nephew. He might not make it throughout the night, so we have to go so sit tight after you gear up. So, we sat around then more guys came to the garage this is the first time I met Petey Q, Spider half-brother same father different mothers and his crazy ass crew Mister Blade, Tommy Machete, Puerto Rican Joe, Merk, Bullseyes, Knock Daddy and Sammy Green.

Spider walks up to his brother hugging him and shaking hands and bumping chest with all of them. Then he huddles up with them talking and telling them what they have to do then Brenton and his boys Ayden, Jairo and Nico. Brenton came over to me and said, "can I talk to you for a minute please?" I walk over to the side with him and I looked him in his face talking low, "so what the fuck do you want?"

"I just wanted to say I'm sorry about early today okay I don't want you to tell your dad what I said to you please." "Okay only if you do something for me."

"And what's that?"

"I need you to take out Duck and watch my girl Shamika's back with his crew after its done don't worry I'll let my dad know all about it." "when are you going to do that?"

"Right now, hold on." I walk over to Spider saying can I talk to you for a minute dad." He just winks and smiled walking over to the side with me saying, "what is it you want Shorty my daughter?"

"Look I want to ask you if I can get Brenton and his people to take out Duck for tapping that crack."

"Yeah, I wanted to talk you about that good looking out we tested that shit and he's been doing that for a while now. Some of our other people tested their shit too and the same shit yeah tell him to take care of this other business and thanks again, baby girl." So, we both walked over to Brenton standing with his boys, look me and my daughter over here was talking, and you got my okay to make that move on Duck after were done with this shit here all right." Before he walked off, he winked his eye at me he must have heard the same shit about me being his daughter. He just let them know what they were thinking was true. I pulled Brenton to the side Look for now on don't come to my house talking crazy or I'll let my dad know about it all right. "Sure, thing it will never happen again Almasi." "Good now keep everything we talked about under you hat, or you will not have a head to put your fucking hat on nigga you hear me? I hear you Ma. Then soon as it got dark outside Spider got the call, he quickly goes in the small office on the right so he can hear and after a few minutes, he came out saying loud, **"Kila mtu aifanye!"**

"Everybody keeps it down! **Utulivu!** (*Quiet Everyone!*) The entire room got Quiet and looked up at Spider."

"Okay my brother Petey Q is going to hit Dumar's son house in West Philly 65th & Samson street. You Brenton and your crew are going to be his right-hand man's hold up in Yeaden Windsor street 59th street 5910 light that shit up! X Jerome and Almasi you're going to back them up that would make seven of y'all. I want X and them to go in first."

"Brenton you hear me?"

"Yes, Sir I'll do that."

"Just follow orders, nigga **Ondoke nje!**" (*Move out*)

"I'm ready to go and the three of us jump in the black work van with X behind the wheel." He drove up to the gate and Fat Jerome jumps out and opens it. X pulls out as Jerome jump back in the van as Brenton and his crew is in a dark blue Tahoe truck is right behind us. We ride out to Yeaden it takes us about an hour to get there because it's still cold outside it not too many people out. Its dark so we park a block from the house X turn to me and said, "you and Jerome go in the back. I'll go around the block after you kill everything in sight and jump in the truck okay! I'll call Brenton to move in the front he calls him he picks up "Yo Hit **mbele walikuwa wanak wenda nyuma** *(Hit the front were going in the back. All right I got you.)* One!

"Okay Almasi. Jerome its show time let's go!"

We both put on our black mask and jump out the truck, me and Jerome sneak up towards the back of the house we make it up to the back door. I'm on the right Jerome is on the left. I nodded my head and he get up to the door and kicked it in Boom! I stayed low and just in two seconds three-gun men came at us. Me and Jerome we open up on their ass and get lower from right and left Kapatataka! Katakackat! Tackapackta! Tackapackta!

Hitting them in the head, stomach and chest most of the blood splashed up on the walls and floor. The rest of the people who were in the front room started shooting at us as we came toward them. They started running out the front door me and Jerome just slowed up. Soon as we slowed up, we can hear the shots ringing out loud. They shot up and killed all five of the men who were running out the front door.

Now we make our move out the door and running past the men laying on the ground in big pools of blood. Me and Jerome run not even a half a block and X came riding up on us saying **Ingia***(Get in)* I say to Jerome, "what he say?" He said, "get in!" We giggled about it and jumped in the truck and they took off laughing, "were going have to get up on some more Swahili."

We drive back to the garage it took us less than a half an hour to get back. X parks the van across the street from the garage and we all walked to the side door. Spider is sitting in the back with this dark skin dude and three of his men Spider stood up and said, "this is my daughter, Almasi" "Almasi this is Emillano Vagus a very good friend of mind he's been working with us for years." He already knows X and Jerome. He shakes hands with both of them smiling, "what's up brothers good seeing you again."

Spider said, "X is my number two now go get us some chairs, Jerome so we can all sit down and talk. I need you in on this as well okay. Sure thing **Nahodha**(Captain) he walks to the side getting more folding chair for all of us to sit down. His men they all stood up not too far from him Emillano saying, "now that everybody has a seat, I wanted to tell you **Hermiano** *(Brother)."*

"I appreciate you seeing me while you in the middle of your war, but I have a real problem with these Gorilla Boulevard motherfuckers!"

"I know you guys do business with them but there really growing there moving in on our action with a lot of the black crews."

"I need your help because we been working together for a very long time now."

"So, what is it you need from us?"

"Well after you done dealing with Dumar and his people were going to need you to hit Khalil Walker and his muscle. We can't get close enough to them without somebody getting wise to what we're doing other then that we would do it."

"Okay I know we been working together but we get paid for work like that and were not cheap **Hermiano** *(Brother)* But you can't give us some kind of discount here? Yes, we can as long as you come down on them keys, we can."

"Okay its 27,000 dollar a key we been selling them to you for 23,000 a key. I'll drop that down to 20 and we can have a deal here?"

"Make it 18 and we have a deal!"

"Okay that's fair at 18 and I have 50 large right here and now to show you we are for real."

"That's not showing me you're for real, that's just showing me your trying to get out this real cheap over here."

"Okay then what about 65? Come up just a little more like 80 and 18 for the keys drop down next week."
"I'll give you the 80 only if you take out that mean asshole Khalil and the price on the coke drops after four months."
"That gives me more time to talk to my peoples about the adjustment okay."
"Sure, that sounds good, but could you front me some keys until that happens?"
"Sure, I can do that, so we have a deal?"
"Yes, we have a deal." Spider and Emillano both shake hands. Then Spider phone rings he puts up his finger and announced, "I have to take this hold on for a minute." He jumps up and he walks a few feet from where we all were sitting. Then he come back to the table and announced, "let me walk you and your men out to the door." He looks over at X and Jerome They both stood up walking with him and Emillano to the front of the garage side door. Emillano went to the two vehicles with Spider X and Jerome they stood out there watching them take off from under the dark bridge. They came back inside and sat back down, and he looked at every one of his team and announced, "you guys did a great job just got word that Dumar's right hand man is dead. Evan is dead and my brother Petey Q got Kalear too he's dead as well word is Dumar got out of town. So, all of y'all can go home. Jerome I'm need you to take Almasi home I talk to you later all right."
I'm getting out of here too so me and Jerome go get into his dark green truck parked on the right. X lets us out it only take us a half an hour to get to my house he parked only a few doors from my house and said, "I holla at you later, Sis!"

I just laughed as he watches me go in the door as he pulls off down the street. I take off my vest and my boots flop on the couch watching TV. I talk to Big Boom on the phone for a little while then I made me something to eat and watch some more TV until I fell asleep.

FINISHING THE JOB

The next day I sleep in late when I got the call from Spider it's like 1 O'clock in the afternoon. "Yo what's up, Shorty?" "I'm just sleeping in late that's all what's up with you?" "Well I'm need you to come past the spot that dude I was telling you about is stopping by and I have a really nice surprise for you as well."
"Okay I will be there in about an hour or so I'm going to take a cab."
"All right just get here talk to you soon. I get myself together I go wash up and get dressed. I called a cab and I waited downstairs for about half an hour and the cab called me on my phone telling me he was outside. I locked up really good and jumped in the cab it only took 15 minutes to get there. I tipped him and I went up to the door and X open the door. He let me in, and said, "he's in the living room waiting for you, sis."
"I'll be right back as he went back out the door." I walked in the living room and Spider is sitting on the couch as he patted the seat next to him, "have a seat, baby girl." he said. "He'll be here in a few I wanted to tell you the big surprise. I have for you first I have to give you your money from yesterday." He hands me a fat envelope I just put it in my inside pocket of my coat and his phone rings. He answers it right and yelled, "okay, here I come right now." He walks to the door open it and this tall dark skin man walks in with him. He introduced him to me, "this is Almasi."
"Almasi this is Layne West the man that can help you find out your real name without anybody knowing about."
He shook my hand and said, "nice to meet you, Almasi." "please have a seat brother." He sits down," well I can help you, but I don't know if he told you I'm really expensive." "Yeah, he told me that too."
"Well I'm not trying to be funny, but do you have 50 large for me to do this to get started?"
"Yes, she does homeboy here you go." He hands him an envelope Spider continued, "this is 50 to get you started and you will get 20 when it's all done.
"30 and were all done"

"Okay then 30. How long will it take?"
"Give me two weeks and I'll have everything you need. Is that's cool?" I looked at him and nod my head, "yeah, that's cool."
Spider stood up, "good, I'll walk you to the door, homes give us a call when it's all done."
"I sure will man I'll be in touch, okay and nice meeting you Almasi."
"I'll have what you need in a couple week okay you two have a good day." Spider stands in the door watching him go to his car and he came back sitting down, "now it's time for your surprise come with me. I get up and we walked outside up to this big black Chevy Trailblazer and he hands me the keys, Happy birthday. I hope you like it?" I started jumping up and down like a schoolgirl at the playground.
"No, I love it. Thank you!"
I'd hugged him and said, "wow, I can't believe it you did this for me. Well after you spend all your money on your crib, I thought I'll help you out a little."
"Come on let's go for a ride." I jump in. Soon as I put my ass up in that truck, I knew this was for me, I was hooked on big trucks the first time I drove Spider's Range Rover. We drove around for a couple hours we stopped to get something to eat at TGIF Friday's on City line avenue and talked about everything but the deadly game. Were all in but at this point in my life, I was loving it. I dropped Spider back off at his apartment and I took my new baby home with me. I'd called up Shamika and she came over to my house and we went out to the club that night. We had a really nice time until we were walking to my new truck. when this guy kept staring at me really hard.
I just keep walking real smooth playing it cool as Shamika is tapping me on the arm and said, "that guy is really checking you out, girl. Why don't you get his number?"
I giggled, "I'm cool girl just keep walking he looks like one of them dudes that was shooting at me on a hit I did in South West Philly will you come on and get to the fucking truck bitch."
"What you are doing hits? Damn, I'm thinking you was bullshitting me talking about training and all that shit here he comes too."
He came up with about four dudes I'd jumped in the truck soon as I close the door, he yelled out, "that's the bitch, Cherry. I know her ass anywhere!"

I' pulled off with the quickness out of the parking lot from 8th street. I'm speeding up the street I looked in my rearview mirror and my heart was beating like an 808 drum on a hard-funky hip hop track. It's a Cadillac Escalade is hot on our ass I make it to the expressway exit to get on and he's coming up on me fast. I tell Shamika, "grab the wheel so I can get my shit." I put some guns and a few grenades in the truck just in case and the first night I'm out this shit goes down. Good thing I was ready for any kind of bull shit that jump off as time goes by after doing hits.

I stack a small little arsenal along with the hand grenades and I'd had three of them. So, I did the same thing I did to the DEA guys that were on our ass after the hit for the bikers. I had Shamika holding the wheel of my new whip I reach back and find my MP-5 machine gun, the clip and I slapped it in. tha I get the grenade holding it in my hand along with my machine gun. I'd yelled at Shamika on three where going to switch you get behind the wheel and I'll start shooting at their ass holes to get them off are ass okay. All right you ready? Yeah! Okay One two three! I jump on the other side and she jump behind the wheel I'd rolled the window down really swift and I started spitting hot shit at these motherfuckers. The truck is swaying from side to side, but I hit the windshield and cracked it a little too then I yelled to Shamika slow down just a little. What is you crazy girl? "Just do it, okay! It's going to work but soon as I said that to her, they sped up and was right beside us. Shooting at us just missing our ass.

Good thing Shamika was ducking as well peeked up just a little. I came up and I toss the grenade like a fast ball like I was Darrell Strawberry. I yelled at, "Shamika punch it, bitch. Come on!" She speeds up Kaboom! I looked back and the truck was on fire and I see it crash into the wall. Doom!

While were driving off Shamika is yelling at me, "where did you get a fucking grenade, bitch?" We both started laughing, "I got it from my daddy, Spider."

She drove to her house in South Philly. She lives on 24th street.

It takes us a half an hour to get to her spot soon as she pulled up in front of her house. She looks me in my face, "are you going to be all right going home, girl?"

"Yeah girl, I'm right in center city I'll be home in ten minutes don't worry about me girl. I'm good go head in the house. I'll call you when I get in the door okay."
"And you better do that too, bitch. I'm not playing. We both chuckled as I got out of my truck with my gun, I watch her go in the door. I jump back in my truck and I took off. I went home soon as I got in the door, I called her up to let her know that I was cool, and we talked about what happen to us for a little while. Then I took my ass to bed after the kind of night I'd had I'm fucking drained.

FINDING OUT WHO THE FUCK I AM!

Two weeks blaze past and its springtime now. We have not heard a word from them bitch-Made niggas that made a move on Nokey Blaze peoples. The sad news came that his nephew Little Jasper died. I'd felt so fucked up about that I wanted to go out and kill everything moving for real. I'm up cooking me something to eat when my phone rings I get it and check my caller ID its Spider. "Yo, what's up?"

"Hey, what's up wit you, Shorty?"

"Nothing. I'm just fixing me something to eat."

"Okay, look that dude called me saying he's coming by later on today with that information you wanted. He said he was going to call you too."

"Okay, I'll be looking out for his call."

"All right then Shorty I holla at you later **Moja** (One)."

"Moja!" I go upstairs and get dressed soon as I'm done my phone rings and it's the dude Layne West.

"Hello is this Almasi?"

"Yes, this is her. Who is this?'

"This is Layne we met at Spider's crib about that information you needed."

"Yeah, so what's up? I won't give it too you over the phone meet me at Spider's in a half an hour all right."

"Sure thing, I see you there."

Now my mind is going in all kinds of directions but I'm trying to keep cool about this shit. That whole half hour it went so slow because I was so anxious to find out who the fuck I am. It's almost time so I go to my whip and jump in. I'm feeling really nervous about this bull shit I don't know why. I drive to Spider crib in a rush. I get to the house my heart is beating fast soon as I ring the doorbell. X came to the door and let me in bumping fist with me smiling. He asked, "what's up, sis?

"Nothing much where is Spider at?" He's in the office with dude go head he's back their waiting on you.

"Okay then, I see you later. I need to holler at you about something."
"Okay I'll be around, Shorty." We both laughed as I'd walk to the back room my heart is still beating hard but I'm playing it cool I knocked on the door. I hear Spider's deep voice saying, "come on in, baby girl." I walked in the door it was like slow motion soon as I go in and sit down at the long wooden table looking up at Spider and the guy Layne West. He said, "Hi. How are you doing, Almasi? "To tell you the truth I'm real fucking nervous so let get right to it! Tell me what's up." He looked up at me reading off this piece of paper he had on top of the table. He said, "Well, I found out your real name is Chantoya Williams. Your real birth date is 1-17-78, your 18 years old, not 17 like your mom, Dotty said. You were assumed dead after all these years when your father got killed. His name was Leon Williams and your mother's name was Teja Williams."
"What about my father? Did he have any other family?"
"Yes, he did. He had a brother name Billy they call him big Billy Bob. He writes numbers in the black bottom in South West Philly. He has three girls Tye, Delilah and Nikkya there all maybe a few years older than you."
"They all live in the city?"
"Yes, I can find that out for you as well that all goes with what you paid me, okay. So, you and Spider don't think I'm going up on the price. I know I'm high, but I get the job done."
"I see that so what about on my mother's side?"
"Yeah she has three brothers and a sister. The guys names are Arthur, Elvin and Dylon they all live here in South Philly. Along with their sister name Danielle.
"I'm going to need those address when you get them please."
"No sweat I'll dig around for you and have that for you in about another month or so is that okay?"
"Sure, just don't forget about me all right and thanks for everything."
"No problem, Almasi and Spider did tell you that you do have a brother and a sister, too right?"
"Yes, he told me that he said my brother's name is Mustafa and my sister name is De-Wanda, but I don't know what to tell them if I rolled up on them."

"That's up to you how you're going to do it? But my work for now is done. I'll come and give you what I got when I get it all right here you go." He hands me three pieces of paper with the information. He smiled and stood up. Spider hands him a fat envelope he sticks it in his inside jacket pocket. He shakes hands with Spider then he shakes hand with me and said, "good luck to you, sweetheart. You'll be hearing from me soon, okay."

Spider looks at me while I'm looking at the papers.

"I'll walk him to the door stay right here. I need to talk to you, okay. I'll be right back." He walks out the room while I sit there just looking at the names typed on this paper. Thinking of my next move how I'm I going to tell these people who I am because this shit is all fucked up for real. After a few minutes Spider came back in the back room closing the door.

He sits next to me and announce, "I know how you can play this."

"How am I going to explain this shit to these people when this happen over 18 years ago?"

"Well you can tell them the truth but leave out some of the fucking details that's all, Shorty. You know what I'm saying."

"Your right, but will they believe me?" That's the whole fucking thing about it."

"You can't worry about if anybody is going to believe you, Almasi. Just as long as you know the real truth is all that counts here all right."

"Yeah, you're right about that too but for right now I'm going to take my time with this. I'm a fucking ghost."

"See your getting it together already if you want to cry it's all right. You need to get it out you just don't be fucking crying your whole life because a lot of people in life have been dealt a fucked-up hand."

"You just be the one to turn that shit into a sure nuff winner like you're doing now. Take your time letting these people know who you really are."

"At least you know who you are and its better than most people who go their whole life not knowing shit, you are ahead of the game right now, player."

I stood up and gave him a hug, "thank you for everything."

"Just like I tell you all the time were family for real, you hear me."

"I know that daddy." We both started laughing.

"So, what's going on right now with those peoples? We are tracking them down as we speak soon as I hear something, I'm need you to move in on their ass for me, okay."
"Sure, I'm in, anything else lined up?"
"Yeah, I'll know that later on.
"Today, I'll call you so don't go anywhere far. I'll walk you to the door."
"I have to holler at X about something, okay."
"I have to get up out of here. I talk to you later and y'all need to do that thing with Duck."
"Okay, I'll talk to him about that too by the way can I get something to hook up Shamika and them now that were going to take Duck's funky ass out?"
"Sure, talk to X tell him I said to give it to you, and you make sure you get that shit from them and make sure the shit is right or it's coming out of your pocket. I'm not taking any shorts you know how I roll, Shorty."
"Yes, I do. I'll get the shit done. Good, I'll call you." He hugs me and he goes out the door real smooth. So, I walked in the living room where X was just chillin watching TV getting his puff on so what up with you?
"Nothing much just working matter of fact we have to go and take care of that thing with Duck, sis."
"I'm ready to go so when you want to do it?"
"Right now, fuck it you ready?"
"I was born ready nigga were going to go tool up at the garage?"
"No, we can tool up right here." I have some tools right here."
"I'll be right back." He walks in the other room and he came back with a big black duffle bag and set on the floor and he reach in the bag handing me a gun and a silencer. He said, "we have to take out the crew on the first floor on the low so the others up stair don't get spooked."
"Yeah I feel you on that one I say to him where is the big man at?"
"He's on his way soon as he gets here were rolling out. Sounds good to me who's truck are we going in? We're going in my truck he's at the spot right now bagging shit up we don't need mask for this one here just going to tell the girls to step out and we just smoke his whole crew and get the fuck out of there.

Soon as he said that coming in the house is Fat Jerome his brother Fly Ty and Damon. They all speak, bump fist and hug. Fly Ty said, "he's still there I made sure he had enough shit there to make sure he stays busy." We all started laughing X replied, "all right, my niggas mount up it time to punch in and go to fucking work." He points at me and yelled, "Yo, sis you're with me, let's go!"

Me and X go get into his truck while Fat Jerome, Damon and his brother Ty jumped into their truck parked not too far behind us. We all drive to this three-story house on 15th street. The second floor is where we bag up dope and third floor are where we cap up coke. Duck had four of his boys on the first floor his brother Chez, Big Josh, Salem and Jocko as muscle.

They all know us, so we don't have to go in with force he calls Fat Jerome before going in the house X called up Gill the phone rings three times before he picks up. X yells, "where the fuck you at Gill?"

"I'm two blocks away I be right there, nigga."

"Don't get fucking snappy with me, young X I'll fucking put my foot in your ass if you fuck around on me, man. I'm not them other niggas, okay!"

"All right man, I hear you, X man. I'll be right there." He hangs up. Then he calls Fat Jerome the phone rings one time he picks right up and said, "Yo, me and Almasi is going in and smoke them right quick then I'll text you."

"Y'all go upstairs and we'll be right behind y'all **Moja** *(One)*."

"Moja." We get out the truck and X knocks on the door then Big Josh peeks out and opens the door with a big ass smile on his face, "Yo, what's up, X?"

We both step in as he closes the door as they all speaking to him." Chez is sitting on the couch with Salem playing X-Box and Jocko is sitting by the window.

"You know why I'm here to check up on you youngins to make sure shit is rolling smooth." Chez stand up and come over and shakes X hand and said, "Man everything is all good? Is there something wrong because you usually send the Fat man to check up on us."

"No everything is good I'm just making sure y'all niggas is doing your fucking job that all. As you know I'm running this by the way so I can see shit is all good like you say it is, right?"

“Yes, everything is smooth as a baby’s ass X man. Who is this you got with you? “

He snaps, “Don’t fucking worry about who I got with me, young boy.” Soon as he said that he pulls out his gun with the silencer on it and he shoots Chez right in his face Poooffff! Then he quickly turned and shot Saleam in his neck Poooffff! He holds his neck with all the blood pumping through his fingers gushing out like a fucking waterfall. I had my gun out soon as we stepped in and shoot Big Josh in his chest twice Poooffff!

Pooffff! Next, I shot Jocko standing by the window in the middle of his head Pooffff! He slumped up on the wall with all the blood and his brain fragments all over the back wall. X quickly put his gun in the back of his jeans, and he pulls out his phone and text a basketball. He said to me, “open the door for them.” I open the door Fat Jerome came in first along with his brother Ty and Damon close the door real swift.

X said to them, **“Kupata msichana nje kisha kuwavuta** (“*Get the girl’s out then smoke them.”* They all are nodding their heads going up the steps. Fat Jerome walks up on the second floor. Duck was in the bathroom fucking one of the women he had bagging up the dope. Fat Jerome did not see him when he got up there asking one of the girls, “where is Duck at?” The girl just pointed towards the bathroom. Fat Jerome and Fly Ty started banging on the door real hard. He’s yelling on the other side of the door asking, “who the fuck is that?”

“It’s me Jerome get your ass out here right now nigga so we can talk motherfucker!”

After a few minutes he open the door giggling, “awwww man, I was just getting some exercise that’s all my nigga.” He looks at Damon and said, “tell the girls to go downstairs while we talk to the man who supposed to be running the spot.”

“Okay man, it’s cool everything is running real good, Jerome.”

Damon yelled, “all you girls down stair right now. Let’s go! Move your ass. I’m not fucking playing wit y’all come on!” The six women with nothing on but shoes on their feet started walking down the steps. “Who is on the third floor?”

“Just Sammy and the girls.”

“Okay get on the horn and call him down here right now, motherfucker.”

"He keeps calling him on the phone and he's not picking up Ty."
"Damon go up there and tell that nigga to come down here so I can talk to him see that why I'm here I heard you been fucking up!"
"Man, Ty was just here man he tells you everything. It's all good, brother!"
"**Ng'ombe** Shit (Bull shit) what did you say you know I can't speak all the Swahili shit like you guys." Trying to laugh everything off. The girls came downstairs with me and X. I say to all of them, "if you don't want to join them ass holes in the afterlife you keep your fucking mouth shut! Then Damon and Ty went upstairs finding Sammy in the corner of the room fucking one of the girls who capping up the crack. They told all the girls in the room handling the drugs to also go downstairs. Then they dragged Sammy fat ass down to the second floor with his pants down they stand him next to Duck inside of the room. "See y'all both in here fucking the girls instead of working! You know X is downstairs and he heard you been here fucking up that's why I'm here, nigga!"
"I'm sorry man. It won't happen again man. I swear to God Jerome, man you know I take care of shit around here, man it will never happen again!" I know it won't he pulls out his gun Poooofffff! Sammy standing there start pissing on himself. Fat Jerome shot him too Poooffff! Both of their bodies are laying side by side. Fat Jerome calls X down stair with me and announced, **"Yamefanyika** *(Its done)*." He hangs up X quickly calls Gill outside with his crew, "Yo, let's move youngins!" Then he turned to me whispering, "Gill and his people are going to clean shit up for us." I just nodded my head as I went to the door letting Gill in the house. Gill looked at both us and said, "I got it from here." X called Jerome saying, "come on were getting up out of here. Fat Jerome, Damon and Ty came downstairs and went right out the door waving at everybody."
Then me and X is ready to go out the door as Gill said to the girl, "everything is going to be all right. I'll make sure everyone of y'all get a big fat bonus if you keep your mouth shut! You already know what happens if you open your mouth right, girls?" All the women nodding their head yes with deep fear in their eyes.

Gill calls his boy Jimmy on his phone and said, "bring in some big bags in here and I need the rest of y'all to start cleaning this dog shit up off the floor!" He hangs up and looks at both of us X just nodding his head as Jimmy came in the door with a big bag of money. Gill points towards the women all huddled up talking to one another in groups. X stood there and watched Gill's boy Jimmy give each of the women a stack of bills then he taps me saying, "all right let go!" We quickly walked out the door to the truck. Soon as I got in and asked him, "where to next?"

"We are going to your girls new spot the shit should be there. When we get there, I need you to make sure they got enough shit and roll out. You are going have to get some of your own peoples to keep an eye on them you got anybody in mine?"

"Not right now only one person I could think of right now is Shamika's brother Blue."

"Well try him out and if he fucks up you know what you have to do, right?"

"Yeah, I do, but Shamika will not like the shit."

"So, what, she knows the rules as well if she fucks up, she's done too you can't let that kind of shit hold you back from getting money."

"If you do your ass will stay broke and fucked up like them you hear me?"

"Yes, I hear you." We drive to Wilder street this small little block near 23rd street right before we were going to get out the truck X's phone rings, he just said, "good". He looked at me saying, "it's here and now your responsible for this spot here and three others. I'm going to give you Fat Jerome and his brother Fly Ty to watch your back until you put together a crew of your own."

"I have to get out of here and put together a crew?"

"Well you ask for this shit when you ask me to hook your girl up with product. So, Spider talk to me about it and said, "you're ready for this along with your other duties this is what it's like when your moving up."

"To me it's more of a test."

"That just what it is a test and I know you're going to past with flying colors lets go holler at your girl right quick soon as we get out of the truck."

"It's a young boy coming up the street with a backpack on his shoulder he walks up to X bumping fist with us. X said to me "Almasi this is Little Dun-Dun. This is Almasi he bumps fist with me and said, "what's up?" Then the three of us walked into the house. Tamika Shamika's sister open the door for us with all smiles saying, "hey what's going on I didn't know y'all was coming up in here?"

"I was looking for Duck crazy ass to come today?"

"Well you won't see that nigga coming up in here anymore!"

"Where is your sister at? Back in the kitchen with Julio."

"Look Julio need to be on the door at all times along with Ali where fuck is, he at?"

"Taking a shit."

"See this is a new spot for y'all and the first thing y'all do is fuck up!" Soon as he said that Ali is coming down the steps.

"The next time you step off you have Julio take you place for now on do you hear me?"

"Okay, X man it will never happen again."

"I know it won't nigga now get on post and keep your eyes open that's what you people are getting paid for, you feel me?" He nodded his head, "yes as we walk to the kitchen Julio is sitting with Shamika drinking beer laughing and joking around. X walks up and grabbing the beer out of his hand and he throw it up against the wall. "I need you to stay on the door from here on out and no getting high or having a good time over here if you are doing your job! I don't mind but you guys are just toolaid the fuck back for me. Go get on post and let this be the last time I see y'all doing this shit! I'm going keep coming back here to make sure y'all shit is tighter than a frog's ass in water!"

"All right Dun pull the shit out so Almasi can see this shit so I can get the fuck out of here before I have to kill somebody up in this motherfucker!" Dun unzip his backpack setting in on top of the round white table. I looked at it and said, "this looks like it's just 20 gee packs here" Shamika looking up at both of us and replied, "were going to need more then that!"

"Well sell what you got there when you get down to your last four then call Dun and he'll bring you more. This is a new spot so were going to see how it goes all right."

"You're right. When your done you give all the money to Almasi and sis you give it money to Rocket. I'm taking you to him after we get out of here now everybody got it right?" We all nodded our heads yes. X waves for me to follow him then he stops and said to me on the side, "see what I mean you have to keep your eye on these niggas like I said right!"

I just nodded my head as we go out the door. We quickly jump in the truck as he drives us to Rocket's spot, he's a block away from my old spot on Taylor street. He parks on the block pulling out his phone calling him. "Yo what's up? come to the door. We jump out the truck and this skinny nerd looking dude come to the door X said to him, "Rocket this is Almasi. Almasi this is Rocket."

He just nodded his head handing me a card saying, "this is my number just call me when you have the drop. I'll tell you where to meet me. Okay and he quickly went back in the house." X taps me on the arm, "let me drive you back to the spot so you can get your truck."

Soon as he's driving off down the street, I ask him, "so when is that job for that Puerto Rican dude?"

Spider said, "real soon so just stay hot and ready but we might have something tonight let me check with Spider, okay."

"Just let me know when you want to strap up." X just looked at me and smiled we pulled up near the house I bump fist with X who said, "don't forget to call me."

"I got you, sis." I'd walked to my truck pulling out my remote unlocking the doors. I jumped in the only thing I'm thinking of is putting together a crew to watch my back with these crack spots I got now. So, while I'm driving home, I call Shamika she picked right away and said, "yo what's up with you girl?"

"I'm on my way home check this out I need you help now that you got me into this shit."

"What I got you into?"

"What? You're the one who ask me to hook y'all up when Duck was tapping y'all shit."

"Yeah, I did tell you that, but I did not know X was coming to the new spot what happen to Duck?"

"He's taking the dirt nap. Along with his whole crew so you and your peoples better get your shit together with the quickness or you're going to join Duck and them sloppy ass motherfuckers." She gets really quiet on the other end of the phone. I ask her, "look I called to ask you about your brother Blue. I need him to watch my back I have to put a crew together could you give me his number?"
"Sure, let me call and ask him first I don't want him to bite my fucking head off."
"Okay do that and I'll call you back. I'm at my house now. I'll call you and let you know. One."
"So, I go in the house to chill waiting on her call a half an hour later. While I'm on the phone with Big Boom I tell him to hold on while I take this call, he said to me, "he'll call me back, later so I click over. Its Shamika, hey he said yes but you can call him right now he wants to talk to you his number is 267-9986999." I got it "Thanks Shamika look come over Friday so we can kick it."
"Sure, I'll be there but my sister wants to come she's feeling some type of way. You can bring her it's cool that way y'all can meet Boom he'll be here too. Good, I can't wait to meet this man who got you all hot and bothered."
We both giggle as I hang up still chuckling to myself. Later that night I'm on the couch chilling then I get the call from X. Telling me to gear up so we can punch in and go to work. He said to meet him at the garage under the bridge on 25th street. So, I'd slipped on my sweat suit, real swift my boots grabbing my two Glocks and putting on my vest while I ran to my truck. I take off it only took me 20 minutes to get there. I'd parked across the street from the garage and walked in quickly. I came up knocking on the door on the right-hand side but I'm looking around it seem like someone was watching me from a distance. Fat Jerome opened the door fist bumping and asked, "what's up with you, Almasi?"
"I'm good but I wanted to ask you do those niggas know where this place is at?"
"They might because there close by why?"
"When I was coming in it seem like somebody was eye balling me like a motherfucker, Jerome!"

"Really come in here and tell everybody back here." We walked to the back of the garage where X is sitting down at the table with Gill, Brenton, Fly Ty and Damon Gee. I notice two new faces in the crowd. X looks up and said, "you know the rest of the men this is two of the men you have not met yet this is Alijah and Ayden. Fellas this is Almasi." They just nodded their heads. "Alright now roll call is over.

I want Brenton, Gill and Ayden hit the back of the spot. Damon you're behind the wheel then you, Jerome, Fly Ty and Almasi hit the front door! And I want Alijah behind the wheel do what y'all do best and everybody split up give me a text when you're done! just like my man Spider always says, "let's go to work good people!"

Fat Jerome said, "Yo Almasi, said she thinks somebody been watching her before she came in here."

"All right then Brenton, Gill, Ayden and Alijah go check that shit before y'all roll out and hit that spot in two-man teams. Go around the block do a really good sweep leave no stones unturned." The four of them rolled out the door swift. The minute they stepped out X looked up at me and said, Almasi watch the big gate on the left! Damon, Jerome cover the door on the right!"

"Fly Ty you're in the middle! **Nenda**/*(Go)* All of us ran and get on your vest and grab our machine guns and moved in position. Then X came and stood by me with a smirk on his face. The we can hear the shooting outside I'd looked over at X. He stands there nice and calm saying, **Shika msimamo wako** *"Hold your position all of them"*, nodding their heads. He looks at me and said, I just said hold your position, okay! So were all standing there, and X yelled out **Sasa** *(Now!)"*

Damon, Fat Jerome, and Fly Ty ran outside the door. He said to me, “you stay right there get ready!” All of you here is machine gun fire and gun shots ripping out loud he taps me on the arm said, “help me close all this shit in the back! We have to get out here the fucking cops will be here before you know it!” We quickly went to the back of the garage closing the big closet door where all the guns are at. Then he hit a button and a big steel door slides up covering it. I was like, “damn this is some James Bond type of shit here! It’s kind of fucked me up for a minute.” We quickly jumped in his truck parked on the left. He drives up to the big steel door he sticks his hand out the window pointing the remote at the steel door. It opens up swiftly and he drives out quickly. I said to him, “what about the others?”

“They know what to do! We will meet them at our other spot you never been there before just hold on!” He drives out towards the expressway X pulls out his phone he hits the speed dials someone said, “yeah, we’ll be there in a few minutes alright.” He hangs up. He just looks at me not saying a word and he jumps off on the first exit and he pulls up to this dark ass junk yard on the right-hand side. Soon as he pulls up and standing at the door is a tall dark skin dude who looks at X and he quickly open the gate. I said to him, “who is that?”

“Oh, that’s Nick he holds it down for us out here that’s who I just called we have about ten spots just here in South West Philly, Shorty. X bumps me on the leg and then he winked. He drives to the back of the junk yard in the dark and he parks and said, “come on”. He walks to this beat up funky looking trailer on the right-hand side. He opens the door walking in and its three ruff neck dudes I never seen before and he introduce them to me, “this is Almasi.”

“Almasi this is Tony, Monk and Hot Rod. He runs this yard for us.” They all speak as he hits one of them playful saying, “yo, get up and let the lady have a seat, nigga!” Tony gets up chuckling as X said, “where the hell is your manners at man? I taught you guys better then that! They all started laughing as we sat down. Tony is standing up checking me out. X said, “how are things going Hot Rod?”

“Smooth brother, so what’s going on tonight with y’all?”

“You know the same old thing taking out fools who think they can fuck with us you know.”

“Look I got a job for y’all I need for you to do?”

"Okay when?"
"Tonight, but I want you to take my girl here with you."
"Are you sure about that?"
"Yeah, I'm sure have I ever bullshited you plus the others will be here soon to back y'all up." He pulls out his phone and he scrolled up until he reaches the picture of this dark skin heavy set ugly dude. He's pointing at the picture this is the target they call him K.G. Clout or Mister Clout his real name is Keyon White! X is showing everyone the picture on his phone and making sure they all get a good look. He showed me last looking me right in my eyes and I know just what that means, "I'm the one who has to punch his ticket to meet Jesus. I'm waiting on the call from the girl at the bar it's at 60th and Woodland Avenue she's going to tell us when he shows up with his peoples."
"I'm using your crew because they know my crew on sight that's why they're going to be in the trucks to take care of his men on the outside. Your crew is going to smoke his men on the inside."
"So how are we going to get close to him?"
"That's why you're taking the girl with you trust me she will not only get close to him she will blow his fat ass brains out on the barroom floor!"
"Okay, Almasi go in the bathroom back there and change your clothes it's on the right-hand side. I have you some outfits and a makeup kit back there for you already." Tony yelled, "oh shit that's why you had that shit back there I thought you was having some freaks coming over here or something."
"Go head Almasi and change I be getting the call soon after that were going to go hit them niggas on Annie street who tried to sneak up on us tonight."

So, I go in the back of the trailer and just like he said he had about four hoochie mommy outfits in there all my size too. I put on this tight white outfit on. Where you can see my pink thong up my ass and this white blouse is real sheer where you can see my nipples. To top it all off he had this blonde wig to wear so I put it on and looked in the mirror. I'd fix it all up I'd put on some make up after doing the wig really nice. When I was done dolling up, I'd looked just like the type of Ho that would be in that kind of bar. When I came out for them to see me. X said, "now you tell me if she is not going to get close to his fat black ass or what?" All of them nodded their heads yes going off with big smiles on their faces checking me the fuck out with deep lust in all their eyes. I can feel all of their eyes right on my ass wanting to fuck me right then and there. Tony said, "damn your right, this will work because its sure nuff working for me for sure, Dawg!" They all started laughing. "Okay Hot Rod, where is the pocketbooks I told you to put up for me?"

"I got them right back here. But he could not take his eyes off of me he reaches in the back on the left pulling them out walking towards me and said, "here you go, sis. Can I say that you really look good fuck that shit?"

X smirk and said, "that's the whole point and before you get any Ideas if you don't know that's Spider daughter so if you don't want your balls cut the fuck off and stuffed in your own mouth you need to be cool all right. Your Dick can get hard all you want there will be no touching." They all started laughing it off and he looked up at me with Hot Rod saying, "I heard he had a daughter doing hits, but I did not know it was her. When she first came in here nobody was paying her any mind but Gawd dam she's sexier than a motherfucker! Almasi said, "I have to say yeah this is going to work just fine, X. You know what the fuck your talking about Dawg. I'd didn't like all of them staring at me, but this is for a job and I'm the bitch that was born to do this shit. I have to stayed focus on just that blocking out these assholes."

Soon as I said that, "X get the call he was waiting on he replied, "alright, thanks baby." He hangs up and announce, "alright, he just walked in there it is fucking show time niggas let's roll out."

"Yo, Monk go in my truck and get the tools for my girl. Here it's in the back and don't touch shit back there all right or I will come back here and kill you."

"Awww come on, X man you know I don't roll like that.
"I know I was just fucking with you; brother just go get that shit for me, please." He just shook his head walking out of the trailer. He said to Hot Rod, "I'm need that sexy ass beast you got out there for my girl so we can get this show on the road over here."
"Yeah, I'll bring it around front." He quickly walks out of the trailer to get the car I was going to drive to the bar. I ask X, "do you have a cigarette?"
"Yeah hold on, sis."
"He reaches in his pocket pulling out his pack handing me one of them and his lighter lighting it up for me and said, "you know the drill two in the head and get the fuck out of there."
I say to him, "damn, I wish I had my truck here so I can get one of my grenades out of there."
"My nigga Tony got that here."
"Yo Tony, go get my girl a few of your grenades."
"Oh shit, what she know about a fucking grenade?" X looks at him and answers, "I hate to tell you this Tony, but she knows more about it then you do. She was trained by the fucking best. She was trained with the Black Militia Force with Mister Irving himself so I would not be talking a whole lot of shit, okay. Talk what you know because I don't think none of you peoples would last a fucking week out there with them." He grabs them from under the desk handing me two of them brand new. I put them in my pocketbook and wink at Tony, "thank you". He just nods his head and said, "there you go girlfriend, have fun." But what after X told him about my training with Mister Irving he looked at me kind of different I can tell but him and the others lusting after me did not stop just like what that bitch Dotty told me a long time ago all men are fucking dogs they will stick their Dick in just about anything with a fucking hole in it. Soon as he said that Hot Rod came back in the trailer handing me the keys and said, "look here sweetheart, I don't care how fine your ass is don't put a fucking scratch on my baby or your daddy Spider will be buying me a new one!"

"You hear me, X man. I'm not fucking around if she fucks up my car, you niggas are getting enough money to replace this motherfucker!" X looked at him and smirked, "don't worry you know I got you nothing is going to happen to it all right calm down, nigga. I heard you I'll be responsible for it okay!" Then Monk came in behind him smiling as he is looking right at my tits handing me the gun with the silencer on it. I checked it out really quick and X hands me a brand-new box of bullets I sit down and load the bullets into the clip, and I'd slapped it in. I looked up at X and I put it in my pocketbook nodding my head and he got up and said, "all right good people time to ride let's go!"

He walks me to the car soon as I walked up to this whip, I was like I want to keep this shit after the hit it was a candy apple red Corvette with fat ass mag tires no wonder, he said not to put a fucking scratch on his baby. I jumped in and I turned the key and I can feel all this power under my ass. I just looked at X and smiled his phone rung and they talked for a minute. he hangs up and said, "all the boys are in position around the bar, so you got a lot of back up. Almasi meet us back at the crib and I'll take you to our other spot we have more work to do tonight, Shorty. Don't get lost in your new toy over here all right." I just laughed and I took off heading towards the gate up the dirt road kicking up dust. Soon as I got up to the gate the boy Nick quickly opened it and started seeing what this motherfucker can do with me roaring up the road. I know there right behind me it only takes me less than a half an hour to get to the bar. Shit when I pulled up and parked across the street from the bar called the Woodlands Good Times lounge. It's a lot of people standing around outside of this joint and soon as I step out the car. It was all eyes on me for sure niggas was breaking their necks just to speak to me, but I know how to play this part. I pay no mind to the nothing ass niggas eyeing me down. I look like that boss bitch. You know the girl who wanted the big-time niggas doing real things in the streets. The ballers and shot callers wit money none of them drunks or drug head begging ass niggas that hang around bars. I'd strutted up in there like I own the fucking place switching my ass and rolling my eyes at the sorry ass niggas trying to holla before I even got all the way up in the bar. I can see this nigga Mister Clout checking me out with two bitches on each side of his arms at the bar. So, I walked up to the bar getting near him but not too far and I can see his men all around too the bar is crowded with niggas, but I can tell who his men are standing around. They sure nuff was not trying to blend in they wanted it to be known who they are to let niggas know what time it is. The bartender came up on me really quick with that I want to fuck you right here in the bar look on his face. He greeted me with, "hey baby what is it you want because you can have it all. All you have to do is just ask me for real." I smiled and wink, "well for right now I'll have an apple martini with a slice of lime if you have it. Mister, I can have whatever I want."

He chuckled, "coming right up, baby. Can I ask you what is your name if you don't mind me asking? My name is Eddie, sweetheart."

"Oh, Mister fast Eddie, my name is Destiny. Well, I'm please to meet you."
"I hope my Destiny is to get to know you a whole lot better baby because you sure looking good tonight."
"You would do a whole lot better to get to know me fast Eddie is to get my drink a little faster for me then it would be a whole lot better to know a woman like myself. You know what I'm saying."
"Oh baby, your right about that, sweetheart."
"See your still talking and not getting me my drink Mister fast Eddie, because your moving just a little slower."
I'll be right back while he's making me a drink, I can see Mister Clout trying to get my attention but I'm just playing the shit off like he's not there. I can tell this nigga is not use to that kind of shit having women jumping at his feet all the time. "Then Mister Fast Eddie came back with my drink with a big cheese smile, "here you go Miss Destiny this is on the house from me."
"Oh, why thank you, dear it took you long enough to go get it now." He started laughing then I can see Mister Clout walk past me walking to the door and his two men on his back walking fast behind him. He walks to the door of the bar looking out standing in the doorway talking to his men for a few minutes later he came right up next to me leaning towards me and said, "well Gawd damn, is that your car out there across the street, baby?" I just sip my drink nodding my head yes slow and sexy because he's eating it up from the door. He said, "well shit that is one hot ass fucking ride you got over there with your fine self."
I looked up at him and reply, "well when your one hot ass bitch like myself. You got to have a hot ass car you know what I'm saying, Big Dawg." He burst out laughing, "oh your right twice, sweetheart. You're one hot ass bitch and I am the big Dawg around here for sure, baby. So, what's your name Miss Hot ass bitch with a hot ass whip?
"Oh, you're going to have to watch saying that word whip you'll be the one who just might get whip before the night is over wit."

He began laughing even louder, "Oh I like you girl what's your name honey because you have to be one bad ass bitch to whip me at the end of the night, little Miss red Corvette." "Oh, you got jokes my name as well is Destiny things can get a whole lot hotter and better for you if you send your little playmates away and deal with a real woman who know how to handle a big Dawg like yourself." He started laughing real loud again and the bartender came back over towards us and he looked at him and said, "Yo Eddie, you better go take a walk and don't come over here until I need you okay." He just had that sad look on his face and backed up walking the other way talking to the barmaid on the other side of the bar. Right about then I can see the boys that were in the trailer with me earlier. I turned to him and said, "that was not nice, big Dawg and you never told me your name anyway so what's up with you, Mister Big Dawg?"

"Oh baby, I'm sorry about that I just wanted to get to know you and I don't need no niggas trying to beat my time. When I see something, I want you know what I mean let me buy you a drink and we can talk about this all right. My name is Keyon."

"Sure, so what about the two-bar room Hoes you had on your arm when I came in the door, Keyon?"

"Don't worry about them, baby there nothing. I want to holla at you let me get a little closer to you and I can tell you what I really think about your fine ass. I know you're going to like it because I see that glow in your eyes that you like me."

"You just might be right come over here a little closer to me, but don't you want to see what I'm working with first, Mister big Dawg? I mean Keyon!" He started laughing, "I sure do let me see that money maker you got back there because you look like you're the type of woman who need a big money baller like myself." I stand up and then I'd turned around real slow and sexy so he can see my ass. When I sat back down and looked him in the face his eyes got wider with a big giant ass Mister Kool aid smile on his large ass black ugly grill of his. He screamed, "lord have mercy!" Then I said to him, "you know something about me Keyon I love me a big strong man something I can hold onto you know what I mean, big Daddy somebody who know how to put it down."

"Oh yeah, I know just what you are talking about, sweetheart." "I like you where are you from girl?" Soon as he asked me that I know it was the right time seeing the two men X send in there with me standing on each side of his bodyguards and I was easing out my pistol from my pocketbook nice and smooth from under the bar and holding by the side of my leg. This nigga was so busy looking at my tits thinking about my nice ass.

Another thing I learned from that bitch Dotty once a man thinks he's going to get some pussy that's when he drops his guard. He's more vulnerable and he never know what hit his ass until it happens.

"I'm from New York I came up here about a year ago after my Boo got shot in the head because he was selling more weight in some other nigga's territory."

"What you don't say, Ma?" I quickly whipped out my gun putting it on the side of his head. Pooufff! Pooufff! I shot him twice in the head his large frame fell sideways with the blood shooting out and it slashed across the bar and even on some woman face screaming. Sitting not too far from him freaking her the fuck out.

Simultaneously Tony and Monk pulled out their guns and started shooting his two big goon bodyguards Pat! Pat! Pat!

Pat! Pat! Pat! Tony shot the dude on the right-hand side in the head and chest and the boy Monk with his crazy ass shot the dude on the left-hand side in the face and neck. They both hit the floor with the blood rolling across the floor. Some of the people slipping in the blood fall to the floor trying to get out of there. Its loud screaming and people falling down rushing towards the door all at the same time. I ducked down and headed towards the door with Monk and Tony on each side of me pushing our way out of this joint as the whole bar goes wild with panic scrambling and yelling towards the front door of the bar.

We were all pushing with all the people crashing into one another until we made it out. All you can hear is people yelling and more gunshots ringing outside. When I looked up, I could see Fat Jerome, Fly Ty and Damon blasting at the other men they had outside. I made a fucking bee line towards the red Corvette. I toss the bag with my gun in it in the back seat and jumped behind the wheel. I'd started up the engine and I took off like a rocket to the fucking moon or something. I'd took off down the street when I got about three blocks away, I snatch off that God damn blonde hooker wig they had me put on, but I had to play the part and it worked. Soon as I got about six blocks away, I can hear all the sirens from the cop cars but dam near home free the real nice part about this shit there all going towards the scene of the crime.

I just smoked that fat horny fat motherfucker he didn't know what hit him. It took me a half an hour to reach Spider crib I park across the street. I got my pocketbook from the back seat and I put that fucking fur ball in my bag. I walked up to the door I ring the doorbell. Spider open the door and greeted me with a smile, "Yo what's up, Shorty!"

"Don't fucking laughed at this Hoochie mommy outfit your boy X picked out for me to wear!"

"How you know it wasn't me who picked it out? While he was laughing. "Yeah, you just might have been the one who did that shit!" We both started snickering.

"Don't worry about we all know you don't really dress like that plus it worked, right?"

"And you got the job done that's all that counts, baby girl you want a beer?"

"Yes, I'll take one, please and what is he talking about putting in some more work?"

"Yeah he told me about them niggas trying to sneak up on y'all tonight."

"Yeah that shit was crazy. We both walking inside of the kitchen and Spider go in the refrigerator handing me a beer I quickly go get the bottle opener out of the drawer.

I open my beer he hands me his beer I open his for him and I hand it back to him, other then business how have you been?"

"Real good matter of fact I'm going to be a father again Sheila is pregnant."

"Wow, congratulations, Big Poppy so how many is that now? This is number four now."

"Damn you're not fucking around over here, Daddy O."

"Look before everybody get here, she asked me for you to come to the baby shower next month and some of them are not invited so Sheila told me to ask you while a lot them niggas is not around. She wants you to be there because she likes you so please keep that shit to yourself." Soon as he said that I can hear all them coming in the door while I'm sipping on my beer nodding my head yes talking low, "tell her I'll be there."

Its X, Gill, Damon, Fat Jerome, Fly Ty, Brenton, Ayden and Alijah. Gill came in the kitchen and said, "you should keep that shit on when we go do this other hit." X came handing me a backpack saying, your stuff is in the bag don't listen to this nigga over here! You can go in your old room and change. Rashida is back there now just knock on the door and tell her you're just changing your clothes.

I looked at Spider and he put his hands up in the air and said, "what you think you was going to be the only one? She's not taking your place were just seeing if she's going to be another member of the family like you, baby girl." I take the bag and I'd walked to the room I'd knocked on the door I can hear her voice on the other side of the door saying, "Yeah!"

"It's me Almasi I'm just changing my clothes right quick." "Okay you can come in when I'd open the door and walked in, I'd looked at the girl and she had two black eyes and I can see bruises on her arms and chest. I just said to her, "hi, how are you doing?"

"I'm good what about you?"

"Same here, girl. I'm good. What's your name again? I'm Almasi and you? I'm Rashida I heard about you. Well I hope it was something good what you heard as I'd took my clothes out the bag taking off the black happy hooker outfit off. She just sat there watching me not saying a word after I got done I put the other clothing in the bag and I walked up to her looking her right in her eyes saying, "you don't know me like that but while your here your cool it looks like I've been where you at right now. She looked up at me crying saying thanks for saying that I really don't know what's going to happen to me now. Check this out while your here with Spider and what ever happen to you, he's going to look out for you like he did me. if you want you can come stay at my house, I'll talk to Spider about it, okay? She's nodding her head yes okay then let me go talk to him all right. I'll be right back. Spider is in the front room talking with everybody and I come up asking him, "can I speak to you for a minute?" Sure, we both walked to the back room we all call the office. "Hey, look I talked to girlfriend back there and she's all fucked up in the head why don't you let her come stay at my crib until she gets some training or what every your bringing her in to do? Okay I was going to ask you but now that you seen her that will be fine with me just as long as you let her know what's up if she's going to be down it won't be until after she heal up. She has to roll make her understand that shit. "I will so I'll come back and get her after we put in this work."

"No that's all right you can take her with you to your crib we got your truck out there the boys brought up here for you we will make sure that nigga Hot Rod gets his corvette back so you can go now she need somebody to talk to right now and he hands me my truck keys." So, what happen to her, Spider? Well she was working in one of the spots selling crack and these dudes who robbed the joint gang raped her, so I said to myself I had to help her and brought her here like we did you. Then it hit me they set this whole thing up for me to see her and they brought my truck here too. I did not mind because I was really feeling bad for this girl because the same shit happened to me. Okay she got any clothes here she took with her. Just a little bit of shit she took in a trash bag back there I'll give you some money for her to get some more stuff all right. He reaches in his pocket and hand me a big roll of bills I stick in my pocket and said, "I'm going to get her and I'm out of here."

I walked back in the room and he said, "it's cool come on get your stuff were going to go get you some new shit tomorrow, okay." She's still crying with what I don't have any money I don't have shit. Don't worry about that right now Spider just gave me some loot for you all right so let's go. She grabbed the trash bag she had her stuff in she slanged it over her shoulder, and she followed behind me outside. I see my truck I'd pointed my remote towards it unlocking it and we jumped in before we took off I looked her in the face and said, "you're going to be all right but I'm going to tell you right now I'm going to help you and everybody in the gang is going to help you but there going to want to know if you're going to get down putting in some work or if not right after you heal up your going to have to hit the bricks!" So, they told me to ask you this before anything else is going to go down. Now if I was you, I would get down and get these ass hole back like I'm going to do or you're going to go back to wherever the fuck you came from and the shit just might happen to you again.

And I took off driving to my house she's not saying nothing right now. So, I don't push it, but I let her know what was up from the door. We get to my house I'd parked and we both get out she looked up saying, "this is your house?"

"Yeah this is my house I brought it putting in work for the gang." She looked up at me and, "you're not just bull shitting me, are you?"

"Why would I say that when it was not true. I know I don't know you like that, but I was in that same bedroom you were in for months until I build up my chips."

I open the door with my key and came in my house and I close the door and asked, "are you hungry?"

"Yes."

"Okay then I still have some bake chicken in the refrigerator you can heat it up in the microwave. That sounds good we walk in the kitchen and I say to her have a seat and I'll put in for you and I have some iced tea. Do you have any family?"

"I do but there all fucked up on that shit so I had to go for myself that why I was in that house selling crack so I can get myself some money." I can dig it honey, I was doing the same shit and my mother is all cracked out and my father is dead."

"Well at least you know who he was I don't know who the fuck my father is or was."

"To tell you the real truth I just found out who he was just a few months ago." Then the microwave started beeping and I get a plate for her and I place the chicken on the table in the bowl for her and I get a big glass and I poured her some iced tea. I pour me a glass and she took some of the chicken from out of the bowl putting it on her plate. I went and got the rest of it out but when she was eating it was like this girl hasn't eaten anything in days. After we both ate, "I say to her I'm going to show you where you're going to sleep after I do these dishes. Heads up if you dirty a dish you clean it. I'm not cleaning behind your ass just to let you know okay?" "Okay that sounds fair and that goes for everything else around here I'm not your fucking maid you feel me. "Yes, I feel you. Come on get your things over there and follow me."

She picks up her shit and follows me up to the side room. I hooked up just in case someone would sleep over, so we go up the steps and I point to the room and she just smiled then I see tears coming from her eyes. "I never had my own room before I always had to share."

"Well I had my own room but the whole house was fucked up and I had to clean it all the time."

"Me too."

"Well this is your room until you tell me otherwise."

"What do you mean otherwise?"

"What I ask you earlier are you going to put in some work or are you going back to your next fucked up situation?"

"No, I'm going to put in this work and get my own crib like you did."

"That's good to hear but you gone have to do a whole lot shit you don't want to do to get to my level. I still have a long way to go inside of the gang myself."

"Well I'm not trying to sound cocky, but I know I can do it too!"

"Good that's what I want to hear go get some sleep you have a big day ahead of you."

"So, what happens tomorrow?"

"Well you're going to soldier your ass up that's what you're going to happen to you. Don't worry you're going be all right just get some sleep. I'll holla at you later."

I went to bed to only thing I was thinking about getting that extra money for that second hit, but I know I'd did the right thing to helping this girl out. That same shit happened to me. So, I had to help her no matter what I just hope she knows how to deal with this lifestyle.

PUTTING MY CREW TOGETHER

It's the end of April and it's nice outside. We have sunshine up the ass now I got up around 11 O'clock fixing breakfast for the two of us after I was done. I can see Rashida walking up slow, but she smiled saying, "I smelled the food it woke me up." As she's standing in the doorway of my kitchen mad flavor is jumping off for sure. "Come in here girl and have a seat I fixed you some." Her eyes got wide looking at the food I cooked beef bacon, eggs and some home fries with butter biscuits. With a wide grin she said, "Thank you." She sat down and I put the plate in front of her then I sat down next to her and started eating in between bites I said,

"Well you look better today."

"Yes, I'm a whole lot better so what was you talking about that soldiering up thing last night?"

"Yeah. they're going to take you to the gun range today so you can build up your skills then after you get shit up under your belt then they will send you out for some more training."

"What do you mean more training?"

"Military training!" she just nodded her head the phone rang I answer it."

"Yo what's up, Shorty? How is it going with Rashida?"

"Good, she's in good hands."

"That sounds like a winner look X will be by to come get her to take her to the strap yard to get busy."

"Okay look Spider X was telling me to put my own crew together. I want those two guys from the junk yard that help me last night with the hit."

"Which two doe?"

"Tony and Monk, I can really use them two there really good with a gun. They know what to do in a tight ass spot as well there the kind of niggas I need on my team."

"Okay, I'll let them know they keep asking to move up so it will work out, but it's your crew and you let them know that." "I'll ask them if they can take orders from a woman and see what they have to say so who else you had in mind?"

"Blue Shamika's brother so what you think?"

"I think that's a good look with Blue all of his men are not all that, but I know you would get them niggas together, okay. Tell girlfriend X will be there in one hour I'll need you to come here to the spot to talk about the next thing we got up on deck I'll see you when you get here one. I turn to her well just like I said, "X is coming by to get you and take you to the gun range in one hour so you can go get ready." "What do I put on to go to the gun range?"
"It's not a fucking fashion show type of thing just wear some Jeans and a top that's all its nothing to it you're going to do just fine."
"Can I ask you something?"
"What's that?"
"Did you get them niggas back that did the same shit to you?"
"What they did to me? No, not yet but its next up on my agenda but when it does happen, I'll let you know when it goes down because that's when I'm going to have a real fucking party." She started giggling,
"Wow I didn't know you had a laugh in you over here. Go get ready they hate when your late or dragging your feet, so you have to be on your fucking toes. They're going to be much harder on you because you're a female. I want you to know that from the door. I have to go get ready as well." We both finish eating our food then we both went upstairs. I just put on a sweat suit and some sneakers I did my hair pulling it back in a ponytail and I talked to Big Boom on the phone until X came. I can hear the doorbell I told Boom I talk to him later and went to the door letting X in the house. Soon as he came in, he hugged me and said, "how are you doing today, family?"
"I'm good what about you?"
"Busy you know me. Did he tell you that thing is up?"
"Yeah, he did. Well this time you don't have to dress like a hooker were going to hit their ass tomorrow night far as I know he might move it up I don't know we will find out together this afternoon where she at? She came down the steps saying, "I'm right here. I'm ready. Good, let's go I don't have all day look I holla at you at the spot, Shorty."
"Shorty? I didn't know they called you that?"
"Yo, you don't know her like that, so you don't get to call

her that okay so watch your mouth all right. Almasi did not tell you that you have to watch what you say when people out rank your ass, okay. So, pump your breaks okay you call her Almasi do you follow me? He looked her in her eyes with a real mean scowl on his face like he was not playing no fucking games with her. Yes, I follow you. Okay long as we got that shit straight like I was saying I holla at you later Almasi. One. He is cutting his eyes at Rashida. He bumps fist with me pointing at her to follow him to his Jeep outside. I came out right behind them locking my doors and jumped in my truck driving to the spot for our sit down about are next thing with the Gorilla Boulevard niggas. It only took me 10 minutes to get to the crib I came up to the door ringing the bell and Fat Jerome open the door for me bump fist with me and yelled, "family!"

Everyone is in the office were all waiting on X to get back before Spider lay it all out for us. "Okay then so how you been?"

"Good." We both walk to the back room with some more small talk until we got to the door of the back room puffing on our Newport's. Spider is sitting at the head of the table I walk in, go over to him, bump fist with him and we hugged "what's up, baby girl? Have a seat when X get back, we will start everything."

I just nodded my head looking around the table at everybody there they all speak. Gill, Brenton, Fly Ty, Damon then Ayden and Alijah came to walk in the room and Spider wave his hand at Brenton to stop them at the door putting his hand up saying loud, "where the fuck you guys think you're going?"

"Were going to go sit down."

"You both can go sit down in the front room and wait for me there when I'm done. The two men stood there with a puzzled look on their face."

"What you can't hear what I said?" They both backed up walking in the other room as he slams the door. Spider said, "I want you to check both of them out."

Brenton nodded his head, "yes, but I'm thinking to myself I already knew that Spider was checking them out as he speaks from the door, I know his ass don't let too much get past him. Soon after that X came back and sat down next to Spider at the table and said, "she's there with your brother, Petey Q and his peoples she's cool."

"Good, I know my brother is going to work the shit out of her to see if her ass can take it all right. Here it is Emillano cut a deal with us now we have to deliver on our end. He gave me most of the product at a way lower price before us doing the hit in good faith. I just found out that the Gorilla Boulevard niggas is having a big cookout in Fairmont park and most of their big men will be there later on but were going to hit them soon as their big man is on his way there. He laid out a map of the park and everybody stood up to get a better look at it as he's pointing on top of the map. I want you, Brenton and your men right here. Petey Q and his people are going to be here I already talk to him about it. Shorty and X, I want you and your peoples here."

He paused, took a couple puff of his Newport and then continue, "we smoke his ass and get the fuck out of there we are doing it on Saturday not Friday. My peoples I have on the inside gave me the real low down. Now whatever y'all do make sure we kill Khalil the rest of his peoples is all gravy. The main target and nothing else so now I let y'all know what's up. X, I need for you to give everybody their cut and we can get the hell out of here and get back to work."

X stood up going to the back of the large room to the safe pulling out these fat envelopes handing them out to everybody, and he gave me two of them. When I looked up at Spider, he just winked his eye and wave his hand on the low for me to keep it to myself and I did play it cool. I just smiled and stuck both of them in my pockets walking out of the door along with the others filling up the hallway with chit chat, a few inside jokes and a whole lot of bull shit.

I talk to X and Fat Jerome for a little while I asked for Tony and Monks phone numbers. soon as he gives them to me, I text both of them on the spot because I'm on a mission for sure and soon after they text me back. I text them both the address telling them where I was going to be at and for them to meet me there. They texted the thumbs up emoji they'd be there. I roll out the door and got to the crack spot on Wilder street were my girl Shamika is working at. Soon as I get there, I park across the street from the spot and I see that little nigga name Dun-Dun. I'm watching him serving people out there but then out of nowhere I see three big ruff neck niggas roll up on him.

I'm ready to jump out my truck to help him getting my pistol when this big greasy ass niggas bear hugs him. He elbows the dude in the head Bam! Then he gets low and he sweep kicks the two other dudes bum rushing him one hit the ground sideways and the other one flat on his ass then fast as lighting he whips out his gun and shot the fourth dude coming at him. The dude started running and he shot him in the ass while he was still running around the corner. He quickly came up on the two men he knocked to the ground he mashed his gun to one of their heads while he kicked other dude on the left really hard. He yelled, "you wanted to fuck with me, motherfuckers see what you get now get the fuck out of here before I kill you both!" He just stepped back still holding his gun the two men got up off the ground and started running their ass off. I got all the way out of my truck giggling thinking to myself this little nigga is nobody to be fucked with for real still laughing I walk over to him and said, "yo what's up?"

He put his gun up sticking it in the back of his jeans looking me in my face and said, "hey what's up, boss lady you didn't see all that did you?"

"Yes, I did I seen it all, baby boy." I bump fist with him. "Well please don't tell X about that shit."

"Well that depend on if you're going take the job, I'm offering you?"

"Oh, I'm down, boss lady. Whatever you need I'm the man for the job, baby."

"Okay good just come with me right now up in the house for a few your off post your rolling with me from here on out alright." He walks behind me up to the crib I knock on the door and I see Tamika peeping out the window she open up the door and greeted me by saying, "hey what's going on and Dun man you need to get your ass back on post!"

"He's cools he's with me."

"And who are you?"

"Putting her hands on her hips rolling her eyes at me. I speak a little louder and announce, "I run this shit that's who I am!"

Shamika came from out the kitchen, "hey what the fuck is going on, Tamika?"

"What? This bitch come up in here saying she's running shit up in here!"

"She does run shit up in here and I told you that already. You are a dumb bitch!"

"What the fuck are you high or something? You're going to fuck things up for me then you need to bounce!"

"Really? Your taking this bitch side over mine!"

"When you're wrong oh hell yes you about to fuck up our money up talking all that bull shit your saying just shut the fuck up all right."

"Look, I came here for you to call your brother up and to tell you you're going to need a new person outside because I'm taking Dun-Dun here. He's going to be down with the crew I'm putting together." Shamika looks at her sister and yelled, "well you just heard what the woman just said right?"

"What? You want me outside come the fuck on now, Sis?"

"What about Julio?"

"What about Julio? Are you as good as he is with a gun bitch?"

"I'll tell you that one hell no!"

"Oh no you want to talk shit you're on post until we get somebody else so let's go right now!"

"Yo Dun give her what you got on you so she can get her ass out there and if you don't go outside just keep going and don't bring your black ass back here!"

Dun steps up handing her what he had on him and said, "it's a Gee pack." He hands her the caps in two plastic bag she takes it. Shamika announce, "you can give me the money holding her hand out. Dun-Dun hands her the money with a smile on his face. Tamika is mumbling under her breath and rolling her eyes. She turns looking at me and her sister again with her eyes on fire. That bitch was hot for real putting the two bags of caps in her pocket. She stomps towards the front door slamming the door really hard Boom!

"Okay now that is done. I'll call Blue up right now." She started dialing waving her hand for me to follow her. I looked over at Dun-Dun for him to stay where he's at without saying a word. I knew this nigga was going to work out we both walked in the kitchen where Julio is leaning on the wall. He waves at me with a big smile and I just wave back. We sat at the little dark brown table as she's talking to her brother Blue, "hey what's up? Look Almasi is here right now. She wants you to come to the crib. So, she can talk to you about her putting her crew together."

"Okay tell her to sit tight I'll be right there." She hangs up and said, "he said he be right here sit tight."
"So how are things now?"
"To tell you the truth, girl a whole lot better now that y'all took care of Duck's funky ass and his peoples. I'm glad X took care of that shit and not Brenton and his crew them niggas is sloppy."
"Why you say that? Because if you ask me, I think he got a snitch in his crew every time they do something somebody get locked up."
"Why didn't you tell X about that shit?"
"I just did." Her eyes grew wide and a deep smirk on her grill.
"Okay your right." Then it's a big knock at the door Shamika looking over at me and said, "that's him right now. Julio, could you get that for me please?"
"Sure thing, baby." He quickly gets the door I say to her real low is you and him a thing now? I can see in both their eyes that their fucking. It's all over both their faces.
"Oh no, he's cool, but no he's not my man or anything like that but he's all right for right now. You know what I'm saying, girl."
We both started laughing when he came back with Blue and two of his boys. He walks over to me with a big bright smile and said, "hey, what's up? It's been so long since I've seen you last." I'd stood up and he hugged me, and he said, these are two of my most trusted men this is Mookie. I shake his hand and he greeted me with, "hi, how are you doing?"
Blue chimed in, "and this is Foxy, and I shake his hand as well he just nodding his head with a smile. I can tell both of these guys been around the block a few times in the deepest part of the gutter doing their thing for real. Another big knock at the door Shamika looked at me and I just said, "It's my peoples I want everyone to meet one another over here. I'm working on a spot for all of us meet for right now. I'll have my own spot real soon."
"What about your house?"
"Oh, hell no, not with what I want to do."
"Hey Julio, could you get that Dun go with him?" He pulls out his gun holding it by his side. I love the way this kid moves. This is the kind of person I need around me at all times. Blue was going to say something, but I just put up my finger and he just stopped that let me know he was going to really be the person I want with me rolling to put in some mad work and lock shit down.

Dun and Julio came back in the room with Monk and Tony. I stood up and bump fist with both of them. I turned to everyone and introduce them, "this is Tony and Monk we already to put in some work together."
"Okay, this is Blue, Foxy and Mookie this is the crew we are going to meet at the garage until we get our own spot. I'll know by next week what's up. Now what was you going to say Blue I didn't mean to cut you off brother but I wanted to talk to y'all all at the same time so we can get everything straight. You know what I'm saying."
"That's all right, Ma. I'm cool with that what I was going to say is this is all BSN right?"
"Yeah, everybody here better be or they about to get smoke out of this, motherfucker!"
Everybody burst out laughing loud breaking the ice like that made everybody feel good. After that I was ready to put them to work. All I need is my orders from X and it's on and popping!" We just talk shit for a while when I get the call, I'm excited now it was a rush to me at the time its X saying, "yo, mount up come to the bus graveyard across the street not at the garage, Shorty."
"Okay, I'm on my way I'm bringing my new crew with me."
"Good we have a lot of work for them. One." I looked up at everybody and yelled, "everybody get your shit together let's ride this is not a fucking drill." I can see in each one of their faces who was really who. I got up and hugged Shamika.
"Call me all right! I'm out of here."
"Yeah, go do your thing, girl." We bump fist and I rolled out towards the door with all these real thug niggas with me now. I feel more powerful but I'm going to put some of them to the test. I said to Dun-Dun, "you're with me in the truck everybody got their own shit to ride."
"Okay playa, you drive." I toss him the keys man he looked like he was going to jump 50 feet. I could see it in his grill, but he played it off real cool about it.

This is the first time we all are rolling out as a group after we put in some work in. I know somebody is going to come up with a name but for right now I don't care what niggas in the street call us long as they know that were not playing any games wit their ass. We get outside he got behind the wheel and he could not stop smiling. He pulled off and he looked at Tamika on the corner he just winked his eye at her, and he pulled off really fast. I know that bitch was hot about that shit I did not feel bad for her she got what was coming to her for talking shit. I told Dun-Dun where to drive at I tell him to park across the street from the bus grave yard. We step out of the ride and I waited for everybody to park so we all roll up in there together.

It did not take them long and we all strolled up inside of the bus graveyard and I can see X standing with Fat Jerome. X stepped up and shook everyone's hands as Fat Jerome bump fist with me. He waves me to the side away from everybody else talking low, "look, we are going to go hit them boys who did you wrong Buck, Willie, Eddie, and Bones is all in there they been fucking up bad. Spider said, "it's time for all them niggas to go. Your crew don't have to know about it, okay." Now there both in the spot-on Taylor street but it's about eight of them so y'all is going have to hit their ass hard. Come on in here and I'll let y'all know how we want y'all to do this shit."

X stood there and I said, "look we are going wait to it get dark before we move on them. I want all of y'all to be ready so don't go off and get high. When were done with that were all going to the warehouse for a few? I want all of y'all to be there its mandatory if you really want to be down? Now all of y'all can break out of here about 12 or 1 to make your move they will still be there."

"How you know they will still be there?"

"Because I made sure they had enough coke to cap up they got from our peoples and they don't know were setting their ass up, so they all be there for a little while. You just be ready to do what you do best, Shorty."

"Don't worry you know I'm ready to do this shit!"

X said, "I'll text you the address I want this shit done tonight. I bump fist with him and said, "we'll get it done let me have the keys to the garage so we can all camp out there until it's time to punch in and go to work."

"Here I should have got you a set of you own by now, but I'll make sure you get your own keys this week all right make sure I get them back from you, Shorty." He hands me the keys, "I holla at you later!" So, I wave to everybody so we can roll out of there soon as we walked away, I'd gather everybody up out the bus graveyard outsides and she said, "they want it done tonight. I don't want nobody go get lost when it gets dark is when we make our move if you're not there I know where you stand at with this thing I'm putting together. We're all going to go hang out at the garage until we get the green light and keep shit super tight before we smoke about 20 niggas tonight."

All of them nodded their heads yes laughing as we all quickly drive over to the garage, I tell everybody to park all along the bridge and spread out a little, so nobody knows were all in there ready to fuck somebody up. With all this fire power and specially the Poe-Poe driving by. So, it doesn't take everybody long to roll up in the garage were all sitting around niggas is telling all their war stories and a whole lot of crazy ass bullshit until we get the call. All of them don't know how long I been waiting to get these ass holes back for what they did to me.

A couple hours past and we get the call I jumped up and said, all my niggas, it's time to tool up I just got the call." Its dark outside and I tell Dun-Dun you with me, Tony and Monk. You two are with me too make sure all of y'all put a vest on. Dun-Dun asked, "you have vests, Ma? You're in the big time now, nigga so start acting like it, homey!"

"Follow me, baby boy I went to the back of the garage with Dun-Dun right behind me. I open up the steel closet I hit the button on the left it open slid to the side. His eyes just about pop out of his head and he rubbed his hands together, "shit you was right I I'm going to start acting like I'm big time. This shit is off the fucking hook, boss lady!"

"Grab everybody one and hand them out for me, please."

"You got it, boss lady!" Dun-Dun grabbed five vests and one for himself. I came up on all of them and said, "Blue, you, Mookie and Foxy you three are going to hit the back of the house. Were in the front make sure they don't get out the back if you see them running out there y'all smoke their ass don't rush inside shooting because y'all just might hit one of us. Shoot only if they run out the back just text me a thumbs up when y'all get in position, okay. Now this one is very personal to me so don't fuck this up!" They all nodded their head yes.

I'm thinking to myself this is all of their first big audition for me and I'm going to see what these motherfuckers going to do. I gear up putting on my bulletproof vest on and black bandanna around my neck. I double check my guns and my machine gun. I tell everybody "were rolling out Tony you drive me, Monk and Dun-Dun are going hit the front door all right, let's go!"

We all quickly jump into our vehicles heading towards Taylor street in the dead of the night it only a few blocks from the garage. It didn't take us no time to get there. The house is in the middle of the block. Blue, Mookie and Foxy drive towards the alley way on the left. I wait for them to get in position we parked not too far from the crib were about to roll up in and wait a few minutes. It seems like a fucking whole hour to me. Then it came I looked at my phone and said, "let's do this! Tony make sure after you hear us spraying the place you roll up to the door and come and get us okay, let's go!" Soon as I jump out with my machine gun, I pulled up my black bandanna over my face staying low. Monk is behind me and Dun-Dun took the lead we all quickly rush up to the front door. Dun-Dun gets on the left, I'm on the right and I point at Monk with his big ass. He ran up the steps and he kicked in the door. Boom!

Dun-Dun rushed in first with me right behind him them niggas are in fucking shock while all three of us started spraying their asses. I looked right in the face of that nigga Willie as I rip him apart with hot fucking bullets then I quickly started blasting on the next nigga. I didn't know him I really didn't give a fuck neither and Dun-Dun started spraying Bones and some other niggas. These guys are supposed to be tough guys but crying like a bitch and screaming like one too, but it really didn't matter he had to fucking go along with the rest of the assholes that's in the spot! Fucking debris is flying everywhere glass, wood, the drugs and blood from their bodies is flying all over the furniture and the walls. Monk big ass ran towards the back seeing niggas running to the back of the house shooting everything that fucking moves only two of them niggas made it out the door but after Big Monk killed about four of them in the kitchen. He did not run after them two niggas because he knew they were more men waiting outside.

Blue, Mookie and Foxy was out back and after he heard the machine guns echoing out in the darkness. He just smiled and quickly walked back towards us in the front room. Then I come eye to eye with this nigga the main big mouth motherfucker that was doing all the cheering while they were raping me. Buck sitting back on the right-hand side on the couch I stood in front of his ass his eyes became wide and he did not have a gun in his hand. I quickly pulled down my black bandanna so he can see my face. I open fire on his ass ripping him the fuck apart into his chest and his head. The blood splash all along on the back wall with his brain fragments looking like little pink peanuts dripping down slow and thick. Then I looked to my left the nigga that was cowering on the couch next to him is Eddie.

He jumps up off the couch trying to run. I turned and started shooting him in the back and the back of his head opening him up it looked like fucking watermelon exploding when I'm at target practice. Dun-Dun dumped hot led in his no-good ass. Blood was flying all over the place and Eddie fell face first. Watching him die would be a memory I will never forget as long as I live. It was like a weight lifted up off my chest seeing him lying on the floor bleeding out and smoke coming off his back and his head opened up where you can see the white meat. You can see the back of his fucking skull with his brains hanging out.

I'd yelled out, "let's go!" Me, Big Monk and Dun-Dun quickly ran out the front door soon as we all ran outside Tony came speeding up right on time. All three of us jumped in as he sped off down the street getting ghost from the set.

Soon as we went back to the garage were all putting up our bullet proof vest and I get Dun-Dun and Tony to help me. I make sure all of them is back in the steel closet and locked it up really good. I'm bullshitting with both of them. When X came inside of the garage, he walks up to me, patted me on the shoulder and said, "good job and then he turns to everybody saying, "all of y'all did a really good job tonight!"

He pointed at me, "you're coming with me your peoples can follow us to the warehouse just let them know I want them all to be there." When I looked at him really good, he was dressed really nice I know something is fucked up but I know I have to play along with this nigga. "So, what's up?" In a laughing voice he said to me, "Don't fucking worry about it just get your shit together and come on all right." I just smile and get my shit then I pull my crew together. "Look X, wants y'all to follow him to the warehouse all right." All of them nodding their heads but I can see in all their eyes that there all down for me now.

Me and X started walking towards the door on the side we quickly jump in his black Range Rover park not too far from the garage. I knew it was something going down if he got the Rover out, he only brings that motherfucker out when he's rolling out somewhere on the town to get his swerve on. He waited for everyone to come out and get in their whips. He asks me for the keys then quickly jumped out and locked the place up with and jumps back in. He puts the keys back on his key ring and pulls off hitting the highway. It takes us about an hour to get there and he pulls up at this really nice apartment complex on City line avenue.

He parks in this really big well-lit parking lot. I can see a fleet of expensive whips all over the place not one fucking hoop-Dee in sight. He jumps out and said, "where here let me wait for your crew to park. Me and you are going in there together so just chill, Shorty and fall back a little all right. I just smile as everybody is parking their cars.

Everyone got a spot to park in and X stands in front of all of them with his hands up in the air saying, "just follow me brothers and I want all of y'all to have a really good time." He taps me on the arm smiling.
"Yo X, what is this shit a party or something?"
"You are fucking right it's a party. It's all for you. You're getting your button tonight, sis. So, enjoy yourself! This is what you always wanted right so here it is, family. Tonight, is your night!" He started smiling as we all walked inside this joint and it was off the fucking hook too before I join the gang places like this, I only seen shit like this on TV. We all walked to this first-floor apartment, but this place is huge and luxurious the whole place smell just like fresh white linen. He smiles and knocked on the door three time and then he knocks two more times that's the knock I know that shit's real good now that I been down for a while. Opening the door is Fat Jerome smiling, "hey girl, what's up?"
He hugs me and bump fist with X. X stand by the door waving in the fellas inside saying, "please come in everybody here is family." They came in with their mouths open, its music playing and all this food on the tables with people serving food dressed in all white with the funny ass chef hats on. I see this long ass fancy bar stock with all kinds of liquor niggas can't pronounce right.
I see a bunch of people at the bar I can tell they are big shots and shot callers from the door there all sitting at the bar with their women on their arm smoking big cigars getting their drink on. Then I'd see these sexy dressed waitresses walking around dressed in all black serving champagne to everybody. My crew quickly went and grabbed a glass of champagne soon as the girls came up to them along with me and X taking a sip. I see Spider and the big man himself Nokey Blaze and whole lot of niggas I don't know at all. They are all well-dressed men and women but if there here I know there down with the BSN or they sure nuff would not be in the same fucking room with any of these niggas. Spider looked at me smile, waving at me and X over towards him. I walked over to him he hugs me, "yo, what's up, Shorty? Nokey Blaze then chimed in, "see you really live up to that name I gave you. I heard you been doing your fucking thing, girl."

"Thank you." He taps two men standing beside him smoking big cigars and introduce me, "this is the girl I've been telling y'all about. Almasi this is Trevor Tee and Jasquez two of my long-time family members they were down with me from the start of it all." Jasquez quickly shake my hand saying nice to meet you, Almasi."
"Welcome to the family you have a lot to be proud of sister."
"Thank you so much."
Trevor Tee said to me, "I heard a lot of good things about you I'm glad you're down wit us."
"Thanks."
Spider whisper in my ear, "look if you want to change its up to you?"
"Yeah where at?"
"Over there yo Jerome show Almasi to the room where we have some gear for her."
I looked at him and reply, "just as long as it's no fucking hooker shit, I'm good."
They both started laughing loud. Spider said, "that was work, Shorty we would not do that shit to you, baby girl. Go get change the tattoo dude will be here soon." While everyone is eating, drinking and talking shit with one another. Jerome came over showing me to the room on the left-hand side of this luxury apartment. I go in the room and shut the door behind myself I looked around and this room is bigger than my whole fucking house and it had its own bathroom inside of it with brand new wash rags, towels and some fancy ass soap too. I wash up and I see two big shopping bags on the king size bed filled up with clothing all my size too. Now I'm all excited and happy trying on the jeans that fit me just right I throw on the matching top and some brand-new Nikes all white at the bottom of the bag when I pull the rest of the clothes out as I'd laid them on top of the bed.
I change and am all excited to go talk to everybody inside of the party. Soon as I came out the whole room started clapping and Spider is waving me over towards him standing right next to Nokey Blaze. Spider began to while the crowd grew quiet.

"If you don't know why your here, I'm going to fucking tell you. Our girl here worked her way up from nothing now today were going to give her what she away wanted her button. He points towards this chair while everybody is looking at me with big smiles on their faces.

I sat down in the chair and Buck Shot stepped up with a tattoo gun in his hand and said, "now you're going to be BSN for life, sis. I'm proud of you." He turns on the tattoo gun loud buzzing sounds with everybody cheering loud then this big fat black dude I never met before steps up and introduce himself, "I'm Hanky, nice to meet you, Almasi and you can drink this while you get your tattoo, sweetheart." I take the bottle of cold champagne out of his hand and I open it right quick soon as it popped everyone just went wild. I started drinking it while it was shooting up and fizzling from off the top of the bottle with everyone one laughing and cheering. Buck Shot went to work giving me my BSN tattoo on my right arm. That is when I started noticing everybody with their BSN tattoo. I never pay that shit any mind until then. Spider yelled out, "okay turn that music up loud over here now!"

Some people are dancing, smoking drinking and having a good time while I'm getting worked on. People are passing me blunts and drinks, but I wave off the coke. I didn't get down with it at the time. I met some of Nokey's peoples and I met his son Philly for the first time. He was really cool too and he looks just like his Pop and all of them are showing me their BSN tattoo while I was getting mine proudly. Just before he was done with my tattoo Nokey Blaze came over with this tall black woman and said, "hey Almasi, I want you to meet Jane Doe." She smiled and she shook my hand, "hey what's up? I heard a lot about you girlfriend. When I looked up, I seen her BSN tattoo on her arm and here I'm thinking I'm the only one." She said to me, "keep up the good work, fam. You're making us all proud over here."

She smiled and walked with Nokey Blaze talking. I quickly wave Spider over to me and he came with a beer in both his hands handing me one and asked, "is he almost done?"

He said, "I'm almost done."

"Look, who is that woman?"

"Oh, that's Jane Doe from North Philly. She is a fucking legend she has her own crew but their fucking tight and really on top of their game."
"Why do they call her Jane Doe because she's getting money like that?"
"No, they call her Jane Doe on how cold she is killing motherfuckers like she doesn't have any feeling. She's cold or dead like when they put you in the morgue, they toe tag and bag your ass and you don't have ID on you. They put Jane Doe you get it now?"
"Yeah, I know what you're saying now!"
"Yeah, she's one bad bitch like you! We both started laughing then he said to me, "she got a big ass body count. She just might take over if Nokey steps down keep that one to yourself all right, Shorty."
"I'm thinking you would take the spot. Well, I'm up next if I get it, I get it if not I'll keep rolling along." It took about half an hour to get my tattoo done. I went over and talked to my new crew with Dun-Dun, Tony, Foxy, Mookie Big Monk and Blue really enjoying themselves getting their drink and puff on. Rubbing elbow with some real gangster niggas just like themselves and really feeling apart of the BSN family.

This was a real highlight of our life and specially for me because all of it was held in my honor. X, Fat Jerome, Fly Ty and Damon smoking and joking and I had a really good time. After having a good time everyone was going home around 4 O' clock in the morning. X drove me back to the garage to get my own truck so I can take it back home with me. I drive back home but soon as I get out of my truck Big Boom is standing on my doorstep with them brown eyes and sexy tight body of his. To me this was the cherry on top of my ice cream Sunday, I was really excited, but I'd played it cool.

I NEVER KNEW SEX WAS SO BEAUTIFUL

I'd quickly walked up to him and said, "what are you doing here?"
"I'm here to see you, baby." Well I'm glad you're here and I kiss him right in the mouth. we kissed slow and sexy he did not know but right then and there I was ready to go. I ask him to come inside we both walk in my house both of us smiling from ear to ear. He came in and sat on the couch checking out my place. I ask him, "would you like something to drink?"
"Yes, do you have beer?"
I sure do. I will be right back. I quickly get the beer for both of us when I sat next to him real close then he notices my tattoo and said, "damn, you're really down now."
"Yeah, I just got it, tonight. It's nice, right?" I sit up and show it off to him. I can feel his eyes all over my body not just looking at my arm.
"Yeah, it is nice because it's on your pretty ass arm, baby." Kissing me on my neck that was the fucking spark to this flame I got going on inside of me for this man.
"Why, thank you."
So, we talked for a little while then we started kissing and getting into it. I stop him and said, "let me see where Rashida is at before things get any hotter than it is right now."
"Who the hell is Rashida?"
"I told you about her on the phone she's staying here until we train her to do her thing wit the gang."

I get up and go up the steps to see where she's at I go check in the middle room and she's knocked out sleep. I go back down the steps and I grabbed Big Boom by his big ass hand, and I lead him upstairs to my bedroom. I close the door behind me. I locked the door and I tell him to have a seat baby and relax. He sat on my bed looking up at me my heart is beating fast, but I walked up to him standing in front of him. I'd gently place my hands on his big wide shoulders rubbing them while he started feeling me up. I had butterflies all in my stomach as he gently started taking off my clothes. I was doing the same thing. His body is so muscular as I'm rubbing him up getting more excited to make love to him. He's feeling on my titties and rubbing my ass really good and not too fast. When he started fingering my wet box and sucking on my titties. I have tingles up my back and all over my body with me getting more hot, wet and super excited for what comes next.

He laid me down nice and soft on top of my bed in his really big strong arms. This was like a fucking dream come true to me he was making me feel so good. Then he started pulling my panties down off of me, but he took his time it was not rushed or forced he knew what he was doing. I lifted up a little to help him get them off and I cocked my legs open thinking he was going to get on top of me. But he started licking on my stomach and he started working his way down with his long thick wet tongue. Wow! I was feeling so sexy with my mind floating up to the clouds getting wetter with the anticipation. Then he made it all the way down licking the inside of my thighs I'm on fire right about now then he started licking and sucking inside of my soaked Coochie. I thought I was going hit the fucking ceiling I never had a man lick my pussy before! With his thick long tongue wiggling around when he first started licking me. I could not take it jumping up and down screaming trying to push his head back off of me. Instead he quickly grabbed both of my hands holding them together while he kept sucking lapping and slurping on my kitty.

Then I just let myself go then it tickles at first then it started feeling really good like something I never felt before. I had sex before, but this was my first time somebody really took their time to make me feel good pleasuring all my senses. I have chills up and down my back, my head started getting light when he started sucking and just concentrating on my clit. Wow the things you find out when you have somebody who know what the fuck, they are doing makes a world of difference. Gawd knows. He's fingering and licking me at the same time and I just was about to lose my mind. Right before I was about to cum, he stopped, and I looked up and he got up on top of me, but he was not rushing or trying to go to fast.

I love how he got up on me and when I see his man hood coming towards me, I think I was going to past the fuck out, but he gently slid it up in me and started pumping. The more he stated pumping and stoking the better it started feeling now I'm all into it now pushing back on his thick dark sweet meat hitting my spot. I'm grunting my ass off, but it was so fucking amazing I could not put words to how good I was feeling at the time. It was like the earth was spinning underneath my whole body filled with so much wonder and joy I never knew ever exist.

Shit, I was trying hold it but after the first twenty minutes I climaxed and the only time I did that is when I use to play with myself in the bathtub. It never happened with the two stupid ass boys I did have sex with they were the ones who got their shit off not me. They came before I could get my rocks off. But this is nothing like that at all now I have a real man! This right here has more passion and sensuality to it. We were both feeling one another loving every minute of it too. I never knew this would happen to me I don't know why. This is like the ultimate in sexual pleasure words just cannot explain it.

Then he turns me over and started hitting it from the back that felt even more better wit each stroke from his hard-sexy muscular body and this nigga got whole lot of fucking stamina. too because I was tired after a while, but I hung in there I don't know how but I did. I was really enjoying every moment of it sweating up a storm like I was running the fucking the 100-yard dash or something. And he really started hitting my spot again and the sensation I was feeling from this man is really rocking my world and after a while I just let myself go for the first time in my life and I climaxed again. I think he know I did because right after I did, he did the same thing, but he started going into fucking convulsions and I can feel all his baby gravy all inside of me super-hot. I almost was ready to cum again feeling it inside of my pussy I blast off to another planet or something while he's grunting and yelling really loud and I was too.
After that he kiss me and held me in his big strong arms, and I felt safe, protected and loved I never knew sex was so beautiful after all the bull shit, I been through. I fell a sleep because that real good fucking he put on me knocked my ass right out. I get up after a while so I can go pee, I go get my housecoat from behind the door. I slip it on, and I looked down at him and he is fucking knocked out too. I smiled and unlock the door and I make a dash to the bathroom and I came back sitting on the side of the bed getting my cigarette pack from off my nightstand. I light one up and I'm puffing floating on fucking air after I started smoking feeling really good. I can see him sit up with a big smile on his face he said, light me one up, baby girl.
"Sure!"
I lit one up for him and hand it to him as he sits up even more looking me in my eyes and announced, "I have to tell you something." First thing I'm thinking he's going to tell me he's hooked up with some bitch or something I'm ready to get pissed off after a really nice time we just had. I said to him, "what is it you have to tell me Boom?"
"Well I did come to see you but I'm on the run right now so can I stay here for a little bit?"
"Yeah, sure baby. I thought you was going tell me you were linked up with somebody or something?"

"Oh no plus I would not do no foul ass shit like that to you baby. I'm not just saying that shit. I don't have anybody I stay up in the fucking woods all the time with my crazy ass father making money."
"So, what happen why are you on the run baby? Well the FBI and the ATF had an undercover snitch motherfucker in our camp while we were selling guns, they raided the place and I came here to see you and ask you can I stay here for a few days until my friend Frank call me and tell me he got a safe house ready for us.
"If you don't mind telling me but who is us?"
"My Pop's and his boys. Oh, and I forgot I brought you a gift too."
"Oh yeah other then you are bringing your fine ass to my bed. We both started laughing while were kissing still laughing out loud. He jumped up and said loud, "I'm going to go get it right now." He turns on the lights looking for his boxers and his jeans he fumbles around he finds them, and he slips them on right quick.
Throwing on his shirt and out the door he goes. I follow him down the steps. I sit on the couch waiting to see what it is he said he has for me in a few minutes. He come back in the house with a dozen roses in one hand and holding this box in the other hand he hands me the roses first. "Thank you, baby! why you didn't give this to me when you first came in the door, nigga?"
"Then you would have knew I was going to ask you something that's why." We both started laughing as he hands me the box, I put it in my lap looking up at him and said, "so what is it?"
"Open it up and see, baby." I open the top of the box and I looked inside and two guns a Glock and Colt 45 pistol with a pearl handle on its really nice too.
"See there custom-made by me Almasi and he smiled. Thank you, baby, so you made both of these guns for me?"

"Yeah, I did that's what I do all day long make custom made guns and machine guns for people who have the loot, baby girl. I know you're really good with a gun, so I'm made them just for you the 45 and the Glock hold 15 shot clips and you can put a silencer on both of them too there in the box. as well you can really fuck something up with both of them. As I pick up the 45 and started holding it in my hand pointing it and I reach in the box getting the silencer putting it on the front of the gun really tight. When I heard Rashida coming down the steps, she stops halfway coming down and spoke, "hi, you doing I knew I heard another voice. I say to her, "yeah this is Boom. Boom, this is Rashida. He greeted her "hi, how are you doing?"

"I'm good I did not want to bother y'all I was just seeing who was in the house that's all I'm going back to bed nice to meet you."

I asked, "Who let you in the house Spider?"

"Yeah, he said he's the only one with the key, so he let me in."

"So how are things going now?"

"Real good I'm really getting the hang of it."

"That's good you'll be in the game before you know it."

"I hope so I'm going back to bed. I'm going to let y'all talk." She went back up the steps. Then me and Boom soon went back upstairs for round two after we talked for a while enjoying one another. This is the first time I can really let my hair down with a man. This shit is like a fucking dream and I really feel good I have not felt this way in a very long time.

OLD ENEMIES AND NEW ENEMIES ALIKE!

Well just like he said Big Boom stayed at my house for three days, but I wanted him to stay longer because they were the best three days I had in my life. He treated me just like a queen. I can get use to that shit nothing but sex and romance just what the fucking doctor ordered. But he did say he was on the run from the law and he had to hook up with his Pops and the War-Dogs a bunch of crazy ass black revolutionaries who still think there living in the nineteen sixties or something. A week blaze past and I was waiting on when we would have to make the move on the Guerilla Boulevard niggas. While I was waiting, I got the good news on our new spot. I hooked up for us at Washington Avenue the old Cole warehouse and we can move in this week right before I was going text everyone after I got the good news from the girl who hook shit up for me with the realtor. I get a call from X telling me to meet him at the spot right away. "I'm already washed and dressed so I quickly roll out the door to my whip and drive over to our crib it only takes me less than ten minutes to get there. soon as I ring the doorbell Fat Jerome open the door for me and said, "Yo, what's up?"
"Nothing much big man, what's going on?"
"From what I heard so far is that those Guerilla Boulevard niggas change their location."
"Yeah, well let's go back here and find out the whole story then."
We both walked back to the room we all call the office Spider sitting at the head of the table with everybody sitting around the table X, Damon, Fly Ty, Brenton and Gill they all speak to me with smiles and waves as I take my seat the whole room is filled with chatter and smoke. Spider lifting his hand up and everybody got quiet. Spider's voice sound like it was coming from a bullhorn, "now that everybody is here, they change shit up on us, but it is a good thing. We have an inside man on top of shit there going to have it at the picnic tables near the tennis courts." X said, "well that's perfect for us!"
Spider yeah, "tell us brother. We can hit them at the strawberry mansion bridge."

Spider clapped his hand and said, "you know something brother, I love it!"
"Okay you're going to quarterback this one, right?"
"And you know it!" Everybody sitting at the table laughing, "alright than anything else on the table?"
Brenton said, "yeah, I have something were having fucking problem with the Gook's their trying move in on our heroin Market with a shit load of weight."
"Well take Almasi and her crew and take care of their ass!" "Okay, you heard the man, baby girl. You got the call-I pick up the ball were ready."
"I'll take care of it!"
"Good now if were done here I like to go see my wife." I stood up lighting up a Newport as X came over to me as were all walking out the door. "Sis, double check on your crew and make sure their ready to go on this Guerilla Boulevard hit." "Okay, I will we can move into our new spot today I'll run it down to all of them then."
"Good, we don't need no fuck ups on this all right now what about the Gook's you don't need any help with that do you?" "No, I got this shit."
"So, when are you going to make your move on them?"
"After I get some real good Intel on them then I'll take care of their ass. Good, I'll call up Black Jeff from 16th street he's down with us now but I'm need you to do something for me while I holla at these niggas."
"What's that, X?" He taps me on the arm while we both walking towards the front door of the spot soon as we got to the doorway, he started talking low saying, "One of his boys Frankie the Pro is working with the police. I'll drop off the files to show Black Jeff that one of his boys is a fucking Rat."
"Tomorrow where you going to be at your new spot you hooked up right?"
"Yeah most of the day I'll be there."
"Well I'll swing past with that I want you to put it up then I'll hook up a sit down with Black Jeff and his peoples at your new place all right."

"I'll be there along with Spider so he knows it's no bull shit so we can have this shit done. It's something else but I can't talk about it right here because it way too many ears up in this motherfucker right now. Then I see him looking over at Ayden who was not in the meeting sitting on the couch bull shitting laughing and talking with Brenton he bumps fist with me as I'd looked at all of them right quick and I walked all the way out the door to my truck.

Soon as I got to my truck and sat down in the seat before I pulled off, I started texting everybody. I started with Dun-Dun telling them all to meet me at the garage at 25th street under the bridge in one hour. I go home and get some more money from out my safe. I go to the garage and wait for everybody and I call the girl, La-Nesa I knew from back in the days from around the way this bitch is on the ball plus she's super smart and she really know her shit. She runs a hair salon for her aunt Dee-Dee but she wants to hook up with me and do her own thing because her family don't want to pay her right and they talk a whole lot of shit on top of that too. With all the hard work she put into the place.

So, me and her have a hair shop in the works. I got her to hook up the spot for me and my crew first and in a couple of months me and her will open up the hair salon but I'll be the silent partner so I can get on track opening up all cash businesses. I can watch all the influx of money we get from the dope spots. I ask her to go and pick the keys up and bring them to me at the garage and I'll give her the rest of the money for me and her to get rolling with the hair shop. A half an hour went past and La-Nesa comes to the garage tapping on the door like I told her too. I go to the door and let her in, and she is smiling from ear to ear with the keys in her hand saying, "I told you I get it done for you!" I close the door and said, "come back here we walked to the back with the card table near the 007 steel closet.' I point to one of the chairs and said, "thank you so much, baby." She hands me the keys.

"Now, I got something for you girlfriend." I reach down into my backpack bag and set it on top of the table, and I unzipped it. I announced, "let's get this show on the fucking road!" We both start laughing as I hand her five stacks.

"You got a bag for all this?"

"Shit girl, what you think I got this expensive ass coach bag for its not just to look good, but you can put a whole lot of shit inside this bitch, girl!" We both laughed as she started putting the money in her blue coach bag that match her outfit. Soon as she did that, I hear a big knock at the door she looks at me I say to her, "it's cool, my crew is on their way here. You look like you're a fucking nervous bitch calm down your all right with me?" I pulled out my Glock walking to the side door. I peek out the little window on the door. Its Fat Jerome I open the door and he step in. I close the door behind him he hands me a big plastic bag filled with envelopes saying, "it's pay day that for you and your crew. I got to go, sis. I have a lot of stops to make. "Okay. Big man Thank you. Are you alright?"

"Sure, you know me I'm all good look I'm having a get together with my family and I want you to come stop by the crib Sunday if you're not too busy, aright."

"I'll be there big man. I'm family too, nigga." I give him a quick hug. We both laugh as I open the door for him. As he made his swift dash to his whip as I stand in the doorway watching his back. He pulls off I close the door back walking back to where La-Nesa is at sitting there waiting on me I quickly open the 007 closet setting the plastic bag filled with loot. I sit down and said, "now back to you girl what is you going to call the place? Platinum Diva."

"I like that shit, girl. How soon can you get this done?" "Well, I already have the location at 22nd street and its lots of parking available."

"I say about two or three months to do it right."

"Sounds good to me girl so let me know if you need anything else and I'll walk you to the door." We both walked towards the side door, but I walked her all the way to her car parked not too far from the door. I bump fist with her, and she jumps in her car. As I stand there watching her pull off going down the street. I go back inside the garage feeling really good about getting things done and the first person to show up is Dun-Dun banging on the door. I let him in and greet him, "hey, I got something for you, brother." As I wave him towards the back of the garage and I quickly open up the steel closet. I look at the envelopes and I see the one marked with my name on it. I take that one out first then all the others were blank, and I toss him one of them as he catches it in midair asking, "what's this boss lady?"

"It's fucking pay day, nigga and good job by the way." He opens it up real fast he said, "damn, I have to work three whole fucking months busting my ass to get what you just gave me."

"Well like I told you before welcome to the big time, nigga!" We both started laughing loud then my phone started ringing, "I answer it and its Blue. "Yo, Almasi were outside the door."

"Okay, I'll have Dun-Dun open the door up for yawl."

"Yo, Dun open the door for them, please.

"Sure thing, boss lady. So, what up with that place you were talking about for us?"

"I'm glad you said that because we move in today. I just got the keys from my girl so we can move in."

He smiled walking towards the side door and opens it up as Blue Foxy and Mookie came in and right behind them is Tony and Big Monk. When all of them came to the back of the garage standing all together.

"Well, I'm glad all of you could make it." All of them started laughing then I started tossing them the envelopes towards all of them catching them smiling. I yelled out to them, "its pay day boys!"

"X and Spider told me to tell all of y'all good job, but we have a whole lot of work to do today! I just got the keys to our new headquarters at 23rd and Washington Avenue were going to move in today.

"Were going have to clean the joint up but I'm going to make some calls to get people to help us out. I'm going to need the rest of y'all to make the rounds while were fixing our new spot. When we get it fixed up, I'll have some keys made for some of y'all, okay. Let's go to work!

SMOKING A SNITCH

Three days later we got our new spot cleaned up and ready to go. It could take a little more fixing up, but I'm really proud of what we done so far. I'm feeling great because this is my own base of operations and I have big plans for me and my clique to do some major fucking damage. X told me he's breaking in our new place today with a sit down with Black Jeff from 16th street. To tell him about his boy Frankie the Pro.

An hour blaze past and Spider along with X, Fat Jerome, Damon Gee and Fly Ty came in with Black Jeff and four of his goons Beast, Lamel, Mazzy and Kuty. We all sat down at the long wooden makeshift table and chairs. I had hooked up in the room on the right we dove it as the war room. Spider sat at the head of the table with X sitting on his right along with Black Jeff and his goons stood up behind him. I sat on the left with Dun-Dun and Blue sitting next to me and Foxy, Tony, Mookie and Big Monk standing up behind us ready to get busy.

Spider bang on top of the table getting everyone's attention and said, alright good people, were here to talk to you Jeff about your boy Frankie."

"What about Frankie?" He barked.

Spider putting his hands up in the air yelling, "First off nigga, calm down. I'm trying to tell you your boy is a snitch."

He sucked his teeth and waved his hand, "Man, get the fuck out of here, man not Frankie anybody but him!"

X said, "yeah, but we have proof right here and he slid the file over toward Black Jeff and he just looks at it. He doesn't even touch it rolling his eyes at everybody in the room with a cigarette dangling from his fat dark lips.

X pushed it open and pointed to the file, "there it is right there, and you won't even look at it, nigga. What's up with you?"

"Me and Frankie came up together and I know he's not a fucking snitch!"

"Spider yelled, "we have a big fucking problem then because you agree to being down with us when we started selling y'all a whole lot of fucking weight of our product!"

"Yeah, we agree to that but not to where we have to sell out our own peoples fuck that!"

Beast, Kuty, Mazzy and Lamel pull out their guns pointing them at Spider. Then reacting really swift in a blink of an eye all of us pulled out our guns Myself X, Fly Ty, Fat Jerome, Damon Gee, Blue, Dun-Dun, Foxy, Tony, Mookie and Big Monk making a loud clicking sounds were all pointing them right back at their ass.

Spider smirked, "if you motherfuckers want to make it back out that fucking front door, I would put them fucking guns down if I was you!" Soon as he said that coming from the left and right side of where Black Jeff and his men were all at popping up like fucking commandos with machine guns all in their hands is Petey Q and his crew dressed in all black Mister Blade, Puerto Rican Joe, Merk, Sammy Green his brother Bulls-Eyes, Tommy Machete, Knock Daddy and Zoro all of them had machine guns pointing up at all of them with a shock look on every last one of their grills. I see that look in their eyes those niggas were shook. Spider stood up pulling out his Glock pointing at Black Jeff and said, "what the fuck is up now, motherfucker? Did you really think you could fuck wit us nigga you really are fucking crazy like niggas said you are!"

X yelled out, "and stupid too!" Everybody started giggling loud with that sinister look of death in our eyes the shit was like letting out air from a fucking balloon or something all their face is blank knowing there not getting out of here alive. Some of them looked like they were going to cry like a little bitch, too. Then Spider said, "yo Brenton bring that snitch ass nigga out here! Brenton came out holding a gun to Frankie the Pro's head along with Gill, Ayden and Alijah.

Spider shouted, "I knew you could not take care of this shit so I had him brought here so you can see what we do with snitch niggas! Okay Fanya Sasa (Do it now)" Ayden is standing behind Alijah Kapacka! Ayden shot Alijah in the side of his head he fell to the floor with blood gushing out of his head. Spider said, "this is how we get rid of fucking snitches and anyone working with the police!" Spider looks over at Brenton nodding his head towards him Kapacka!

Brenton shot Frankie the Pro in the middle of his head his whole face looked like fucking raw hamburger meat at the butcher shop he fell backwards to the floor. Doom! With blood squirting out of his head all over the floor Spider looking over to Black Jeff and his men said, "it's up to you if you still want to follow this low life fucking snitch, motherfucker. Here this ass hole doesn't think I know him, and Frankie was working with the Poe-Poe the whole time. We put y'all on!" Black Jeff yells, "that's a fucking lie! So why you did not open that file because you knew you were in one of those pictures with the fucking cops! I set your ass up. I wanted you to look at them, so you know we knew about your ass! Yo what's your name? Mazzy."

"Go over there and look at your bitch ass boss selling you and your crew out y'all never notice all of y'all get locked up but him and Frankie don't!"

Mazzy walks over to the table and he looks in the files seeing the pictures he looks up at Black Jeff and his eyes are on fucking fire. Black Jeff yelling, "Yo, Mazzy man that's some bull shit man they doctor that shit with photo shop, man! Tell him we will go down to the death if we have too fuck, these nigga, Mazzy man! He yells out is Mazzy I'm not dying with you, nigga!"

"I'm not scared to die but not for your fucking ass not the way you and Frankie been acting all funny and fucking all of us over. I see you right there with them cops because I know these police, I seen you talking to them all the time before that's not photo shop, Dawg that's real fuck that! And I suppose to die for your snitching ass no fucking way nigga!" He steps off to the side as Petey Q and his crew let him walk over towards them and Bullseyes took his gun out of his hand.

Spider anyone else before it's too fucking late? Beast, Lamel and Kuty stepped off too looking over at Black Jeff with a surprise look on his grill yelling, "you bitch made motherfuckers! Oh, it's like that you fucking sell out niggas as much as I did for you no count ass niggas!" As Bullseyes and Tommy Machete take their guns out of their hands Spider smiled and said, "looks like you're the next up to meet the big Kahuna in the sky motherfucker! Fuck you!"

Soon as he said that Petey Q and his men open fire on his ass shredding him apart with bullets with his flesh and blood flying in the air as his lifeless body hit the floor really fast and hard with everybody standing there looking at the bloody mess with smoking floating up in the air coming off of his bullet riddled body.
X walking up to Mazzy, Kuty, Beast and Lamel and said, "you guys made the right decision now. I don't know which one of y'all is going to run your fucking crew but if we hear any more bull shit that went on in the past you four Negros here are good as dead too, you feel me?" All of them nodding their heads, "yes, I'm glad to be still alive, Spider steps up and points at Mazzy, "you're the one I'll have my people come talk to you and you run shit for now on, okay?"
"Yeah, I'm wit that but when will I get something to hold it down?
Tomorrow night if you go down there and show my peoples where the Gook's hang at, I give you my word."
"Sound good to me he shakes hand with Spider now can I have my gun back?"
"Sure, Bulls-Eyes give this man his gun back.
The dude name Beast said, "what about me?" Spider looks him right in his eyes. "Can I trust you?"
"Yeah you can trust me."
"Okay Petey Q, **Kama yeya anajaribu kitu unajua cha kufanya** (*if he tries something you know what to do.*" All of them started laughing as Bulls-Eyes hands Lamel and Kuty their guns back still laughing Lamel said, "what did he say?"
"You really don't want to know. Just don't make any funny ass moves or you're going die right where you are fucking stand, nigga."
X walks up to me and said, "alright this is your place, baby girl gets your peoples to clean this shit up for me, alright."

Tommy Machete and Knock Daddy is going to show y'all where to dump the bodies. Ayden see if that pussy ass snitch Alihjah got a wire on his ass or not for me if he does make sure X get it!" Me and my crew in our new place clean up all the blood and the bodies from off the floor. It took us about four hours to get everything clean up. You never think about death all that much until your cleaning up thick blood and tossing body parts from niggas inside of a construction size trash bags like they were yesterday garbage and some of them we had to hack off their arms and legs to make them fit inside the bags. When I first did it, I threw up all over the place and I could not get that fucking smell out my nose. It was like my nose hair kept the smell of death burning inside of it for days on end or something and shit smells, but dead man shit is even worst. Now I'm an old pro at the shit like it's another day at the office or a fucking walk in the park.

Later on, that night we had Kuty, Mazzy Beast and Lamel went home but the next day they came and did what Spider and X ask them to do to show us where the head of the Gook's stay at. His name is Vien Hy. He's the leader of the Quai Vat gang that mean's Monsters in Vietnamese. Mazzy told us he has about eight bodyguards around at all times and they only sell weight and a lot cheaper than we do. The product is more powerful than any of the shit we use to get off the fucking Italians. I know dam well their cutting it too much the cheap ass motherfuckers that's why we don't fuck with them anymore.

So the next night we go down there to smoke this motherfucker driving around the block a couple times to see how they move were all parked near 15th and Tasker street right before were going to make our move this Vietnamese lady come out from the playground with a young street tough kids with her on each side of her saying in broken English and this heavy ass accent, "don't shoot, don't shoot I want to talk to Glock Mommy boss lady big boss lady." Dun-Dun got behind the wheel holding his gun on her she's waving her hands saying, "no! No, I want to talk to the boss lady Glock Mommy. She run shit you know who I'm talking about!" He looks at me, "what did she say?"

"She said you want to talk to you."

"Okay then."

"No, boss lady it just might be a trick to get you in the open."

She said, "no tricks I need to talk business no tricks."
So, I step out the truck while everybody is on standby. I hold my Glock by my side with Dun-Dun, Tony and Big Monk right behind me she's points towards the playground. We walk inside and sitting on the Bench is a young Vietnamese dude wearing a wife beater cut up jeans on with all these crazy ass tattoos all over his arm and chest with these mirror sun glasses on and a cigarette cocked in his lips.
He said, "Thank you for coming."
"What is this all about?"
"I know y'all came down here to kill Vien Hy right?" I just looked at him with a smirk on my face.
"Well you know those guys you let go yesterday are setting you up. If you run up in there you do know that shit, right?" "No, I don't? Well a couple of them guys cut a deal with the Italians to kill two birds with one stone."
"Why you say that give me the break down."
"Well here it is they get you to kill Vien then that stop all the big weight flowing for a while and the Italians give them that weak shit to sell to take the BSN spot. You get it now."
"So, what is it to you and who the fuck are you, anyway?"
"I'm the answer to all your fucking problems, boss lady. My name is Quan Kauu."
"So, Quan why should I trust you it just might be you setting me up, too?"
"Oh no boss lady I would have had you and all you people killed soon as you was going around in circles if you don't believe me or you don't trust me send in the men how said where Vien Hy is at and see if I'm lying to you or not?"
"Okay, I'll do that Quan. But before I go here is my card call me and we can do business."
"Why you want to do business with me if I'm down here to kill your boss?"
"Because he's not my fucking boss he wants me dead just like the Italians want you guys dead, too. Plus, I need you guys to help me fight the Italians from what I heard about the BSN they hate Italians. You guys don't do business with them anymore and they hate y'all because they can't control your organization like they did back in the days. I know for a fucking fact they can't fuck wit y'all because your too fucking strong right now and I know that shit for sure."

"How you know all this shit, man?"
"Because I'm smart and I did my fucking homework and I know when to make my move. Do what I ask you with them two dudes telling you where Vien is at and call me tomorrow." He got up from the bench and he walks with the old lady and the two street tough kids smoking cigarettes strolling to the other end of the playground real smooth and they were gone. Dun-Dun Tony and Big Monk started nodding their heads with Dun-Dun saying, "I believe him send in those three motherfuckers and sit back and see what happens?"
"I'm with Dun we can't trust them motherfuckers we just kill their boss and their friend."
Tony chimed in and said, "yeah I knew when Spider let them live, they were going to fucking try to pull something right from the door. I see in their eyes I got a real bad feeling about them niggas." Then I got an idea I go in the back of my truck and get my machine gun. and I called Dun-Dun over to me and I hand him the machine gun real fast.
"Hey Dun- Dun. I want you to go around the block and sneak up on their car if they pull off really fast like there making a run for it. I want you to kill all three of them motherfuckers! Spray the car and make sure their dead too and I also hand him the extra clips." He put them in his pocket, and He bumped fist with me, and he went off into the darkness going around the block like I ask him.
Me, Tony and Big Monk went back to the truck I told Big Monk to drive. As I hand him the keys, we all jumped in while I called Blue and he picked up in the first ring and said, "what's up? Are we doing this shit or what?"
"Look these niggas is setting us up I'm send them in their first you guys. I want y'all to act like you're going with them and then Jet! You hear me?"
"Yeah, I hear you, Almasi. I don't want any of y'all to get hurt with these assholes setting us up."
"Okay, I got you! I call up Mazzy, "hey, what's going on? Are we doing this or what?"
"Yeah, I want you guys to go in first and my people will be right behind you."
"Okay you want us to go in right now?"

"Yeah right now, motherfucker. Move your ass. Let's go!" I hang the phone up Mazzy behind the wheel of his gray Chevy Impala he started up his car and he pull off. He made a quick right turn not where the house is on the corner Dun-Dun popped up shooting Rat tat tat tat kackapacka! Dun-Dun strayed the windshield with glass flying in the air hitting the driver. Mazzy in the head and neck and all the blood shooting up on the glass. He also hit the dude Beast in the chest head and stomach on the passenger side. Dun-Dun got low spraying bullets in the back seat hitting Lamel in his head chest and neck. He ran towards the playground the car swaying from side to side and crashing into group of park cars on the righthend side. Kadoom!

We heard the machine gun fire I told Big Monk behind the wheel to go around the block so we can pick him up and keep rolling the fuck out of there. I was on the phone calling him to see where he was at, he picked up. "Yo where the fuck you at nigga?"

"I'm in the playground! Meet us on the other side on that little block and we'll come and pick you up!"

"Okay I'll be there, Boss lady!" Big Monk made a quick left turn up the little block from off 15th street near the playground. We can see Dun-Dun running up he jumps in the back seat and he dam near fell on the truck floor with the machine gun still in his hand. Tony helps him up and asked, "you all right brother?"

"Yeah, I'm good. He's laughing his ass off now Big Monk took off towards Broad street." I told him he can slow down after he makes the turn. I quickly called Blue to see where they were at and make sure they got away as well. He picked up after three rings, "yo, you, all right?"

"Yeah, I got the fuck out of there when I heard the shots once you told me they were trying to set us up!"

"Yeah, but I took care of their ass. So, Dun did you get them?"

"Yeah I got all of them they should be all dead. I sprayed that motherfucker just like you told me too boss lady! Good all right Blue meet us back at the spot. Okay one!"

An hour later we meet back at our new headquarters so we can all talk about what happen tonight. So were sitting around in the what we all call now the gangster lounge. I brought a nice black leather couch set some end table and a 50-inch TV but were all waiting on the fucking cable man this week to hook it up. But we have ourselves and some music to entertain us with some hard beats flowing. Drinking beer getting our puff on talking a whole lot of shit me Blue, Dun-Dun, Tony, Mookie Foxy and Big Monk. Foxy said, "man when you went into the playground Almasi I'm thinking were going have to run up in there and start blasting, niggas from the gate."

"Blue told us to chill out and make sure we get word before we make our move. I'd said see that's what I'm talking about don't make any moves until you know shit is right. Because if we would have run up on them niggas up at the crib, they told us they just might have blown us the fuck up and keep getting up." Everybody started laughing loud.

"Big Monk well that Gook gangster ass nigga was telling the fucking truth."

I said, "yeah and he was right if we knock off that boy Vien were helping out the Italians."

"So, what about him what happens now?"

I said, "well he's was like he was going take care of him from what I got in so many words."

When he said to me, "he's not my boss that let me know he's going to take over I'll call him and find out what we can get from him." So, the rest of the night we all got high and everybody when home and the next day I'd linked up with the boy Quan Khuu. We got a shit load heroin that's really powerful too and we don't have to step on it too hard. It's some really good shit after month or so the money was really rolling in. Spider was really happy that I'd made that move because not only it put us back on top it was raining money like a motherfucker.

But with that the gang gave me more shit to do, but I bumped up money wise and so did my crew. I heard Vien was dead.

Spider told me why he had that boy Alijah killed because he was working with the FBI. He found that out with his inside peoples on his payroll. He wants everybody to make sure we keep on our toes and not to fuck up. Do things right and for me to keep my eyes on everybody no matter how tight you get with somebody background.

THE BBC IS WHAT THEY CALL US

Its August 1997, and shit is crazy right about now in Philly. The long hot days of summer is blazing by. Me and Boom are in love and were ready to move in together. La-Nesa and I got our first hair shop open Platinum Divas is jumping off just like we knew it would. All the fly bitches come get done up and all the big ballers bring them to us because mostly all of BSN come do fucking business with us. Like real family do it's a real good look on both ends we plug in motherfuckers that can handle shit real hustlers down with our network. From all over the city it makes good for business. I put my two girls on with them running two houses each Big Kim and Queisha with my old crack slinging crew. Little Row-Row, Jagger and my aunt Lisa I still call her that. Big Kim with the dope and Queisha with the coke. Big Kim didn't want to sell heroin at first but once she started seeing all the money flowing in her whole attitude changed.

The gang sent Rashida for some military training with the War-Dogs while me and my crew is busier than a one legit man in an ass kicking contest. After waiting so long we got the green light to do the Guerilla Boulevard hit. Its Saturday afternoon Fairmont park strawberry mansion bridge 11:45 a caravan of three black trucks and a Benz wagon behind them is driving into the park all of us are in position. Mookie and Gill are on the lookouts on each side of the bridge in the park. Foxy was over by the tennis courts keeping an eye on the Guerilla Boulevard peoples setting things up for the big cook out. Mookie and Gill on post just in case the cops roll up on their job is to jam them up. Now were posing as street sweepers cleaning the park with light brown jump suits on me. Dun-Dun and Big Monk is on the right-hand side of the bridge on the left-hand side is Mookie and Blue.

Soon as they were coming Tony behind the wheel not too far from us in the park on his walkie-talkie with the loud cracking sound announced, "here they come!"

All of us can hear them as they all make that big right hand turn on to the bridge speeding from the other direction is Fat Jerome in a big black GMC truck coming towards the four trucks. The caravan with Sammy Green in the other truck right behind him. Fat Jerome jumped out of his lane right into the front of the four-car caravan crashing right into the lead truck. Kaboom!

He jumped out of his truck right after the crash he rolled on the ground jumping up blasting at the trucks fucking them up right from the door.

Soon as Fat Jerome crashed into the lead truck, we all sprang into action. I quickly pulled my lucky black bandanna over my mouth and went to work with my machine gun running up on the vehicle spraying bullets into the trucks like a mad woman possessed or something **Kapacka! Kapackacka! Katapacka!Katackpacka!** Machine gun fire echoing loud with glass flying everywhere as I hit the first three niggas trying to blast back at me from out of the truck. I never gave them a chance to get out or make any other moves. I pen their ass down right where they were at. Hitting them all center mass in the chest, neck then the stomach watching them fall to the ground. Inside of the truck with blood gushing out and splatter all over the truck and the ground like Niagara Falls of blood. Seeing their twisted fucked up expressions on their faces while I send each and every one of them to hell to go smoke blunts and talk shit with the devil personally. Because none of these no-good motherfuckers are going home to see Jesus! Next, I started with head shots seeing all the blood flying in the air as their heads explode from the shells from my machine gun obliterating their faces. I know when it's all said and done their own mother will not be able to recognize their ass turning them into one big fucking bloody mess.

They all looked like their faces just came out of a fucking meat grinder. I made sure I did not get any of their blood on me after they fell to the ground on my black Reeboks. I'm in my zone when I'm in the middle of the shit I stay focus spitting the hot shit in my military stance pivoting to the next target. In the other truck just a head of the one I just shred up giving them first class tickets to Valhalla courtesy of BSN travel agents we aim to fucking please!

I came up swift and silent on the next truck spraying four more of them Niggas like they were roaches in my kitchen, but I'd got a bigger rush doing this shit here. I can see their flesh being ripped right from their bodies.

As I kept shooting keeping my head on a swivel looking both ways. Then I can see Fly Ty, Damon Gee, Ayden, Brenton and Fat Jerome shooting shit up all you see is their muzzle flash and shells flying out. Along with Mister Blade, Puerto Rican Joe, and Merk every one of them dressed in all black and with their mask on. Machine guns in tow running on the right- and left-hand side of where the trucks were stopped at spitting hell fire. Going to work on their ass as well on everyone inside of the trucks. These niggas never knew what the fuck hit them they were all overwhelm the men they did try to jump out to fight back. All killed within minutes of trying to get out then Fat Jerome waved his hand for everybody to stop shooting. Fat Jerome, Damon Gee, and I stepping over a bunch of bloody bodies looking inside of the truck to make sure that Kahlil is dead. Fat Jerome seen him slumped on the back seat on the left-hand side of the truck all shot the fuck up bleeding from out of his head and chest with his pistol still in his hand dead.

I looked inside still holding my machine gun with my heart beating fast when I looked at him. His whole body was ripped up with bullets with thick globs of blood coming out of his mouth. Fat Jerome yelled, **"Tulipata!**(*We Got Him*)" he pump his fist up in the air. Sammy Green who was driving behind Fat Jerome that crashed into the lead truck Puerto Rican Joe, Merk and Mister Blade. All of them hopped into the truck super quick and took off at the same time. X in another truck came speeding up as Fat Jerome, Fly Ty, Damon Gee Ayden and Brenton quickly jumped into the vehicle taking off going the other direction. Tony came picking us up as me Dun-Dun, Blue, Mookie and Big Monk jumped in the truck and sped off up on Ford Road getting the fuck out of dodge.

We all went back to our warehouse to chill out and get our groove on. We found out in the after math of the hit when were all sitting around getting our drink and puff on. When the news came on with the news announcer said, "fourteen people dead from gun battle on the strawberry mansion bridge. With police on the scene calling it the strawberry mansion bridge massacre." After we heard that shit, we were all going off we all could not hear the rest of the broadcast with all of us yelling and celebrating. I have to say we all got really fucked up that night. Spider was happy about the job we did now he call us the body bag clique and that's how the BBC came to be, and it stuck.

September 1997, a month later me and Big Boom move into our new huge ass luxury apartment on City Line Avenue. I'm still keeping my house I'm thinking about renting it out but I'm feeling good because me and Big Boom is starting our life together. After him and I had all the new furniture put in our place and we were fixing up the bedroom and when we stop to take a break my phone rings. I answer it while still checking out my sexy ass man thinking of all the freaky shit were going to do tonight to one another smiling when I hear X voice asking, "yo what's up, sis?"

"Nothing just fixing up our new place, that's all."

"Look, I hate to give you this bad news on your big day, but somebody just shot and killed Fat Jerome along with three others of our peoples about an hour ago."

"Who?"

"You did not know them it was Marco, Brody and Maximo."

"What the fuck happened, X?" Well he was making his money drops like he always does in South Philly and these guys made a drive by on him and the others that's all we know right now."

"So, nobody knows who did it then?"

"Well were talking to some people's right now but you know fucking well were going to find out who did this shit before the day is out. So be on standby and I'll let you know when we find out more, okay. I just wanted you to know because I know you and him were really tight."

"Yeah, your right that was my boy, okay then keep me in the loop X one." Big Boom walks up to me and asked, "what happen baby?"

"Bad news that was X telling me that somebody just killed my boy Fat Jerome while he was making his money drops."

"Damn that's fucked up, baby."

He hugged me. I'm feeling sad because this guy was always nice to me and I got to meet his family, his wife and kids so I quickly call his brother Fly Ty and he picks up on the first ring.

"Yo, what's up Almasi?"

"I just wanted to tell you how sorry I am about hearing about your brother you know that was my boy."

"Well thanks, sis he really loved you too. I just found out who was behind that shit and I'm calling everybody to ride out with me. You down?"

"You damn right I'm down. Who did it?"

"The Italians did it!"

"How you know?"

"My peoples just were talking to this dude that was there saying it was two white dudes."

"Okay. where you at right now? I'm on my way to the holdup spot."

"Okay I'll meet you there."

"Hey baby, I got to go I'll be back later on all right."

"You want me to go with you because if they hit Jerome you just don't know they might just hit somebody else?"

He looks at me with his eyes getting wide.

"I'm cool baby plus when we all sit at the table you can't be in there when we're talking about BSN shit." My phone rings and its Fly Ty again I'm going out the door right now "Ty, what happen?"

"Look somebody just hit Nokey Blaze son, Philly and two of his homies in front of his house so keep your eyes open and be careful okay. I see you there all right. He's not..." She cut him off.

"No, he's shot up really bad but the two guys that was with him did not make it."

"Did I know them?"

"No, but you met them at your party at the luxury warehouse."

"Okay, I'm on my way. One!" Big Boom overheard what he just said and announced, "I'm going with you. I don't give a fuck what you have to say!"

"Okay baby, but I don't want you to feel some type of way when we all meet in the back room."

"That's all right just as long as I know that you're alright. I'm good fuck that!" He quickly went to his backpack getting his two Glocks.

"I got my shit in my truck lets go." We both swiftly went to my truck and I took off hitting the expressway blasting some hard beats all the way there. It took us about hour to get there. Soon as I got to the door, I felt funny because Jerome always came to the door to let me in. Damn, I'm going to really miss that nigga. I rang the doorbell and Bullseyes came to the door opening it wide looking Big Boom up and down mad dogging him. "Who the fuck is this?"
As he's looking up at Big Boom.
"That's my man, nigga so chill the fuck out all right!" He just smirked at me Spider came from out of the other room seeing Big Boom and greeted him, "Yo, what's up, my nigga." They both hug and shake hands.
"I'm good brother what about yourself?"
"As you see shit is fucking crazy man. How's your crazy ass Pops?"
"Just like you said still fucking crazy."
"So, you need anything before we all go back here and rap brother?"
"Yeah a cold beer would be cool." Spider pointed to the refrigerator and said, "it's in the refrigerator help yourself." He waves at me so we can go to the back room with Bullseyes looking him up and down. Spider started laughing "yo, Bullseyes if I was you, I would not fuck with that dude man. He will kick your ass in a fucking heartbeat, and I'll let him because your fucking with him." Bulls-Eyes yell,
"yeah right, I can take that motherfucker!"

Big Boom step up to him, "what you say, nigga?" I quickly grab Big Boom's arm and Spider get in between the two of them and screamed, "I don't have time for this shit all right Bulls-Eyes, man. Kuanguka Nyuma(Fall Back). He looked up at Big Boom and he kept walking towards the backroom Spider say to Boom, "I'm sorry about that man we will be back, all right." I turn to him winking my eye at him with a smile. He smiled back at me while I go in the back room with Spider. Soon as I get back there sitting around the table is X, Petey Q, Tommy Machete, Puerto Rican Joe, Knock Daddy, Damon Gee, Fly Ty, Brenton, Gill, Ayden and Bulls Eyes take his seat. Spider looking up at everybody saying, "I holla at everybody letting them know what was going on."

He took a puff of his cigarette and continued, “Almasi, you need to start texting your people while were back here to tell them to keep their eyes open were at war again, but these motherfuckers are not a fucking push over. Plus, like I tell all of y’all don’t underestimate nobody in this fucking game. We did not get to where we are overlooking niggas! We took care of Guerilla Boulevard niggas, but the Italians can hit us both ways by farming out fucking jobs to niggas who want to make some money. With the people that they have as well, so don’t get it twisted about them having manpower okay. Now they just kill Fat Jerome and four of our soldiers then they turned around. They also killed three more of our soldiers and almost killed Nokey Blaze son, Philly. He’s in critical condition but we have our people around the clock watching his back. Nokey is fucking pissed off and he wants everybody to lay low and don’t do shit. The cops are keeping very good eye on us after the massacre on the bridge shit is way too hot to make a move. So, I want everyone to go home and lay low keep doing what you have to do but be very fucking careful.”

Spider phone rings and he get it. He is just nodding his head and said, “okay, all right. One.” He looks back up at all of us talking, “Alright X, will let y’all know when we are going to get some get back for them killing our brother and friend Jerome.”

He looks over at Fly Ty and said, “I know you’re hurting; man, and you want them niggas to pay but I need for you to chill, okay.” Fly Ty looking up at Spider and said, “okay but how long doe, Spider?” “I’ll talk to you when everybody gets out of here. alright family. Just trust me okay you know I never lied to you.” Fly Ty just nodded his head

Spider said, “okay everybody, that’s it!” Everybody got up from the table he waves me and X over along with Fly Ty as everybody started walking out of the door. He points at the chairs as we all sit down with him saying,

“I just got a call Jasper is on the fucking rampage he just hit the Italians. He just killed one of their Capo Fat Nicky DiFronzo. Two of their soldiers over there on 9th street in the Italian market now they know were coming for them so there going to be ready for us. So, Jasper just fucked up things for us but soon as I get word from this crooked ass cop. He’s going to give me the names of the two spaghetti hit men that killed Fat Jerome.”

"I want you and the body bag crew to take care of this shit. Jasper open the door up for us I'm bringing him in on this because he does what he wants because he's Nokey Blaze's brother. So, Ty you down with this?"

"Oh, hell yes!"

"I had to do that in front of everybody because somebody just might be talking a little too much and tell Nokey what were really up to as you know niggas will do anything to move up in rank. So, I know I can trust everybody here keep this shit within yourselves right here. If it leaks out what I'm doing I will kill one of y'all for letting it out do all of y'all understand what I am telling each of you?"

All of us just nodding our heads okay.

"I have to go make arrangements for our boy. I'll let everybody know when we're going to have everything the sad part is that I have to look his wife in the eyes when I'm doing this shit." We all get up and walk out the room with X right by my side and said, "I talk to you later. I'll call you." I walked over to Big Boom sitting at the bar in the living room saying, "come on baby soon as we walked out the door and standing by my truck is Bulls-Eyes. Big Boom said to him, "so you're just itching for this ass kicking right nigga?"

"I was waiting on your ass talking all that shit in the house lets go, pussy!" He quickly came towards Big Boom he just sidesteps him hitting him right in the back of his head Plow! He went down face first Boom!

I'm thinking he's going to pop back up and start fighting he just laid there. Big Boom looked over to me and said, "you ready?"

The guys that did hang around thinking they were going to see a fight just stood there with their mouth open. Puerto Rican Joe and Knock Daddy help him off the ground Bulls Eyes thought he could beat Boom because he's been beating up people for a very long time what he did not think about most of them people were scared of him and the BSN.

Me and Big Boom just jump into my truck and took off while he was laughing. I'm thinking this is going to be a big thing later on, but I have bigger fish to fry. I was thinking about some real get back on the grease balls who killed my friend. It took us longer to get back home because of traffic but when we did get back home, we both christen the place right. Big Boom surprise me with a candle lit steak dinner he cooked and them I had his ass for dessert as me and him had some real buck wild sex after we both got high. After all the shit went down, I'm glad I have a man I can be with and we both enjoy one another at the end of the day

What stays on my mind all the time now is my little sister Robin? I still make sure she all right buying her things for school or whatever she need living with that junkie bitch and make sure she don't sell the shit off in the streets and I want to go get her now that things is really flowing with me other than that things is good with me and the game is the game. Some win and some lose.

PLOTTING ON THE SPAGHETTI HIT MEN

Two weeks later, I got the call I've been waiting for the motherfuckers who killed my friend Fat Jerome after we had his funeral service. The whole BSN came from all over the city. Our peoples from out of town as well but so was the FBI and the local asshole police watching us, we knew them Dick Heads were taking pictures. We did not care because we had to show everyone in the city if you kill one of us the whole Black Syndicate Nation will show out and heads will roll. Even the punk ass cops knew that it was just a matter of time nobody fucks with the BSN and get away with it. We all meet at our warehouse on Washington Avenue, but I did not have my whole crew there because of Nokey Blaze's orders of chilling out with so much heat on us. I didn't like it I felt funny about this shit, but Spider was super smart bringing in Jasper's crazy ass this was the first time I met him to tell you the truth I did not like this guy.

I learned about being in this game you don't always have to like the people your working with just as long as we get the job done.

We all met up in the wee hours in the morning, so nobody gets wise to what we were all doing this was the first time I did not have my crew in on something like this. It was me, Fly Ty, X and Jasper and three of his goons, Jay the Joker, His brother Sean Jiggy, and Kenny Shoes. Spider got all the Intel on the two Spaghetti hit men. He's sitting at the head of the table giving us the run down and said, "the guy we are hitting first is Carmine Smooth News Deluca. He's the brother of Slick Sammy Deluca one of their Capo. He's really smart and careful too. "I paid this cop a lot fucking money for this information here so listen up really good." Spider can see that Jasper is not paying attention bull shitting with his crew. Spider screamed while pointing at Jasper, "yo! Are you listening to me over here, nigga?"

"Yeah, I'm listening and who the hell are you yelling at motherfucker?"

"You nigga were in the middle of this shit and your fucking around. Jasper man come on!"

"Okay say what you have to say, nigga. I got some hot pussy to get to over here!" He's looking over at me with a smirk on his face trying to be a smart ass.

"You done, nigga?"

Now on this first thing I'm need you and your peoples to sit on his house at 3rd and Porter street when he comes out to get in his car, I want to tell X and Almasi now and they will do the rest."

Jasper yell, "so what we just get sloppy seconds over here now. How about they sit on the house and they tell me and my boys when he comes out and we smoke their ass!"

"Look I don't want to argue with you man just as long as we get this shit done. Is that cool with you, Almasi?"

"Yeah, I'm good with it just as long as we get them, we will sit on the house and let y'all know when there coming out." Jasper yelled, "so when is all this shit going to happen over here, Mister boss man?"

"Tomorrow night."

"What? No way I can't do that then I have a lot of shit to do."

"Like what? You were the one who wanted to do this shit because they tried to kill your nephew that's what you told me!"

"Yeah, I did say that shit, but I have things to do then make it the next night and me and my peoples will be there guns blazing you know what I'm saying."

"Look tomorrow night is the best time to do this shit because he's going out to his kids dance recital. I paid a lot of money for this information because you said you was going to fucking help me here, Jasper man?"

"Look nigga, I'm not dumb here you need me to do this shit wit you, so my brother don't go the fuck off on you so why don't you take my men with you to get this shit done and that way my brother know I had something to do with it. You can do the shit as you plan without me being there how about that shit will that help you out?"

"Yeah that does help me out."

"Okay then like I said before you two sit in the house and let X and Almasi know and they will kill him and his men." Jay the Joker looking up at Spider and said, "sounds good to me, brother." The other two men just nodding their heads yes. Spider said, "look, I want to know if your brother questions them what are they going to say to him?"

"Don't fucking worry my boys will not rat you out okay, nigga."

"I have hard core soldiers I roll wit!"

"Well I don't know them like you do so I'm fucking asking?"

"Look I'll tell my brother I sent them to do the hit all right, nigga. Don't worry about it he will just yell at me like he always does, that's all." Spider just looked up at him because he doesn't trust Jasper ass at all and he's rethinking the whole thing because if they say something, he can wind up dead disobeying Nokey's orders. So, it supposed to be all good on the surface.

The next day way across town Nokey Blaze is with his wife Tyshana in Chestnut hill laughing and talking shopping at one these little boutiques along the street. He's walking with his wife by his side when this dark blue sedan sped up and open fire on him from out of nowhere Pat! Pat! Pat! Pat! Pat!

Pat! Pat!

The first shots hit his bodyguard Dylan shooting back at the drive by assassins hitting him in the chest and neck with blood flying everywhere hitting the ground. Nokey is hit in the arm and leg. His wife is hit in the arm and shoulder as he jumps on top of her pushing her to the ground and his bodyguard Dylan was killed instantly what's really fucked up about it. Dylan was his long-time friend and top man. Fat Hanky son he is feeling really bad seeing him lying in a big pool of blood. Checking on his wife making sure that's she's alright. There both hit but there still alive pulling out his phone calling for help covered in blood. An hour later I'm chillin with my man Big Boom curled up in the bed after having knock out drag out sex, giggling, talking to each other. I pick up the phone and its Spider and he said, "where you at? Home?"

"Yeah, what's up?"

"Meet me at your spot in an hour they just shot up Nokey Blaze in Chestnut Hill."

"What?"

"Yeah call up your crew, too. I tell you the rest when I see you there, okay. **Moja** (one!)"

"Okay **Moja** *(one!)"* I hang up in the fucking daze. Boom asked, "what happen, now?"

"Somebody just shot up Nokey Blaze I have to get dressed."

"I'm going with you."

"No, the fuck you're not. I got this shit, honey."

"I know you do a lot shit with our gang but you're not in this shit, all right."
"I'll be all right." I quickly go in the bathroom and I get myself together. The only thing I can think of is I hope this man don't die and he's all right. I washed up fast and got dress. I grab my guns put one in the front of my jeans and one in the back. I go in my backpack in my closet and I get about four hand grenades, four more guns inside of my bag. I check all of them and I got my machine gun soon as I'm about to take it to my truck. Big Boom standing in front of me with his eyes getting really wide and he said, "I don't want anything to happen to you, baby that's all. I knew you were in that shit before me and we even linked up with me knowing this shit, but you are my whole world now and I love you for real."
I kiss him. "I know you do, baby but I have to do what I have to and just like you said I was in this shit before you and I fell in love. I will be back by your side all right don't worry. You have to think positive okay."
I kiss him and I break the machine gun down into two parts putting into a big gym bag with extra shells and clips and I quickly walk to my truck with Big Boom helping me with my bags. I just looked at him with a smile and I pulled off hitting the expressway while I was driving, I text everyone with my emergency Emojis a skull and cross bones. It was telling the BSN to meet me at our warehouse. It took me about hour and a half to get to South Philly soon as I get there the first one at the door is Dun-Dun, then Spider is right behind him as the three of us is waiting for everybody to show up. He told me what happen to Nokey Blaze. He said,
"he's all right but that thing we were planning is rammed up I just made a call to that friend of mine I am waiting on his call right now as we speak." Soon as he said that everybody started coming in Mookie, Blue, Foxy, Tony, Big Monk all of them wondering what was going on.

Spider looking up at all of them in the face real serious and said, "my crew is on their way as well I'm going to let you guys know what the fuck is going on here. Look Nokey Blaze was just hit I'm waiting on a call so I can put everything in motion." Then X, Fly Ty, Gill, Ayden and Brenton came in the door as Spider said to all of them, "take a seat everyone." His phone rings and he said, "hold on." He puts his hand up in the air walking away from everybody talking on his horn. He talks for a little while and he came back and announce, "that's what I was waiting on, X. I need you, Fly Ty and Gill to go pick up the list for me right now then we can go to work."

The three of them get up as he gives them the address to go get this list for him while we all were waiting on the other side of town. Jasper is going the fuck off fighting for power, but he doesn't know where to start but Spider knew just what to do making his move. In less than an hour after getting the list he started with the Spaghetti hit men we were going to hit in our first plan of action but a whole lot bigger from the door.

Later on, that night we do the first hit Mookie, Foxy and Blue sit on the house at 3rd & Porter but Spider had his bomb maker Brenton to make a bomb and Foxy puts a bomb under Carmine's car and his wife car as well. Blue had the detonator for Carmine's car and Mookie had the detonator on Carmine's wife car, Jenny. Mookie and Dun-Dun are around the corner with Fly Ty as our wheel man waiting along with Tony and Big Monk with Damon Gee as their wheel man. After waiting for two hours being patient and out of sight in the dark. Carmine came out of his house with his bodyguard Billy Waddles. Blue quickly calling me on the walkie-talkie saying, "here they come, sis!" I hit Tony he just laughed driving really fast going the wrong way up the street soon there about to get into the car me and Dun-Dun jump out on their, ass lighting them up with the hot shit Rat tat tat kapacka!

Kapackacka! Rat tat tat tat! Kacpackakaca! I hit Carmine in his face, chest and neck watching him fall back with the blood shooting up all over his face hitting the ground Boom!

Dun- Dun cut that fat motherfucker in half with his machine gun like it was a fucking chain saw. When he hit him in the stomach his intestines flew out like a fucking giant bloody ass slinky toy hitting the ground hard screaming in painful agony at the same time.

Big Monk ran up on the house with the three-hand grenades I gave him to get busy he tosses all three of them inside of the window and he ran jumped back in the truck with Tony with the quickness. We were right behind him as Tony took off down the street and at the same time Damon Gee took off flying up the street right behind us. Soon as we got about twenty feet from the house riding down the street Kaboom! Right after that we all rolled up to our next target at 13th & Dickerson at Esposito's grocery a little corner store Willie third leg. Esposito is in there with uncle Richie Red Esposito's along time soldier with a lot power because his brother is the under boss of the family. Frankie Fat Neck Esposito there in there with another long-time soldier Charlie Crazy Charlie Lombardo a close friend of Willie and Willie's mother Annie. She's behind the counter.
Tony drove up letting us out on the left-hand side of the street Me, Dun-Dun and Big Monk ran up in their spraying place with no remorse or hesitation. Katakacka Rat tat tat tat tatacka kacapacka! Ripping them grease ball motherfuckers to shreds blood and debris flying everywhere killing everything in there that fucking moved and grandma too. we all put some hot shit in her wig, and we ran out of there and jumped back in the truck riding off getting ghost like a fucking piper.

To top the shit off when we go back to the warehouse and packed up to jet Mookie set off the detonator while the cops were investigating the murder. When we found that out, we all laughed our ass off because it killed two cops then Foxy set off his detonator killing Carmine's wife. The kids were not in the car but to me I would not have gave a fuck if there were in there. They were fucking lucky, but Jenny ass was not she die just like her husband did on the same day. We were just showing all of them Italian assholes that were not nobody to be fucked wit from the door. They started it and were going to finish the shit for sure.

After this shit went down, we all knew we had to lay low because most of the cops are working for the Italians and as much as they talk shit their white and white people don't like to see no kind of their people get killed. As long as we kill each other they don't give a fuck but when we kill them, they go ape shit. I knew I'd be cool because I move all the way up on city line avenue and I had La-Nesa hook up some apartments for Dun-Dun, Foxy, Big Monk, Blue, Mookie and Tony in Jersey to lay low. I knew the same crooked cop will turn the fuck on us in a heartbeat. Spider said he won't, but I don't trust no fucking body. While we were all laying low Nokey Blaze from his hospital bed order another hit two days later killing five more of their peoples at 11th street making all of them to go into hiding like Nokey try to tell them its 1997 not 1967. He was letting them know they don't have the power they once had and after months went by shit cool off fast and the BSN was taking over shit fast in the city. We all started making more money hand over fist. Philly Nokey's son healed up and he was okay just like his father Nokey Blaze. He laid low while Spider ran shit and he hook up another pipeline of cocaine flowing.

A month later I found out I was pregnant. Big Boom and myself could not be happier. I just was overlooking a lot shit until I had my beautiful baby boy nine pounds and ten ounces in July of 1998. We both gave him Boom's government name, Byron Wilson Junior aka Little Boom. We both talk about getting married but we both don't want to fuck things up because were getting along so good. We both stack up some more chips and got another place in Jersey but still keeping our places within the city as well. We were rolling like that the life have a lot pain in the ass things going on with it, but it also let you do shit you would never get to do if you were just a regular ass nigga trying to keep your head above water. So, I take the good with the fucking bad, so I never bitch about it like most niggas do. The life is bittersweet sometime, but it is what it is.

THE FIGHT FOR POWER

Three years blaze past faster than you can blink your fucking eyes. It's the summer of 2001 my whole crew stayed loyal to me and that's what I love about them being real family not no fake ass shit people have within their organizations. Our shit is ten times tighter than the mob was back in the day and we all were moving up in life in the deadly game and balling out of control with no fucking shame and taking over the game. We all got closer as time went by going over to one another cribs. All of our families spending a lot of time with each other.

My man Dun-Dun running and owning his own businesses like me with all his bars and coffee shops. There's one nigga in our crew Foxy who I think I helped him a little too much. I don't what that nigga is thinking. Shit, everybody knows he's fucking lazy and he became a real dope head motherfucker overnight. That nigga Dun-Dun do all that shit on his own. Like all the others owning and running shit they all build up from nothing. I just gave the little nigga Dun-Dun some advice here and there. He is just fucking Charlie Hustle for real.

That nigga Foxy just don't see that he wants people to hand him shit everybody is eating good. Mookie have all his clubs and strip joints. Tony have his cigar shops; Big Monk is running his own truck and auto shop parts stores. He's the only nigga that's stuck on fucking stupid for real. He's starting to make me feel like he's not happy with things when he eats just like everybody else. He just fucks all his money up all the time on tricking with bitches and buying coke liquor like a newborn fool and everybody in the streets is talking about his ass like a dog. I just want to talk to him before he makes the wrong move or fuck up some of our money then were going have to give this nigga the dirt nap for sure.

Big Boom told me to talk to him about it because we were really tight and made our come up together in the streets and when I set up the meeting with Foxy at Blue's barber shop. He called it Blue's Be-Dazzle Barber & Salon a very good cash cow and laundering tons of loot just like I do with my salon Platinum Divas and Platinum Diva's beauty and supply store I have jumping off.

I talk to Blue about it and he said yes so, this nigga Foxy can feel safe when we all meet up. Foxy agreed to link up with us so we can talk and get things off his chest at Blue's barber shop he owns in South West Philly he got about eight of them all over the city. Now working on number nine it's a nice sunny day and I roll up in there with Little Boom with my bodyguard Jagger this nigga is about 350 pounds of all fucking muscle no fat with tattoos all over his body. After this nigga did a little time he turned into a fucking monster. I knew him from back in the days when we use to sling crack in South Philly on the block together this nigga made a big come up as well inside of the BSN. Doing hits, moving money and whatever we ask him to do. I really trust this nigga and we got close over time as well. So were all coming in the door of the barber shop with my son holding his hand as he is taking little steps, he gets excited when he sees his uncle Blue Jagger standing by the door keeping an eye on things like he always does getting on post. I go over and talk to Blue with my son it not too many people inside of the barber shop, but we still step to the side in the back-room office where he did his books and take care of his business. In his little office he had his high-tech camera surveillance system, so he keeps an eye on things inside and out he has on the right-hand side of the joint.

He fixed it up really nice with a glass desk, black and red lamps, gold frame pictures of himself and his family hanging up on the walls and on his desk, black carpet and 50-inch TV on the wall. He closes the door and he had on the air and it smelled really good inside of there. You see that he is getting excited to see you nigga. He picks him up and said, "yeah, he knows his uncle love him, sis?" I kiss him on his cheek, and he does the same thing back like we always do. We both say at the same time hard fast and smooth in rhythm family!

"I'm good look your boy Foxy is acting really fucking funny now. What's up with him?"

"Man, I don't know that nigga is fucking lazy if you ask me, Almasi. To tell you the truth everybody is doing their thing once we all came up together. I don't know what's wrong with him shit!"

"Look another reason I came to talk to you before he comes were going to expand like in a month or so and Spider told me to ask you if you're with it?"

"Oh, hell yes, I'm with it. Well were thinking about moving in B-More and you head up the crew on your own. It's time I know you been waiting on something like this."

"You are fucking right I'm down and I pick my own crew, right?"

"Sure, thing but carrying the BSN flag and your going have to kick a lot of ass and flip them things fast."

"You are fucking right. I got my tattoo for life just like everybody else that's really down but how many of us is moving in on B-More?"

"Well I'm thinking about a good 100 niggas and you run it." "How many joints you're going to give me to start with?"

"About 500 and then I'll bump it up when you clear a good fucking path can you do it?"

"Shit, I can do it with 300 but I'll clear a good path, but I think I'm need more nigga to wreck shit then sail it back with 100 hard core niggas."

"Okay, I'm with that. So, did you hear the rumors about Nokey yet?"

"What about Nokey?"

"He's thinking about stepping down?"

"No, I did not hear that shit."

"Who told you that?"

"Philly that's what he told me the other night when were all kicking it like hood fellas at Mookie's club."

"Oh really, I did not know that shit."

"Will Philly take over or Spider will step up and do it?"

"I think Spider would take it he's up next?"

"So, what about Jane Doe you think she would get it? Only if Spider turn it down that's the only way, she would get it plus Jasper would go the fuck off about that shit."

"I know he would have a fucking aneurysm popping all the veins in that big ass pus head of his!"

We both laughed and fill the rest of time with small talk about our families and the places we've all been and are going to this year. we all going to fly out to Las Vegas like we all did last year and had a really good ass time.
Me, his wife Taye, Dun-Dun and his main girl Tawni because that nigga is a fucking player for real for real, but he brings her around more, so I know that they have this thing going on with the two of them. After a little more time, past while we were chit chatting about all kinds of shit everything, but the bloody game was both in then Blue said, "Look Almasi, I don't think this nigga is coming to our little meeting here?"
"Yeah, I can see that now. I'll wait just a little bit longer and if he doesn't come in the next 15 minutes or so I'm going to get the fuck up out of here. This nigga done wasted both our time if you ask me."
"Well I'm also glad you came here to see me so I can tell you about the Chopper posse niggas up the street. I'm need your help moving their ass out off the block."
"Okay, I'll send Rah-Killer and the boys to clean shit up for you."
"Yeah, I'm going to need that for sure she moves like our old Body bag crew!"
"Yeah that was the good old days when we were all coming up in the world but she's holding it down for the body bag crew now."
"Yeah, I heard. I remember when she just came out of fucking training now, she's running shit."
"I know she remind me of myself just like I got started just let me know when? ASAP!"
"I don't trust these monkey ass niggas you know what I'm saying. That's why I want this shit done. He handed me back little Boom.
"That nigga is not coming like you said, sis."
"Okay, that's a done deal, Mister Blue I'm going to get up out here and let you go back to work."
"Yeah I have a million things to do and no time to fucking do it. You know what I mean." We both laughed. "Well tell your wife I said hi when you see her and make sure yawl come by the house next Sunday I'm cooking."

"Oh shit, you know were going to be there if your cooking because you throw down like a motherfucker. As he opens the back-room door and were walking inside of the barber shop towards the front door. We both started laughing some more as I am carrying my son out the door to the car with Jagger right by my side.

Soon as he opens up the Benz truck door for me with him, he said, "come on and get in Almasi because these niggas coming up the street look fucking shaky for real." I quickly jumped in the back of the truck he closes the door really fast and he whips out both his Glock pistols by then these two dread head niggas came running up on him. I quickly place Little Boom at the truck floor reaching to get my gun soon as I got it and looked up Jagger pointed and shot both them niggas Pat! Pat! Pat! Pat! Giving them two slugs each and he got low and shot another nigga riding up in the car. Kapacka! Shooting him through the window of his car glass and blood flying in the air and the car swayed and crashed into some park cars on the left. Kaplan!

Jagger quickly jumped behind the wheel of the Benz Truck and took off like a fucking driver in the Indianapolis 500 going down the street burning rubber. Jagger said, "I told you I had my eye on them motherfuckers." Soon as we went inside of the barber shop to see Blue somebody told them niggas that you were there?"

"Yeah and I know just who it was, too!"

"Yo, let me take care of the shit for you Almasi!

"No, I got this brother." He drives us back to our crib at city line avenue fighting traffic the whole way there he's cussing and fussing when I came up in the crib. Big Boom is sitting up watching movies with his boy Hugo from his War-Dogs crew puffing up a storm. I speak to him still holding the baby with Jagger standing by my side. I said to Big Boom, "can I talk to you for a few, baby?"

"Yeah, give me the baby as he gets up and I hand him the baby smiling. He looks at Jagger and said, "okay homey, I need to talk to my wife, alright?"

I said to him, "no, I want him standing right here so he can tell you what just fucking happen to me!"

"Okay, let's go out here on the deck." The three of us walk out on our big deck and Jagger sat down at the bar not too far from us and I sat the baby in the chair, and I said,

"Yo, the Chopper posse niggas just came at me! Are you all right?"

"Shit! No, I'm fucking pissed, and I want to kill everything moving right about now. Good thing Jagger peep them niggas from the door or you would be laying out me and the baby." "Hey man, I'm sorry about what I said to you, Jagger. Thanks for looking out for her."
"It's all right as you know nothing is going to happen to Almasi when I'm around her, brother."
"So, how they know you was down there in the first place to be coming at you, baby?"
"It was Foxy, and I know its him that nigga been acting really funny now that everybody is doing their thing and he's just getting high blowing all his money. He thinks I'm helping everybody get further in life more than him. When in fact everybody is putting in the work. He set me up today we supposed to be meeting at Blue's barber shop to talk about things and these two dread lock fucking gun men came after me."
Jagger looked up at me and said, "just let me take care of that nigga for you?"
Big Boom said, "yeah let him do it and you don't have to worry about that nigga no more."
"No, I got something for his ass trust me. Meanwhile I'll call up Rah- Killer and have them take care of them Chopper posse nut ass pussies. Me and Blue was just talking about them niggas."
"What about?"
"He wanted me to move their ass from down the street and when we came out, they came at me and I had the baby with me."
"I really want these niggas to pay."
My phone rings and its Spider, "Yo, what's up, baby girl?" "Some more dumb shit that's all!"
"What happen?"
"Some dreadlock assholes tried to come at me today that's all but don't worry Jagger smoke all three of them niggas!" "So, what's up with you, big man?"
"I just wanted to tell you that Nokey is stepping down and I'm taking the spot!"
"Well congratulations, brother! I'm really happy for you." "Thank you, but I want you to take my spot."
"What?"
"Yeah, I want you to take my spot you down? So, what about X, Fly Ty, and Damon Gee they were down longer then me?"

"They don't want it and I would never give it to Gill dumb ass he's too drunk with power as it is now!"
"So, you mean to tell me X don't want it at all?"
"No, he said he's getting out of the life so it's all on you?"
"Yeah, I'll do it then if X don't want it."
"Good, I'm having a big dinner on Friday and let everybody know what's up."
"Okay, I'll be there see you then. One!"
Big Boom said, "what's going on now?"
"That was Spider he just told me that Nokey Blaze is stepping down and he's taking the top spot, but he wants me to take his."
"Jagger pumped his fist and said, "I always knew you be running shit soon. Sounds good, sis. Congratulations your one spot away from running the whole fucking thing, right?"
"Yeah, you know it." I gave Jagger a high five with him smiling Then I looked at Big Boom and he did not look to happy about what I just said to him.
"What's wrong, baby?"
"Nothing we can talk about it when were all alone, okay!" I give Jagger the baby and ask, "could you take him in the other room while I talk to this man, please."
"Sure, thing Almasi he looks over at Big Boom holding the baby and walking inside of the house he gives me that look as he's closing the deck door really fast holding the baby. "What the fuck is up with you, nigga? You're not happy for me to move up or something."
"No, it not that..." I cut him off and asked,
"So, what is it then you tell me?"
"You're going to be a fucking target that what let one of them other niggas take that shit not you!"
"So, what I did not talk about it with you first, so you don't want me to take it then!"
"No, I don't want you to take it, alright. You ask and I'm telling you not to take it!"
"Nigga, I worked my way from out of the street to get here and we have all this shit because of what I did and your standing there talking shit. What the fuck is wrong with you?" "What I'm saying is I don't want you to take it because you never asked me about it and you're going to be a high-profile target after that can't you see that, baby!"

"No, you don't want me to take it because you never move up in your father's shit and you want me to say on the same level as you. I know what the fuck it is, nigga. I didn't want to say this, but I pay all the fucking bills in this motherfucker and I'm taking it so we as a family don't have to go back to the fucking gutter or live off the land like your father and all them fucking end of the world nuts. Fuck that!"

"Oh really, fuck you, Almasi and he started walking really fast from off the deck and he started yelling at his boy "Hugo come on let's go right now man, Come on!" Hugo got up with his hands up in the air and he went out the door with him and Big Boom slams the door behind himself.

I walked back inside of the house still pissed off. Jagger just looked at me I put my finger up at him and I sat down at the bar and I'd called up Rah-Killer she picks up after two rings and answers, "Yo, what's up, Almasi baby?" **"Nimepata Kazi Kwako** *(I got a job for you)* **Sawa Mimi Kuna**!'

"Juu Ya Usoku wa leo *(Okay, I'll be over tonight)"*

"Nina kuona kuliko *(I see you then)* Okay, little sis **Moja! (**One)."

"**Moja! (**One)" I hang up Jagger looking over at me and he announce, "Damn your Swahili is really tight now, girl!"

"Yeah now it is you have to get yours down too, nigga. I'm getting there when I was in the joint my shit was tight, and I was learning a lot I have to stay focus now that I'm out."

"You will get it just stay with it like I did you will get it."

"Your right." He hands me the baby back and asked, "you want me to make you a drink?"

"Yeah, make me a drink, please let me put the baby in the room and you and me can have that drink. I can really use one right about now!"

"So, I changed the baby and then I laid the Little Boom down in his room." Me and Jagger sat at the bar and got twisted talking about back in the days. After a while I was twisted and then I sat on the couch and fell asleep. It's a big knock at the door Jagger walked to the door asking, "why niggas knock so fucking hard like there the fucking cops or something?"

I'm half asleep when Jagger let Rah-Killer in, and she has her girlfriend Kitty with her. I sat up and looked at her and I pointed toward the deck doors she started towards the deck with Kitty trying to follow behind her. Jagger steps in front her putting both is big ass hands up stopping her cold in her tracks and said, "where the fuck you are going at, bitch?" "What? Fuck you, nigga." Rah-Killer cut her off and cover her mouth, "Yo Kitty, watch your mouth and shut the fuck up alright. I will be right back!" See looked up at her rolling her eyes she was going to open her mouth open again and Rah-Killer said, "don't say one fucking word now sit the fuck down and keep you fucking mouth shut!"

She is blowing out air as Kitty sat down pouting like a little kid as me and Rah-Killer walk out on my deck. She closes the deck sliding doors and we both sat down at my bar. I looked up at her and said, "what the fuck is wrong with you bringing that bitch to my house, Rashida?"

"I'm sorry but the bitch thinking I'm creeping out on her and she would not shut her fucking mouth unless I took her with me!"

"I don't care about how you live your life but don't bring that bitch around no BSN people no more because you don't want me to bring this shit to the table because you will not live to see the next day. Now you know you and me go way back so this time I'm going cut you a fucking break all right because I already know about your two other side bitches and niggas is already talking.so you need to slow the fuck down me myself I don't care how much pussy you suck and fuck but you need to fucking honor that fucking tattoo you got on your right arm there from the door."

"Your right Almasi thank you and I'm sorry about this shit it will not happen again okay, and I will away honor the BSN as long as I live. Y'all really save my life on the real." "Well act like it alight, bitch" We both started laughing. "Okay, we got that shit out of the way now did you hear?" "Yeah, I just heard the shit this afternoon. Congratulations I away knew you make it up there, but I heard Jane Doe is really mad about you getting it instead of her so watch your back okay!"

"Well thanks for letting me know that shit now why I'd called you over here is I need for you and your boys to clear off the block near Blue's barber shop in South West Philly you know where it's alright?"

"Yeah, I know just where it's at, Yo."

"Yeah, the Chopper Posse pussies are getting out of fucking hand they tried to take me out today good thing Jagger was with me or I be laid the fuck out!"

"Don't you worry the body bag crew will live up to our fucking name like when yawl was doing your thing!" **"Nzuri!(***Good)"*

"**Kuwaua Wote** *(Kill them all*)"

"**Unajua Vizuri** *(You better know it)"* We both started laughing and she bump fist with me as she stood up and I pointed at her and said, **"Tahadhari ya tunachozungumzia** *(Take care of what we talked about)"*

She smiled and replied," **Mimi Nitakuwa mtoto** *(I will baby*)" I got up walking behind her soon as she opens the deck door the girl Kitty jumped up and screamed, "damn, well it took you all fucking day!" Rah-Killer sucker punched her in the mouth. Plow! She fell backwards on the floor holding her mouth bleeding Rah- Killer yelled, "I told you to keep your fucking mouth shut your going to get me killed with your bull shit!"

"Now get the fuck up before I put a fucking bullet in your funky ass!"

"Get up bitch!" She got up off the floor holding her mouth bleeding rolling her eyes not saying a word while Rah- Killer grabbed her pulling her out of the door. Jagger shut the door looking over at me and I said, "I know! I know! Just keep that shit under your hat for me, please." "Yeah, for you I will, but you know that stud bitch is out of fucking control. You know that shit, right?"

"Yeah, I know that shit."

"Man, and that other nigga her right-hand man Nugee is a fucking psycho for real!"

We both started laughing, but he was right the new crew is fucking crazy for real Rah-Killer, Nugee, Billy Blunts, Bullet head Joney, Gino Gats, Willie Black, Mick Molly, Crowbar Carl and Lace Lawless. Behind their backs niggas on the streets call them the Psycho body bag crew but they get the job done.

A whole four days blaze by and that nigga Boom did not come home after me and him fell out over me taking the number two spot in the BSN. Spider held it down for a long time now I have some big shoes to fill. Now, I have to work hand and hand with the top man Spider but now that Rah-Killer brought that strange bitch to my spot. I moved to my other condo not to far from the one I was in because you never know niggas get caught up and run their fucking mouth. So, I got my girl Tanya whose Jagger's little sister she come and help me out with the baby from time to time. She's a really smart kid she's going to college. Jagger doesn't want her to get mixed up in the life. I already know she is sneaking around seeing Gino Gats who is down with the psycho body bag crew in BSN, but I didn't rat her out. I knew soon enough he was going to find out but for right now it's our little secret.

So, I get dressed to go to the dinner Spider was having so I did my hair first and my make up this was the first time in a long time beside going to the club with Shamika. I get dolled up without it being a fucking hit. I put on my new black and white dress I got at Sax fifth avenue and some small heels shoes, but they were fucking Sharp. I look in the mirror and I can get use to dressing up. I felt beautiful only if my man could see me like this is the only thing, I could think about, but I blew that off that thought. If he wanted to act like an asshole that's the fuck on him. I missed him, but I was not going to apologize for who I am and what I want to do fuck that. I love him, but if he can't deal with it then fuck him. I'm going to make my mark in this world if I played by the rule's niggas set out for me, I be just another lost ghetto whore with my hand out something I would never be not in this lifetime.
After I got dressed, I put my gun in my pocketbook and made sure I had an extra set of clips, then I called Tanya in my bedroom and she came in and I shut the door. I pointed to my bed and she sat down looking up at me. "Look, I don't want you to sneak that nigga up in my house when I'm gone, okay?"
"Okay, I won't do that?"

"Yeah you say that shit I already know you had him in my other condo a couple weeks ago when me and Boom when out to the movies. See, I don't want niggas knowing where I live at and you know if Jagger catch you and him together, he's going to kill both of y'all on the spot."
"Who told you that nosey ass white chick across the way at the other place?"
"It doesn't matter who told me I don't want your fucking brother to find out he will go the fuck off and if he finds out I know he will not keep working for me. I need him so your fucking everything up for me here, girl and that is the fact of the matter."
"Well, I tell him if it makes you feel any better then."
"Shit, do what you want to your grown but leave me the fuck out of it, but you need to go out with the guys in your school or something not some nigga in the game."
"Well my brother is in the game just like you are too, Almasi."
"That don't have nothing to do with what I'm saying to you girl you're really smart and you don't have to fuck up your life like we did we hand no choice in the matter. You do so you need to get your mind right. I have to go you think about what I told you, girl!"
She just looked up at me with a smirk on her face like those young girls do. As I walked out the door before I get mad and have to kick her little skinny yellow ass. She came behind me soon as I got to the front door, I said the baby is sleep right?
"Yes, he's knocked out."
"Okay, I'll be back a little late. If you need anything just give me a call all right?"
"Okay, but I'll be all right, so you go enjoy yourself I got this Almasi."
"Alright remember what I told you girl see you when I get back you here." I go out the door pointing at her with a smile on my face she smiled back as I got my keys out my pocketbook walking down the long hallway towards the elevator, but I still got Big Boom on the brain.

I would never think this nigga take that shit this far maybe I have to find out the hard way some men don't want their women to succeed in life. I'm hurt, but I'll never let his black ass know about it. It takes me about a half an hour to drive out to Spider's new house in Chestnut Hill. His place is really fucking nice too when I park my truck in the huge ass parking lot filled with all kinds of expensive whips parked shit it looks like the new car show out there for real. I get out looking up at this house my eyes got really wide shit this joint would make all them niggas who suppose be balling and shot calling look like a fucking outhouse in the back woods down south. I said to myself this is what I want one day as I walked up the long wide well-lit path looking up at the tall fancy ass black lamps. Along the path up to the house and the palm trees wow I never seen one in real life.

Once I thought about it, I just had to walk up and touch one, so I did real quick hoping no one see me doing this shit. I can smell the fresh cut grass in the air while I'm walking. I'm looking at this garden alongside of this mansion is beautiful and the lawn looks like five football fields to me as I walked up to the doorway. When I looked at the door thinking to myself. Shit even the door knob and the doorbell looked like motherfuckers with a lot of loot so I'd ring the doorbell smiling and this short pretty dark skin Hispanic lady in a black and white maid uniform with the funny looking white hat too came to the door with a very warm smile ask, "yes, may I help you?"

"Yes, my name is Almasi Samuel. He is expecting me?"

"Yes, he is. Well come in, please everyone is in here. My name is Mary, nice to meet you, Almasi right this way." I'm looking around playing it cool, but this joint is off the fucking hook. I walked into this giant dining room with this long ass table and walking up to me dressed in a beautiful white dress and white high heels shoes that cost more than most people cars. I know because I saw them same shoes online walking up smiling is his wife Sheila who hugged me saying, "hey girl, I'm so glad you're here!"

"Well thanks for inviting me to your lovely home. Why thank you, dear. I've always dreamed of a house like this now that we have it." I just want to get used to it we always had big apartments, but this is really big girl.'

"I tell you what Sheila, I can get used to it if it was me."

"Shit, one day girl you're going to have something like this with your skills and ambition. Come have a seat at the table next to me all the other guests are on their way. where is that man I keep hearing about?"

"Well me and him had a big fight so he could not make it." "Girl you know men they are like little kids sometimes. He'll come around I know you have not met our older son Shamink she waves him other

"Come here, boy. I want you to meet Almasi." He shakes hand with me smiling and said, "I heard so much about you it's so nice to meet you."

"The same here, Sheila saying, yeah he's in law school at Temple."

"Oh, really that's nice. Do you like it? Yes, I do I have one more year and I'll be done. Sheila said, "he better finish or me and his father will kick his ass for wasting our money!"

"Oh Mom, why you say things like that you know I wanted to be a lawyer from the time I was a little kid."

"Yeah, I know. Baby, I'm just messing with you that's all then she took me by the hand, and I want you to meet my sister Tyonna and her husband Nick."

I'd shake their hand smiling, "nice to meet you."

"They both own three BMW dealership so if you need a new whip just let one them know and they can hook you up at a real nice price." They both started laughing then walking in the house is Trevor Tee and his wife Ruth. She hugs both of them, "hey, you met Trevor at your coming out party.

I said "hi, how are you doing, and this is his wife, Ruth."

I shake her hand with her and said, "I just love your dress girl nice to meet you."

"Thank you so much." Soon as I said that Xavier my man X came in the door with his wife, Tachell. I never met her before after Sheila hugged and kissed them and with some small talk. They came over to me and hugged. X introduce his wife to me and said, "this is Almasi when I'm breaking them for her, I called her Shorty like we did back in the days." we all started laughing. She looked at me saying, "don't pay him any mind its really nice to finally meet you. I heard so much about you. You're like a living legend with all these guys. I can see they really care about you and I want to come to your hair shop I been hearing some really good things. You have to hook a sister up for real. Well, I'll give you my number and I'll set up an appointment for you?"
"Yeah, I would like that Almasi or should I say, Miss diamond?" We all laughed. With her saying, "yeah, I know Swahili really good for some time now."
"Yeah, me too. Now I'm really good at it."
"Good, you always can use it around niggas who don't know what time it is. You know what I'm saying." Then Spider came over to us speaking to everybody hugging, kissing and he came over to doing the same to me, "what up, baby girl?"
"I'm good. I really love you. Homey, it's fucking fabulous brother."
"Thank you, I knew you like it. Me and my wife are just getting use to the place." Then Mary the maid came over to Spider saying, "Mister Samuel, you have to come to the door right away!"
"Why what happen over here?"
"Just come please it's your brother and some other guys out there yelling." Spider quickly runs over to this end table pulling out his gun sticking it in the front of his pants. Trevor Tee, X, and my self is right behind him something told me to bring my gun with me what niggas don't know once you're in the life you should away have a fucking gun on you no matter where your fucking going.
Too many forget to carry their gun with them, and they wind up fucking dead and if I'm going to go, I'm taking a few niggas with me for sure! We all run outside, and Petey Q is face to face with Jasper crazy ass jumping up and down yelling. I can see Petey Q's peoples, Puerto Rican Joe, Bullseyes and Knock Daddy is ready to do something and so is Jasper peoples too. Jay the Joker, Kenny Shoes and Sean Jiggy they can't wait to get into it. I can see it in their eyes just ready to fuck things up for Spider.

Spider get in the middle of them yelling, "loud nobody asked you to fucking come here Jasper so take your goons and get the fuck out of here before you get hurt! What?"
"Nobody is going to lay a fucking hand on me nigga not without everybody taking the big fucking dirt nap!"
"Look, I don't care who your related to nigga your disrespecting my home and even Nokey would understand that I'll do what I have to!"
"Well I came to give you and your fucking number two bitch a fucking message!" I just looked at him not saying a fucking word I wanted to shoot that nigga right in the middle of his fucking big ass head. Spider yelling even louder, "just get the fuck out of here, Jasper!"
"I came to tell you that this shit is not over I will run the BSN one day and you two assholes will be the fuck under me really soon!" Then Jay the Joker pulls out his gun laughing loud along with Sean Jiggy and Kenny Shoes. Why he do that shit for? Then everybody pulled out their guns all you can hear is clicking sound from all the guns everybody pulling out pointing at each other.
X holding his gun at Jasper head yelling, "you want to set it off, nigga lets go then!" Jay the Joker laughed walked up pulling Jasper by his arm and said, "come on Jasper. you said what you wanted to say, let's go home!"
Spider said, "I think you better listen to your top goon over there and go the fuck home before you can't!" He back up putting his gun in the back of his jeans saying, "remember what I said, nigga you and the crack baby you have for your number two!" Him and Jay the Joker along with Sean Jiggy started laughing looking over at me. I wanted to kill all three of them right then and there putting his gun in the back of his jeans smiling but Kenny Shoes still holding his gun out pointing it at every one. Moving his hand from side to side with a serious expression on his dark grill like he wanted to shoot all of us standing there.

Jay the Joker yelled, “Yo Kenny, let’s go another time for this shit all right. Let’s go!” He started backing up holding his gun then he puts it in the front of his pants mad dogging everybody standing there. Then Jasper and Jay the Joker jumped in Jasper’s white Range Rover and Sean Jiggy and Kenny Shoes got in his black Benz parked beside him. They took off up the long road as we all just stood there not saying anything. Spider is pissed off as he waves everybody to come back in the house. Soon as we came in the house Philly came with his woman LeRinda and his two bodyguards Fat Hector and Black Leon. Soon as he came in the door Spider walks over to him and speaks to his woman and shake hands with both his men. He said to LeRinda with a big smile on his face, “I need to holla at him for a minute you don’t mind, do you?”

“Oh no, I’ll go get me a drink or something its cool winking her eye at her man, Philly.” He winks his eye back at her right quick. Spider waves to Mary with a big smile and said, “could you please get this fine lady a drink while I talk to my man, Philly. He points to his men, “You go with her please all right.” They just nodded their heads as they walk away Spider took Philly in the other large room on the left and said, “you just miss the fucking fireworks.”

“What happen?”

“Your uncle is what happen he came here talking shit!”

“Yeah, he’s been on the fucking rampage since he heard about you taking the top spot. I’ll get my father to try to talk to him but as you know he’s not going to fucking listen. I also heard Jane Doe is not to fucking happy about your girl Almasi getting her spot too.”

“Really, who told you that?”

“She did she came over to my phone store with her goons but she’s going to be alright, but my uncle is the fuck out of control. We might have to take care of him I hate to say that shit. Look, I’m with you my father made the right choice and you fucking deserve it. I’m with you 100%, okay. So, don’t worry about my crazy ass uncle let me get back to my wife to be.”

“Yeah, she’s fucking gorgeous, man.”

“Yeah, she is but she’s the one.”

“Good, long as your happy let’s go in here and eat. I have some really good food waiting on us to grub on.”

"Good, because I'm really hungry with that long ass drive over here to your fucking house, man." They both started laughing as we all walked into the big lavish dining area you can feed about 50 people at a time at this long ass wooden table. This the kind shit you see in them top notch fucking gangster movies. We all eat at the long ass table and the food was fucking great, too. Prime rib with bake chicken with this fancy ass wine sauce it was delicious then Spider came to me and said, "I need to talk to you in my den area about a few things."

I walked into his big den this is like the ultimate man cave with all of his big boy toys. It smelled like weed and black & Mild cigars still lingering in the air, mix with the air freshener. He points at the seat next to his desk. Then Petey Q came in with his boys, Trevor Tee, Philly and X came and sat down real smooth. He sat down looking up at Spider waiting to hear him speak puffing on their cigarettes. "Well, if you guys don't know our man, X here is getting out, so I'll have my brother Petey Q with you Almasi and I'm letting everyone know were sending Blue to B-More. Me and Almasi been talking about it and Trevor Tee here is going to take New Jersey and Buck Shot is going with him and his boys so they can have things locked down. I'm thinking about sending Brenton to DC. What you think about that, Almasi?"

"Yeah, but let's wait until we finish up with the Chopper Posse, niggas and some other niggas trying to make a come up then after that they can roll out and plant a flag for us." "Sounds good to me, Petey Q you can go talk to Brenton and let him know what we're doing okay."

"Sure, I do that first thing tomorrow Spider. Good now we all get back to this party but my brother in law Nick need to holla at me about these New Jersey Russian mob cats trying to muscle in on him."

"I need all of y'all to leave the room, so he doesn't feel so uncomfortable everybody started laughing but Almasi. I need for you to stay because I'm need you to take care of his little problem for him."

Petey Q, Philly, Trevor Tee and X stood up still laughing "Petey just tell Nick he can come back here after y'all roll out."

"I will." He looks at me winking his eye. As him and X walked out of the room a few minutes later. Nick came in the room as Spider points at the chair in front of his desk, so you said you have a little problem.

He sat down screaming loud, "I was thinking we were going to talk alone here?"

"Well, I have Almasi, here. She the one who is going take care of your little problem for you so tell us what happen okay you do trust me, right?"

"Yes, I do but I don't want my wife to know what's going on as well. Don't worry this will be just with us here in this room Tyonna will never know what happen just as long as you keep your mouth shut about our little arrangement about all the dealerships okay because I already know you tell your wife everything! As Spider is snickering looking over at me and Nick face is getting twisted up yelling back at Spider, "No, I don't!"

"Yes, you do nigga just tell us what happen so we can help your ass out and keep this shit to yourself. That's all I'm saying, Nick!"

"Okay, look these two Russian goons came to my office telling me they wanted to be partners with me I said no and then they came and blew up about five cars in the showroom. So, I put in the claim to pay for them soon as I got things fixed up. I told my wife that if was some kids fucking around, they did it again and the insurance company did not pay me! So, they said they would give me the money to take care of things. My dumb ass took the money and they been leaning on me so much I can't even pay my employees until you came and help me out and I really need your help to get rid of these guys."

"Don't worry were going to take care of this for you what's the names of the first guys who stepped to you at first? Some asshole guy calling himself Artyom and the other one name was Nikon."

I looked at him and said, "are you sure?"

"Yes, that what they said."

"Why you know them or something?"

"These were the same guys Damon Gee and that dirty cop Eddie Wilson was talking about moving in on the Albanians on their chain of motels in Philly, Jersey and Baltimore we can move them out and use some of the motels as stash spots for the heroin were moving."

"No, but I have some people whose holding down the stash spots already. Thanks, but that's all I need for right now."
I stood up and said to Spider, "I'm going go back in there and talk to your wife and her friends. Sure, thing you got this, right?"
"Oh yeah, I got it down. I'll holla at you about the details later all right."
"Yeah when everybody is gone come on Nick, we have to get out there as well to make everything look good all right."
"Yeah, so you guys are going to help me out and take care of this shit, right?"
"Like I told you just as long as you agree to me being a silent partner in the business were all good for helping you out."
"Yeah, I told you I'll sign the papers." Spider pulls them out of the desk saying, "I have them here is a pen and you can put your John Handcock on it and all your problems will be over with. He hands him the papers and the pen. He looks it over and said, "okay, this look really fair."
"I told you I'm not greedy. I'm you brother in law, nigga." They both laughed as he signs the papers and he look at me saying, "okay, we have a green light, Almasi." you can go to work as he puts the papers back in his big desk smiling.
I just smiled walking out of the big den area into the living room at this long big bar is Tyonna, LeRinda, Tachell and Sheila. There all laughing and drinking having a good time when Sheila said, "I know your one of the guys, but you can come hang out with the girls tonight what are you drinking?" "Just beer."
"That's not a drink, girl how about having a real drink with us?"
"Sure, I'll have an apple Martini." She waves at the bar tender and said, "Al give the young lady an apple Martini and make me another My-tie please."
"So, your enjoying yourself other than that all of the business my husband is getting you to do?"
"Yes, I am."
"Good, because I have something, I need for you to do but I have too many people around to talk to you about it. You don't mind if I give you my number and you call me so I can tell you what it is, do you?"

"Oh no, I'll give you mine give me your phone and I'll give you a number where you can reach me any time." She hands me her phone and I put it in real fast. I give it back to her and she smiled saying, "you just don't know this will mean the world to me if you can do this for me." Now I'm standing there sipping on my drink wondering what it is she wants me to do the whole fucking night. Then the fellas came over to the bar and everybody is having a really good time telling old war stories and every kind of dirty joke you could fucking think about. I slow down drinking while everybody got twisted, I knew I had to drive back home. After a couple hours I was ready to go home. Sheila walked me to the door talking low and said, "don't forget I will call you real soon I need to get this done for real, aright?"

"I'll take care of you!"

"Sure, just call me and we will talk about it. I had a really good time thanks for everything. Sheila, she hugged me smiling, "you all right to drive, girl?"

"Yeah, I'm good. I slow down when everybody was getting their groove on."

"Smart girl, but if you didn't, I would have had one of these goon gun men to drive you home."

We both started laughing loud as I quickly started walking to my truck in the large ass well-lit parking area. I'd drove home listening to Fiesta bye

R. Kelly featuring Jay-Z the best of both Worlds mix tape banging all the way home singing the songs the shit was hot. I played it over and over again until I made it home soon as I walked in in the door the whole house is dark with Tanya sleep on the couch with the TV blasting. I turn it off and I walked over to her shaking her and she looked up at me saying, "I didn't hear you come in the baby is in his room and Jagger was here to check in on us. He just left not too long ago."

"So how did everything go?"

"Real smooth I fed him, and I gave him his snack later on and he went to bed after watching Rug Rats and Sponge Bob." We both giggled and she got her backpack, she said, "okay Almasi, just give me a call when you need me. When do you go back to school?"

"I have to get ready the end of this month. That's why I need some extra money for books and shit."

"Look, I'll help you out if you get your mind right and do what I ask you before your brother find out and he'll cut you the fuck off then you'll be up shit creek without a fucking paddle."

She just looks at me with a smirk on her face and she quickly walked out the door with that look on her face I did not care if she got upset. I'm only trying to help her young silly ass out. I quickly walked behind her locking the door and I went and check on little Boom. He's knocked out so I went to my bedroom taking off my clothes thinking about Big Boom's ass and he still didn't call me. I laid down in my big bed and it seems like it was bigger without him beside me. The booze started to kick in and after a long day I had I quickly fell to sleep.

THE PSYCHO BODY BAG CREW GETS BUSY

The week blaze past still no word from my so-called man Big Boom. He still did not come home while I get all my Intel from Damon Gee on these fucking Russians. He's getting all his information out this dirty ass ex-cop name Eddie Wilson but when it comes to getting dirt on people Damon Gee is one of the fucking best. He had so much on this ex-cop his ass would do life in prison if Damon told on his ass but what he did is have him doing all kind of shit for him. I finally found out what Sheila wanted me to do she wanted me to take care of this asshole dope head freak name Crazy Marco. She sent me a picture of him on my phone, so I know what he looks like. He raped her girlfriend coming out the after-hour joint in North Philly her name is Kalisa from her old hood and there still tight like sisters. So, I'd put Rah- Killer and her psycho niggas on Foxy after he set me up at Blue's barber shop and what really piss me off about that was that I had the baby with me, so this nigga really has to go.

None of them could not find him so I got Damon Gee to tracked down the boy Crazy Marco and Foxy this nigga did it in two days. He's really good now I know why Spider love this nigga when he went to work and that's why I had to bump up his pay he's worth every fucking dime.

We took care of Foxy's ass first he told me that Foxy is hiding out in Elkins Park with his brother Toby and his old lady Nyesha and Foxy's girlfriend Catrina. I called up Rah-Killer and them crazy ass motherfuckers giving them the address of the house where he was laying low off the grid at a real nice two-story joint with a big lawn. A real quiet area of the city nobody would be looking for him, so we all drove out there I'm in my other truck with Jagger, Damon Gee and Fly-Ty to make sure they really take care of this motherfucker. We parked not too far from the house that way we have a front row seat to all the action we sit there, and check shit out for a little while then I pulled out my phone and I'd called Rah-Killer saying, go and make sure you get his funky junkie ass!"

Soon as I said that the psycho body bag crew drove up in two cargo work vans one in the back of the house the other in the front with Billy Blunt behind the wheel driving up on the lawn right near the door. As Bullet Head Joney, Gino Gats and Rah-Killer jumps out with their machine guns blazing like wild men on a mission charging in the door with Bullet Head Joney kicking in the front door.
Doom! Then Gino Gats going in first with Rah-Killer right behind him Rat tat tat tat kackapacka! Kaplow! Echoing really loud all we can see is muzzle flash from all the windows down stair with all the machine gun fire and people screaming lighting their ass up then we saw them running out jumping back in the work van. soon as Rah-Killer jumped in the van she text me and I read it in all cap letters **TULIPATA!**(*We Got Him.)*
I tapped Damon Gee behind the wheel, "let's get the fuck out of here they got him!" he took off down the street soon as we got about five blocks away then my phone goes. Bing! I looked at my phone and it's a picture of Foxy's bloody body. I show it to Damon Gee while he's driving, he just smiled and hands it back to me then I hand it back to Fly-Ty. He looks at it and he show it to Jagger sitting next to me and said, "yeah, that's him he's never looked better! As he hands me my phone, I say one down one to go."
All of us started laughing Damon Gee replied, "do you want to go take care of that other thing right now?"
"Yeah, why not? You know where he's at, right?"

"Yeah, he hangs out in front of the store on Park side Avenue with them other dope head niggas." So he drove to North Philly on Park side Avenue I had a picture of this nigga so I know what he looks like and I know I have to take care of this myself so I'd pull my hair back in a pony tail then put a stocking cap on my head so I can put my blonde wig. The trick bitch looking special. I'll blend right on in then I'd quickly screw on my silencer I had in my pocketbook I say to, "Damon pull up over here." So, he pulls over not too far about a block from where all these niggas are all standing and sitting around. I watch him for a little bit and everybody in the car is waiting to see what I am going to do not saying a word. I just watch them drinking malt liquor talking shit, so I waited to see if he makes a move back to the store. But after an hour or so I see him get up off the step walking towards the store that's when I knew that was the right time. I jumped out real fast putting on my blonde hair wig with the big floppy hat and some dark sunglasses on. I have on this jacked up looking played out black sweat suit and my big ass pocketbook on my shoulder walking nice and smooth up to the store. When I walked in this raggedy ass Korean beer joint where you buy your beer and go.

He was standing by himself and nobody is in the store while he was waiting on his malt liquor. I'm holding my gun with the silencer on it inside of my pocketbook, but I look where the cameras were at, I wanted to shoot his ass in the store but after where I see the cameras was at. I said I get him outside the door then I'll blast his ass. So, he gets his malt liquor. He looked at me, but he did not pay me no mind as he walks out the door, I walked up behind him saying, "yo so you like raping young girls, right?" Soon as he went to yell at me with his mouth open,

I whip out my gun Poooff! Poooff! Poooff!

I put three in his fucking dome he fell near these park cars on the left I looked both ways up the street and nobody seen me do it. Damon came driving up the street nice and smooth and I jump in the car and he did not speed off he drove nice and normal up to broad street and we were gone. An hour later, when I'm at the warehouse I'm in my office at my desk working the phones, I called my babysitter, La'Wanda, my girlfriend Shamika aunt checking up on my son. Then I'm calling around making sure everybody is doing their jobs, picking up money and making sure all the crack and dope spots have enough products.

Soon I hung up talking to some of them niggas I get the call from Sheila saying, "I just got the good news from the hood girl, thank you so much!" She was really happy saying, "don't worry, I'm going to take care of you thank you so much, Almasi!"

"You're welcome, Sheila look I have to get back to work and stay on these niggas ass, so they don't be sleeping on the job I talk to you later. Sure, thing baby and thanks again look I have my girl Tyonna on her way to you as we speak with your money its twenty large, okay."

"Why thank you, Sheila all you had to do is give me ten and it would have been all good!"

"No, your family and you did me a big favor, girl. I will never forget it. You know what I'm saying now if you need anything just let me know all right?"

"Sure, thing Sheila, I holla at you later, girl. **Moja!** (*One)*"

"Moja! (One)"

Soon as I hang up with her, I get a really good idea. I get up and I walked to the door calling Damon sitting in the gangster lounge with Fly Ty and Jagger watching basketball highlights of the playoffs of the eastern conference with the Los Angeles Lakers versus the Philadelphia 76ers game on. They were going off with the Sixers kicking their ass I wave Damon over to me to come in the office. He put up his finger for me to wait after he seen the end of the high lights. He came over with a big smile on his face and asked, "what up?"

"Come in I have a job for you."

"Yeah, what is it, sis?"

"Have a seat because I trust you with this so I know you will keep this shit to yourself."

"Oh, you know that shit I'm not like these other niggas gossiping like bitches that why people always want to do business with me because I know how to keep my mouth shut." "I know I need for you to go check up on my old man he has not been back home in a while it starting to make me think of some real foul shit, he said he would not do to me."

"Okay, I'll get right on it after I take care of a few things, okay?"

"Sure thing, do what you have to do and let me know all right?"

"Yeah and as you know I will not say shit about this with nobody, okay and I need some money so I can pay off this fucking ex-cop working for me."

"Yeah how much do you need?"

"Sixty large right quick."

"Is this guy worth that much, Damon?"

"He sure is especially on this thing I been working on."

"Yeah like what?"

"Remember that crooked ass cop that turn on us and we lost that big ass shipment and we took a big loss?"

"Yeah, it took us about three months to make that shit up! But we smoked his ass doe!"

"Yeah, his wife Natalie don't know that well she owes some money to this Venezuela cat, so we give her some of the money to bail her ass out then she gives me the introduction to Tony Bolivar's people. After I get the goods on this judge for him for his boss, he heard how good I am on getting shit on people."

"Yeah sounds really good to me I hope you can pull this shit off it will be a big come up for all of us."

"I know, and you know fucking well I'm going to pull it off you know me I'm the fucking best, sis. That's why you want me to do things for you!" We both started laughing. I'm thinking to myself this shit is going to be fucking huge if we hook up with these Venezuela cats we can really expand and take over the whole fucking city as well. Damon Gee phone ring and he pulls it out of his pocket looking at it and said, "see that just is what I'm talking about this motherfucker it the crooked ass cop I was telling you about right here. I have to take this I'll be right back!"

He put his phone to his ear walking out of the office talking with his hand going up and down like he always does. I sit back in my big office chair tripping off of him and I see him coming back opening the door and said, "he's ready with that thing I was telling you about and the rest of the Russian info as well. I need that loot right now, Almasi so I can go meet his ass."

"Okay, hold on." I stand up and walked to the right-hand side where I have my big Scarface poster on the wall in a frame. I slide it over and I hit the keypad super-fast and I hear that clicking sound letting me know it open. I swing the steel door open really quick and go into the safe and I pull out six stacks and close it back. I'd slide the poster back over it and I put the loot on the desk looking up at him saying this information better be right on the money or this flat-footed cock sucker is dead, you hear me?"

"He knows not to fuck with us, and I'll check it out myself, okay."

"Okay, if not you know what's up. If it's not right, I'll smoke him my motherfucking self!"

"Do you have a bag or something I can put this loot in, sis?' I sit down looking up at him and I'd reach in the bottom desk drawer and pull out a plastic bag. I had stuff in there and I hand it to him. He looks up at me smiling putting the money inside he winks his eye at me, and he rolls out of the door. I sit back down in my big office chair and I light up a cigarette blowing a big cloud of smoke thinking about taking care of these Russian cock suckers.

Then its Tyonna tapping on my door I wave her inside she just smiled handing me this fat ass envelope and said, "Sheila said to give you this."

"Thank you, baby. You want a drink or something before you go?

"No, I'm good. I have some more stops to make maybe next time thanks, any way, girl I talk to you later all right?" "Okay girl, you take care."

I sit back and I count it and I'd quickly toss it in my safe on the wall behind my Scarface poster looking up at the poster saying the world is mine too, motherfucker!

Then I get the call from one of Blue's people his name is Black Duke I met him a few times at the barbershop and when he was moving a few things for Blue.

"Hey Almasi, Blue told me to call you to tell you we just got hit and he's in the hospital all shot the fuck up the Chopper Posse niggas did it."
"What?"
"Yeah him and couple other guys too!"
"Who?"
"Lou-Lou and Wink I don't think they're going to make it!"
"Yeah I seen them around. What hospital is you at? Are they at Graduate?"
"Damn the fucking meat market, yo!"
"Yeah that's where them white motherfuckers brought him here."
"Okay, I'll be right there!" I hang up really fast and I checked my gun and stuck in the back of my jeans and I run out of the office.
"Yo, Jagger lets go man somebody just shot up Blue and his boys!"
"What? Who?"
"The Chopper posse pussy did it!"
"Yeah were going have to see them motherfuckers right quick!"
"Don't worry I'm let the psycho niggas out on their ass trust me!"
"You should let me take care of them motherfuckers like I did before when they tried to make a move on us!"
"Yeah, the wrong move too!"
We both started laughing walking fast towards the door to go outside to the whip. We get outside Jagger holds the door for me to the Benz wagon and he takes off like a jack rabbit going after some fresh pussy in the woods. it only takes us about twenty minutes to get to Graduate hospital the fat dark skin security guard at the front knew just who Jagger was and greeted him,
"hey what's up brother?"
Jagger came over shaking his hand an going in his pocket right quick and he shook his hand again with two hundred dollars and said,
"Yo, keep your eyes open for anything strange or out of the way and everything will be Gucci, brah!"

"Sure, you know I'll be looking out for the cookout!" "Good check this out I'm going to be having some my people rolling up in here be looking out for them, okay." He came inside while he's talking on his phone while I'm at the information desk. the older white lady that looks like Liza Minnelli that just gain a little weight she said, "Blue was still in surgery we have to go to the waiting room." I turned to Jagger while he still holding his phone up to his ear and said, "Come on he's still in surgery we have to go to the waiting room. I need for you to call some of our people to get up here and be looking out for my nigga!" He put his phone back in his pocket and said, "way ahead of you, sis. I got Willie Wack-Wack and Nails Nathen coming up here as we speak. I'm on it!"

"Are they the two who did that work up in New York?"

"Yeah, that's them. I'll make sure we have some loot to grease a few palms up here, too!" We both get to the waiting room and his wife Taye sitting in the row of chair she sees us, and she quickly stood up and came over towards me hugging me, I ask her in her ear, "how are you holding up, baby?"

"Well, I'm hanging in there the doctor Said there still working on him, but he just might make it but he's not out of the woods yet."

"Okay baby, he's a really strong dude he's going to make it alright. Look we have some people coming up here to watch your back and I'll take care of the bill. Did you eat something, yet?"

"No, I can't eat I'm a fucking nervous wreck!"

"I know girl just let me know if you need anything?"

"Well, I need a drink right now to tell you the fucking truth!" I wave towards her and said, "come on."

She walks with me and I ask, "do you like Belvedere Vodka?" "Shit girl that's my drink. you have some?"

"Yeah, I have some of everything in this pocketbook, girl. I have blow, weed, Volumes you fucking name it!" We both laughed and went inside of the lady's room giggling. We both stand by the sink as I put my pocketbook up in the sink and pulled out my steel flash handing it to her with her saying, "damn, you're really old skool under all them sharp ass clothes you wear girl. Thank you!"

Then she takes a big swig from off the flash and I light up a cigarette and she stick her hand out for me to give her one. I'd blow out a big cloud of smoke and say to her,

"look before the cops get here, I want to tell you that they're going to fucking harass the shit out of you. I'm telling you this shit from the door because Blue is down with BSN, okay just know that, Taye."
"Okay, I hold it down plus I don't know shit, anyway, Blue keep me out of all that bull shit."
"Good that what I want to know, okay."
"I got you, Almasi. I just hope he make it that's all I really care about." She hands me back the flash and I drink some and puff off my cigarette smiling to keep this bitch calm down with her husband under the knife. Willie Wack- Wack and Nails Nathen arrived along with Shamika, Blue's sister, Dun-Dun and his peoples his girl Tawni and his two goons Chrome and Booby Hill, Mookie and Tony.
We call him Tony Smokes now and Crazy ass Big Monk there all waving at me to let me know there all in the house. There were standing with Jagger in the waiting room but just like I told her soon as we came out of the ladies' room and went back in the waiting room and sat down. Here the fuck they come the fucking cops came in asking for her. It was two uniform fucking clowns I did not know them I know most of them cock suckers soon as I see them. Taye went on the side and talk to them. She did really good talking to them while she was crying and all that shit then an hour past and now the ball busting twins came in and I know both them motherfuckers all too well. Detective James Schultz and his nigga sell out fucking partner Detective Kenny Williamson they been trying to put me in jail for the last three years and they been on my ass. They still can't get the goods on me for a very long time that's why I been very careful on who I fuck wit and people who be around my peoples. Soon as they came up on her I stood up and looked both them right in their eyes. Detective Schultz smirked, "why look who is here, detective Williamson? Our favorite drug pusher the queen herself Almasi.
Detective Williamson laughed, "yeah and she don't look to happy to see us neither. Well were glad to see you and we knew you be here with your best flunky got all shot the fuck up."

Taye yelled, "my husband was nobody's flunky! Now what is it you want?" And when she looked up at them man if looks could kill, she would have blasted both these asshole cops head the fuck off for sure.
"Well, we need to talk to you alone." Detective Schultz. eyes get wild looking at me. Taye looks over at me nodding her head and when he went to grab her by her arm, she snatches it back saying you said talk not touch okay. He puts his hand up in the air saying, "I'm sorry could you step to the side and speak with us, please?" She nodded her head yes but she's very upset then that motherfucker detective Williamson stare at me and I say to him, "you fucking sell out!"
He smiled and said, you're fucking sell out selling poison to your own peoples, bitch!"
"That's Ms. Bitch to you, nigga!" Detective Schultz called him and said, "come on, Williamson we don't have time for black trash today we have a job to do!"
"Your right!" Looking me in my face really hard then he walks over towards the right-hand side talking with Taye. Jagger steps up along Willie Wack-Wack and Nails Nathen with Jagger and said, "fuck that coon ass, nigga, I'll take care of his ass soon enough!" So there talking to Taye and she do the same thing crying and carrying on, I have to say this bitch is good there talking for about twenty minutes while were watching on the side. As soon as they done, they walked up to us to talk shit with detective Schultz and said, well we have the fucking streets safe with this fucking crime wave happening. We are just waiting to see if their little friend is going to buy the fucking farm over here!"
They both laughed and Jagger yelled out, "that was very fucking disrespectful you fucking cracker!"
"What you say to me you black piece of shit!" Detective Williamson grabbing his partner and announced, "Yo, Jimmy its cameras in here and just like what you told me a few minutes ago we don't have time for no black trash don't you worry were going to see them on the streets!"

"See you assholes later!" Jagger was pissed he looked at me and I'd just nodded my head all of us standing there knew what that means that a green light on the ass hole cops everybody knew even the cops you don't fuck with or disrespect nobody in the BSN. I do mean nobody.

After three hours of us all in the waiting room to find out my friend Faith this short gray hair doctor came out to me Shamika and Taye jumped up walking over to the doctor and Taye looking over at me and we all go over with her. I can see she's shaking like a leaf in a fucking hurricane. The doctor name was William Goldberg he looks her right in the eyes and said, "well, he's alright for right now. He made it out of surgery so that's the good news but he's not out of danger. It's a wait and see how things goes over night. He lost a lot of blood."
"Thank you so much, doctor. Can I go see him, now? Sure, but he'll still be sleep but you can go see him he's in room 577." She turned to me hugging me really tight then she started hugging Shamika as the doctor just smile and walk away really quickly, we all were glad he's still alive that give us some kind of hope.
I tell Taye were all going up together first let me tell everybody what's going on wait for me by the elevator. I walked over to be with all the boys is standing but we can see a whole lot of people starting to come in the waiting room these young girls tell us some real dumb shit happen at club Jump off between GTG German Town Gangsters and the Hadid Ajundi. It means Men of Iron in Arabic there a group of Muslims killers who want to take over the drug game in Philly. I know one day were going have to clash with these niggas. That's the same group that Lane West told me my brother Mustafa Gats runs. We used to go to club Jump off, but it started getting a little too wild over time so me and Shamika started going to the club Elite. Mookie whose was down with my old body bag crew we both started feeling safer at his place because if anything jumps off in that joint is like fucking suicide with all the BSN there all the time.

I wave at everybody around me and said, "he just came out of surgery it's still touch and go but he's alive he's in room 577. Make sure we post some of our people up there. Two good people too. I don't want no fuck ups and keep your eyes open. Some dumb shit just happened at club Jump off between GTG and the Hadid Ajundi so stay clear of their bullshit **Sawa** (Okay!).
Dun-Dun said, "don't worry I'll make sure shit is cool Almasi and I need to talk to you after you go see Blue all right?" I just nodded my head with a smile on my face. I quickly walked over to Taye waiting for me and she hit the elevator button and we both jump on with three other people waiting as well. I really did not want to see him like this but long as I know he's still alive I feel good about that so far."
I sit with Taye and Shamika for about an hour I see that Dun-Dun put his peoples on post. Chrome and Booby Hill, I hugged both of them and I'd told Taye if she need anything to give me call. She asked me to leave the flash I had with Vodka in it and a few pills. I gave them to her giggling, and I rolled out soon as I got on the elevator. I run into some of them Hadid Ajundi niggas with the thick ass beards and the tattoos in Arabic on their arms and chest and there both staring at me they must know me, but I don't know them then one of them said something smart talking in Arabic, said, "***Iinaha alkarz*** alqatil Its Cherry the killer!"
They both started laughing really loud then I say to both of them looking them both in the face real loud, "***La alsmi hu*** al'ah Almasi No my name is Almasi, brother!"
They both looked at me in shock they did not know my old man Big Boom taught me a lot of Arabic and I helped him with Swahili. The bell rang loud to the elevator. Before I stepped off the elevator, I say to both of them,
"***Ladayk' Iikhwat laylat Jayida*** Have a good night, brothers!" One of them looked at his homey and said, "what did she just say?"
"She said have a good night, brothers. Soon as I started walking Jagger came up to me saying you ready? Yeah, let's get the fuck up out of here!"
Then Dun-Dun came up to me with this tall dude I never seen before saying, "this is my man, Ty-Kim." I shake hands with him then he said, "this is Jagger and Ty-Kim shake hands with him with Dun-Dun."

"Congratulations."

"I'm so happy for you!" Then Tawni came up handing me a gift-wrapped box with a red bow on it and she said,

"I know everybody is proud of you!"

I say, "y'all didn't have to get me anything now."

Dun-Dun screamed, "open it!" I looked over at Jagger smiling and I opened it and it's a diamond platinum watch.

"Wow, this is really nice you didn't have to do this man!" "Yes, I did with you helping me all this time, girl!" I put it on my arm real fast and I show it to Jagger.

He smiled and said, "shit that really off the hook, Almasi!" Dun-Dun said, "I'm glad you like it!"

Tawni boasted, "I help you pick it out!" I hug her and then Dun-Dun announced, "let's all go get something to eat?"

"Sure, where you want to go?"

"Let's go to Gino's and get a cheese steak?"

"Shit sounds good to me you ready? Lead the way, nigga!" Before I rolled out, I went and said goodbye to Mookie, Tony Smokes and Big Monk. I bull shit with them for a little bit and We all are laughing, going out the door Me, Jagger, Dun-Dun Tawni and his bodyguard Ty-Kim. We all bought some cheese steaks from Gino's we made a fast pit stop at one them beer to go joints getting my favorite, Heineken and we drove out to the Park eating and then we got our smoke on talking about old times and talked a lot of shit.

I said, "look Dun, I'm going to need your help with this Russian thing so I'm putting the old band back together. You know people I can really trust also with a whole lot of things now that I moved up in the world."

"You know me, Almasi. I always got your back no matter what Foxy was a real asshole junkie."

"You did what you had to do everybody knows that shit but it's funny how you put it the old band we did make some sweet music together." We both started laughing while we finish smoking our blunts.

The Next day Rah- Killer and the boys hit three of the Chopper Posse weed spots and moving them off the block from Blue's barber shop killing about four of them. The psycho body bag crew hit about four of their weed spots killing another four motherfuckers, eight dread head niggas all together what I like is they made sure to get the ones who shot Blue. I know some how they would be back because there just like cock roaches they just hide and pop back up again, but we have bigger fish to fry and really get this money.

FIGHTING TWO MOBS AT THE SAME TIME

Four months blazes past the summer is over too soon like always when you're having fun and working your ass off too when its nice outside its our busy season putting in work. Blue is recovering from his gunshot wounds he was really lucky were all happy he's going to be all right, thank Gawd. I just did not want to lose another man down with the gang because after Fat Jerome got killed that shit really broke my heart, but I had to play it off just like everybody else that's down with our family of BSN.

Its October of 2001, after plotting for the last four months on these Russian mob cats I found out all the information Damon got from that crooked ass cop was really good and we can get to work on their ass. I also found out about Big Boom no good ass as well.

Damon told me he's living with this stripper Ho bitch name Wanda White. Her stage name is Black Orchid there living in a brown stone in North Philly on Diamond street. I'll go see them and deal with all the bull shit but first I have to take care of some these Red Fellas that's leaning on Spider's brother in law Nick.

Our first target Nikon Popov he the big man's brother and Artyom Kuzwetson is his top-notch goon a stone ugly ass Scarface cold killer from Odessa with over 79 bodies to his credit that's just here in the states. He probably killed over another 100 niggas in Russia alone. So, its Friday night Me and Jagger following Nikon and Artyom in our black Cadillac Escalade there both in a white Jaguar in Maple Shade, New Jersey on route 73 while there making their rounds picking up money from all the businesses their leaning on. Mookie is behind the wheel of a dark green work van and Dun-Dun is riding shot gun up the road across the street at the parking lot of Verizon phone store near Nick's BMW car dealership. Not too far from them is Tony Smokes with Big Monk in a black Pathfinder with the big ass road bar in front of it in the Fed Ex parking lot. We have Chrome one of Dun-Dun's men near the bridge keeping an eye out for the cops, so we don't get jam up if anything goes sideways. We have everything covered to smoke these motherfuckers and take over there shit as well.

So, Me and Jagger park as we both watch the two Russian thugs make their first stop in New Jersey Chili's Grill & bar. We both sit tight puffing up a storm on our Newport's watching everything moving all of us have earpieces, radios so we can be in communication with one another but I'm quarter backing the whole thing. They stay in there for about an hour and then they came out there and drove not to far and pull up at the Kazumi Sushi joint. I said to Tony and Monk,

"You guys need to be coming up the road because there not going to be there to long!"

Tony said outloud, "I'm coming up the road right now, sis doesn't worry we will be in position!"

I said, "do you hear that Ty-Kim?"

Ty-Kim and Booby Hill is in a dark blue Chevy Impala both said, "**Ndiyo** (*Yeah!)"*

"I read you loud and clear we on our way as well we will be 100% in a few minutes!"

"Nzuri (Good!) and just like I said they didn't stay to long, but I knew that because the last time we watch them they did the same thing. So, we have their ass clocked so soon as they pulled up out the parking lot, we see Ty-Kim pulls right up behind them driving and Jagger pulls out get right behind Ty-Kim Booby Hill. The two Russian goons are driving towards the BMW dealer on route 73 and I say to Monk and Dun-Dun, "**Inaonyesha Wakayi** (Its show time!)" With Monk behind the wheel yelling, **"Wewe ni bora kujua.** (You better know it!")

Soon as he said that Ty-Kim speeds up on the Russian ass hole's hitting the back of their Jaguar. Doom!

I yelled out to everyone, "get there ass right now. Tony!" They speeded up crashing into the passenger side door is Tony Smokes and Big Monk in that black Pathfinder with the big road bar on the front of it Kadoom! Hitting the Jaguar car, he crashed into them so hard that it flips over upside down Boom! Dun- Dun jumps out with his machine gun with the silencer on the tip on the left taking aim Poouufff! Pooufff! Pooufff!

Hitting Artyom in the face neck and mouth and Dun-Dun walked back to the truck taking his time nice and smooth getting in and Mookie takes off down the road at the same time. Booby Hill jumps out their whip he is on the other side on the right with a pistol and a silencer on the tip of it as well he bends overlooking his target right in his face shooting Pooouuufff! Pooouuufff! Pooouuufff!
Hitting Nikon in the eye, neck, and the top of his head. He quickly walked back to the car jumped in and Ty-Kim pulls off real smooth and Jagger followed him as we head towards the Tacony bridge. I can hear Mookie saying, "I'll see y'all back at the spot were going hit the Betsy as he takes that Sharpe left up to the ramp and all the rest of us keep going straight and then we can hear Chrome saying, "it's all clear y'all keep it moving!"
As Ty-Kim pulls up to the toll booth ahead of us and we pulled up to the toll booth as they take off hitting the Tacony bridge were right behind them smiling at the fat white lady in the booth she smiles back as Jagger handing her the four dollars and were off to the races driving up on the right hand lane Then I say loud to everybody, "check this shit out ,y'all that white lady in the booth she have summer teeth!"
Jagger laughing asked, "what the fuck is summer teeth, Almasi?"
"Well some are green, and some are yellow!" I can hear everybody laughing really loud as were riding up the road and soon as I see the sign saying welcome to Philadelphia, I know were all home free Jagger said to me,
"where to home or the warehouse? No, I want you to take me to North Philly!"
"North Philly why what's up, Almasi?"
"I'm going to go talk to my ass hole baby daddy he's linked up with this skank ass Stripper ho name Black Orchid!"
"What? Get the fuck out of here I did not know that shit that's fucked up!"
"Yeah, it is what it is playa! So where is this joint?"
"8th and Callowhill."
"I know that joint I use to go there all the time."

"Well that's where were going, nigga!" Then he gives me that look knowing I'm really piss off about this shit. I don't say a word while he's driving to this nasty ass hole in the wall stripper trick spot. So, it only takes us about a half an hour to get there it was nowhere to fucking park, so we park about three blocks away because it's so busy at this fucking joint. So, me and Jagger quickly walked up to the door and the big black dude at the door looked at me all funny when I stepped up to hand him my money to get in with Jagger right behind me. He looked at me then he looks at Jagger not saying a word his eyes said it all taking the twenty dollars out my hand. He's about to hand me the change I said to him, "I'm paying for the big man right behind me too."

He said, "oh no, Miss he doesn't have to pay I know him he's down with the BSN." I looked him in his face really. Jagger steps up saying, "do you know who this is?"

"No."

"This is Almasi, my boss!"

"Oh snap, the boss lady Glock Mommy in the fucking flesh nobody is going to believe this Shit!"

"Oh, here is your money I'm sorry Ma!"

That's all right he hands me the twenty dollars back and I said to him, "you want to make some real money?"

"I sure do, boss lady."

"Tell me where the bitch Black Orchid dancing is at?" He waves both of us to the side saying, "I'll take you to where she's at if you give me a few?"

"Sure thing, brother. Do what you have to do big man what's your name?"

"My name is Glenn, but everybody calls me Goliath."

"Well by the looks at you they gave you the right nickname. Now go do what you have to do, and I have a few things to tell you when you come back." He smiles he goes back to the front door while me and Jagger stand on the side checking everything out the whole place is dark filled with neon lights, but the stage was lit up for the Hoochie mommies doing their thing. The joint smelled like beer its real smoky in here its packed with horny men jumping up and down looking at women shaking their ass. Shit bitches doing whatever they have to do to get that paper. I'm not mad at them just one bitch in particular.

I see big dude Goliath call one of his boys over to watch the door then he came back over to us and, "okay I'll take you over now."
I said to him, "hey Goliath, I have a few things for you to do if you want to make some real money. If you got some heart your fucking pocket be busting out larger then a horse Dick."
"Well, I'm the nigga for the job, boss lady. I'm down!"
"A nigga like me need that fat paper right about now!"
"Okay, come pass my office tomorrow at 23rd and Washington Avenue around 4 P.M. Okay?"
"Sure thing, I'll be there!" I'd hand him three one hundred-dollar bills for taking us over to where this nasty ass bitch is dancing at. His big black face lit up smiling knowing its Christmas day for thugs and knuckle dragging niggas in the streets who kick ass for a living for real!
I smiled back at him as he walks us over to the table sticking the money into his pocket and I see Big Boom sitting there and his jaw damn near hit the fucking floor when he saw me. I should have had my gun out and blow his fucking head off where he's sitting. I walked over and I sat down looking him in the face saying, "what's up with you?" He just looks up at me even doe its dark and smoky in this dump all I can see is this guilt glowing in his eyes. I look up at the stage seeing this light skin nasty ass ho bitch and I asked, "so that's the skank ass bitch?" He nodded his head yes all fucking nervous and shit. I never seen this nigga like that he must know I'll kill his ass where he stands without blinking my eyes.
"Look Boom all you had to do is be a fucking man about it. If you wanted to step off, you should have told me so and look me in the face and told me like a man. What makes you think I would not fucking find out about this shit?"
"What you forgot who the fuck I Am nigga. A thousand niggas move on just one of my phone calls and I would not find out your fucking some low life skank Ho from North Philly that done fucked every nigga in the city with a few dollars!"
"I didn't know how to tell you for real, baby."
"Well now that it's all over with you and me just make sure that you do for your son and come see him some time so don't get lost into strange pussy like you're doing right now motherfucker. Remember that you're a father of a beautiful little boy don't forget that shit you hear me!"

"I hear you; I'll be by Sunday to see him."
"Look, I'll let you know when you can see him, okay but you and me will work something out and I'll let you know like I said because you done lost all your rights and privileges when your dumb ass jumped up and rolled out the spot with your boy Hugo and never came the fuck back all right!"
"So, you can kill all that shit call me Sunday and I'll let you know if its cool depending how I feel, nigga!" He sips on his beer with his head down low and he act like he could not look me in the face mumbling, "alright."
Now I'm getting out this fucking joint all right he stood up coming towards me like he wanted to hug me or something and I put my hand up in his sorry ass black face.
"Sit your ass back down I did not make a fucking scene in this motherfucker, but I will if you try to act like you really care about me, nigga !I should have come in here and lit you and that skank ass ho up with the silencer I got in my pocketbook and nobody in this fucking flea circus would have not knew who the fuck did it. You know I'm that good right, nigga?" He just looked up at me as I pulled out my gun with the silencer on the tip showing it to him and I'd put it back in my pocketbook. He looked like he was going to shit on himself. I point my finger in his face making like it was a gun yelling, "So have a nice life, motherfucker!"
And I looked over at Jagger waving my hand and quickly walked away from him rolling my eyes pissed off.
He sat back down looking up at me with them sorry ass eyes of his, but I don't even look back at him as I'm walking out with Jagger right by my side to the front door. I wave towards Goliath and asked, "how about you put in some work, tonight?"
"What is it you want me to do, Ma?"
"Come with me right now and I'll tell you." So, he follows us out of the bar to our truck walking three blocks up. I jump in and reach in the glove box I pull out a stack of bills and I hand it to him and said, "that's two large I want you to kick that nigga I was talking to ass and that nasty ass stripper bitch he's with. I want you to slap that bitch around really good, too. Don't kill them just fuck them up, alright, can you do it?" He put the money in his pocket really fast smiling from ear to ear and replied,
"I sure can, boss lady!"

"Good and report to work on time, tomorrow too so don't get to fucked up on that loot I just gave you!"
"I won't I'll get the job done! Good now you sure about this shit?"
"Yeah, I'm sure!"
"Wait until the bar is closed and I want you to kick his ass now he's no punk so it's not going to be easy. You might need some help big man and for Gawd sakes don't let him get to his truck he got his gun in there and he's really good with that motherfucker."
"So, don't let him get the drop on you."
"I got this trust me." "Okay now how I know you are going to get the job done?"
"Give me a number where I can reach you, I'll send you a picture on your phone and I'll send it to you. boss lady!" Give me your phone he hands me his phone and I put in my number and I give it back to him don't call me if you don't fuck his ass up now!
"Oh, don't you worry boss lady I'm going to fuck his ass up real good. I want to be down with y'all!"
"Good I holla at you later! Jagger drive us the fuck out of here before I change my mind!" He pulls off really fast as I say to him "what you think?"
"That's a really big dude I think he can get it done."
I called Shamika and told her to meet me at the warehouse. I had something to tell her she said she was on her way. He drove us to the warehouse it doesn't take us long to get back to the spot soon as we walked in everybody is chilling in the gangster lounge. I spoke to everyone and bumped fist its Mookie and my girl La-Neesa sitting in his lap, Dun-Dun and Tawni and her girlfriend Kalindi talking with Chrome, Big Monk, Tony Smokes and Ty-Kim is talking really loud watching sport center highlights of the basketball games.
The whole place is smoky with the fat funky beats banging out and everybody have a bottle of fire water having a real good time. I go in my office area and go in my desk, get me a red plastic cup and I walked up on Dun-Dun and Tawni drinking Cristal champagne the good shit. I'd pointed my cup towards them and said, "I can really use a drink right about now." Dun-Dun sat up saying sure thing, sis. He picks up the bottle and he poured me a good cup full and Tawni is puffing on a blunt she smiles and quickly past it to me saying,

"here you go looks like you need some of that, too!" We all started laughing as I yelled out, "you're fucking right I need some of that is a real fucking understatement right about now, fam!"
They all started laughing loud at what I just said as I started puffing and I passed it back to her we kick it talking shit to one another for about half an hour then my phone goes Bing!
I quickly reached in my pocket of my jeans to look at my phone and I looked at the pictures of Big Boom all beat the fuck up with two black eyes and a busted lip and that bitch of his with her lips all swelled the fuck up and blood running out the side of that nasty ass hoe's mouth. I started laughing saying, "wow, that nigga really did it!"
Dun-Dun asked, who really did what? I hand him my phone I went to holla at Big Boom and that stripper bitch he's fucking, and I gave this big thug nigga two large to kick their ass and he really did it too! Big Man was not fucking around neither. Dun-Dun and Tawni is looking at the pictures on the phone laughing their ass off with Dun-Dun in a laughing voice, "well looks like that nigga past one of your tests, so far."
Tawni yelled, "damn he fucked their asses up real good shit y'all can use a nigga like that to put in some more work for y'all for real!" I replied, "your right about that shit, girl!" I wave Jagger over to me while he's sitting with Big Monk and them watching the DVD of the fight, he quickly came over smiling as I hand him my phone and he boasted, "I told you that nigga was going to get the job done well. His name is not Goliath for nothing!" Everybody started laughing shit I got a few niggas I want this nigga to go holla at right quick shit he can make a few dollars off of me.
"I don't mind paying him he does some good ass work from what I can see!" Everybody is snickering then Shamika came in the door by herself she came over to him bumping fist with me then she bumps fist with everybody standing there asking,
"what's so fucking, funny?" I need a good laugh right about now too, shit!" I smiled and I gave her my phone showing her the pictures of Big Boom all beat the fuck up and that slut bitch she was cracking up.
"Oh, this is some funny shit!" I told her all about Big Boom stepping out on me soon as Damon Gee told me about the shit saying, "well it could not happen to a better guy if you ask me!"

We all started laughing some more really loud. So, we all got high for another hour or so with the gang then me and Shamika went inside of my office so we can talk one on one. she knew I was really hurt about this shit deep down inside, but I have to play it off around everybody else. Soon as we went inside the office Shamika asked, "are you all right, girl?"

"No, not really because I really loved that man and he did me like that and we were talking about getting married too. I feel like a fucking fool!"

"You're not a fool girl you just were in love that's all your fucking human too. No matter how hard and cold hearted you have to be in this game with all these crazy ass niggas." "Yeah, I know but he was the only thing I knew. I'm thinking we were so happy, and he's been fucking that bitch the whole time."

"Look at it this way good thing you found out now then later on. It's all fucked up now but you're going to come out on the other side like you away do, girl. Time will heal all that hurt you have now trust me."

"That sounds easier said then done! What you need girl is to meet somebody for real. Yeah, but who?"

"Don't worry you will meet somebody, girl. Its somebody out there for you. Don't you worry you will meet somebody that really wants to be with you and love you for real not just somebody who just want some pussy."

I looked up at her and I glanced her in the eyes really good saying that's what all men is like for real, girl."

"Who are you kidding!"

We both started laughing then her phone started ringing she reach in her pocketbook getting her phone looking at the caller ID she said to me I have to take this hold on. She walks on the other side of the room talking and I can see her whole face change all happy and giggling when she got done. She walked back over to me and I said to her, "who the fuck is that?" She started laughing girl, "that's my new boo I was telling you about his name is Carlo."

"Oh, that's Carlo I was thinking you was bull shitting me." "No, girl, I've been seeing him here and there."

"So, what about Julio?"

"Girl that nigga is in jail and I'm not fucking wit him anymore after I found out about him."

"What about him?"
"Shit some niggas told me he was fucking this sissy motherfucker up in the jail. I ran to go get checked out."
"What?"
"Get the fuck out of here are you sure?"
"Yeah, I'm sure that why that nigga love getting locked up so he can be with his fucking butt buddy, boo!"
"Damn, I did not know he was a Homo thug. I would never think that about him well it takes all kinds in this world."
"Yeah girl, I'm telling you right from the door I'm not fucking with no man who fuck niggas in the ass. I'm not wit that shit! That nigga is not going to give me the fucking Heebie-Jeebies and I be all fucked up and die from that shit!"
We both started laughing loud as we get out puff and drink on in my office after another hour or so we all went home after getting twisted. We all chilled out for the next two weeks getting ready for our next target and we know that the Russians is really watching their backs but we know when and where to hit them so that kind of shit don't bother us, we still will get the job done no matter what.
Two weeks blaze past like the wind in a hurricane storm and it's the day before we were going to hit the Russians again I'm in the bed sleep when I get the call 3 O' clock in the morning I pick up the phone from off my night stand haft sleep trying to knock the cob webs off my brain and its X saying, "I didn't want to wake you up but the GTG just made a move on us once more and they killed Petey Q outside of his house in the North East coming from Mookie's club."
"What? When he said that I was woke up then because it shocked me because Petey Q run a very tight ship wit his crew. Yeah also Mister Blade and Sammy Green is dead too Tommy Machete is hanging on to his life by a fucking thread. I quickly sit on the side of my bed said," where the fuck was Bulls Eyes and Knock Daddy? I said there is something wrong here, but they said they rolled out with some bitches before Petey Q and them left with Sammy and Mister Blade. The shit still doesn't sound right to me because Bulls Eyes and Knock Daddy never leave his side now, they roll out with some bitches come on now.

"Yeah, I was thinking the same thing well Spider wants everybody at the strap yard tonight, so he told me to call you. I'll be there I'm on my way!" I quickly get dressed I called Jagger up and tell him to meet me at the strap yard in North Philly. He said, "he doesn't like this shit he wants to meet me at my house I told him no to meet me there."

So, I had to call somebody to watch Little Boom while I was gone. I called my girl Milly a rich hippy chick white girl who lives at the condominium not too far from mine. I helped her out with her crazy ass rich spoil trust fund asshole dope head boyfriend name Brad when he was beating her up one day. I was riding by and I jumped out my Benz wagon and I pistol whip his ass with my 45 and we became fast friends.

She loves Little Boom and she always ask me how she can pay me back so she would baby sit for me in times like this when Tanya went back to school or was not around running the streets or something. So, I called her and told her I was bringing the baby past her house she said sure any time. So, I got all my guns I checked both of them really good and made sure I had extra clips too. I went and got Little Boom together right quick. I changed his diaper and that boy dropped a fucking load too so I'm getting him dress. He was half sleep, so he did not fuss that much I made sure my doors were locked up and I turned on all the alarms. I quickly drove over to the condominium about four blocks away. I got the feeling the whole time I was being watched.

I dropped Little Boom off to her and I hand her some money and she pushed it back to me said, "you don't have to do that you're the kind of friend I need in my life. I don't want your money, girlfriend." I do what I I always do. I'll buy her something she never turns that down when I do that. I go back to my truck when I drove off, I looked in my rearview and I can see two dark color cars following me, so I put my gun in my lap. I see the cars speeding up on me one of the cars pulled up beside me and the other car crash in the back of my truck. Doom!

The other car a dark color, Ford Sedan I can see the mask gun men hanging outside of the window shooting Pat! Pat! Pat! I ducked down really low even doe I know I had bullet proof glass on my truck and windows the impact of the bullets made me react but I'm still driving with these motherfuckers hitting the back of my truck.

I'm holding on to my Glock in one hand on the wheel ready to make my move on them they could not break the glass still shooting at me. I'm maneuvering from side to side trying to get away from them but there still hot on my ass, so I cracked the window just a little sticking my gun out the crack. I started shooting Kapacka! Kapacka! Kapacka! I hit one of the gun men in his shooting arm he drops his gun then I quickly turned my truck into the side of the dark Ford Sedan. Doom!

And then the car behind me came up and hit me from the back really hard again. Kadoom! But this time he hit me so hard it made my truck flipped over upside down. Kaplang! My truck started sliding down the street I was freaking out sliding upside down. I can see the sparks flying I'm scared to death I was about to shit on myself then the truck slid into the group of park cars on the left-hand side of the street Kaboom! My head hit the steering wheel and I blacked out from the impact. I don't know how long I was out all I know is these two men one black and one white. I'm in a daze and my head is throbbing the two men is pulling me out of the truck and soon as we got a good twenty-five feet away from my truck while there dragging me away. Kabooom!

We all can feel the heat from the flames and the big black man said in a loud excited voice, "are you alright, Miss? I nodded my head yes. I feel like I'm under water while there talking to me then the white man said to me, "can you walk?"

I just nod my head yes and I'm really dizzy the two men help me to my feet and they quickly walk me a little Further from my truck on fire. As the flame grows higher with black smoke gushing out then the truck went up again. Kadoom! That shook me down to my core I was shaking, and my head was hurting really bad. I just sat down on the sidewalk as the group of people he was with started walking up they all seen what happen when the car hit me and made my truck flip upside down.

They did not see them shooting at me 15 minutes later while I'm in a daze the cops came up two funny looking white dudes. One is tall and goofy looking and the other one is fat and mean looking like a bulldog both of them are young guys. Asking me what happen, and I told them that the car came from out of nowhere and hit me from behind and made my truck flip over and all my ID was inside of my truck.

They both said that was all right just as long as I'm all okay. I gave them my alias that my name was Dana Brown and they jotted it down in there little black report book not really giving a fuck about doing that too. They don't know I have about five difference driver's licenses being in the life you have to be ready for all kinds of bullshit and believe me. I could fall off the planet earth in a matter of hours and get out of the country with my eight different fake passports and just one fucking phone call with a pocketbook filled with loot rolling like a boss bitch.

Ten minutes past by in a blink of an eye the paramedics came and check me out. They ask me do I want to go to the hospital at the time I did not get a good look at the two men my eyesight was still a little blurry and my heart was still pumping really fast like I took five black beauties or something. I chased it with a fifth of vodka but the way I was feeling I said, "yes" really quick the very nice white man that help save my ass.

He helped me to the truck then the nice white guy stood by me while I'm sitting on the end of the paramedic truck saying, "do I need anything and I'm alright but my head felt like I was hit in the fucking head with a baseball bat more then a few times. I'd told him thank you so much what is your name I ask? He said his name is Neal.

I said to him, "can I use your phone Neal?" He swiftly hands me his phone and I quickly called Spider he picks up after just three rings I say really fast, "hey, dad, it's your daughter Shorty out here in the world!" He knows that's the code and that its other people around me, so he knows what's up from the door and not to say my name out loud as well. "Where are you, baby girl?"

"Look I don't want you to get upset dad, but I was in a car accident and I'm going to the hospital." I could not tell him with the cops and paramedics around me that these niggas were trying to kill me.

"Are you all right?"

"Well, I'm really shook up but I'm all right! Do you know where there taking you?"

By this time my eyesight cleared up and I get a good look at this guy and he's a real looker too, Gawd Damn. I ask the tall good-looking black Paramedic guy, "do you know where your taking me my father wants to know?"

"Yes, were taking you to **Lankenau** its closer to where we're at. "I said Lankenau hospital Daddy."

"Okay. I'm on my way." He hangs up and I hand the phone back to Neal and said, "thank you so much, Mister Neal."

"It's okay just as long as your all right, young lady." Then the big Black man came over and chimed in, "you're really lucky, Miss. We were all out there after our little art show. Are you sure you're alright?"

"Right then and there I realize why those motherfuckers didn't kill me it was too many people out there good thing they did not see them shooting at me or the cops would have been looking up my ass with a fucking microscope. I answered, "Yes and thank you so much for helping me. What is your name, sir?"

"My name is Rickey Sanders. I hope you feel better, okay." "Thank you." As the paramedic said to me, "were pulling out to get you checked out, Miss. It looks like you got a real nasty bump on your head here put this ice pack on that."

As he hands me the ice pack, he points for me to step up on the paramedic truck he helps me up on the truck. I get up on the truck and sat down as the other paramedic a good looking young Asian dude said, "alright were out of here as I can see the fire men still putting out the fire of my Benz wagon. All I can think about is I could have been in that motherfucker dead as the paramedic truck pulls off up the Dall yellow lit road everything looks like blur of a very bad dream I can't wake up from. While were on are way to the hospital I got to talking to the paramedic my head is killing me but wow this man is fucking gorgeous. I ask him, "what's your name?" Latrell so I lie to him and say my name is Dana. "Well, it's really nice to meet you, Dana there going to check you out and make sure you're alright." He smiles at me and said, "well you're going to hear this all night but you just had a very traumatic experience so you need to relax, and can I ask you something Dana?"

"Yes, what is it you want to know?"

"Are you married?"

I smiled and said, "no, I'm a single mother of one."

"Okay, how old is you child?"

"He's three years old."

"what about you where is your wife or woman at home?"

"Well, I'm a widow and my wife die two years ago a drunk driver killed her and my little girl."
"Oh, I'm so sorry to hear that."
"It's all right that's why I love this kind of work helping people that's how I been trying to deal with it for about a year. I did nothing now I'm back doing something with my life." Soon as he said that we pull up in the emergency ward parking lot and Latrell said to me, "well were here and I have to ask can I see you again?"
"Yes, I'll give you my number give me your phone and I'll put my number inside of it." Sure, here you go he hands me his phone smiling I put my number inside of it and I give it back.
I asked, "you're going to call me, right? I sure will nice meeting you, Dana."
I get out and I go in up to the counter to check in. It took me about hour to get waited on and they check me out telling me that I had a concussion they did an x ray, and everything looked good. Spider show up with Jagger, X, Fly Ty and Damon Gee. After all that bullshit, I checked out five hours later, but I was a little scratch and bruised up, but I was really glad to be alive fuck that! So, they took me home I went and picked up Little Boom from Milly's house went to my crib, sat around and talked. Spider said he wants us to go ahead with other hit on the Russians.
"Once you get yourself together, I want you on that shit Almasi."
"Okay, just give me a few days and I'll take care of it."
"Now I want the psycho body bag crew to take care of GTG right away because I know it was them who came at you tonight, I want you, Damon to get all the information on GTG I want to know everything Damon you here me."
"I'm on it!" Then Spider yelled out, "now that we got that shit over with let's have some drinks up in this motherfucker. Ty pull that shit out and fire it up!"
All of us started laughing I was playing it off getting my puff and drink on with the gang, but I was really shaking from them fools trying to take me the fuck out. I was lucky that a small crowd was there, and those two regular Joes pulls me out that truck or my black ass would have been deader than Tupac and Biggie. So, we got twisted and everybody rolled out, but Jagger I needed some days off to get my shit together and don't think about nothing but my son and myself.

The three days when by faster then the wind blows in a fucking tornado but what I did do is I got Damon Gee to track down those two brave ass dudes that saved my life and I had him take them ten large each. The black dude told me his whole name Rickey Sanders an out of work dock worker hustling his artwork to get by. He was easy to track down and Damon told me he damn near had a fucking heart attack when he gave him that money and he was really happy to get it too. The white dude Neal Damon found out his whole name Neal Gray a struggling artist making crazy ass erotic paintings for a living he turned the money down at first but when Damon came back the next day, he took the money. I told him when he gave each of them the money just tell them that's for being a good Samaritan. They both got it and he also told them to keep it to themselves as well. They both did not saying a word about it to no one.

I also had Damon look up that knock out fucking gorgeous black man Latrell the paramedic I was not going to step to him with any money .I just wanted to get with him but when Damon looked up his background for me I found out his brother and father was in the life and he was too at one time as well. I also found out where he lives at and where he hangs out at as well. I was going to run into him where he hangs out and tell him my real name and see what will happen but until then I knew I had to get back to work really soon. It was the fourth day of me resting up but was glad to be spending time with my son.

So, I'm playing on the front room floor with the love of my life, my baby boy, Little Boom when Jagger walked up to me with the phone and that look on his face. I knew right then and there that the party was over he hands me the phone he said really low, "its X." I take the phone out his hand saying, "Yo big guy, what's up?"

"just want to know is are you all right first of all before I tell you this?"

"Why what's up what happen, X?"

"I'm need for you to talk to Jagger and calm him down after I tell you this."

"Tell me what nigga, spit it out! My peoples just told me that your girl Tanya just got locked up for holding."

"What? Holding what?"

"What do you think she quit school and was running around with Gino crazy ass selling drugs. I'm letting you know she's probably going to call you because she knows Jagger is going to fucking flip out on her ass!"

"I told that stupid ass little bitch about fucking with that nigga!"

"What the fuck am I going to tell this man?"

"It's only one thing to tell him but the truth that's all Ma." "Yeah, but then I have to tell him she was hanging with Gino as well this is fucked up!"

"Shit, Jagger already know about her fucking with Gino she told him that shit that's some old news over here, but she did not tell him about her dropping out of school to sell drugs that's the thing he's going to go off about."

"So why didn't he say anything to me about this shit?"

"I don't know I'm just giving you a heads up, Shorty."

"Okay thanks, X. I hear some clicking on the other end of my phone that just might be her. I holla at you later thanks again **Moja!** (One)"

"Moja! (One)." I click over and just like he said its Tanya. "Hello Almasi?"

"Yeah, it me, girl."

"So, what's up with you?"

"Hey this is Tanya I really need your help. I'm locked up and they just brought me to the round house. They said I have to see the judge before they set bail."

"Okay, now listen to me really good keep you fucking mouth shut."

"Okay, yes I didn't say shit!"

"Okay Good now what did they locked you up for?"

"Possession of cocaine."

"Now, I want you to sit tight I'm sending you somebody to bail you out his name is Mitchum Wells. He's a tall white dude okay he's going to bail you out. When you get here, I need for you to tell me everything that happen alright?"

"Okay, thank you."

"Now hang up and do everything I told you to do girl see you when you get here!"

"Yo Jagger, I need to holla at you right quick!"

"Okay. I'm coming!" He came up to me and said, "what's up?"

"What happen now?"

"Look, why you did not tell me that your sister was fucking wit Gino Gats?"

"Well, I did not want to tell you that bullshit wit all the things we got going on. I told her she was going to fuck her life up fucking with that dude, but she said to me she's grown and I'm not her daddy. Our daddy is dead and all that bullshit, but I told her well I'm not your daddy, but you better stay in school or I'm going to kick your ass."

"Well she just called me she's at the round house she just got locked up for possession of cocaine."

"What?"

"Yeah, so if she was in school what the fuck is she doing here getting locked up for possession ain't her school in North Carolina?"

"She fucking lie to me telling me she went back three months ago, Almasi. I'm going to kick her ass when I see her.

"Let me get Mitch on the horn to go bail her out and you can kick her ass when you go to pick her sorry ass up at the fucking round house!"

"Yeah, that's just what I'm going to do! Take somebody with you, okay."

"Alright I'm going right now. As I pick up the baby and I'm going to fix his food in the kitchen. So, I set him in the highchair when the doorbell rings and me and Jagger look at each other. He said, "I'll get it as he pulls out his gun walking up to the door real smooth then I can see him putting his gun up and opening the door. I see him hugging Blue and he's kissing Taye on the cheek then bumping fist with Dun-Dun and Tony Smokes. I was really happy to see them all.

Dun-Dun said, "hey, Sis you alright?"

As he kisses me on the cheek and hugged me as we all yelled, "family." I hug and kiss each one of them repeating, "family" really loud as well at the same time.

Then Tony Smoke said, "Crazy Monk is on his way he's talking on the phone."

"Okay, so what's up with y'all?"

Blue said, "we came to see if your all right we heard what happen, so we came to holla at you!" Crazy Monk came walking in and gave me a big ass bear hug lifting me up off the ground yelling, "boss lady, what's up?"

"Put me down with your crazy ass, Nigga." Everybody laughed at us. He said, "Mookie told me to tell you he'll be by later he had to take care of some shit at the club."

"Well, y'all all have a seat. Do any of you want a beer or something?"

Dun-Dun said, "you know damn well were not turning down no fucking beer, fuck that! Everybody started giggling loud Jagger points at me and said, "I'm going to head out now. Don't forget to take somebody with you now!"

"Who doe?" While I'm handing out beers to everybody I said, "Call that new dude, Goliath. I got him working at the pill mill and if he doesn't move his ass fast enuff I'm going to put a bullet in his big black ass!"

Everybody snickering really loud Big Monk said, "see that shit, y'all she is alright, Jagger." He was still tittering pulling out his phone calling Goliath walking towards the front door walking out giggling to himself.

"Taye so what you are cooking, Almasi?"

"Just a little something for the baby that's all. If I knew y'all was coming I would have hooked something up let me fix y'all something while y'all here now, Fam. Blue, it's cool we just wanted to holla at you that's all baby."

"No, it's not going to take me that long to hook y'all something up." I pulled out my big black frying pan out turning on the stove I whip out some ground beef from out the refrigerator. I put it in a big bowl and started seasoning the meat really good then I'd chop up some onions and a green pepper on the counter and toss it inside of the meat. Blue asked, "Yo, did you hear what happen to my sister Tamika, yet?"

"No, what happen? She got popped with 100 keys of shit. Damn, that's fucked up why Shamika did not call me to tell me. Well she's trying to get her out she didn't get time to call you yet."

"Big Monk all I want to know is she going to talk?"

Blue just look at him not saying a word but his face says it all. "Well, if it was Shamika I know she could hold her own, but Tamika is not built like that!"

Everybody but Blue is laughing loud while I'm mixing up the onions and green peppers inside of the ground beef. I toss the ground beef in the frying pan chopping it up letting it cook until the meat turns brown then I put on a big pot of boiling water I quickly put a little cooking oil inside of the boiling water then get my pasta out of the cabinet. Taye said, "oh shit, you are making Spaghetti!"
"No Shit Taye what tip you off the pasta?"
Everybody started chuckling loud while their drinking their beer. She is about to light up a blunt and I say to her, "yo Taye, you can't do that my baby is right there step out on the deck and do that okay, baby girl."
"Oh, my bad, Almasi. I'm sorry." She stands up with the blunt in her hand as she waves towards Blue, Dun-Dun and Big Monk as they all walked towards the deck door when the doorbell started ringing Big Monk yelled, "I'll get that for you Almasi you just keep cooking up that Spaghetti, okay." Everybody started giggling as he quickly went to the door, he peeked out opening the door saying its Mookie.
I see him hugging Monk and he came up in the kitchen and he kiss me on the cheek. He said, "family" as Monk when out on the deck with the others as me and Mookie started talking. "Hey, are you alright?"
"Yeah, I'm good thanks for asking doe."
"Look, I had to come holla at you after I heard what happen and I have to come help you on some get back on these niggas!"
"Yeah, we all are working on that right now, Fam, but never mind all that right now. How is my girl La- Neesa?"
"She's good and me and her will have some good news to give to you real soon."
"What y'all having a baby?"
"Yeah, and something else too."
"Oh shit, y'all getting married?"
"Yeah, but I want her to tell you because you two are really close. So, don't get me in trouble with me telling you that shit!"
"Oh no, I would not do that to you, my brother. I'll play dumb when she tells me, but I'm happy for you over here. Look at you, nigga your handing in your players card that's a good thing brother."
"Well it's because of you I hooked up with her when you started sending me over to her office with loot to get shit done."

"Yeah, that's how it all happened then wow I did not know that well you never know when and where you're going to find love."
"Yeah, you're right about that shit!" After chopping up the meat in the frying pan it's done, I'd mixed in the meat inside of the pasta as I was talking with Mookie.
He said, "man, you always could cook your ass off, girl."
"When I was young, I had to take care of my little sister and my junkie ass mother could not cook to save her fucking life, so I got really good at it and I love to do it to tell you the truth." I made a small bowl for Little Boom, but I let it cool off before I gave it to him as the others come back in the kitchen laughing and talking, they all one by one hugging Mookie. I give Little Boom his food after I chopped it up for him and I say to the others all sitting at my big table, "do y'all want some?"
Dun-Dun asked, "is water wet?"
Everyone started snickering and talking loud shouting, "Oh hell yes!"
Everybody saying it at the same time that what made it even funnier.
Taye jumped up and said, "let me give you a hand, sis." She goes in the cabinet getting the plates while I started making big plates for everybody and Taye help me out by making her man, Blue his plate and Tony Smokes. I made the others their plates. I went and gave them another beer and I made mine and sat down with everybody eating and talking having a good time. I was really happy they all stop by to see about me. It took off my mind of getting back at GTC and the next Russian hit. Soon as we were all done the doorbell rang and I got up to get the door it's my Auntie La'Wanda I let her in and gave her a hug she's going to watch the baby while I go to Jersey so I can do this hit on the Russians. She smelled the food and saw everyone sitting at the table saying, "damn that smell good, Almasi."
"Well I have a lot of it left so help yourself, girl." La'Wanda whispered, "Look, I need to talk to you before we walk in there with the others."
"Sure, what is it?"
"Did you hear about Tamika yet?"
"Yeah, I did what happen?"
"Well, they won't give her bail she still being held by the DEA and the FBI."
"Yeah, where is Shamika at?"

"She's on her way back home she just called me she said she's going to call you."
"Okay, thanks go get yourself something to eat all right. The baby is in there too. Where is my little boo- Boo as I walked with her in the kitchen, she spoke to everybody then she's playing with the baby then she makes herself a big plate of Spaghetti. She sat next to Little Boom. I wave to Dun-Dun to follow me to the deck we both walked out as I close the deck door and we both walked over to my bar as Dun-Dun asked, "what's up, sis?"
"Look, they still have Tamika they denied her bail."
"So, what you think she's going to talk?"
"Yeah, I do but what's fucked up that's my girlfriend sister and Blue is her brother and he's down with our crew here and were talking about taking care of her were going have to really be careful with this one Dun-Dun."
"I know it's fucked up but I'm not trying to sound cold, but this is the life if we have to shut her up were going have to do it."
"I know but that just might make Shamika flip on us doe and Blue too."
"Yeah, but it is what it is, Almasi. Everybody knows what all were getting involved with here. Nobody is a fucking kid here and if they want to act like one, they will grow up real fucking fast in this game."
"You're right!" We both started giggling then we both bumped fist and we walked back inside the house at the same time. Jagger came in the door with Tanya with her face all twisted up she quickly walked to the back room not saying a word. I walked up to him saying, "what you do?"
"I kicked her ass what else I was going to do!"
"You did the right thing she need her ass kicked what Mitch say?"
"He said she did not tell them shit she kept her mouth shut like you told her, but they got her with 10 keys of cocaine in her car and he said to get rid of her phone it just might be bugged."
"Good, I'll go talk to her before we all roll out okay?"
"Sure, thing but as you know she's not going to listen it's going to go in one ear and out the other! Your right she's really hardheaded."
"So, when are we rolling out?"
"We have another four hours, so we have some time to get ready where is Goliath at?"

"I dropped him off back at the pill mill he was mad that I did not take him here with me. I know damn well you don't want that nigga knowing where you live at and he's not a full member of the BSN."

"Yeah, you got that one right!"

"He keeps asking to be down. I told him he has a fucking long way to go before we can bring him in."

"Yeah, your right he thinks he's on the fast track because I got him to beat Big Boom and his bitch up for me. I'll talk to him, okay."

"What happen with the funeral for Petey Q?"

"They did a private thing with just the family that way the FBI and the local asshole cops don't get up dated pictures of all of us Spider said."

"That's kind of smart if you ask me."

"Yeah, it is. What everybody don't know it's going to be a whole new ball game with Spider running things and were going to make a whole lot more money with him running the show watch you'll see. Oh, I know that for sure!"

We both bump fist and walked over to the kitchen with all the others laughing and talking with La'Wanda washing up the dishes singing along with the radio playing.

"Thanks for taking care of the dishes for me. aunt La'Wanda."

"Baby you don't have to thank me, and that Spaghetti was off the damn chain, girl!"

"Thank you, I'm glad you enjoyed it, Auntie. Girl, you cook like an old down-home, girl from down south you would never know you were a young city girl."

"Well, coming from you I can really feel good about my cooking because I know you can throw down your Gawd dam self."

"Shit, just like they say it take one to know one, girl. So, go do what you have to do I got the baby. I'll finish cleaning up for you, okay."

"Thank you so much, Aunt La'Wanda. I don't know what I do without you."

"I don't want you to find out neither, baby.

Look, I need to talk to you in private right quick before you go, okay. It's really deep, too?"

"Sure, what's up?" She looks around at everybody with her eyes getting wide saying, "I'll talk to you."

I said, "okay, when your done and when you put the baby to bed you and me will talk." I walked towards the deck as I wave everybody to follow me out to my deck. So, we can go over what we have to do, tonight."

I asked, "Taye could you stay here with my aunt and give her a hand." she just nod her head yes with a big smile on her face she know it's a nice way of saying she can't hear what we're talking about but she know what's up and know what time it is with us. Nobody that's not a BSN member can really hear what we're talking about. I know Blue tell her shit but not when were first talking about it that a big fucking no-no from the door.

"Y'all ready to go?"

"Yeah were ready. Okay, let me go holla at this girl before we jet give me a few I'll be right back. I'd quickly go to the back room. I knock on the door and walk in she's on the phone. I yelled at her put the fucking phone down and hang the fuck up bitch!

Tanya is rolling her eyes at me with the phone up to her ear and her other hand on her skinny ass hips. I slapped the shit out of her. Packa! She dropped the phone holding her face yelling, "what the fuck you do that for?"

I quickly get the phone off the floor and I went to the window. I open it and tossed it out the window. I watched it smash on the ground below in the street and close the window back down. Tanya yelled, "what the fuck you do with my phone and I did what you told me to do. Fuck!"

"No, you just fucked your life up over some Thug Dick! You're nice looking girl. You can get some Dick anywhere you dumb yellow bitch!" She stood and yelled, "I wanted to be down none of y'all was going to put me on, so I did what I had to do fuck that!"

"You dumb ass young bitch now they're going to be watching your ass and your phone just might have had a bug in it they know who you are. Why you think they jacked your ass so fast now you're never going back to school!"

"I didn't want to go anyway!" I slapped her again she fell to the floor then she tried to jump up and sucker punch me, but I blocked it and give her a super hard right cross to her face. Blam!

"You want to go bitch, come on!" She stood back up with her yellow face getting red like a white woman putting her hands up to fight me.

I said to her, "you really want me to fuck you up, right?" She yelled in deep anger, "Fuck you bitch!" Soon as she when to make a move to swing at me I'd hit her with a fucking left upper cut. Pang! And another rock-hard right cross in her jaw. Woop! Shit, I knew that one hurt she hit the floor on her ass crying. I stood over her yelling you're not a street bitch. A Nigga out there would eat your little yellow ass up just stay there and cry you sorry ass bitch! I be back later on, and you better stay here. If not, I'll find you and kick your little yellow ass for real do you hear what I said?"

"I want you to stay in this house until I get back say it!" She is sitting on the floor holding her jaw and her eyes filled with tears

"Okay!"

"I can't hear you say it a little louder bitch!"

"Okay!"

"Okay what?" And I acted like I was going hit her again she yelled out, "I'll stay here in the house until you get back!"

"Good, I'm trying to save your fucking life, dumb bitch!" She is laying on the floor crying really loud and I went out the door slamming the door. Boom! I walked in the baby room where aunt La'Wanda was with the baby changing him and I asked, "what is it you wanted to tell me Auntie?"

"Look, I really need some money or I'm going to lose my house." She goes to her pocketbook pulling out some papers handing them to me I looked them over and it was some foreclosure notice papers. I read them while I stood there looking up at her face, she's really upset.

"Why you didn't tell me about this shit sooner, Auntie?" I looked at her and her eyes were so sad with tears falling from her eyes.

RUSSIAN HIT NUMBER TWO

"To tell you the truth I was shame!"
I hand the papers back to her saying, "come here with my arms out to hug her.
I said, "don't worry about nothing I'll take care of it, okay."
She said with tears running down her face, "thank you so much. I'll baby sit for you for nothing if you're going to do this for me."
"What come the fuck on with that! I'll be right back." Looking her right in her eyes filled with tears. I quickly go in my bedroom and go in my stash in the top of my dresser drawer and I pull out a few stacks. I came back in the room and handed it to her and said, "here take that, okay that's just couple stacks and I'll have your house paid off in the morning. I'll send La- Neesa to take care of it okay, auntie, trust me. Look I have to go." I kissed her on the cheek and reminded her, "your family and don't you ever forget that shit, you hear!"
She looked up at me and said, "God bless you, Almasi!" She's wiping the tears from her round brown pretty face that's filled with so much wisdom.
"I hope so Auntie look I really have to see you in the morning. I'll have that business taken care of for you, okay!" I went over and kissed my boy in his crib and waved at Auntie with a big smile. She smiled back at me saying "Okay, you be careful you here and I want you to keep an eye on Tamika's man, Mark."
"What did you say? I said keep an eye on Tamika's man."
"He ain't her man. I can tell he's a fucking cop or something that was the deep part I was talking about baby. "Oh, Really Auntie, tell me some more when I get back okay, I have to go."
I walked out to the deck waving to Dun-Dun, "I need to holla at you." I walked him back to my bedroom and I close the door behind me. He stood there asking, "what's up now?"
"Look Auntie just told me about Tamika's man Mark she said she thinks he's a cop."
"See I told you we just might have to dust her fucking coat. I know it's a real sticky situation but were going have to find some way to take care of her ass."

"I know I'll get Damon Gee to really dig in really deep and find out before we make that move on her ass all right?"
"Sure, I'm wit that but he can't take too long finding out if she's working with the cops before they fuck up everything, we fucking built."
"Yeah, you're right and we both going have to have proof so Blue and Shamika don't flip on us. Yeah but no matter how it goes one of them is going to be upset because their family." "Yeah, your right but were all family."
"True that! Let's go take care of this business and you and me can talk about this later."

We both bump fist as I opened the door and we walked back out to my deck where everybody is ready to roll out. I'm thinking to myself this is something that is really fucked up and it just might break up our friendships. We all built up over the years were all really close. Yet, one thing I know is blood is thicker than mud and one wrong move and everything can go down the fucking drain. If I tell Spider about this before Damon Gee get that information, he'll have her killed at the Drop of a hat. I really have to tiptoe around this shit for real. We both walked out on the deck looking everybody in the face and I said, "alright let's go, y'all."
All of us rolled out the front door going to the parking lot where Tony Smokes hooked up two work vans. Dun-Dun got behind the wheel of the dark blue work van I'm riding shot gun and Big Monk in the cargo area. Blue drives the white work van with Taye riding on the passenger side there going to drop her off right quick with Mookie and Tony Smokes riding in the cargo area. They drop off Taye first at her mother's house in North Philly we drive to an old abandon factory near front and Erie. Soon as we got their Booby Hill, Ty-Kim, Chrome, Nails Nathen and Willie Wack-Wack is there waiting outside for us we all go inside, and we sit around with two gas lamps. They took out the work vans like were in the fucking woods or something so we can see one another and its cold in there too. Were all sitting on these old boxes and milkcrates in the back the whole place smell like funky ass trash and garbage mixed with fucking cat piss, but we all put up with it while everybody is gathered around me as I run it down to my crew.

"The Russians have three bodyguards in the back of the hotel. Nails and Willie. You two will take care of them nice, smooth and quiet-like. Now in the front they have two bodyguards, Ty-Kim and you. Chrome will take care of them two the same way while me Dun-Dun, Jagger and Big Monk go up to the room and wait on the call from one of the girls. Damon Gee made sure they were paid really good to do this. Tony you take care of all the cameras and the alarms doors the whole nine and come pick us up after we smoke their ass. Mookie and Blue y'all get the girls out of there as fast as you can it will be a limo in the back unlocked. Damon will have there with the keys under the floor mats to get them out of there. Everybody got it!"

Everybody nodded their head yes.

"Okay, let's get the fuck out of here this place really stinks!" Everybody started laughing as Dun-Dun and Big Monk grabbed. The lamps leading everybody out there once we got to the door, they turned the lamps off, and everybody carefully went to their vans and cars. As we all take off in the darkness driving in different directions of the concrete jungle that moves and flow like a living organism.

An hour and a half later were all in position in Maple Shade, New Jersey at the luxury hotel call The Loft. It's 2 A.M., a cool breezy morning and the number two Russian mobster Ivan Poppv and his top lieutenant Yulian Lagunov are there in the VIP suite on the fifth floor with three sexy young women. High price thousand dollar a night prostitutes Butterfly, Dedra and TaJae'. Two white girls and one black they all look like they're worth the kind of loot they be asking for the night plus tips. Things are getting hot and heavy with the Red Fellas getting their shit off snorting a shit load of cocaine in giant piles on the tables and off of the hooker's ass and fake titties sucking and fucking their brains out.

While were sitting in a really nice room right across the hall from them dressed in all black ready to make our move on their ass. We are all set with our machine guns with silencers on the tips and have earpieces, radio's so we all can be in communication with one another. Where all on channel one what I call being on one page before motherfuckers get sprayed. The boys love when I say it, they get a fucking kick out of it when I spit it to them. They start giggling their ass off, but we all know this is not a fucking game just some sick twisted humor before putting in this work.

Now soon as we get the call, we all have from TaJae' all the other girls are paid off as well to go along with the plan. We wait another hour to use it seem like five hours but were all pros at this shit so we wait patiently until we unleash hell on these motherfuckers, and they will never know what fucking hit them.

3:10 A.M. TaJae' make the call for some champagne but she's not calling room service she's calling Tony Smokes he hacked into the hotel's computer system. He makes the switch of the image on the fifth floor and he calls Nails Nathen and Willie Wack-Wack said, **"Wakati wa kuwaweka usingizi** (Time to put them to sleep.)"

Nail Nathen said, **"Unaijua** (*You know it!*)"

Nails Nathen and Willie Wack-Wack is dressed in all black creep up on the first two bodyguards Yuriy in a black BMW and Vladimir in a dark blue Cadillac Escalade Nails Nathen swift and silent come up on the driver side of Yuriy's Black BMW. He has earphones on listening to hip hop music Masta Ace sitting on Chrome. Nail Nathen with a silencer on the end of his pistol he points and aim slowly. Poouufff! Poouufff !Poouufff!

Putting two in his head and one in his chest at the same time Willie Wack-Wack is getting busy he slips up on the back of the Cadillac Escalade Vladimir is drinking coffee trying to stay woke on post to keep his eyes open after partying all day. It's kind of fucking hard for him Willie Wack- Wack taking aim at the same time as Nail's Poouufff! Poouufff! putting two in the back of his head soon as he seen him slump forward Willie talking in his earpiece and we all can hear them yell, **"Tayari kwa ndugu hii mwisho** *(You ready for this last, one brother?)"* Nails Nathen replied,

"Hebu kupata show hii kwenye barabara *(Let's get this show on the road!)"*

They both creep up on the last body guard Mikhail sitting in a black Benz about twenty feet from where the other two bodyguard were parked at staying low Nails Nathen saying to Willie were going on **Tatu**(*Three).* Willie Wack-Wack saying fast **Wakati wa kupungua** Slumping time! **Unaijua** You know it! They quickly reach the black Benz Nails Nathen on the right Willie Wack-Wack on the left, Nails say **Moja**(One), **Mbili** (Two), **Tatu**(Three)! They both stand up at the same time shooting into the car Poouuff-Poouuff! Poouuff- Poouuff!

Willie hitting Vladimir in the neck and mouth. Nathen hitting him in the head and eye soon as they seen he was dead they both say at the same time to Ty-Kim and Chrome **Nenda**(Go!)

Ty-Kim quickly jump out the white work van Ty-Kim swiftly came up on Pavel in a light green BMW Wagon he's half sleep and at the same time Chrome is creeping up on Damir in a blue Audi with a local black prostitute name Quansha Damir wanting to get his shit off just like the boss's up in the hotel. She's sucking his Dick really good and he not looking out on post he's just pushing the back of her head on to his rock-hard trouser snake while she's doing him well mumbling crazy shit to her in Russian.

Ty-Kim is closer to the Pavel's BMW in the dark he takes aim on his target Pooouufff! Pooouuufff!

Hitting Pavel twice in the middle of his head the blood squirts all up on the window as his lifeless body is leaning back in the black leather seat with the white smoke floating out of his skull.

Simultaneously Chrome come up on Damir leaning his head back while Quansha is giving him a million-dollar blow job for 50 bucks. Chrome knows he has to kill her as well saying to his self well this bitch is going have to die with a Dick in her mouth Pooouufff! Pooouuufff! Pooouuufff!

Hitting him twice in the chest and once in the head when the glass fell down and rained down on the top of her head, she looked with her eyes getting real wide in shock seeing the blood running down Damir chest and head she went to scream before she could have got out a sound Pooouuufff! Pooouuufff! Chrome hitting her in the middle of her head and when her head went down, he hit her in the top of her head and her wig flu off seeing her nappy ass head with blood gushing out.

He just smiled thinking to himself that bitch stop sucking that Dick when she seen that blood shooting out giggling to himself. With Chrome saying to us in the ear pieces, Nenda Ndugu Na Dada(Go brothers and sisters) so were up next. I stood up and looked at Jagger, Dun-Dun and Big Monk.
I quickly opening the door with Dun-Dun right behind me and Big Monk Jagger walk across the hall I posted up on the right holding my machine gun Dun-Dun post up on the wall near the door on the left with his weapon and Big Monk standing in front of the door. Jagger bending down behind him Big Monk putting his large hand over the peekhole but Tajae' came to the door saying, "hey baby, that's the champagne laying on the bed saying yes go get it. I want to pour it on my dick, and you suck it off with some cocaine!"
In his thick Russian accent Taja'e said," I'm down with that honey but you're going to have to tip me a little more. Ivan you're some kind of freaky daddy!"
Ivan laughed, "yes, I am baby!" They all started laughing louder it sounded really funny to all the girls with his heavy Russian accent. She puts on her housecoat from out her overnight bag on the chair winking her eye at him real sexy he quickly grabbing her hand with his big hairy ass hands of his said, "I want to put cocaine on my balls and I tea bag you baby. You wash it down with champagne you down with that baby? I pay you extra!"
"You have to pay me extra any way, Ivan baby for that freaky shit but if you're paying extra, I'll take care of you. Let me go get this champagne to pour on your big Dick daddy, okay!" They all started snickering she act like she's looking out the peek hole she opened the door and Big Monk quickly hands her the hotel key to our room right across the hall as she walks fleet-footed to the room opening the door as Big Monk gets in his gun stance with his machine gun walking forwards with Dun-Dun right behind him on the left and me on the right and Jagger right by my side. Soon as they see us there all in shock Big Monk yelling, "don't fucking move and put your hands up in the air or I'll kill you where you stand at!" Ivan and Yulian are upset but they put their Hand up in the air and Yulian is yelling saying in Russian, **"Vse vy mertv(***You all are dead!)"*
Big Monk yelled back at him,

"Net, vy budete cherez neskol'ko minut) No you will be in a few minutes!" Both men are in shock that this big black man understand and can speak Russian. I quickly yelled to the two-white girls Butterfly and Dedra, "get something to cover yourself up and move your ass right fucking now!" Both of them started moving swift grabbing something and running out the door as Taja'e is standing in the doorway across the hall waving them in and quickly closing the door. Soon as they left, we all get ready to smoke their ass staying in our gun stance with our machine guns.
Ivan stood up off the bed yelling in Russian, **"Trakhat Tebya**(Fuck You!)"
Big Monk yelled back, **"Trakhat Tebya Tykrasnyy otmorozok** (Fuck you, you red scum bag!")
As I nod my head at Dun-Dun, Jagger and Big Monk we all open fire on the two men Pooouufff!
Poooffff! Poooffff! Poooffff! hitting them all over every part of their body ripping them apart with blood flying in the air hitting the walls, the bed and all over the furniture in this very nice luxury hotel suite. We just painted it with a fresh coat of blood and human flesh.
While we were smoking the two Red Fellas Mookie came up to the fifth floor rushing the girls out of the room to the back door exit with the quickness. Blue was waiting behind the wheel of the long white Lincoln limo Mookie got all three of them down the steps and inside of the limo taking off from the parking lot and out to the street flying up the road.
We were right behind them running down the back-exit door soon as we reach the bottom of the stairwell and opened the exit door. Tony came speeding up in the back of the parking lot swift smooth and silently. We jumped in the large white Benz work van right after Big Monk getting in last banging the side of the van letting Tony Smokes know were all inside. He took off up the dark road I put my machine gun on the van floor in front of me and I took off my black mask and I looked up at Big Monk I asked, "I did not know you knew how to speak Russian, nigga?"
"You never ask!"
"Wow where did you learn to speak Russian?"
"Shit, Almasi to make a long ass story short I learned that shit in the Navy I was a navy seal."

Dun-Dun said, "man talking about not knowing a motherfucker you thought you knew all these years!"

I said, "you can say that the fuck again!" We all started laughing all the way back to Philly and me and Dun-Dun broke his balls the whole time.

But we all went home we did not party like we normally do after a big hit I guess were all too grown for that shit by the time I got back in the door at home. It was five O' clock in the morning I went to check on Tanya to see if her little fast ass was still in the house. She was in the back room sleep now if she was not in that back room, I would have gone and tracked her down to kick her little light skin ass again. I went to see about my baby boy Little Boom he was sleep in his crib I'd lean over and kissed him and I looked up over at aunt La'Wanda sleep on the bed she got up after I kissed Little Boom with her saying really low are you all right?

"Yes, I'm good I'm going to get some sleep so we can take care of that business okay aunt-Tee."

"Okay baby." in a real groggy voice and she rolled over going back to sleep. I just smiled turning the lights out and went to my bedroom taking off all my clothes and I'd flop down right on the bed.

I was fucking exhausted. The next morning, I got up around 11 O'clock what woke me up was smelling the food Aunt-Tee was cooking the aroma was banging. I quickly went to the bathroom and washed up and got dressed. The first thing I did was called La-Neesa and I told her to buy my aunt La'Wanda a new house in West Oak Lane. I gave her the account numbers to pay for it and after she got that done to come past my condo, pick her up and show her the new house and give her all the paperwork to it as well. She said, "no problem she can get that done today. I replied," Good."

I hung up with her and came in the kitchen and said, "damn, Auntie you got it going on up in this joint!" She blushed and said, "I sure do. Are you ready to eat, baby?"

I used Dun-Dun's line is water wet?"

"It's sure the hell is girl sit your smart ass down and get your grub on alright!" We both laughed as I sat down and ate eggs, beef bacon, and grits with some sweet rolls. I had my favorite drink a big glass of iced tea. I said to her while I'm throwing down eating, "damn, Auntie, this is really good. "Look Auntie, I need you to stay a few more nights I have to go out and check some things out."

"Sure baby, you know I'm here for you. All my kids are grown, and you already know my man Ronny dumb ass is still locked up so, I can stay!"

We both laughed as Jagger came in the door and said, "man, it smells really good up in here."

"What's up ladies, good morning?"

Aunt La'Wanda said, "hey baby, let me make you a plate."

"Please do, Auntie, I'm hungrier than three dogs for real!" He sits down with big smile on his dark brown face as me and Auntie is giggling only thing, I can think is running into that fine ass hunk of a man. All I have to do is accidentally run into him at the bar he hangs out. Damon told me about I might have to beat a few chippies away from him because that nigga is fine. I hope he can fuck as good as he looks because its been a while for me now that me and Big Boom is on the outs. I can go get me some, too.

I'm daydreaming a little bit at the table as my auntie and Jagger are jaw flapping and bullshitting with one another. My phone ringing and I knew it was work when I saw that number on the caller id. I knew it was Spider I quickly get it and just like I said when I hear that deep as voice like he smoked ten packs of cigarettes.

"Yo, what's up, Shorty?"

"Nothing, just eating some of Auntie's good ass cooking that's all what's up wit you, big man?"

"Well I know I been working the shit out of you, but I need you to meet me at the scrap yard in about an hour we have some our New York peoples coming up to holla at us **Moja** (One!)"

"**Moja** (One!)" Well there goes my plans of getting some strange dick from some fine black motherfucker!

"Who was that Almasi?"

"Spider! He wants us at the scrap yard in an hour so soon as your done we have to roll out, okay."

"Sure thing, sis this grub is off the hook. Hey, Auntie you can come over anytime and hook a nigga up!"

"Why thank you, Jagger let me go in here and get the baby and feed him too Now that my bubble is burst about getting some I sit and wait on Jagger while he's busting a grub my aunt- Tee bring my baby boy boom and he wants to jump out of her arms right into mine. I grab him with that smile that just light up my life every time. I'm kissing him then I put him in the highchair while still playing with him with them cute chunky cheeks of his while aunt-Tee is giggling. Coming up to him with his food she started feeding him this give me my time to slip out of the door right quick before he starts crying. Jagger was done eating and he knew what time it was too smiling getting up out of his seat heading towards the front door. I spoke low to Auntie, "let me know if that girl Tanya left."

Auntie winks her eye at me, and I'd wave at her and flew out the door. Jagger held the door open for me, but I double check to make sure I had my gun in my pocketbook. I made sure the clip is in really good with Jagger smiling at me saying, "you have a name for yours?"

"Yeah Kesha! From New Jack City?"

"Yeah, she's the only black gangster bitch other then Queen Latifah in set it off." We both just giggled and stepped fast to my whip in the parking lot area of my condo.

It took us less then a half an hour to get to the scrapyard. Jagger parked in the back of a large stack of old cars, so nobody knows were even in there. We get out and walk through the stacks and long rows of old car ready to be scrapped.

CHILL OUT I'M TRYING TO GET SOME

We both walked up to the brick shack on the right-hand side of this big ass yard that smell like dog shit and cat piss mixed together. When a bad smell is in the air it lingers around, and you can't get it out of your fucking nose for real. Jagger bang on the door really hard on the thick steel gray door with rust and graffiti covering it after a few the door swings open. It's Ty-Kim he quickly hugs both of us and said, "family."

I smiled and looked up along with Goliath he looked me right in my eyes and said, "hey, Boss Lady."

"Hey, what's up, big man? So, you're in the yard holding it down right?"

"Sure nuff, boss lady."

Ty-Kim said, "Almasi everybody is at the **Meza** (Table.)" Walk them to the room tell Booby to come up Goliath I looked at Ty-Kim announced, "before I step off **Ni jinsi gani anafanya kazinje.**"

"How is he working out? **Nzuri(**Good!)So far!"

"**Sauti Nzuri**(Sounds good)."

"Right then and there I got a flash back of Fat Jerome."

I miss my homey he was always at the door holding it down for us and that nigga loved my cooking when he came to my crib. As me and Jagger step off really towards the war room on the left-hand side of this dark dim brick room. The three of us stroll to the thick brown wooden door Booby Hill is on post. He steps out from behind the doors with a cigarette cocked on the side of his thick lips smiling. he bumps both our fist saying **Ndugu**(Brother!)Da Da!(Sister!) I say to him he's **Mtu mbaya**(Bad Man!) He smiles with Goliath uttering what did she just say?

I looked him in the face talking low I'd said Bad man now **Fanya kaziyako(Go do your job!)** Booby say she said go do your job nigga! Goliath okay Ty-Kim said come up! Waving his large black hands with his hard-dark game face on doing his job on look out. Booby lets go then as me and Jagger walked in the smoky large room with everybody sitting at the large long table Damon Gee, Brenton, Ayden, Philly his two men Fat Hector and Black Leon is standing up behind him Rah-Killer, Gill, Gino Gats, Chrome, Bulls Eyes, Puerto Rican Joe, Knock Daddy, Black Leroy and his crew standing up behind him Fat Lou-Lou and Gavin. Spider sitting at the head of the table with a cigarette cocked in his thick lips blowing out smoke with his eyes on everybody in the room leaning back.

He is chilling with a big ash tray filled with blunt leaves and cigarette butts, two guns in front of him on top of the table sitting to his left is a nigga. I don't know I quickly walked up to him bumping fist with him he stands up and the nigga next to him with Spider, "this is Almasi"

"Almasi, this is Black Scooch from New York and his number two Big Nizzy I say to my self-dam that's a real big nigga!"

They both bump fist with me while we sat down really quick with Spider looking up and down at the table loud,

"Now is everybody here?"

Philly saying, "no Jane Doe is not here"

Spider said, "so, where the fuck is, she at? I don't have all day with her bullshit!" Damon Gee Looking over at Spider who said, "she down with Jasper so you won't see her here and they also hooked up with the 3rd street mob boys to add some more muscle and transportation."

Everybody is looking at each other with that strange look on their grill I would never forget this shit as long as I live. I'm thinking to myself this nigga is making moves like that he won't be that easy to take down because we all know that the 3rd street mob boys are no fucking joke and their all hooked up with the Colombians. They are well organized we even tried to get them to hook up with us, but they turned us down because we did some hits for some of their rivals. "You sure about that Damon?"

"You know if I tell you something Spider its gold you should know that by now."

Spider smirked and agree, "you're right Ndugu (Brother). Well, anyhow our New York brothers are here so they can help us with our move into Jersey and B-More. Buck Shot you're going to D.C. With Brenton. He just looked up and nodded his head with his cigarette hanging from his fat dark lips. Spider phone rang he puts it up to his ear just nodding his head then he quickly cuts it off and said,

"Yo Rah, Knock Daddy and Bulls Eyes go to the back and get that thing from Nails and Willie. Put it in the truck for Fly-Ty for me please." Rah- Killer Bulls Eyes and Knock Daddy get up from the table walking towards the door soon as they walked outside the room Spider just looked at me with that wicked grin and I knew what was up.

The three of them walking towards the back door on the left-hand side of the brick shack soon as they got to the back door Knock Daddy quickly pushed the door Open with Bulls Eyes and Rah-Killer walking behind the two of them walking up from out the darkness is Fly-Ty who said, "over here motherfuckers hurry up I got to get up out of here!"

The two men quickly walked towards Fly Ty with the trunk open of the old beat up Ford truck on the right popping up out the dark on the left is Nails Nathen and Willie Wack-Wack both of them with guns in their hands pointing towards the two men with shock expressions on their grills knowing right at this moment they were set the fuck up to get smoked.

Rah-Killer has out her pistol out on the two of them standing behind Knock Daddy and Bulls Eyes taking aim she screamed, to the two traders, "Yo, you two cock suckers are dead for selling out Petey Q!"

Fly-Ty in a split second with no hesitation shoots Knock Daddy in the side of the head from the right Kapacka!

Blood shooting out of his head falling to the ground. Rah-Killer Nails Nathen and Willie Wack-Wack shoot both of them Patka! Kaboom! Packa! Pat!

With all of the, shooting at the same time their airing them out hitting them in every part of their bodies like it was target practice. Rah-Killer blasted both of them in the back of their heads with blood gushing out the large holes in the back of their domes. Their lifeless bloody bodies falling to the ground swiftly making a loud thumping sound then Rah- Killer looking down at both of the dead men in a large pool of blood.

She pulled out her phone and called Spider he picks up on the first ring. Rah-Killer said, "**Kutenda Wake** (Its Done!)"

"**Nzuri**(Good!) Come on back so we can drink on it!"

"**Ndiyo!**(Yeah!)"

Nails Nathen, Fly Ty and Willie Wack-Wack began laughing Fly Ty pulls out his phone calling Goliath he picks up after three rings, "Yo bring your big ass back here I got some work for you to do, nigga!" Willie Wack-Wack, Nails Nathen and Rah-Killer started to giggle we heard the gun shots while we were all sitting there. They double cross Petey Q to be down with Jasper and paid with their life I know Jane Doe ass is next. An hour later they walked back in the room where we are all sitting soon as they came in the room and sat down Spider said,

"for those who don't know what just happen we just had to take care of Knock Daddy and Bulls Eyes!"

He looked over at Puerto Rican Joe and said, "Joe, I'm glad I did not here about you being down with that funky ass shit or you would have joined them. We heard the news on Tommy Machete he's still in a motherfucking coma."

"I know and I'm glad you know I was not down with that foul shit. We family!" Spider got up out his chair and went and hugged him and said, "my nigga!"

As they both laughed with Spider he said, "yo Fly-Ty, go get one of them niggas to help you bring that yak and weed so we all can smoke and drink to this shit. Those niggas sold my brother out and thought I would not find out about them!"

"You got it Spider!" He went and got Ty-Kim so they could pick up the beer, Henny and Weed. Spider talked business and making sure everyone got their money with the New York niggas. He told all of us what he wanted us to do. Me, myself I don't care how long the meeting goes just as long as I got my paper right. Now that I'm getting more of it, I have to do a hell of a lot more too. By the time he was done working shit out we did not know it was dark outside. Fly-Ty asked Spider, "are we going to the warehouse after this?" Spider looking at his watch and said, "Yeah, it's 9 o'clock I was waiting until it got dark for them to get rid of the bodies. I know he'll get Ty-Kim, Rah-Killer Fly-Ty, Nails Nathen, Willie Wack-Wack and Goliath to chop them up and put them in big construction trash bags. Then drop some of the bags in the Schuylkill river and the city dump.

Spider said, "y'all need to go take care that thing right about now its dark outside now. Yo Leroy get some of your boys to give them a hand for me." They all just nodded their heads yes. Spider said, "Well on that note this meeting is over we going to the warehouse to get our drink and puff on and show these New York niggas how we party!"

All of us started getting up walking towards the door the whole room is filled with smoke and loud chatter. I looked up and seen Black Scooch checking me out then walking out the door with his big ass bodyguard on his back. I'm walking with Spider I whisper and asked, "what's that nigga's story?"

"Well his wife and kids were killed by this local drug crew called the Wild Boys from the Bronx he got all of them niggas back when he linked up with us. As you know we gave them a hand airing them niggas out. Leroy crew took care of that shit for some territory to pump our product and they turned out to be some really good partners."

I was thinking to myself Black Scooch seem like he's on the up and up, but his number two man looks really shaky to me for real. I have a bad feeling about that nigga, and I don't know why. Me and Jagger quickly walked to our whips outside walking through the stacks of old cars in the dark. We jump in and Jagger head towards the expressway with the dull yellow lights going by like a blur it took us less then a half an hour as we arrived at the luxury warehouse. We all are sitting at the long fancy ass wooden bar. Jagger is sitting on my right with Fly Ty right behind him on my left is Rah-Killer.

She yelled at the bar tender name Ronelle,

"Yo Ronelle bring that fat fine ass over here and give me another fucking beer!" She quickly turns to her and replied, "Hold on, Rah. I will be right with you."

She looked right at her ass mumbling, "she lucky were in here I would have reached over grabbed that fat ass!" I just laughed when Black Scooch came and lean on the bar beside me real smooth with his fine black ass smiling holding two Heineken beers.

He said, "somebody told me you like Heineken."

"Well somebody told you right, brother." He hands me the beer now he got closer thinking to myself I'm really checking this nigga out from head to toe, and So far, everything is looking really fucking good from here I must say.

"So where is your back up?"

"I told him to go socialize a little like I'm doing right now so why do I need back up for you?"

"You better have some back up for me, nigga if you want to keep your dome on your fucking shoulders."

"Wow your funny where you from Almasi?"

"South Philly what about you where you from?"

"Harlem, USA but I live in the Bronx now."

"Okay then **Mchezaji** (Player!) What did you just say to me?"

I replied, "okay then player."

"Look, I'm down with y'all but I don't know all that Swahili shit y'all be spitting."

"Well you better learn then **Ndugu**(*Brother*)that means brother and you need to learn fast around me."

I wink my eye at him he started laughing looking me up and down. I know he's lusting after my body and I'm doing the same thing to him. I giggled, but I can see in his eyes he done seen and done a lot but there is something really deep about him. I want to find out more about him for real. Jagger got up out of his seat and stood over Black Scooch and asked, "you all right, Almasi?"

"Yeah, I'm just fine Jagger **Ondoka Nje Ninajaribu kupata baadhi** *(Chill out I'm trying to get some)."*

Black Scooch smiled and asked, "what you just say to him?" I replied and I just smiled.

"I can't tell you that, but you already know by the way you're looking at me." Jagger chuckled, **"Sawa Na ufikie** *(Okay then get to it!)"*

"So, I guest you're not going to tell me what he said too right?"

"No, he said okay then get to it."

"So, is there some where you and I can go to talk?"

"Sure, but I don't think we're going to do too much talking doe."

He smirked and said, "you really get right to the point." "Well, I know what I want when I want it you know what I'm saying."

"Oh, I'm feeling you on that, baby girl."

I'm thinking to myself that's not the only thing I want. This fine black motherfucker to be feeling for real. I feel good about this right here this is the first time I'm letting myself go and be sexual with a man. I don't know if I'm really horny or just really confident of myself or both. I said to him, "hold on let me get us something to set the mood up for us so things can really get hot up in this motherfucker.

"Okay Harry handsome." He laughed burst out in laughter as I quickly called Ronelle over to me from behind the bar.,

"Yo, give me three bottles of. cold Cristal Champagne, baby girl and a big bag of **Pigo**(*Blow).*I'm going have me a real party! She just giggled saying coming right up looking over at him smiling.

He leans over to me real close and asked, "what the fuck is Pigo?"

"It's blow you know coke. I'm going to put some on my titties and let you lick it off my nipples if you know how to act handsome." He rubbed his hand together, and licked his lips, "oh, I know how to act baby trust me, Miss dark and Sexy."

I giggled as I am still sizing his ass up, he looks like he got a nice package down there. I'm going see if he knows how to work that motherfucker.

After a few minutes Ronelle came and sat the three cold bottles of Cristal on top of the bar and then she said, "here you go, Almasi. She handed me a big zip lock bag of cocaine I put it in my pocketbook and pulled it up on my shoulder. I turned to him and said, "you ready now?"

"Oh yeah, let's go baby and have that talk." I winked at him. I'd took him by the hands holding one bottle of champagne and he picked up the other two. I pulled him down the long large hallway towards the room on the right-hand side of this giant ass Luxurious apartment. Soon as I open the door and he walked in he was impressed.

"Gawd damn, is this yours?

"No, this belong to the whole gang so lean back and relax nigga. Have a seat." He sat down on the bed looking up at me with them sexy brown eyes of his. I stand in front of him and said,

"I hope you ate your Wheaties as I sat the coke and champagne on top of the large nightstand by the king size bed. You are about to be in for the ride of your life, nigga. It's been a long while for me for real."

"Me too it's been a while for me as well."

"What for real you're not just saying that shit I'm still going to give you some pussy over here, so you don't have to front now nigga. I looked him right in his face. No, I'm telling you the truth, Almasi.

"All them Hoes out here want is a few dollars to suck my Dick to get their cash flow up and get the bag. I'm not with that shit because that just shows me there about money for sex there not into me. So, I don't fuck wit them like that maybe when I was younger but not now bitches like that is a dime a dozen." If they willing to suck Dick or fuck a nigga for a few dollars ain't no telling who else, they will fuck or suck off you know what I'm saying. I need a ride or die bitch like what I lost not a bitch who suck any old nigga Dick in the game type of bitch."

I knew I was right about this nigga the eyes never lie.

"Oh yeah, well I get to turn your gangster ass out, then right?" He started laughing then I just stood in front of him taking off my clothing slow, sexy and seductive looking down on this super-hot black man while he was rubbing on my ass and feeling me up really good. I was getting hot this nigga has some big ass hands and I'm helping him take his shit off when I took his jeans down all I can see is his hard-On popping up out his black and red boxer shorts. All I can think of is I can't wait until he rammed that motherfucker up in me and make me cum until I passed the fuck out. When he got down to my matching red lace bra and panties his eyes got wider rubbing on the inside of my legs and I pushed my breast into his fine dark grill as he started pulling down my bra licking my nipples. He quickly went down on me he did it so fast it just about took my breath away. Wow that's what the fuck I'm talking about and started licking on the inside of my pussy pulling the panties to the side of my legs. I quickly reach over to the nightstand and popped the bottle of champagne.

I started drinking some while he was licking me out. I was pumping my snatch in his fine dark face as he got both his hands on my ass eating me out like a fucking world champion. Shit, I even put my leg up on the bed and I'd spread my big legs a little wider to make it better for him to get all the way up in there. This nigga really knows how to eat some Coochie, too! He was sucking right on my clit I have thrill bumps running up and down my back slowly pumping it to him working my hips flowing like waves in an ocean smooth and steady. Oooh this feels so amazing I just don't want to cum to fast! I pour some champagne down there and let him lick it with some champagne flavor. This nigga was lapping it up too with his long fat tongue of his and he's getting all the way up in there making that loud sucking and slurping sound and that's turning me on even more. I'm drinking champagne in one hand and holding the back of his head with my other hand the shit is feeling really good but I'm down for the main event. I want this nigga to Dick me down and make my shit real creamy.

So, I quickly pull away from him giggling looking him right in his eyes with his chin dripping with champagne. My pussy juice running down the side of his dark debonair face. I can see this nigga was ready to go with fire in his eyes raging with lust and that I'm about to fuck the shit out you look on that gorgeous black mug of his fill with wild cum boiling anticipation. I can see his Dick shot up out his boxer shorts.

I'm said to myself there is that black motherfucker come say hi to mommy's hot wet kitty and I turn around putting both my hands on the end of the bed. Nice, slow and sexy putting my juicy black ass up in the air for him to hit it from the back pulling my red panties all the way down to the floor. I don't have to see his face but know this will really get this niggas attention. What to do next and let his next move be his best move. He came up behind me I looked back and damn this nigga is holding a hand full of fucking meat pointing right at my wet coochie waiting. I braced myself for impact he's poking around for a few. I reach back with my right hand to give this nigga a hand and he slide it in nice and slow. Wooooppp!

Gawd dam I can feel the head of his Dick is like a helmet on a fucking soldier ready to go to war. He took his time and then boom he got it all the way up in me and I grunt while he's pumping slow and then he started going faster like a train on a track. The smacking sound of our hot flesh have a sizzling rhythm to it and I'm saying to myself, "Oh yesssss!"

I'm pushing back on his thick black love rod and now we have a super-hot groove going on and the shit is really feeling good now. This is how you start a motherfucking fire from the door this what I was waiting for him to knock this shit out the park and yell his name out loud while he's going to work on my wet hot pussy. The more he stroked my wet Kitty with his large hands on my hips pulling me hard now this nigga is hitting my spot really good too. This nigga knows how to throw that Dick I can't front on him he got me talking in tongues right about now and were both feeling each other. Then he started smacking me on my ass at the same time and I'm loving it. I felt that volcanic sensation and I squirt my whole head gets light, but I feel like I just got shot out of a fucking cannon hitting the stars as he's still pumping me like a fuck doll.

I keep pushing back on his tube steak harder I know after a while his ass will let it go it feels to fucking good until I can feel his hot nut shooting up in me. Shit, it about time I can hear him yelling, shaking like twig in a hurricane. He pulls out fall on top of the bed covered in sweat laying on his back. I lean over and kissed him with him saying, "I'm out of breath. Oh, baby that was good!

"I know that was just round one, so you better rest up for round two Mister sweet Dick." He started laughing I lean over and get my pocketbook getting my pack

Of Newports. I light two cigarettes this nigga is falling asleep. I pushed him hard with a big smile on my face to wake him up. He sits up and he takes the cigarette out of my hand I'm puffing hard, but I pull out the coke. I dumped some of it out on top of the smooth surface. I put the rest of it back in my bag I pull out an old business card using it to shuffle up the white powder and I make four lines. I rolled up a hundred-dollar bill and I snort up the two lines real fast. I pushed him so he can get up and get some of the coke to snort. He sits up on the side of the bed next to me.

I hand him the hundred dollars bill he bends over and snort the other two lines of white powder I looked him in his face, and I see his eyes get wide. I knew he was ready to get that sweet big black Dick back up for another hot fuck. All I want to do is cum about three more time and I'll call it a night. We do some more freaky shit I put some coke on my titties and let him lick it off like I promise him. I also mixed it with champagne, and I put it on my pussy lips as well. He loves the way my pussy taste with coke and a lot of Louis Roederer with my Coochie. I have his black ass whipped before the night is over for sure.

Shit round two was just as good as round one now I know this nigga know how to work it. We kick the Willie Boo-Boo for another hour or so, smoke a couple blunts and snorted a lot blow. This nigga still did not get enough but I have to go plus I'm sore and I came about six times. I rolled over on the bed and said, "hey baby I have to go the next time you're in town look me up, okay."

"I have to take a shower baby-boo."

"It's a shower in here?"

"Shit, this bathroom in here is as big as some people's apartment." I get up and I get new panties and bra out of the dresser drawer, a wash rag and two towels. He follows me to see the bathroom on the left-hand side of the room. He walks in there looks and said, "your right can I join you in the shower?"

"Sure, come on after that I really have to go to go get my son, baby." Tears form in his eyes and he lower his head, I use to have kids, but some motherfucker killed them along with my wife. I act like I did not hear the story. I hugged him and said, "why don't you tell me about it?"

"I want to buy then my Dick won't get hard. All I want to think about is your super-hot snapper right now."

"Look, it won't be like this will be a one-night stand or something that's up to you. We had fun and I want to see you again. I like that baby he leaned in and kissed me, Will you come to New York with me one time, baby?"

"Yes, I'll come to New York and fuck your brains out again baby just as long as you keep that big black sweet Dick hard for me and we can paint the fucking town red if you want?"

"Good, then we will do just that. I took my towel off I had wrapped around me while were both kissing, and he pens me on the wall. I turned the water on and we both jumped in feeling each other up. We really got it on inside of the large shower and he made me cum again. This time I think I'm going to hit the fucking ceiling. He hit it from the back-doggy style then we both washed one another off after we both got our shit off. We got dressed I'm nice and high now and I'm floating on air after cumming seven times. I wish I had more time it would have been more after we got dress, I gave him my number and he gave me his too. I said to him your going has to tell me that story about your family the next time we get together.

He Kissed me and said, "I will baby." I called Jagger and told him I'm ready to go. Jagger said he's getting busy as well he just finishing up with the two hoes he had. He'll be right with me after he wash his Dick off. I told him that was Too much information for me and we both laughed after a little while.

He called me back and said, "he was in the parking lot in the whip." I walked up to Black Scooch and asked, "how long are you in town?"

"For another week."

I replied, "good now you can take me out to dinner before I give you some more pussy and if you're a good boy I just might suck your big black Dick for you."

He said that sound really good to him and I kissed him. He replied, "let me walk you to your car Miss Dark and Sexy. Come on, baby." He walks with me smiling puffing on his Newport. I can see that look in his eyes that the pussy was really good to his ass. He'll be back for more of this right here for sure. Soon as I reach the car, I said to him, "now don't forget dinner, nigga and call me."

"You will be hearing from me soon take care." He opened the door for me to my Benz black wagon. He closed the door after I jumped in and Jagger pulled off nice and smooth. He stood their waving goodbye to me and I waved back smiling. It took us about a half an hour to get back home. It's the wee hours in the morning soon as we both walked in the door aunt-tee ran up to me kissing me and said, "you didn't have to do that you could have just paid off the old house."

I looked at her and asked, "so, do you like your new house or what?"

Jagger smiling giving her a high five and said, "you go girl!"

"Yes lord, I do. Your girl La-Neesa took me to go see it. I just love it thank you!"

"I'm glad you like it Auntie look I'm going to go take a nap I'm pretty tipsy right now, okay."

"Sure thing, girl go ahead and go lay down. I got the baby." I waved at Jagger as he is heading towards the front door walking out still smiling at me. I go over and kiss the baby I went to my bedroom I quickly toss my pocketbook on the chair then I flopped down on the bed. Soon as I got to the foot of my king size bed and I didn't even take my clothes off. I fall asleep I was out for some hours getting sleeping off some of my high I got back up and I looked at my clock and its 9:30 P.M.

I can hear the TV in the front room I walk, and the baby Little Boom seen me jumping right into my arms with Auntie watching the Wire she looked up at me saying you all right? I just nodding my head yes while I'm rocking the baby in my arms. She said, "good, I'm glad your all rested up."

I said, "has Jagger came back yet."

"No, he went outdoor when you went to bed and he never came back."

"Okay, did you feed Little Boom?"

"Yes, I did, and that little boy can eat, too!"

"I know Auntie he's a big boy over here!" We both started laughing and coming in the door is Jagger he walked up to me bumping fist with me asking, "you good?"

"Yeah, I'm good I had to sleep some of that off."

"I know the feeling, baby girl. I'm going to make some coffee you want some?"

"Yes, I do!"

Auntie La'Wanda said, "that sound good I want some too, baby I love when you make that French Blend stuff."

"Okay, I got you Auntie coming right up." Jagger went in the kitchen making a big pot of coffee in the coffee machine. He's on the phone talking to one his girlfriends after a few it was ready.

Jagger said to both of us while we're on the couch watching the wire said, "hey ladies, its ready to go. I pick the baby up walking in the kitchen sitting down with aunt-tee right behind me as Jagger hangs up the phone placing my big cup in front of me and Auntie cup as well pouring me some first and said, " hey, don't let the baby knock that over on you, Almasi."

Little Boom wiggling around in my arms and I said, "you're right so I put him in his highchair. Then he pours Auntie a big cup then himself. We sat around the table laughing and talking about all kinds of shit enjoying each other company. Tanya came out from the back room and joined us kicking it with us. Jagger was happy that I got in her ass and straighten her ass out really good. She told him I whip her ass she did not know I could fight that good. He laughed the whole time while she was telling him the story. Before the week when by Black Scooch call me up and took me out to dinner and I had his big black sweet Dick of his for dessert before he went back to New York. I went to New York to go see him too and were getting along really good it nothing to serious were just going out and having sex when I can see him.

A WAR WITH JASPER

Two months go by fast the first week of December X is out of the game. He went down to Miami selling boats to rich white motherfuckers and his wife Tachell open up an art gallery they both say it's all on the up and up. I know that nigga got something else going on with the gang knowing about it but I'm not a hater. So, whatever he got going on then Gawd bless him he is a good friend of mind, so I wish him all the luck in the world. Everything with me in the game is K.I.M.

Keep it moving and were really making some really good money now that we move out the fucking Russians in the New Jersey operations. The Albanians running the motels we were stashing coke and guns they are really some tough motherfuckers. We really had to go toe to toe wit their ass for real. But after we smoked about eight of them the rest of them fell in line for right now, but I don't trust their ass.

December, Friday the 7th it is two in the afternoon. Ty-Kim's trusted men working under Dun- Dun the first two men do the drop off, Antonio and Chaz at the motel 6 in Maple Shade, New Jersey then Keon and Lamont come at night. One took the guns and the other take the coke to Pleasant Beach New Jersey motel 6 that's the drug and gun route. Soon as Antonio and Chaz drop off the coke and guns in a big towel truck four mask men with guns came and took the whole shipment and then a half an hour after the men took the coke.

Antonio called Ty-Kim he yelled, "the shipment of guns and coke was jacked." Ty-Kim told both the men to stay where they are at he was on his way.

He calls Dun-Dun and then Dun-Dun calls me telling me what happen. Jagger and I were in my office at our Washington avenue warehouse when I got the call.

Dun-Dun said, **"yo Mtu alichukua usafirishaji wote**." *Somebody took the whole shipment!"*

"Mini nipo hapo *"I'll be right there!*

Sawa(Okay!)" I quickly put on my leather coat from the back of my chair and I get my lap top computer putting it under my arm telling Jagger,
"come on somebody just took the whole shipment at the motel."
"Get the fuck out of here!"
"Yeah we have to roll right now." We both quickly walked out of my office I walked up to the gangster lounge where Fly-Ty, Chrome Booby Hill and Black Duke they call him the new guy now that he's rolling with us. Blue is laying low getting himself together are all sitting around talking shit. I looked at all of them and said, "okay, it is time y'all earn your fucking pay, let's go! All of them jumped up with Fly Ty saying, "Yo, where are we are going, Almasi?" While he's checking his two Glock pistols.
"Were going to Jersey to kill a fucking trader, my good friend."
"Well, I'm really down for some shit like that!" All of them started laughing putting on their coats and checking their guns all at once. Me, Jagger get outside as we jump in my Benz wagon. I put my lap top computer in the back seat and sit down in the passenger seat as Jagger get behind the wheel and he takes off towards the expressway with my gang of thugs following behind us in two trucks Fly-Ty and Chrome in one and Booby Hill and Black Duke in the other its fucking ice station zebra outside with a wind that will blow straight up your ass with freezing you down to your bones for real. It takes us about hour to get there. Jagger pulls up in the parking lot and we both jump out right quick and I wait for the others to park soon as they park I walked up to Fly-Ty I'd taped on the window and he rolls it down really fast looking up at me I say y'all wait here until I call y'all **Sawa** *(Okay!)* **Tu niambie wakati msichana** (*Just tell me when baby girl!)*

I just smile and I turn to the other truck as he rolls his window down shouts to Chrome, **"Unasubiri hapa mpaka nitajuwta** *(You wait here until I call you.)"*

"**Nimeipata** (I got it!")

Black Duke said, "what she says?"

Chrome laughed. "She said to wait here until she calls us new dude!"

"I'm not new all right." I just laughed and I wave my hand towards Jagger as we both go in the motel office sitting there is Antonio and Chaz with the motel manager. Behind the counter Arben as I looked at him, I can tell he's pissed off. I said to him, "what's up?" He replied, "things are real fucked up. That's what's up!" I looked at the two men looking up at me, "Calm down I got this man."
"You just give us a room I can talk to these guys okay!"
"Take room 107 at the end of the hall." Jagger stepped up and took the key out of his hand and points at the two men, "come on we have to talk." I checked both of them out Antonio is really calm but other dude is real fucking nervous they walked in front of us then I see Dun-Dun and Ty-Kim pulling up in their truck getting out. I wave them over to us as were walking towards the room on the end. Jagger opens the door telling the two men to go in he walks in the room with them walking up to Dun-Dun and Ty-Kim.
Dun-Dun said, "So, what you think? One of these niggas had something to do with it that's what I think."
"So, how do you know which one of them is it?"
"Shit that's easy hold on."
I open the door, "Yo Jagger, toss me them keys!" Jagger toss the keys smiling I grabbed them midair handing them to Ty-Kim, "go in my back seat and get me my laptop for me brother."
"Sure thing, Almasi." He quickly walked to my truck getting my laptop and he hands it to me.
"Okay, let me make this quick call and I'll be right in." I made my call and I tap Dun-Dun saying, "let me show you what I did!" As we walked in the room and Ty-Kim closed the door behind himself. I walked up to both of them sitting on the bed, "Yo give me your phones, Antonio." He looked up at me and asked why you want my phone?"

Jagger pulled his gun out mashing the gun up to his head "you heard what the lady said give her your phone or I'll get the phone after we clean your brains off the fucking wall. Now give me the fucking phone!" He hands him the phone Chaz just hand over his phone looking over at everybody in the room. I take the phone from Jagger and I hook them up to my laptop and I looked at both of them and asked, "all right now I want you two to tell me right now which one of y'all made an outside call?" They both looked at me like I was crazy. Dun-Dun said, you know damn well there not going to tell you that, right?"

"See, what they both don't know is I know who phone is who. I wanted to see if they were going to fucking lie!" I get on to my computer and I type in some commas and each one of their phones pop up on the screen. I looked at both of them and asked again, "I'm going to ask you one more time who made the outside call? Chaz answered, "well it was not me I know that shit!"

"You want to know what you're right, Chaz." I nod my head towards Antonio Jagger stepped up putting his gun to his face while I'm looking at the screen,

"What makes you so stupid, nigga that I was the one that made sure you guys had your phones, so I know where and when you made and you my friend have been really busy for the last couple days. You've been plotting this shit from the door so you might as well tell me who you are talking to because I can call them right now if you like or you're going to tell me?"

I picked up my phone calling Nail's Nathen, "saying are you almost here?"

"Yeah I'll be there in a few I hang up looking at Antonio so you're not going to tell me anything?"

"No, I don't have shit to tell you! I looked over at Chaz saying, "you want to get up out here?"

"Yes, I do because I didn't do anything."

"I know that Chaz, but you can't open your mouth about this shit if you want to keep a job."

"I know that!"

"Okay, I want you to go home and I'll have Ty- Kim to call you when we have another delivery okay."

"Sure, can I get paid now?"

"Sure, Ty-Kim pay this guy and take the towel truck with you. And make sure you take it back to the scrap yard before you go home." Ty-Kim handed him his money I asked, "who have the keys to the truck?"

Chaz pointed at Antonio. He's pissed off yelling, "you sell out, motherfucker!"

"Look, I did not know what the fuck you were doing, nigga. I don't care what the fuck you say. Fuck you! I'm out of here." As Antonio hands the keys to Ty-Kim holding his hand out for them. Ty-Kim snatched them out of his hand, and he gives them to Chaz. He gave Antonio the finger and went out the door with Dun-Dun closing the door behind him. Soon as he went outside my phone rings and its Nails Nathen saying, "I'm here, Almasi."

"Good bring up that package for me were in room 107 brother." After a few minutes it's a small knock at the motel door I looked at him and yelled, "so, you have nothing to tell me, right? Ty-Kim get that door and let Nails in here for me." He opened the door and Nails is pushing this woman inside she yelled, "get your fucking hands off of me!" Antonio looking up in shock he yelled, "Mom?"

"Yeah, it's me. What the fuck you got me into with these fucking goons? Pushing me up in this funky ass room to do Gawd knows what to me, nigga!"

Nails Nathen closes the door smiling at everyone in the room. I looked up at her and said, "Miss King, please sit down and calm down okay nobody is going to hurt you."

She looks me in the face, and she yelled, "who the fuck is you bitch? Don't tell me to calm down." I stood up and slapped her right in the mouth she fell back with Ty- Kim catching her stopping her from falling on the floor. I point my finger in her face and I said, "now, I tried to be nice to your fucking trick ass bitch. I know you sell pussy in bars to feed your fucking drug habit now jump bad again. I'll pistol whip your ass so bad you're going to beg me to fucking stop! Now listen up your dumb ass boy over here has something of ours. I brought you here to try to talk some fucking sense to your pill popping dumb ass son of yours!"

She stood up straight wiping the blood from her mouth looking over at Antonio. She looked really hard at me and said, "okay if he tells you where it's at are you going to let him go?"

"No, I'll let you go if not I'll do what I have to do now. I know your life is not fucking much but you do want to walk out here. You're an old pro you know what it is this nigga of yours got the game all fucked up for real. So, what's it going to be Linda?" She blew out some air and said, "shit Antonio, I brought you up the best way I knew how but I did not show you this fucked up part of the game with niggas like this. You can't fuck wit people like this and not pay a fucking heavy price. Could you tell them so I can get the fuck up out of here, please?"
"I can't, and they will kill me! And I thought you was giving up the life, Mom?"
"What? Nigga you not a fucking baby. I'm grown and I raise you until you were a man, motherfucker."
"I do what the fuck I want to do shit you do that's why I'm fucking here! They're going to fucking kill you and your worrying about them what about me, nigga! So, you're going to let them kill me for your bull shit! Okay! Okay!"
"Mom, now I'll tell them, but they have to let you go!" Linda looks up at me with her eyes getting wide and said, "see he's going to tell you what you want to know all right." I looked up at both of them and said, "sounds good you tell us where it's at and who's behind the shit and your mom can go after we get our shit back!"
Linda yelled, "you did not say that shit you said for him to tell you where your shit at and you will let me go!"
I stood up pulled my gun out and yelled back, "look, I'm not playing any more games with you two scum bag motherfuckers you tell me who is behind this shit. Where is my shit or I'll kill both of you assholes and track down it my motherfuckin self the hard way now start talking or I'll blow your moms fucking ho ass head off first then you nigga!" I got up on Linda mashing my gun to her head making her wig go sideways and I looked him right in his eyes showing them I'm not playing any fucking more. He looked up at his mother and announced, "alright, it was Jasper who step to me a few months ago!"

"And what else nigga spit it out, motherfucker!" It was Sean Jiggy, Kenny Shoe's Tricky Rick and Jay the Joker. They took the shit to his stash spot at B & Allegheny 259 East Westmoreland street the end brick house." I pulled out my phone calling Fly-Ty the phone rings about three times before he picks up saying, "Yo, what's up, Almasi?"

"Look I'm sending Chrome out there to you to B line it to Allegheny 259 East Westmoreland street the end brick house and go get our shit. Let me get Rah-Killer and her crew to back you up on the horn when they're ready to go. I want all of y'all to hit them motherfuckers hard too."

"Okay, you going to call her now?"

"Yeah, let me get her on the phone and I'll let you know when to move out all right?"

"Sure thing just let me know **Moja** *(One!)"* I quickly hang up with him and called Rah-Killer the phone rings two time and she pick up yelling, "hey, what's up, girl?"

Hey baby **Nina kazi kwako** (I have a job for you) **Vizuri umemwita mtu mzuri** Well you called the right person."

We both started laughing then I say, "I need you to get your peoples together and back up Chrome to get our coke and guns back at B & Allegheny. He will fill you in when they get there."

"Alright? I'm on it right now I'll call you when I'm rolling out okay Almasi **Moja** (One!)"

I looked up at Chrome it won't take her long to get everybody together then I turned to Antonio and his mother Miss Linda. "I hope your son is not lying or were going to stick you in the same hole that were fucking bury his ass in!" She looked up at me with them fucking crocodile tears running from her eyes.

I point at her sit down until I get the call all right before I change my mind. She went and sat next to her son hugging him with more fake crying and carry on. I wanted to shoot both of them and get it the fuck over with to tell you the truth. A half an hour blaze past while I just sit there puffing on my cigarette when my phone rings its Rah-Killer she said, "I'm rolling out the door right now I got half of my troops together."

"Okay, just as long as you got enough people to get the job done."

"Yeah, I have enough people were on our way to B & Allegheny right now."

"**Nzuri**(Good). I'm sending them right now **Moja**(One!)"
"Okay Chrome she's rolling out the door right now you can go meet her okay." He nodded their head yes. I looked at Antonio and asked, "how many people they got there at the house and don't lie nigga?"
"About three of them at the most- okay get there before they move the shit somewhere else all right."
He asked, "you don't think that dude you let go will tip them off, do you?"
"No, I don't think so but if they not there I will track him down and blow his fucking brain out myself. We know where he lay his head, so I'm not worry about that now go get the shit and take it to American street warehouse. Take the guns to the scrap yard and give them to Black Leroy and his boys he knows where to put them up call me and let me know how you make out."
Chrome went out the door real swift and Jagger closed the door behind them. He stands in front of the door on post with his gun in his hand looking at both of them sitting on the bed. Now I'm sitting at this cheap ass desk in the motel waiting on the call from them and I hate that I have to baby sit these two motherfuckers. Dun-Dun came over to me sitting down said**, "Hivyo unafikiri wasnapata shit nyuma** (So you think they are going to get the shit back?")
"Kama sio kwenda kuwa wata wengi wafu wamelala karibu (If not it's going to be alot of dead people lying around.")
"**Ndio na wafanyakazi hao watakuwa.** (Yeah with that crew it will be.)" We both started laughing.
Linda yelled, "what kind of fucking mumbo-jumbo your talking?" Jagger quickly walked up to them pointing his gun at her head and yelled, you shut the fuck up before I put a hot slug in your fucking head before they go get our shit back!" She went to jump up to say something Kacka! Jagger hit her in the head with his pistol. Antonio then followed to jump up to do something. Jagger hit him in the head with his pistol too. Krack! The blood is dripping down to his face with him holding his head "Oh, you can get some too, motherfucker!"

I just smiled looking up at Jagger to let him know that was enough. He walked back to the door of the motel and he winked his eye at me, and I just smiled some more. Now it took my people less then an hour to arrive at B & Allegheny Rah- Killer have Nugee, Billy Blunts, Gino Gats and Bullet Head Joney with her in the work van we all call the death machine because when they roll up a whole lot of motherfuckers is going to get smoked. Ty-Kim and Chrome see them in the black work van telling them the house where the coke and gun stash is at. They all huddle up and Ty-Kim Chrome Rah-Killer, Nugee took the front door Billy Blunts, Bullet Head Joney, Gino Gats took the back door Rah-Killer texted everybody in Swahili in all caps **NENDA KUWAUA WOTE**! (Go Kill them all!) Rah- Killer and Nugee is on the left Billy Blunts and Gino Gats are on the right Nugee crazy ass kicked the door in Kadoom!

Bum rushed the joint as Rah-Killer, Billy Blunts and Gino Gats ran inside staying low shooting to draw them out in the open. When Nugee came in behind Billy Blunts Rah- Killer and Gino Gats Nugee tossed a flash bang bomb making a lot of smoke and shaking damn near the whole front of the house Tricky Rick, Kenny Shoe's and Jay the Joker jumped in shock. With their weapons taking aim shooting wildly not able to see too good with the noise and smoke firing at the intruders that just busted inside the roe house but by the time they started shooting back at the people coming at them from the front door. Jay the Joker and Kenny Shoes were both hit in all parts of their bodies. They all ran towards the back door Rah-Killer, Nugee, Billy Blunts and Gino Gats did not chase after them knowing at the back door is Chrome, Bullet Joney and Ty-Kim waiting for them. The first one running out of the back door is Tricky Rickey soon as he opens the door all of them cut him with a barrage of bullets hitting him in his head, neck, stomach and legs with blood flying everywhere.

Right behind him is Kenny Shoe's he tried to turn around after seeing his friend Tricky Rickey get riddle with bullets. He's in the back and his legs he falls inside of the door trying to turn around to run back inside.

When he falls to the ground in the doorway. Jay the Joker saw the blood gushing out from his body he runs back inside the house and he runs right into Rah-Killer and Nugee and Billy Blunts but Rah-Killer yelled to the others, "Msimuue don't kill him!"

Billy Blunts shoots him in the hand making him drop his gun and he falls to the floor in deep pain yelling and Nugee runs up grabbing him by his neck shouting, "where is the shit nigga!" Rah-Killer quickly walks up standing over him screaming, "if you want to live Mister Joker man tell us where the coke and guns are at!"
"Fuck that you're going to kill me any way so I'm not telling you shit!" Nugee throws him on the ground and he steps on his hands with the blood gushing out and he's yelling in deep pain as Rah-Killer yelled,
"you still don't want to tell us?"
He screeched in pain, "no!"
"Okay flip him over Nugee and pull down his jeans so Nugee grabbing him flipping him over and he quickly started pulling down his jeans as Rah-Killer pulls out her big Rambo knife sticking it in his face so he can see it real good and she said through clenched teeth, " now I'm going to cut your fucking dick off and I'm going to have fun doing this shit because I wish I had one motherfucker!"
"Okay! Okay! Don't cut my Dick off shit!" She reached down pulling his Dick out of his boxer shorts and she puts the knife up under his Dick meat with her eyes getting wide with a wicked smile on her face.
"Alright, tell me where it's at?"
"If I tell you where it's at you won't kill me right?" Rah- Killer smirked, "no, I won't kill you. Now where the fuck is it?"
"It's all upstairs in the main bedroom on the left."
"Is anybody up there?"
"No, please don't kill me, Rashida!"
"Go check this shit out if your lying I'm make you wish you were dead nigga." Nugee and Billy Blunts quickly go up stair to the main bedroom on the left they slowly walked to towards the door staying low. Nugge pushed the door open and there is no one in there as they both glanced around then they see boxes laying on top of the bed Nugee and Billy looks inside of the boxes seeing the keys of coke and then they both looks inside of the boxes stacked up on the right-hand side all along the wall looking inside seeing the guns. They both just looked at each other Nugee pulled out his phone calling Rah- Killer she picked up real fast and said, "so what's up?"
"Yeah, its here."

"Okay call Ty-Kim and the others and tell them to help take this shit out of here **Moja**(One!)"
Jay the Joker said, "see, I told you where it was at you're going to keep your word and not kill me right?"
"Yeah, I'm going to keep my word, Nigga." she smiles at him then she told him come here get your ass up off the floor. He's holding his hands both of them bleeding he stands up as she waves the knife for him to come closer but he's shaking in fear. Soon as he got closer Rah-Killer stabbed him in his right eye he's screaming in pain and he falls to the ground yelling. Rah-Killer stood over him while he's rolling on the ground then she started stabbing him in his left eye, he's screaming even louder while she walks away pulling out her phone calling, I'd picked up on the first ring,
"(**NiniJuu**) What's up? It's all here were packing up right now!"
"Okay good see you in a few **Moja**(One!)"
While everyone was putting the guns and drugs in the work van very quickly. Rah-Killer and the others putting the last boxes in the work van she talks low to Nugee and said, "put that motherfucker out of his Misery for me, I told him that I would not kill him."
"Well you did not lie to him because I'm going to do it!" As they both started snickering Nugee quickly ran back in the kitchen area where Jay the Joker is wiggling on the floor moaning. He stood over him taking aim shooting him in the middle of his head with one shot and he swiftly ran out the door jumping in the van with Rah-Killer behind the wheel of the work van, Gino Gats, and Billy Blunts. Waiting in the cargo area Ty-Kim and Chrome took off ten minutes ahead of them as they take off from the set.
Ty-Kim call me and said, "we got it all back. Okay I see you when you get back here Moja(One!)"
I looked at Linda she is laying on the bed next to her son. I called and check on the others on post Fly-Ty, Booby Hill and Black Duke there all sitting in the same car now I talk to Fly-Ty sitting behind the wheel.
"Yo, Ty check this out **Nitahitajika wewe kumtunza mtu wakati wanaporudi** I'm going to need for you to take care of this guy when they get back all right?"

"**Kitu hakika mtoto** Sure thing sis." An Hour later Ty-Kim and Chrome came and knocked on the door Jagger let them in pointed at Ty- Kim and said," **Kuchkua Uzinzi huyu hapa** (Take this whore out of here!" Everybody in the room started stare.
"Meet us back at the spot, okay." Ty-Kim just nodded his head yes with a big smile on his face. He grabbed Linda by her arm pulling her out of the room as she's looking back at her son with a sad face.
"Jagger and Dun-Dun take this piece of shit to Fly-Ty and them outside." Jagger and Dun-Dun with their guns in their hands. Dun-Dun mashed his gun to his back and Jagger put it to his head and said, "any funny move and I'll smoke your funky ass right here motherfucker!"
They both take him outside Fly-Ty jumps out the car and said, "Yo Duke, get up here and drive." He gets out and he goes to the driver seat as Jagger and Dun-Dun push him to Fly-Ty mashing his gun to his head said, "get in motherfucker Booby Hill is already is in the back seat. Fly-Ty pushed him in the backseat, and he slid right next to him closing the door.
"Alright Duke, step on it, nigga where going to the yard let's go!"
Not even an hour after all of us roll from off the set to go home Jasper and Jane doe." Her crew hit one of our pill mills in Frankford on Potter street right near Kensington avenue. They came in three black Tahoe trucks Truck one has Hassan behind the wheel. Jane Doe riding shot gun Black Poppy and Cedric in the back-seat truck two is the Stone brothers Logan Stone behind the wheel his brother Marquez Stone riding shot gun in the back seat is Leo Stone and his right-hand man Big Lukas. In truck three is Crazy Chad Sean's cousin Jasper riding shot gun and Sean Jiggy in the back seat. Truck one and three hit the front door and truck two when to the back door. Soon as truck one and truck three stop at the front door Black Poppy Jane Doe and Cedric jumped out with their black mask and machine guns and the same time jumping out of truck three is Jasper and Sean Jiggy.

Jasper running in front of everyone all fucking gun Ho with Sean Jiggy right by his side Jasper post up on the right Sean Jiggy on the left with Sean Jiggy waving his hand for Black Poppy to kick the door in. He's his kicking and then trying to hit it with his shoulders and he could not get the door open. Cedrie came up to help him and they both can't get the door open up above them. Fat Lou-Lou and Gavin open fire on their ass shooting down Black Poppy, Sean Jiggy and Cedrie with blood squirting all over the place hitting them in the top of their head, neck and top of their shoulders and arms killing all three of them. Jasper and Jane Doe duck down shooting up at the window and running back to the truck with Hassan behind the wheel who yelled, "get in hurry up!" Jane Doe and Jasper jumped in as Fat Lou-Lou and Gavin is still shooting at them hitting the truck Hassan took off crashing into the third truck making a hard-right hand turn making their getaway.

Meanwhile at the back-door Marquez Leo and Big Lukas kicked in the back door. Boom! Leo rush through the door first Big Goliath step out the darkness with his Bravo Company machine gun spraying all three of them hitting and ripping every part of their body. The flesh from their bodies hitting the floor faster then rabbit gets fucked hitting the deck then. Goliath already had nine bags of pills by the door on top of the counter by the back door. He puts all of them inside of a large Nike bag he quickly tosses his machine gun on to his right shoulder and the Nike bag on his left shoulder and he quickly checked to see if there all dead.

Laying in a big pool of blood then he runs up the alley in the dark when he got near the end of the alley, he gets himself ready holding his machine gun upward pointing his weapon running towards Logan Stone behind the wheel of the truck. Near the end of the alley shooting him in the truck through the glass flying in the air along with blood and his head slumped on top of the staring wheel. As Big Goliath quickly ran towards his left to his car a dark blue Pontiac getting his keys out popping the truck tossing the big Nike bag inside and jumping behind the wheel taking off like a driver in the Indianapolis 500. He took all the pills to the scrap yard on American street in North Philly.

Fat Lou-Lou and Gavin quickly got out the house and was long gone before the cops showed up. They went and laid low at one of our warehouses in Nice town calling me up telling me about what happened. I'd told them lay low there for a while and I'll call them back and let them know what Spider want to do.

Fat Lou-Lou said that Goliath took all the product to the scrap yard, "okay thanks Lou-Lou." I hang up with him I'm sitting with Dun-Dun, Jagger, Tanya and my Auntie sitting at my bar in my condo chillin having a few cocktails. I got off the phone with him calling up Spider telling him what happen after we got our coke and guns back that they jacked.

Spider said he will meet up with everybody tomorrow and I want you to call and text everybody and tell them to be there as well and he hangs up. I called up Rah-Killer she picked up after four rings she said, "Yo, what's up? Everything is cool right?"

"Well the pill mills just got hit and Spider wants everybody to meet at the warehouse in Nice Town tomorrow and he wants everybody there so tell your crew they better be there. All of them not half of them like today."

"Okay I'll make sure they all be there Almasi **Moja** (One!)" Soon as I hung up with her I call my peoples who live near the 3rd street mob this O.G. Nigga name Rocka I away sold him coke with a big discount price. I asked him about the 3rd street mob he told me he just stays out their fucking way because there real thick, but he did tell me that there having problems with their heroin hook up. Soon as he told me that I said to him that I was going to hook him up for that information. He said, "thank you."

I got off the phone and I called up Black Leroy and told him to have one his peoples to take Rocka four keys of coke and I wanted there today!

He said, "you got it, Almasi!" Now the wheel in my head started rolling around. I know just what to do while I'm sitting back working everything out in my mind. My phone rung its Damon Gee he yelled in my ear, "Yo, what's up?"

"Hey Gee, what up with you?

"Everything is up wit me. I did it, sis!"

"You did what fool?"

"I got us the new hook up with that chick Natalie I told you about so we can sit down with Tony Bolivar."

So, when is it going to happen? This Friday at the Ritz-Carlton 8P.M. sharp."

"Nzuri(Good!) So, our shit is going to be on and popping then."

"Oh, hell yes, sis. I told you I get this shit done."

"Yeah, you said you would get it done. "so how did make it happen?"

"A whole lot of dirt that's all I can tell you right now!" We both started laughing really loud. "But any who Gee good fucking job man I'm really proud of you Dawg."

"Thanks, Almasi well I'll see you at the meeting tomorrow. Check this out Damon didn't you tell me one time you knew most of them dudes from the 3rd street mob?"

"Yeah, I was locked up with most of them and me and El Barero got really cool. I used to hook up a lot shit for him."

"Do you think you can go holla at him for us."

"Well, I'll reach out and see what he say that the best I can do."

"Yeah, do that for me and let me know what he says!"

Alright, but I can't make no promises, but I'll give it a shot."

"That's all you can do, brother. I'll tell you what I want to do tomorrow, okay. I have a sweet deal for him."

"Well tell me all about it then I have to go Moja(One!) Moja!" I hung up with him and we got our drink and puff on for a while Jagger and Dun- Dun went home and I turned in a little early along with Auntie, Tanya, myself and the baby. The next morning the baby woke me up crying at 7 O' clock on the dot. I jump up to change him and gave him his bottle it took me about another hour just to put him back to sleep. I know once I was up, I could not go back to sleep and my phone rings. I get it right quick looking at the caller ID I knew it was Spider and something happen with him calling me so early.

What I did not know while we were all sleep all kinds of shit jumped off and we just got started with this war with Jasper. we never seen him hooking up with the 3rd street mob but I have something up my sleeve and I know it's going to work.

PUTTING SHIT TOGETHER FOR THE HIT ON JASPER

"Yo, what up, Shorty did I wake you up?"
"No, Little Boom got me up and I could not go back to sleep anyway."
"Why, what's up with you?"
"Shit, the cops got a large shipment of our product and plus that Jasper is on the rampage. He hit four of our spots last night they took all the product and he killed about five of our workers."
"Was it anybody I know?"
"No, you might have seen a few of them here and there but nobody you knew I just have to deal with their families running around buying caskets and flowers for all of them. That ain't no type of fucking fun but the really hard part about that shit is looking each one of their peoples in the face you know what I'm saying."
"Were going have to find him and end to this little war with Jasper crazy ass. I have a few Ideas and I'll run them down to you at the meeting tonight."
"Well please tell me about them so we can put an end to this bullshit because its fucking up our money for real."
"Your right about that shit and were still fighting with GTG at the same fucking time."
"Well I'm cooking something up on that one. I'm going to need your body bag crew to hook up with the new crew and wipe his ass out for good. As you know I got somebody on the inside I'm just waiting on them to give me the word before we make a move on their ass."
"Well, just tell me when you know I'm good to fucking go, Spider."
"I know that, baby girl that's why I love you. Look, I have alot of shit to do." I holla at you later. Do you need some help with the spots?"
"No, I got my people on that I'm cool but thanks for asking baby I see you later. Okay then, **Moja**(One!)"
"**Moja!**"
Soon as I hang up with him, I called up Quan Kauu from the Quai Vat that mean Monsters in Vietnamese the phone rings about six times. I'm thinking he was not going to pick up and I hear him shout, "this better be good whoever the fuck it is!"

"It's me, Almasi, Nigga. You should know everything I have to tell you is fucking good in the hood!"
"Oh shit, I didn't know it was you Almasi. My bad what up with you calling me so fucking early?"
"I called to put some money in your pocket, motherfucker Money never sleep my friend."
"You're right. I like that shit I'm going to use that one."
"Yeah, I got that shit from an old movie called Wall Street."
"Yeah well, I never seen it before, but I still like the line. So, what is it you have in mind, Glock Mommy? I need a shit load of heroin and I need it right away."
"I just send you guys your load already what happen y'all got hit or something?"
"Well you can say that but I'm making a sweet ass deal to set somebody up that's all."
"Well whatever you need I can get it for you just let me know where you want it at."
"Put it in the same spot I'll have my peoples to come get it just let me know when you're ready Quan."
"I'll be ready for you by the end of the day, sis. You know I don't fuck around when it comes to that loot." We both laughed while I give him the rest of the details and where he can pick up his money and all that shit. I hang up with his crazy ass and I went in the kitchen and started cooking breakfast. The smell of the food when through the whole spot like a bomb went off in the crib. The first one who came in the kitchen with the baby is Auntie holding Little Boom she still yarning and said, "damn, you're up early, girl?"
"Yeah, I could not sleep then right behind her soon as I blink was Tanya with her eye getting wide said, "it sure does smell good up in here, Almasi!"
I just smiled and said, "have a seat, baby girl. I'll fix you a plate how do you feel this morning?"
"I feel good today where my brother at?"
"He'll be here any minute like clockwork soon as I said that here, he come walking in the door yelling, "why Gawd damn you got it going on up in here, Almasi. I'm right on time then!"
"You sure are, baby boy has a seat."
He walked over and spoke to Tanya and Auntie.
"Hey ladies! What's happening? Tanya is it cold out there! Brrrr!"

"It's fucking freezing out there you'll freeze that junk in the trunk along with your pretty titties right off, baby girl!" All of us started laughing really loud while I started to give everybody their plates of food super-hot and down home delicious. I sat next to my baby Little Boom with my plate feeding him his food and me eating at the same time and this little nigga can eat too.

"I wanted to ask you Jagger if your sister can help on keeping an eye on things at the warehouse for me?"

"Why you are asking him I'm sitting right here?"

"No, she did right by asking me because you went and fucked your life up the first time now, she's asking me all right?"

"But you not my daddy, nigga!

So, I put my hands up in the air "fuck all this shit he's right you went and fucked up on your own so you just chill for a few babies, while I talk." Okay. Tanya can you do that for me, please? She just nodded her head and sit back Jagger understood what I am doing I was giving him the respect. I turn back to Jagger all I need to know can she shoot?"

"Yeah, I wish I never showed her. I only showed her a long time ago so so she can defend herself out there in the streets now she thinks she's a fucking gangster." She's rolling her eyes, but she doesn't say a word.

"I know but what you say about it? Why not she's not going back to school she fucked that up I did not what her in the life, but this is what she wants to do so fuck it." I quickly wink my eye at Tanya right quick without Jagger seeing it. "Okay then I'm going need you for you to hold shit down for me and keep your eyes open for any funny shit going down you feel me?"

"Yeah, I'm wit it, thanks." We got done eating and Auntie help me clean up while him and Tanya are talking, but I can tell by the way there were talking to one another everything was cool with the two of them. I told Auntie I need to roll out of the spot while I go take care of a few things.

"Sure, baby I'll stay here and take care of my little man over here." She went over and rubbed his face and legs making him giggle. I said to Jagger, "give me a few while I get dressed my nigga!" He just nods his head leaning back drinking his iced tea still talking to his sister fucking with her making faces. Well soon as I got washed up and dressed and I'm ready to fly out the door I get a call from Nugee when I look at the caller ID and answered, "Yo, what's up?"
"Look, I wanted to tell you Rah-Killer just got locked up yo."
"For what? What the fuck did she do now?"
"Well she beat up that bitch Kitty toss her out of the spot. She brought in another bitch. Kitty was piss off about it, so she called the cops on her ass while she had her head face down in the other girl's pussy!"
"Okay, I'll call Mitchum to go bail her crazy ass out all right I need you to get everyone in your crew to me at the warehouse I have some shit to run down to all of y'all."
"Okay, I'll be there **Moja**(One)"
"Moja!" I came out of my bedroom and went into the kitchen where Tanya and Jagger are still sitting talking. Aunt-tee took the baby to his bedroom to get him washed and dressed. I point to Jagger, "come we have to roll, and Tanya keep all that shit we talked about to yourself. I'll fill you in on everything to night so if you go out make sure if I call you be ready to move your ass, you hear."
"Can I wait for you at the gangster lounge?"
"Why not you got a gun?"
"Oh yeah, I keep my gun wit me fuck that!"
"Okay then you ride in front of us in your whip me and your brother have a lot of shit to talk about. Why can't I ride with y'all?"
"See now your pushing it just do what I ask you to do and everything will be smooth girl. Now can you understand that?"
"Yes, I can!"
"That is what I want to fucking hear let's go!" She jumps up putting on her leather jacket with a big smile on her yellow ass think she's too cute face of her's. Soon as me and Jagger got in the truck, "I ask him are you cool with this for real?"
He started up the truck and started driving saying, "yeah, I'm good I just did not want this day to come but it is here."
"What are you talking about?"

"The day when she started doing her own thing, I didn't want this life for her. I wanted her to be a fucking lawyer or something but, like she said I'm not her daddy I'm just her brother."
"Well, you can't feel bad about it you did try to put her on the right path now."
"Yeah, but I did not want her to be like everybody else in our family in jail or fucking dead."
"Your mom too?"
"Yeah, she overdosed, and my father is doing double life so he's never getting out."
"Do you go see him?"
"Fuck no that nigga never did a motherfucking thing for me or my sister so fuck him."
"Well I can feel you on that."
"So, what about you?"
"Me? Shit, you would not believe my story, Dawg if I tell you this shit you have to keep it to yourself for real."
"Now all of these years you don't trust me?"
"You know I trust you with my life, nigga so don't start talking crazy. I'm going to tell you!"
"All right spit it out like you say to niggas all the time!" We both started laughing and I said my mother and father were killed. Spider took me to some crack head bitch to raise me up he didn't know it at the time so that's my fucking story nigga."
"Now was that hard nigga!"
We both started laughing loud while he watched his sister Tanya ahead of us with Jagger who said, "so what was it you wanted to talk about wit me beside both of our fucked-up family drama.'
"I got a plan to set Jasper ass up soon as I get the call from Damon Gee he can tell me if everything is in fucking motion. I had him reach out to EL Braero to make a deal. Do you think he will go for it?"
"Sure, he's having problems with his heroin hook up. We hook him up with Quan and he help us set up Jasper crazy ass and we smoke him! Shit sounds good to me, sis. Then my phone rings I looked at the caller ID and I know its Spider. I just looked at the phone again throwing my hands in the air and I hit the button, "what's up, Spider?"
"Come meet me at your place in one hour it's really important."

"Okay **Moja**" (One!)"
"**Moja**!"
"Hey, gear up Jagger we have to meet Spider at our office in one hour. He said it's really important. What the fuck is that about?"
"I don't know but I can hear in his voice that it's really fucking something big!" I called up the three hundred dollar an hour lawyer so Rah-Killer can get her crazy ass out of fucking jail. Shit, that bitch like jail if you ask me all the pussy you can eat, she tells me the stories all the time when she gets high. I don't want to hear that shit for real because nothing in the world can get me off getting some dick, so I know that bitch is crazy!"
It took us about half an hour to get to my house on Washington avenue. Jagger help me unlock the doors soon as we get up in there walking in the door is Spider along with Philly, Fly Ty, Damon Gee and Booby Hill. He wave is hand for everybody to come into my office. His face is twisted up he points for me to sit at my desk and he sits on top of it he said, "as everybody knows everything, we talk about here stay in this room." He looks around the room at every one of us nodding our heads in agreement. Then he said, really loud, "we have a snitch in our camp!" I just looked up at him and asked, "who is it?"
"That's why I came here to show you. I just got this video from your boy Layne West this morning. I came here to show it to you. The only people that know about this is the people in this room right now he hands me the phone I'm looking at it. I don't believe it I see Shamika sneaking up in the house. I asked Spider,
"so, what is this your showing me?"
"That's your girl meeting up with the FBI just wait you'll see it and look who's with her check that shit out Yo." I'm looking its Shamika, Tamika and her man Mike with the FBI dudes four crackers with windbreakers on inside of the Y I can see clear as a bell.

Then they quickly came out as the two of them jumping in Shamika's car driving off down the street. I can see the look on their faces these two sneaky asses bitches she was playing me this whole time. I felt like I was just hit with a brick upside my head. I could not believe it if I did not see it with my own eyes. I was sick to my stomach for real and my whole head got light with shame. I hand him his phone back slowly. He said after Tamika got locked up, I had her followed and watched every day.

"I had to show you because I know that's your girl and I'm showing you proof that she's working with the FBI. We just got hit last night with a big shipment and they locked up Gun Crazy Charley and his crew."

"How much did they get?"

"500 keys of blow I'm not worried about Charley, but the rest of his peoples are not going to hold the line. So, I'm going to have to get the fuck out of town and you're going to have to run things while I'm gone."

"Shit they just might come after me too Spider."

"No, they want me I heard them talking on some other videos that Layne got one for me. They did not name you yet in the indictment, but they did name me Philly and Buck Shot as the heads of the organization. You are going to have to find a way to take care of her. You don't have a problem taking care of this do you?"

"No, I'll get it but what about Blue?"

Don't worry about him I have Dun-Dun taking care of his ass right now. We know damn well he would want to fight for his sisters, so, he'll be dead before the day is done. You feel me? Now you are going to have to be careful on taking care of Shamika she just might have an FBI tail on her ass. So, what about the meeting tonight? We are still going to have it at the City Line avenue joint the FBI and the cops don't know about that spot yet but check this out, baby girl your running things while I'm gone."

He looked me right into my eyes all this time I been doing all this crazy ass shit for the gang now I'm the one who have to hold shit down life is stranger than fiction. I just nodded my head with that I don't give a fuck expression on my face, but I feel really fucked up about this now is the first time I have to kill somebody that is really close to me. I have mix emotion about this shit but Shamika did turn on the BSN, so she does have to go. I have to be the one to get this thing done damn, I have to kill my best friend. I never knew that it would ever come to this, but I have to do it or I'm dead. This is one of my biggest tests in this kind of life I have ever had to face. Spider said in his deep voice, "Yo Almasi, I'll be in touch with you I'm going to get the fuck up out of here all right?" I stood up and I gave him a hug and said, "don't worry I'll hold this down for you until you come back!" I know you will that's why I have you at the head of the **Meza**(Table). Philly then came up bumping fist wit me saying, "I know you got this I smiled and said, "you know motherfucking right I do!" Everybody started laughing and I sat back down and lit up a cigarette watching the two of them roll out the door.

I pointed up at Booby Hill and said, "Yo Booby, I need you to get on post along with Fat Lou-Lou and Gavin at the City line avenue spot for me please. Also, call up Goliath and tell him to be there make sure he's there because tonight is what he's been waiting for he gets his button. I'll make sure he's there Almasi Baadae (Later)." He smiles and quickly walked out of the office.

I looked up at Jagger, Fly-Ty and Damon Gee and said, "were going to have to do this shit real smooth because just like Spider said she just might have the FBI following her around."

Damon Gee said, "the only thing I can think of is to get someone to plant a bomb in her apartment while you get her to hang out with you because she doesn't know that you know she's working with the FBI."

Fly-Ty shouted, "I think that's it Almasi or we can put it on her car. I think that will be easier if you ask me!" Jagger said, "I think so too that will work they will never know what hit them." He looked over at him.

"Fly-Ty, you want to know what both of y'all have a good point why don't we do both and get Tamika ass the same way." Fly-Ty chimed in and said, "sounds good to me I'll take care of both of them if you want?"
"Yeah, I would like for you to do it that way. I know it's going to get done, right."
"So, when you want me to do it?"
"Right after the meeting tonight."
"Okay, I'll call Crazy Monk right now so he can get working on making me two devices. So, he can have them ready by the time the meeting is over you know that nigga is one bad boy when it comes to that shit."
"Hey Damon, I'm going to need you to call up that crooked ass cop and see what's going on with the local cops and FBI for us?"
"I'm on it right now." He pulls out his phone it rings about five times and Eddie picked up,
"Yo, man! How are you doing today?"
"I'm all right, brother. Look I need some more help with some information."
"About what?"
"About the FBI and local cops investigating my peoples."
"Yeah, I can help you out with that just as long as you got the money?"
"Well, you know I got the money meet me at the same place later on tonight and you will get your money, man." At the same time Fly-Ty is on the phone with Crazy Monk sitting in the chair in front of me he hangs up looking up at me and said, "he can do it he'll work on at the meeting." **"Nzuri**(Good)!So, Damon when are you going to take me to go see EL Braero?"
"I can set that up for tomorrow night that's the only time I can get wit him he is only up at nighttime."
"Okay do that set that up because we are going to get all of these motherfuckers all around the same time."
Soon as I said that walking in the door is Dun- Dun, Ty-Kim, Mookie, Puerto Rican Joe and Black Duke. I got up out of my chair opening my office door yelling out,
"Yo Dun, let me holla at you right quick, homey." He smiles he turns to Black Duke and Puerto Rican Joe. He said,

"hey, you two niggas need to get on post right about now you're not here to fucking socialize okay motherfuckers!"
They both jumped and walked to get on post at the door then he's walking towards me quickly as the others sat in the gangster lounge. He bumped fist with me while I stood in the doorway. He gives me a hug then he hugs Fly-Ty and Damon Gee as they both say Family all at the same time as he closed the door behind him. I sit down at my desk and he sits next to Fly-Ty and Damon Gee sit on the side of my desk. I looked up at Dun-Dun, "so tell us what happen wit Blue?"
"Well I took Blue to this fine ass big butt ho name Latrice in South West Philly we all sit in her living room area. She has a really nice spot, so I make us some drinks and we get our puff on talking shit. So, the bitch takes him in the bedroom so she can suck his Dick so I wait for a little while so she can have his ass all relaxed and I opened the door real fast. I stepped inside the bedroom with my gun with the silencer on it I shot him three times in the head. He fell back on the bed but an hour before I took him there, I put plastic on the bed before I had her suck his dick. I wrapped him up on top of the bed with the covers and the plastic we laid out on the bed she was sucking his dick so good when he sat on the bed he never notice the shit if you're going to go out that's the way to go."
We all started giggling loud. "So, after I wrapped his ass up, I called Ty-Kim, Mookie, Puerto Rican Joe and Black Duke to help, get his funky ass out of there right quick. I gave the girl five large and I told her she can buy a new bed and all that. Know what that bitch told me?"
"What?" Were all giggling looking up at him.
"She said she's going to move to a whole new apartment with this kind of loot fuck that bed! Shit I never made so much money sucking a real salty dick like his! Then she said I sucked a lot of salty dick for free. I just hit the fucking jackpot over here!"
We all started laughing but in the back of my mind I'm thinking about Taye is she going to know that we did this too her husband Blue. When he doesn't show up for a while its really fucked up, but we could not see it any other way because how close he was with his sisters being a couple **Panya** (Rats)."

So, we kick it until it was time to go meet up at the City line avenue spot. Right before I roll out the door with Jagger, I say to Puerto Rican Joe and Black Duke,
"stay here and hold it down. As Tanya came walking in the door, I tell her to keep her eyes open and stay here until I call you and say otherwise. She just nodded her head as Jagger winks his eye at her as we all rolled out from there.

MY BEST FRIEND HAS TO DIE

We are all sitting up in this huge luxury condo. This place is beautiful with all white modern furniture, high ceiling with giant picture windows and a breath-taking view. You can overlook the whole city and see the skyline of Philadelphia lit up and it looks like a picture-perfect post card.

I sat at the head of the long table some of them was wondering why I was sitting there not knowing what's going on, but I have to be the one to tell them. Sitting next to me on the right-hand side is Jagger along with Dun-Dun, Tony Smokes, Damon Gee, Chrome, Fly-Ty Willie Wack-Wack, Nails Nathen, Ty-Kim Ayden and Black Leroy. On the left-hand side is Gill, Rah-Killer, Nugee, Billy Blunts, Gino Gats, Mick Molly, Bullet Head Joney, Crowbar Carl, Lace Lawless and Goliath. Booby Hill, Fat Lou-Lou and Gavin is on post and Crazy Monk is in the other room working on the two bombs. I looked up at everybody faces and said, "okay is everybody here?"

Dun-Dun said, "yeah everybody we told to be here is here."

"Okay then I know a lot of y'all is wondering what's going on. Spider had to get out of town with the FBI investigations shit. He just put me at the head of the **Meza**(Table) until he comes back. Now, I also have to tell everyone to be on your toes because we have a snitch in our house but were taking care of it as I speak. We're going to have to send some of us to D.C. to help Buck Shot and Brenton move out this gang that's giving them a hard time moving product. So, I'm sending Black Leroy and his crew to give them a hand up there and I'm going to need half of Rah-Killer crew to go to B-More with Ayden to run shit there.

Rah-Killer asked, "so, who are you going to send from my crew?"

"You pick 'em, it's your crew, Rah. So, you take care of that, okay and I need to holla at you when I'm done here."

"Chrome you're going to take Philly's territory while he's gone out of town. Fat Hector is going to link up with you to give you the run down and then he's going to go get back with Philly."

Chrome asked, "so how long is this going to go on?"

"As long as it takes, he just called me tonight to let me know so we have to have somebody over seeing shit."
"Now the next time we all get together is next week after I come back from New York."
"All right everybody that's it our meeting is over I just want to say before everybody leave out that our man Goliath is at our Meza(Table) because he worked his ass off to get here and I have to say this is the day he's been waiting for a while. Now it's his time to get his button in the BSN!"
Everybody at the table stood up and started clapping.
Tony Smokes stands up waving him over to a chair with a big smile on his face as everybody else got up from the table to get some food and drinks. Tony Smokes had his tattoo gun set up by the chair in the middle of the floor I went over to the bar telling Ronelle to give me a big bottle of gin. She gave it to me and said, "here you go Almasi that's a really big nigga over there."
"Yes, he is and he's one brave ass motherfucker too!" You need to holla at him for me.
She's smiling knowing what I'm telling her to do.
"I will sis." winking her eye at me before the night is over, we will get him real fucked up laid and paid. I walked over to Goliath sitting in the chair as Tony Smokes is working on his BSN tattoo and he is smiling from ear to ear. I hand it to him and said, "I'm really proud of you brother here drink up, Big Man!"
"Thank you, boss lady, I told you I would not let you down!"
"Yeah, I knew that big man or I would have not fucked wit you in the first place. I just want you to enjoy your self-tonight me and the fellas got some horizontal entertainment for your ass so have a good time. Take a few days off and get wit me when I get back, okay."
"I sure will boss lady thank you!"
I walked back over towards the big bar where mostly were everybody is at if they did not leave out the door. I see Fly- Ty standing next to Dun-Dun I said really low, "is it ready yet?"
"Almost Monk said he's almost done soon as he's finish, I'll go and do that."
"Okay, I need that done tonight."
I walked over to the end of the bar with Rah-Killer I bump fist with her and said, "you know what you have to do, right?"

"Yeah, I have to kill that bitch for calling the cops on me and thanks for getting me out."

"Just get that shit done we have enough shit going on. Rah and don't be sloppy with it we have a lot of eyes on us. The FBI is on our ass right about now, Rah. So, who is the fucking snitch?" With her eyes getting wide.

"I'll tell you later on someone just might get word to them I don't want anybody to tip them the fuck off. So, I don't want you to feel some type of way because I'm not telling you right now. I have to keep it on the low, so we get this shit done you know what I'm saying Rah."

"Oh, I feel you, but I think I know who it is any way."

"So, keep it to yourself for me I don't want things to get fucked up okay." I put my finger up to my lips smiling.

"I got you, sis. I'm not saying shit for real I know what's up." Then I see Fly-Ty walking to the back room right then and there I know it's about to go down. I know this is fucked up, but my best friend has to die for what she did. The more I think about it I don't feel bad about it no more. I go to the bar and get me a beer and started sipping on it watching the big man drinking his gin laughing and talking with everybody coming over fucking wit him having fun. After a few minutes my phone rings and it Fly-Ty he said, "I got it. I'm going out the back door. I'll call you when it's done.

Moja *(One)"*

"Moja!" While everybody is chit chatting getting their drink and puff on, I walked up to Damon Gee said, "are you ready?"

"Yeah right about now is a good time lets go." I waved at Jagger from across the room rapping to a few peoples he came over and said, "what's up?"

"We are going to go meet up with EL Braero. I need you so you can watch my back.'

"Oh, you know that for sure let's roll out who's going to hold things down here?"

Dun- Dun said, I'm here! I will take care of everything Fam check this out I need to holla at you about something." "Yeah, what about, Almasi?"

"I'll tell you about it in the car. Damon Gee whose car are we going to take?"

"Mine because its bullet proof." We all started laughing loud walking down the stairs to the parking lot. Soon as we jumped in the whip and Jagger pulls off and out of the large parking lot. We started driving towards our meeting with EL Braero. I turned to Jagger and said, "so how do you feel about being my number two?"
"I'm good with it, but I want to have my own crew doe. Sounds good to me you have some niggas in mind?"
"Yeah, I do, but I have to go holla at them and bring them up to speed if your giving me the green light to do it?"
"Sure, do it you done your time wit me it's time for you to grow."
"You been really loyal to me and to the BSN it's your time that's what Spider did for me now it's your turn, bro." "Thanks Almasi, that really means a lot coming from you. I never had any real family but my sister and you."
"So, are you cool with this Damon?"
"Oh yeah, you know me I love what I do. Shit, I'm your Consigliere. I'm good wit that because I have to keep everybody on what's going on round us or everybody just be killing each other all over the fucking place. We can't get no money doing all that crazy shit."
"Your right and you the best Consigliere anybody can have. I was thinking X was going to step up when Spider asked him, but he said that he wanted me to take it. I was kind of fucked up about that because y'all was the ones who brought me into the gang."
"No, Spider knew what he was doing some time it's not about how long somebody was down, its who is the best person for the job wit us. Gill's been down for a long time but he's drunk wit power and don't know how to deal with people and what there good at. That's why were still around, and the other gangs fall to the waist side, dead or in jail we have to be smart about this game here you know its chess not checkers.
"Your right about that shit."
It took us about hour to get to EL Braero house in the North East we park right in front of his place. Damon Gee got out first and said, "I'll be right back wait here." In the car we watched as Damon Gee walked up to the door ringing the doorbell. EL Braero came to the door shaking hands with Damon Gee they talked for a few minutes and he quickly walked back to the car knocking on the window.

He said, "come on." We both get out and walked up the path to his house the house is big, but it looked like a regular person lives there. I'm thinking he live in a big ass mansion or something this let me know he's really down to earth. Damon walked in first with Jagger then myself and soon as I walk in, I notice he doesn't have any bodyguards all around him. He's all by himself I close the door behind, and he came over to me shaking my hand saying, "welcome please come in and have a seat." Wow I'm thinking this day would never happen he points at a chair next to the couch as Damon and Jagger sit at the same time on the end of the couch. I'm thinking to myself he looks black with his big Afro he's kind of plump but not too big with tattoos all over his arms and on his neck his eyes tell his whole story he's seen and done it all a real fucking tough guy but he can be a real soft touch when he have to be. I already know not to get that shit twisted because he has those killer cold eyes and you will be dead if you cross this dude from the door. Well I'm glad you're here because I been wanting to hook up with y'all for a long time now. I said I'm thinking you guys did not want to deal with us because of other things that wit down with your peoples.

"No, that was with the old crew they had beef back in the day with Black Giovanni and as you already know we were not even around it we had to hold shit down for us and we just build ourselves up and everybody think we're all against them we just doing our own thing that's all."

"Well why is Jasper down wit your peoples then?"

"Look Jasper came to us saying he should be running BSN because he's Nokey Blaze brother and he thinks that he should run shit not Spider I know Spider and he's a hell of a good leader super smart I seen how he made his moves in this game. Jasper is not really down with us he is running around telling people that bull shit!"

"He's just selling drugs with one of my crews we are not his peoples fuck that! Him and Jane Doe is real fucking unorganized if you ask me it's like night and day. I can tell he's not really down wit the BSN because all of y'all have your shit together!"

"Well, he's a real pain in the ass and we want his ass gone and he thinks y'all his new muscle."

"No fucking way that's all bullshit that Jasper is talking about I don't have no problem helping you get rid of his ass."

"What I want to know is are we going to hook up and work together?"
"Yes, what can we start with so we can have this working partnership?"
"Well we can start with your heroin hook up and we will take care of Jasper for you, so we know were all down with one another."
"Sounds good to me and we can share our coke flow as well what do you think? I'm down wit that and your gun hook up we need that as well."
"Yeah, we can do that I'll have the heroin and the guns dropped off wherever you need them as soon as tonight if you ready to roll or not?"
"Oh yeah you can drop it off tonight at two of my warehouses."
"Are you sure you can do it tonight?"
"Didn't you just say how organized we are, brother?" I pulled out my phone and said, "give me a place where you want the guns and how many and what kind?"
"Okay, I need two cases of Glocks and one case of machine guns at Front and Frankford Avenue it's a warehouse on the right-hand side let me make sure I'll have my peoples there. He pulls out his phone."
The phone rings about five times then he said, "yo Mark get your peoples with two trucks so you can pick up what I have coming there and take it to our spot you got it okay, thanks." He hangs up looking over at me and said, "it's your move, sweetheart." I pull out my phone with a big smile on my face the phone rings one time and its Quan Khuu and said, "Yo you ready, sis?"
"You better know it here it is Front and Frankford Avenue it's a warehouse on the right-hand side." okay hold on for a minute I said to EL Braero, "how many white girls you want to dance at your party?" He holds up his hand 4 fingers, "okay make it **Mia** (400) for right now."
"Okay you got it will be there in a half an hour. One." I hang up and I called Black Leroy he picks up after three rings, "yo, what's up Almasi?"
"I need for you to take two case of **Bunduki** (Guns) and one case of **Bunduki machine** (machine guns) to Front and Frankford Avenue warehouse on the right-hand side brother."
"Okay that's not too far from me. I'll have it there really fast."

Okay make that happen for me they have their peoples waiting there to get it thank you, **Moja.**(one)!" I hang up and just look at him, "it will be there before the heroin."
"But what did you say 40?"
"Oh no big man, 400!"
"Damn 400 keys?"
"What you can't handle that?"
"Yeah we can but our peoples took all day just to bag up 100 fucking keys I was thinking more like 40 not 400 were really going to have to step up our production line. Gawd damn!"
"We can help you get that shit out on the streets I'll have my elves come to where ever your bagging the shit we have magic elves all over the city bagging shit up the first of the month is like Christmas all year long to us." He started laughing, "Wow we do about 100 to 300 keys see were independent. That's why we don't work for no body like the rest of them niggas down there in the bad lands. We do that kind of shit in an hour big man this is the big time homey just think of it this way." I looked him right in his face and said, "You're going to be on another level just tell me where the spots are, and I'll have my worker bees come to give you a hand cool?"
"Yeah, I'm going to need that kind of help with 400 keys of shit!" We all started snickering loud. "Just write down the spots and I'll have them come on now this is business, big man. Get on your game time is money."
"Okay." He gets a pen and some paper from the other room writing down the spots quickly he hands it to me I just nodded my head and said, "I'll have the elves there tomorrow."
"Thanks Mommy!"
"I'll wait here until the heroin get there and then you are going to have to tell me where your boy is at?"
"He's not my boy that nigga just be selling a lot of fucking wolf tickets if you ask me."
"He just was down wit y'all because of Nokey. He never really put in no real work he's a fucking clown if you ask me, Ma."
I laughed and you got that one right, brother. He said to me "so where are you from, Almasi?"
"South Philly. What about you, big man where are you from?"
"The Badlands born and raise, baby."
"I hear that can I ask you something?"

"What's that?"
"How long y'all been on your own?"
"For a really long time it has not been easy but were still hanging in there."
"Your right but how long do you think that's going to last? I'm going to keep it real wit you I don't know?" "Well I have a suggestion if you don't mind. And what's that get down wit y'all?"
"Yeah you caught on fast, brother."
"Well, who's going to be the boss of you?"
"No, Nigga you run your own thing we just hook up the supply we are not taking over your thing. You just kicking it wit us and we solve each other problems that all. You have some peoples that you have to get rid of we help you take care of their ass and you do the same for us like what we're doing right now!"
"Your right but let me holla at my peoples and I'll let you know what's up."
"Okay don't take too long all right give me your phone." He goes into his pocket pulling out his phone I stand up and take the phone from his hand and I put my number in his phone saying, "call me and let me know and if shit don't jump, we can still be cool."
Then my phone rings and its Black Leroy, **"Ni pale (**It's There)
Nzuri(Good)
Moja!(One)."
"Moja!"
"What was that?"
"That was your guns is there and the heroin should be right behind it. So, where are you going to drop that loot off for the guns at?"
"I'll have it dropped off to you tonight just tell me where?"
"Well my peoples are there right now." Before we pull up here to 23rd and Washington Avenue it is the warehouse on the corner 2301 big gray door it's your move brother. He's holding his phone he hit his speed dial, "Yo Pete, take that bag to 23rd and Washington Avenue 2301 big gray door, bro okay. One!"
"Okay that's done so what's up with the heroin?"
"Check this out big man that's a different type of bag, my nigga but if your rolling with us I can wait and break it up and cake it up wit you big Fella."
"I don't know that's a shit load of dope your dropping on me plus I'm hooking up old boy for you doe."

"Yeah, your right but you have not done it yet so what's up?"
He smiles, "Well you and me can work that shit out."
My phone rings so I got his ass now I get my phone and said, "yeah what's up, Quan?"
"My peoples just dropped everything off so were good, right?"
"We sure are I'm getting the money right now, baby boy!"
"Okay, get your money, Glock Mommy. I holla at you later one!" I look at him and he smiled and said, "bring your peoples to my spot- on Bills street tomorrow and you can take care of Jasper crazy ass and were going to be working wit each other from here on out is that all right, sister?"
"I'm wit that big homey!" He started snickering loud, I'm Thinking to myself. I knew I get this motherfucker he was thinking about how much money he's going to get off them bricks. Fuck that I know just what was on his fucking mind he's not fooling me!
"Okay what time tomorrow big guy?"
"About 3 is good I'll have him there and you can do what you do I heard some much about y'all in the streets."
"Oh, you heard for real." We both started laughing really loud. On the other side of town Shamika is getting in her whip a pink 2001 Lexus in front of one of her houses in South West Philly soon as she started up her car and was ready to pull off. Peeping her a block away is Fly-Ty he sees her pulling out of her parking spot real smooth he presses the button of his remote for the device. Kabooom! The blast shook the whole block like it was an earthquake flames and smoke flying everywhere.
Along with glass wood and bricks raining down to the ground from out of the dark sky's on fire landing down on top of everybody parked cars and the cars driving by. The shit was loud it could be heard for five blocks or more all you hear is everybody car alarms going off ringing through the streets in the darkness. Fly-Ty pulls out of his parking spot he drives off making a hard-right turn seeing the car on fire he calls me. Soon as I seen his caller ID while I'm still kicking it with EL Braero I tell him hold on I have to take this excuse me big guy I put the phone up to my ear looking over at Jagger and Damon, **"Imefanyika** (Its Done!)"
"**Nzuri**(Good)"
"I holla at you later I'm rapping with EL Braero."
"So how is it going?"

"Real smooth I will tell you about it when I see you later on, all right? Knowing how smooth you are I know you will have him down with us before you know it."

I laughed and said, "you know me, nigga don't I do make a real sweet deal." I looked up at EL Braero smiling his ass off we both can use one another. He has a lot of soldiers in the prisons and on the streets our next move is selling dope on the inside of the prisons."

"Maja chini kwenda(One down One to go!) You got that one right."

"Yeah I'm on my way there right now **Moja**(One)"

"**Moja**"

"Can I ask you something what is that your speaking?"

"Swahili why?"

"I was just asking shit I'm Puerto Rican and I don't speak Spanish."

"Well I can tell your half black, so I'll teach you how to speak Swahili is that cool?"

"Yeah I'm down with that so how do you know I'm half black?"

"I did my homework you might say big man."

"Oh, so you had me looked up otherwise then?"

"Yes, I did I had to do it to find out who I'm fucking wit from the door because if you were foul, I would not be sitting here, brother." I'm not going to fucking lie to you that's why our shit is rolling, and the other motherfuckers is falling off."

"Yeah your right but what's up wit y'all and the GTG niggas?"

"I'm working on that as we speak and as you can tell were on another fucking level with this here!"

"So, what's up with Emillano Vagus?"

"Were still cool why do you ask?"

"Well you know he don't fuck with me. So, I'll make a phone call and if he's not fucking wit you, I'll tell him that I'm fucking with you doe!"

"I know y'all beef go back three years ago I heard you killed a few of his peoples in your little war I know all about that."

"Okay, just as long as you know what you're getting when your fucking wit me, baby."

"I did my homework like I told you and I like what's going on with y'all. I don't bullshit see he has to sell a lot of product, but you have mad muscle I can get more product just about anywhere, but I need muscle to control the market. If I can control the market, I can't get my money you dig."

"You're a very smart chick I like that."

"No, I'm a very smart bitch! And this bitch is trying to get rich my nigga you heard me." We all started giggling I stood up saying, "look we are family now so give me a hug so I can get the fuck up out of here all right, big man." He stood up snickering hugging me man, "this has been a real pleasure meeting with you I did not know what to call you Almasi or Glock Mommy or what?"

"That's cool you can call me Almasi, Glock Mommy whatever my friends call me both big men." Jagger Stood up with Damon Gee and the big man walks us to the door smiling as we go out the door to the car I turned and wave goodbye as I jumped in my whip. Jagger pulls off real smooth and I said, "damn that went really good. I know I need that nigga right now."

"Damon so what about Emillano Vagus he's going to flip when he finds out that were fucking with the 3rd street Mob Almasi."

"No, he won't he know we need some real gangster ass niggas for us to keep this thing going if he can't understand it's going to be too bad."

"I'll talk to him don't worry plus we need a new deal with him any way that was an old deal with Nokey Blaze not with Spider or me he will go for it."

Damon said, "What makes you think he's going to go for it?"

"Because he already knows we can take over his shit right now with just us alone. Now that were expanding, he can get more money in his pocket or he can wind up dead fucking wit us right about now. He has to go wit it or take the fucking dirt nap."

Jagger said, "she's right his people can't fuck wit us right now and he knows it! So, he's not going to say shit. watch!" We all started giggling.

While we were driving back home Fly-Ty rigged Tamika's apartment door on the second floor while she's not home Tamika is hanging out with her girl's Lataya, Joelle and Sierra is going into her apartment in South Philly on 22nd street. She parked her car with her girlfriends who are waiting for her to run up to her place and get some more money she had stashed in her bedroom for them to go buy some more weed. Tamika runs up the steps with her keys soon as she turned the key to the door of her apartment. Kadoom! Her whole place when up with all the debris flying everywhere along with bricks, glass and thick black smoke rushing out of the dwelling. Her friend Lataya parked two doors from the apartment because it was no parking spaces in front of her place, the explosion made the car shake, but they were not hurt but they were real shook up after seeing what happen to Tamika.

We all are talking shit to one another cracking jokes while were riding back to our warehouse. We made it back to the home base soon as I walked in the door, I ask Puerto Rican Joe Black Duke and Tanya did we get a package while we were gone?

Tanya said, "yeah, it's in your office on the desk."

"Y'all did not look in it did y'all?"

Tanya replied, "no and I would have told you if they did." She smiled at both of them. We all started laughing I said, "good job, girl!" As me, Damon Gee and Jagger go in my office soon as I sat down looking up at the brown backpack filled with money, I light up a cigarette blowing out a big cloud of smoke. I lean back smiling pointing at the bag then Damon he knows just what to do without me saying one fucking word. Jagger sat down in the chair in front of my desk lighting up a Newport too as Damon Gee is opening the safe putting the loot from the guns inside of it out of the back-pack bag.

I go in the bottom of my desk on the right hand side getting a bottle of Rum and some red plastic cups Fly-Ty called me and said, **Mbili Kwa Mbili**(Two for Two), Sis!"

"**Ninaipenda**(I love it)"

"You are coming back here?"

"No, I'm going home. I see you tomorrow all right. Sis!"

"All right fly guy I holla at you and thank you **Moja**(One)

"**Moja**!"

"After I hang up with him, I'm thinking to myself well they had it coming to them and I did not feel bad about it.

Like I did at first the same thing would have happened to me if I was fucking with the FBI or if I did not get this shit done. I would have got killed so I had to do it. I make Jagger and Damon Gee a drink and said, "lets toast to the fucking snitches going Boom-Boom bye-Bye!"

We all started yelling, "Boom-Boom Bye-Bye!"

Its real fucked up but this is the game were all in, so we all got drunk and high getting our smoke on until the wee hours in the morning and went home. I know I have something really big coming up that will move the whole BSN to another level of the game and I'm ready for it. When Spider comes back, he's going to be really happy wit all the moves I'm making and if he doesn't come back, I got this shit down for real.

CUTTING A REALLY BIG DEAL

The next day I take Jagger, Dun-Dun, Mookie, Tony Smokes and Crazy Monk with me to Bill street at this abandon store near Frankford Avenue. We drive up there in my black Tahoe truck we meet up with EL Braero a little before 3 O'clock and his peoples they tell all of us to go inside the spot. So were all standing around in this big space in the dark waiting on Jasper to walk in. We did not have to wait long soon as he walked in the door one of EL Braero men name Pete turned the lights on. Jasper is with four of EL Braero's men Big Wokey, Butter, Maro and Vegas with all their guns pointed up in Jasper's face. He's in deep shocked because he's been running around with them for months getting money selling crack with them, fucking bitches, tricking and breaking bread with the homies. Going out to eat all over the city having a good time thinking he's really down wit the 3rd street Mob. His mouth is wide open looking up at all of them knowing their going to shoot his black ass if he moves.

Pete holding his gun with both his hand up in the air and said, "just give me the gun Jasper the shit is over, brother." He looks up seeing all the guns on him and he's pissed off looking up at each one of us and said, "what y'all think I'm a bitch up because you low life motherfuckers sold me out for that crack baby bitch over there. Fuck that you got another thing coming!"

I stepped out from in front of Jagger and Dun-Dun with my Glock from in front of my jeans I yelled, "you said that shit before and I didn't like it now I'm going to make you pay for that shit you trick ass motherfucker!"

"What with all these niggas you got with you so you one bad bitch then, now?"

I'd looked around at everybody and said, "lower the fucking metal boys and move back for me. I got this shit just me and this nigga is going to settle this shit once and for all!"

Everybody moves back Dun-Dun grabbing me on my arm and said, "you don't have to do this shit Almasi."

"Yes, I do, I'm going to show this nigga what time it is. "Don't worry he's going to be smoking blunts and talking shit with Lucifer in a few fucking minutes Dawg!" We all have his ass surrounded. Most of EL Braero's peoples backed up standing on the left side then most of my peoples backed up from the right side of the large space giving us enough room to air this shit out we have between us. He's smiling pulling his black leather jacket back with his pistol in the front of his jeans and said, "I've been waiting to kill you bitch for a long time now. They all might kill me but at least I know I smoke your fucking ass first!

I just kept my focus on his ass not saying a word we stare at each other for a few ready to do this gangster duel shit. I didn't have to give him a chance, but this will show all these niggas what kind of skill level a bitch like me have when it comes to the gun shit for real. I put my pistol in the front of my jeans letting him see it along with everybody standing around ready to see how this shit is going to go down. I step out he's on the other side of me still wit that shit eating grin on his ugly black ass mug. I'm about to blow it the fuck off his face. So, then he reaches to draw I got my shit out faster then you can blink your fucking eyes. Pulling my Glock out beating him to the draw. Kapacka! Kapacka! Kapacka! I shot his ass three times before he could pull his shit all the way out. Hitting him in the head, neck and chest with a big chuck of meat flying out from his chest and head with the blood squirting out like the fucking water plug on the corner in the summertime. He falls backwards hitting the floor. Boom!

All of EL Braero's men moving out of the way and all their faces are in amazement that I was that good. My peoples knew what was going to happen to this nigga from the gate and just like he said they were going to kill him any way if I would have lost. But I knew dam well I was not going to lose to a nigga like that he was all fucking talk all the time and he never ran across a bitch like me with mad skills to pay the fucking bills. I was straight out the Gawd damn battle fields rocking that steel. All of them are cheering loud jumping up and down like they were in a football stadium. I just score a touchdown in the last few minutes in the fucking super bowl. I'm still holding the gun with both hands looking down at him in a pool of his own blood his eyes are still wide open. I walked up on him looking down stepping around the blood I made a big gob of phlegm from deep inside of my mouth and I spit right in his bloody ass face and screamed, "fuck you, nigga!" Jagger give me a high five laughing then Dun-Dun and said, "shit you still got them skills from our body bag crew days"! I stick my gun back in the front of my jeans and it's still hot.

Pete walked up to me and said, "shit now I know why they call you Glock mommy man you got skills, girlfriend!" I say to him, "I'm not the kind of bitch you want to piss off you know what I'm saying", and he slapped me five. Then Wokey, Butter, Vegas and Marco gave me some dap real swift still laughing I can see their dark tan faces glowing like a light bulb. I go in my pocket pulling out some money and asked, "can y'all clean up this dog shit up off the floor for me, please?"

Pete came up to me waving his hand and said, "you don't have to do that were all family now I talked to EL Braero last night and plus I seen all that work you put in wit us so that's not even necessary, Ma!"

Waving his hand, he said, "you and your peoples can get the fuck up out of here okay."

He hugged me and said, "I'll be hollering at you real soon mommy."

I wave my hand towards Dun-Dun, Jagger, Crazy Monk and Tony Smokes they all slap me five as we all rolled out the door and Pete close the door behind us. We all walked quickly to the truck jumping in Jagger took off with the hip hop music blasting loud all the way back to our home base. We had a party getting twisted until the sun came back in the sky. Friday came quick like a blur but soon as word when out about Jasper getting smoked Jane Doe and what she has left of her crew got out of town faster then the speed of light.

Now that I gave Jagger his green light to put his own thing together, he went and holla at a dude he did time with five years ago. He kept trying to get him to put in some work with him, but Jagger knew by staying loyal he would be running shit soon. So, he hollas at this bad motherfucker from North Philly name Flip and most people called him Flip Diddy young vicious crazy but very smart and cunning. He has half of North Philly all of South West Philly and Camden on lock.

The reason why is his brother the notorious Seany Shells who bodied more niggas then Chinese graveyard for real. This crew of niggas is mixed with Puerto Rican killers calling them self's BWHS Broadway Hit Squad. They wanted a sit down with the BSN soon as Jagger when to holla at Flip Diddy. I told Jagger that I will sit down with them soon as I get back from New York.

It's Friday night me, Jagger and Damon Gee meet up with the big man himself Tony Bolivar. The meeting went really smooth and he said he love the way we take care of business. It was not even a half an hour that went by and we had a deal, but we stayed for another hour celebrating with him and Natalie who hooked everything up. She received a big fat finder's fee, so she was happy.

Now were on our way, but the next day I went to holla at Emillano Vagus to see what that was up were dealing with Tony Bolivar. He was not happy about the news, but it was nothing he could have done about it. He knew were too strong to make a move on us plus he heard about the 3rd street Mob hooking up with us so now we had twice the muscle we had before.

So, after I spend Christmas with my family. I went to New York with my new Boo-Boo Black Scooch and we brought the year in right sucking, fucking and a tidal wave of orgasms.

SHIT GO SIDE WAYS IN NEW YORK

Three Months later it's the end of March 2002. We've been going back and forth with GTG with a large body count, to me neither side wins because it fucks up our money. Other then that shit been going real smooth with the big guy Tony Bolivar. He's loving it seeing large horse shit loads of money with us expanding in Maine, D.C., Baltimore, Boston, Virginia and New York.

I have not talk to or heard from Spider. I don't know if he's coming back but I'm in the driver seat its lot of work for sure but I'm loving it doe. So, I go back to New York with Black Scooch he take me to his apartment in the Bronx's on Commonwealth avenue.

The 1200 Block and the five houses he owns on 1700 block of Gleason Avenue down the street from his apartment. He owned six more building all in the area. They don't sell out of there they use them for stash spots looking normal as possible. We were chilling after having wild knock down drag out sex and we both got our shit off really good. I'm lying in the bed floating on a cloud when Black Scooch phone rings. I said to him, "hey baby you told me you were not going to do any business while I was here?"

"I'm not I just have to check on something is that all right baby?" I just looked at him now I'm real pissed off right about now so soon as he went out the door. I put my clothes back on fuck that I'm ready to roll back to Philly faster then the wind blows in a fucking hurricane. I put my clothes on and I light up a Newport while I'm checking my guns. Soon as I looked at my second gun, I hear some niggas by the door making all kinds of noises. I ran and turn the lights off and I lay in the bed with both my Glocks. I have them motherfuckers cocked. I act like I'm sleep Boom! I can hear the door came flying open. I know there coming but I just lay there until they reach the bedroom soon as they opened the door. I lift my head from the bed putting on that defenseless woman act on with them so they can have their guard down.

The first two men turn the lights on, and the other two men walked in the room behind them I sit up as the first two men came towards me with a sinister smile on their dark grills. Its Nizzy and his top henchmen Tombstone Tommy I sit up slow with the covers over me acting like they startled me as Nizzy yelled, "yeah, I'm going to keep that pussy warm for my man black Scooch is not going to be fucking you no more!"

I looked at him and asked, "what the fuck are you talking about, nigga? Get the fuck out of this room before Scooch come back here and fuck all of y'all up for real!"

They all started laughing Tombstone Tommy said, "your man is dead, bitch! Now go ahead and cock that hot black pussy open for all of us and you just might live after were done fucking the shit out your fine black ass!"

Kapacka! Kapacka! Kapacka! Kapacka! I shot him right in his mouth and neck then I hit Nizzy in his fat ass nasty neck and head. They both fell to the floor with blood shooting out everywhere. The two men behind them were in shock with blood all over there fucking faces. They did not have their guns out both of them is freaked out from the blood on them ready to draw. I squeezed the triggers at the simultaneously Kapacka-Kapacka! shooting both their ass at the same time hitting both of them niggas in the middle of their chest. I can see the chunks flying from their bodies as they went down. They hit the ground fast. Doom! I'm jumping up from the bed to my feet I slip on my flat shoes thn I put my pocket book up on my shoulder super swift.

Fuck them clothes I brought with me! I step around all the dead men on the floor and all the blood trying not to step into it. I run towards the front door my heart is beating like an 808 drum on a hard ass hip hop track.

I make it out the door looking both ways with my head on a swivel ready to smoke anything that jump out on my ass. I'm on the third floor I can hear more men running up the stair well. I run towards one of the apartments on my left while there shooting at me. Pat! Pat! Pow! The bullets just missing me while I shot the doorknob to the apartment at the same time I crashed in the door. While I hear them yelling "get that bitch! Don't let her get away!"

I run throw these people apartment there looking at me like I'm crazy. I aim towards the window shooting the windows out. Siiisssssszzz! I take my guns clearing out the rest of the glass, so I don't get cut the fuck up. I put both my guns in front of my jeans I climbed out the window as there running in the room still shooting at me. I let myself hang, and I let go dropping myself down to the ground Woooop! I'm one lucky bitch I land on my feet then I ran towards Gleason Avenue where my car is parked. There shooting at me from out of the window. Boom!
Boom! Pow! Katow! Patttaa! Bullets is raining down on me I'd quickly ducked behind this parked car I turn and took aim Kapacka! Kapacka!

I hit two out of the four of them its dark, but I know damn well I took a chunk out of one of them ass holes head some of them backed up from the window. I gave them something to think about! I see one of them fall from the window. Then I just stand up acting normal walking real slow towards my car I hit my remote Boo-Beatt! I jumped in and I pulled off really smooth. Some more niggas were running around but they did not know what kind of car I had. They never seen me come there. So, I was good to go but I knew it was something about that motherfucker Nizzy I got a bad feeling about him the minute I laid eyes on that big black poppy eyed cocksucker. I would not stop until I see the sign saying welcome to Philadelphia. I'm thinking about Black Scooch the whole way home if he is dead, he never seen this shit coming you can't trust none of them niggas from the Bronx. It took me three hours to get back to Philly and I'd thank Gawd I got the hell out of there with my fucking life. I was so happy to be back home. I learned something tonight never go out of town to go get some Dick no matter how good it is in the game I'm in.

Soon as I got to my door, I damn near ran inside I ran up and kissing Auntie and then my precious little baby boy sitting in the living room. I found out later on that week what happen the Bronx Niggas wanted all the Harlem niggas out and big Nizzy was just waiting to take Black Scooch spot to become the new drug king pin in the area. They might have run all the Harlem niggas out. Nobody wanted to fuck wit them giving them any kind of big-time product after that bullshit they did.

They went from bricks to half of bricks to shitty ass O's(Ounces). It is real weak shit too after having to cut it too many times. They wanted them Harlem nigga out, but they knew what they were doing those Bronx niggas was too greedy and did not know how to conduct business. They might have won the battle, but they lost the mother fucking war.

Well when you make moves like that the two-bit cheap nickel and dime hustler you just be fucking your own self out bigger and better things if you ask me.

RUNNING SHIT MY WAY

Its May 2006, the weather is starting to break after all that cold ass winter. I hate the fucking cold, but I love living in Philly doe. I chill out and laid low but still doing my job and shit is working out lovely with Tony Bolivar peoples and I notice that our drop doubled. I got Jagger to stick around until July and train Goliath to be my new bodyguard. He can go do his thing I sat down with his peoples and all of them are good to go and rockin with the BSN flow.

I got a call from Philly while he was on the lamb from the FBI. He's telling me that he wanted his stepson Poochie who just got out of jail to give him a top spot somewhere because he's been holding down the BSN while he was in the joint. So, I brought him on as my other bodyguard but I'm going to keep my eye on him until I can really trust his ass. I trust Philly's judgment but that just me I don't trust a motherfucker until I know I can. So, I have Damon Gee to check him out really good but I'm playing it off while Damon check his ass out.

So now Jagger have to whip both of them into shape and Jagger really was hard on them to get it together too. I'm getting dressed when I get a call from Damon Gee. I get the phone while I'm in the mirror doing my hair, "yo, what's up Gee?"

"Hey, I got some shit to tell you."

"All right then spit it out, nigga!"

"No not on the phone I'm on my way to the spot."

"Yeah in a couple hours after I eat. Well I see you then **Moja!**"

"Okay **Moja!**" I'm done doing my hair when I go in the living room and Jagger is in both them niggas ass again, I'm loving it. Jagger said, "to both of them wait right there as he came over bumping fist with me and said, "Auntie, took the baby with her to do some shopping she said your plate is in the microwave."

"Thanks! What's up wit them two niggas?"

"They will get it trust me. I'm showing them a few things and I'll stay until they have shit down tight all right." They both wave at me and I wave back smiling.

I whispered, "stay on their ass I want them to have their shit, real tight too."
"I don't want no sloppy ass niggas when it comes to my life okay." I looked up at them smiling getting my food out the microwave and I sit at the table.
"Did you here?"
"Did I hear what?"
"GTG again they got into it with our crew in North Philly." "Why nobody told me that shit?"
"I'm telling you now, Almasi. You did say I was your number two man, right?"
"Yeah, I did say that. Well I'm on top of that shit right now and I'm telling you about it now." I send my crew to deal with that shit. I'm giving them niggas a test and see if they're going to work out you feel me."
"Well look at you my nigga good job so what happen doe?"
"Those GTG niggas shot two of our peoples Poke and Sleam at the gas station at Board and Lehigh."
"Are they dead or alive? No, there in bad shape but there both still alive all fucked up, but I am getting sick of this shit doe!"
"We had an inside guy, but once Spider got of town, but I know if he is dead or not."
"So were going have to take care of this shit." I'm eating my food looking up at Jagger nodding his head yes.
"Let me eat and you and me can put our head together and come up with the master plan to bring them motherfuckers to their knees all right, Dawg."
"Sure nuff, sis. I'm going over here and finish drilling these niggas!" We both started laughing as he walks over towards the two of them waiting for him near my door. Soon as I am done eating my phone rings, I looked at the caller ID. I don't know who the fuck it is, but I pick it up any way.
"Yo, who is this?"
"This Top-Cat from the Black Demons M.C. Remember me?"
"Oh yeah, what's up with its been a long time now."
"Yes, it has girlfriend, Look I need to holla at you about some **Biashara** (business)."
"Okay, do you know where my new office is at? "
"**Hapana** (No)"

"**Wapi**(where)?"
"23rd and Washington Avenue it's a warehouse Oon the right-hand side big steel gray door I let my peoples know you're coming."
"Good I'll be there around one all right."
"All right I see you then **Moja**. (One)!"
"Moja!"
I get myself together I get up and wash my plate out while I watch Jagger showing them niggas the right moves with a gun and machine gun. I'm just smiling thinking back when I was getting my training back in the days this shit is life and death for real. I put on my leather jacket from the back of my chair I checked all of my guns taking my time. I put one in the front of my jeans one in the back. Plus, one in my pocketbook because you never fucking know. Now I'm ready to go punch in for the day. I walked up putting them niggas to the test Jagger stand to the side to see what they're going to do, and I can see how these niggas move and act. They both get on each side of me. Jagger get the door smiling I don't say shit I just see if they're going to be in step with me the right way. I stop while Goliath check the doors then he's waiting for me to start walking again. I just look him up and down and started walking towards the elevator in my condo.
Poochie press the button his face is cold and hard. As a rock that just what I need on my team and he's a big ruff tattoos all over his face and neck nigga.
I can tell by looking in his eyes he been down that lonely ass dark road of death and destruction like all the rest of us in the ghetto. I ask him before the elevator came what part of South Philly you from?
"23rd & Tasker street I know now coming up around there is no fucking joke from the door."
"Good you know any Swahili?"
"Very little doe."
"Well you're going to have to work on that, brother. Don't worry were going to teach you."
He nods his head, "yes, as were getting on the elevator. I like that he doesn't do too much talking until I do."

Looks like things going to work with this nigga all I have to do is wait to talk to Damon and he give me this nigga whole run down about his ass. Poochie get the car door for me Goliath is driving my gray Benz wagon I had to get another one and oh yes, the motherfucker is bullet proof. Me and Jagger sit in the back I say put so music on for me please big guy. Okay boss lady he puts in the CD a mix tape Jawn banging that Robin Thicke joint Blurred Lines I just love that song its really hot about this time. Where the fuck is your sister at Jagger? She with Gino Gats I told her to be on time for work I'll call her to see where she's at. He got the phone up to his ear he talks for a few minutes he hangs up saying she's there already sis. Okay good see after I whipped her ass she straighten right the fuck up! We both started laughing while I nod my head to the hot ass beats.

Soon as we get to the spot Poochie jump out and get the door for me.

I stand there while Goliath hit the remote as we all walked together Goliath banging on the door three times then he stops and bang three more times. That's the code letting them know it's us. The door open, up real fast it Puerto Rican Joe opening up the big gray steel door and Booby Hill is standing inside of the door on the right. We stepped in while I bump fist with both of them o while we all get inside. I see Tanya sitting with Gino Gats Ty-Kim and Black Duke there all huddle up talking they all speak to me. Ty-Kim came up to me and asked, "did you hear?"

"Yeah, I heard already Ty Jagger is taking care of that shit yo did you do your rounds yet?"

"Yeah, I'm done you know I don't fuck around it over there on your desk waiting for you. I bump fist with him saying that's why I fuck with you brother. But I'm going to need you later on so don't go anywhere all right "Sure, I hang around looked tell all them niggas I have Top Cat from the Black Demon's coming by."

"I let all them you don't have to check them there cool."

" You sure?"
"Yeah, I'm sure let me get in here and do some work like you did already nigga. We both started laughing as he goes over towards everybody telling them what was up. I go in the office with Jagger and were both working the phones making sure niggas is doing their job. Or I'll have somebody in their spot that same day once somebody fuck up. And everybody had their hands out too even the fucking cops as much as they talk shit and want to lock us the fuck up and we still have to pay some them no good motherfuckers dam if you do and dam if you don't. We're working and talking shit to one another and Jagger send his sister out to get the boys lunch and I had her to go take my little sister Robin to my crib with all her things. I know that bitch Dotty is going to get mad but its time she came to live with me she's 17 now and I don't want that junkie ho has her raped like she did me. I can't wait until she come stay with me. Damon Gee came in the door of the office smiling bumping fist wit me real smooth. We both say family at the same time.
"So, is it you wanted to tell me nigga?
"Well our good friend Emillano Vagus are going to make a move on us real soon. My peoples close to Ouroboros told me this shit. Emilliano hooked up with Ouroboros for more muscle. He got us on the top of the hit list because were not fucking with them no more after we hooked up with Tony Bolivar."
"Okay we will be ready for their ass. And who the hell are the Ouroboros?"
"It's a super gang from out of the Puerto Rican jail system there like the Latin Kings you never heard of them before?"
"No just as long as there out of my way I don't give a fuck about them."
"Well it's a lot of them motherfuckers so we have to lock shit down and keep an eye on their ass for real there no joke."
"So, what the fuck do Ouroboros mean anyway?"
"It's like night and day black and white good and evil like that."
"Okay I get it like Ying and Yang, right."
"See you got it." I'm thinking to myself a bitch like me might just have to gear up for this shit coming at us fast. "So, what's up with this nigga, Poochie?"

"He's good to go and solid as a rock don't worry, he's not down with no cops with that niggas record he's a stone-cold killer from the door."

"Good, that's what I want to hear!"

I picked up the phone and I'd called up EL Braero he picked up after the phone rings about three times and said, "hey what up, sis?"

"Look I need to holla at you about some shit about to go down brother."

"Well whatever it is I'll have my peoples ready for it just tell me when and where to be. We will be there all right don't worry about nothing okay."

"Thank you, big man. I knew things would really work out with us."

"Well as you know you done put us to the test many times before and we always show out for that kind of shit, Glock Mommy. just give me the details and I'll have my peoples in place. **Nzuri**- "That means good right?"

"Yeah it does, so you've been studying then big man?"

"Yeah, I have, and I been learning Spanish as well from my aunt Rose."

"I See you getting in touch wit your roots I like that. I'll come by and give you the whole lay out once I get things together here all right **Moja!**(One)"

"**Moja!**"

I looked up at Jagger and said, "I'm going to need you to call up your boys with all this shit about to come down on us so we can give them a real work out.

"I'll get on that right now this is what they been waiting for."

"I know this is what they were born to do. We both started laughing. But I know this was going to be something that will test us all another war now with me At the head of the **Meza**(Table)."

I have the feeling this time around were all going have to dig down real **Kina**(Deep). Then I heard someone tapping on the glass on my office door. Its Puerto Rican Joe he said, "it's Top- Cat and his men our here to see you."

"Thank you, Joe show them right in, please." I stood up smiling. Its Top-Cat his right-hand man and partner in crime Doctor Jerry, Jo-Jo Outlaw his Vice President, Gee-Gee Thug the sergeant of arms and his son Dream. Damn, he got the right name this nigga is fine he can get some. Along with Dream right hand man Tony Blue and Kay-Kay. I shake each one of their hands as there coming inside of my office.

Jagger closed the door behind them, and Damon Gee put up so more chairs for everybody to sit down. Then he stands up by the wall with Jagger. Top-Cat said, "so you done moved up in the world the last time we met?" **Mimi nina hisia**(I'm Impressed)

"Thank you, yes I did. I worked my ass off to get here too." Then I sat down lighting up a cigarette leaning back in my big office chair.

"I know I heard how much work you and your crew been putting in taking out the fucking Russians wiping out the Gorilla Boulevard niggas. And taking over the cracker ass mob boys heroin hook up!" All of his men started laughing loud. "That's just why I'm here I'm proud of you and your peoples for the good work but right about now you're going to need some help with these Ouroboros motherfuckers."

"How you know that Tee Cee?"

"Because I know everything going down in the streets, we got people in all the prisons and them niggas be talking too." Everybody started laughing.

"I already know you got the 3rd street mob to go down wit you too after you done hooked them up really good there rolling like a motherfucker. Everybody started snickering. "You will just go toe to toe with these motherfuckers, but wit me and my peoples you will wipe their ass off the fucking map. Just like you did wit Gorilla Boulevard and the Chopper posse. I don't know if you're going to have them working for you like you did the Armenians with the gun hook up doe?" Everybody in the room started giggling. Okay so what do you need from us?

"So, you can help us wipe these assholes off the map for us."

"Well I'm going to tell you right now, sis. It's a freighter coming in three days filled with some of the best methamphetamine in the world."

"Okay, you want me to get my people to help you get it right but who is guarding it and who it belongs too?"

"Well, it used to belong to this gang in South Dakota called, 'the Tribal Boys some Indian gang bangers who was cooking up crank for the white biker gangs.' They all got locked up by the FBI, ATF and local asshole cops they are done. Now the FBI is taking the crank out to sea to destroy it."

"So, you want us to take out the FBI and take the shipment?" See this is the best part about this they're going to have some outside contractors and some FBI men to guard the shit. We have the inside track because all of the outside contractors tipped us off about this, but I don't trust their ass that's where your people come in."

"So how you know you can trust us?" He said, "well I trust you more then I trust their ass plus crank is not y'all game." I looked up at him and nodded my head,

"Yeah, you're right about that we don't fuck wit that. So, what do you think?"

"Plus, were going to break you off wit something as a thank you for helping us. Okay we will do it but any man I lose you pay for them from the door."

"Sounds fair how much?"

"80,000 dollars a man.

"Make it 75 that's what the crackers pay for in the army, navy or the marines."

"Okay deal." We both shook hands smiling.

So, when did you become not trustworthy?"

"I was just fucking wit you. That's why I came to y'all in the first place, shit!

We all started laughing really loud.

I still was giggling and asked, "how many men you need?"

"About 15 or 20 that will be good, and I'll help you fuck up each and every one of them Ouroboros you have my word on that Ma!"

"Uwaue wote (Kill them all!)" The whole room erupts into a big cheer. We talk shit for a little bit then me Jagger and Damon walked them to the front door to their bikes parked outside. Soon as they rode off in their thunderous heard.

We went back inside making big plans for our next move. After talking with Jagger and Damon Gee I had Goliath and Poochie take me home. When I got home, I was so happy to see my sister Robin's big beautiful smile playing and talking with my son. This right here to me this was picture perfect moment and that's just what I did I took a picture on my phone. Right then and there I felt like a normal person for the rest of the day. But I know if the phone rings or someone comes knocking on the door. Then shit just change in a flash of an eye and Glock Mommy has to make her appearance like wonder woman in her fucking invisible jet and kill everything on set. A lot of motherfuckers are going to get wet.

So, I feel really good when the phone or nobody came to get me so I can be with my family and that means more than the world to me for real. I spent hours with them having fun, laughing cooking and just being a mommy and big sister nothing but love and happiness even if it's just for a few hours.

THE FREIGHTER JOB WITH THE BLACK DEMONS

The Three days flew by faster than the fucking wind blowing in a tornado. The night of the freighter job Dun-Dun told me the he had everything under control, but I wanted to be in the middle of the shit. I told him I'm going. He just threw his hands up in the air, but he said when you're riding in the back of the truck with the rest of the nigga's doe.

I said, "yeah, but when I got back there my ass was hurting from the hard ass steel of the cargo truck. He had ten men in one and ten men in the other he was driving one truck with Mookie riding shotgun with him with Crazy Monk, Booby Hill, Black Duke, Tony Smokes, Puerto Rican Joe, Ty-Kim, Fly-Ty and Chrome and me. In the other truck he had Rah-Killer driving with Nugee riding shot gun with her. With Billy Blunts, Gino Gats, Fat Lou-Lou, Gavin the new guy Taz Money, Poppy Low Nugee's brother, Jamar and Mister Fat Back Nugee's half-brother.

It took about hour to ride to the docks in the two cargo trucks. We met up with the Black Demons right outside of the docks Top-Cat son Dream had the truck to hook the trailer on to with his right-hand man Tony Blue. And just like us there were all in cargo trucks and six cars. Top-Cat Jo-Jo Outlaw and Dun-Dun worked it out soon as the truck drives up. Top-Cat will take out the driver with his sniper rifle with a silencer. He's already set up with his gun about 2000 feet away out of sight on top of a stack of containers. After he takes the shot and everybody in the trucks and cars move in and get the guards driving behind and in front of it. They had it set up perfect where all the trucks were all around them, we did not have to wait long. The FBI had four cars in the front of the truck carrying the crank and four cars in the back of the truck with the crank cargo. I can hear everyone talking to one another in my earpiece. Everybody had an earpiece all dressed in black. I can hear Gee-Gee Thug from the Black Demons up the road and said**, "Hapa Wanakuja**" (Here they come). I never heard the shot that Top-Cat took I just heard the gunfire all over the place. I'm waiting to jump out to get to the action I don't know this is like my drug being in the shit. After he took the shot while I'm sitting in the back with the others waiting to make our move. I'm the boss and they are doing the whole thing with me waiting like the soldiers. My ego is working overtime now. I know he did not want anything to happen to me, but I wanted to be there. The the truck pulls off really quickly and I can hear Dun-Dun yelling, "**Kila Mtu ainhie**" (Everybody move in). The truck is moving quickly I'm holding on with my heart beating really hard. The door opened fast with all of us jumping out like commandos. Bullets was flying everywhere now I know why he did not want me there the minute I jumped out with my machine gun. I'm in my gun stance letting them motherfuckers have it.
Kackapacka! Kackpacka! Katowoo!
I'm thinking to myself damn there really putting up a hell of a fight for this shit. I smoke about five men jumping out their cars. Soon as I think it's over six more of them pop back up but just like Top-Cat said the guys who supposed to be working with them is trying to double cross them he knows what he was talking about.

The Black Demons is taking care of their ass too. I see Jo-Jo Outlaw, Gee-Gee Thug and Doctor Jerry smoking their ass working them machine guns like down ass soldiers that know what they're doing. While Tony Blue and Kay-Kay helped Dream hook up the trailer super swift. I looked up and there long gone with all the crank. When I see those contractors try to cross us right before my eyes this piss me off so bad. I went into blood lust Black Duke, Tony Smokes and Booby Hill started rolling with me side by side started killing them ripping their shit to shreds.

After we started smoking about eight of them the last guy throws up his hand and said, "they made me go along with them don't kill me!" We're holding our machine guns on him while the Black Demons is mopping shit up with these niggas. Booby Hill ran up on the last contractors working with the FBI he pushed him on the ground hard. Boom!

We are all looking from side to side to make sure nobody else is coming up on us. Our second truck of our men is jumping on loading up getting the fuck out of there and off they go.

Then I can hear Dun-Dun's yell, "okay Unit one gets ghost!" Booby Hill sprayed the dude on the ground in the back before we ran back on the truck Kapacka Tat! Takapacka! Tataka!

Blood flying up in the air right from my far right I can see this guy running up on us shooting. I got low flat on the ground pointing upward spitting hot shit.

I did get his ass watching him fall to the ground fast and hard. Booby Hill and Tony Smokes reached down pulling me up on the truck while Ty-Kim and Crazy Monk is laughing closing the doors. Boom! The Cargo truck is taking off down the road then I can hear Dun-Dun in the ear piece loud and clear, **"Kazi Nzuri kila mtu"** (Good job everybody!) A half an hour later we all are getting out of the cargo truck in the middle of the Acme parking lot with all of our trucks and cars waiting for us. Soon as I'm taking off my bandanna from my face Jagger and Poochie is waiting for me in my truck holding the door open for me. I jumped in the back seat still feeling the rush. Sex or cocaine can never make me feel like this. I got home and I fell asleep I found out later we did not lose not one man a lot of them got hurt but no deaths thank Gawd. Top-Cat called me and thanked me and said he will have our back before shit go down and he broke us off wit a lot of loot as well. I shared it wit all my men who did the job. Dun-Dun came and talked to me a day later and said, "he doesn't what anything to happen to me so I can run things smooth.

I can't lie he jumped in my ass but he's the only one I would let talk to me like that. He did not do it in front of anybody as well, but I knew he was just looking out for me doe. He told me things is running super smooth and he don't want things all fucked up now that I'm running things. We laugh about it later and got drunk and I left him on the floor while I went to bed. When I got up that morning it him and Tawni were on my couch because I called her to let her know where he was at that night.

When I got up, I fixed both of them breakfast they stayed all that day until that night, and we all got drunk together talking shit about back in the days having fun calling over the rest of the old crew. They all came over to my house to. Mookie with La-Neese, Tony Smokes with Nashaen and Crazy Monk with Danielle and we all had a fucking ball too. Real family we were doing what we always do live life and enjoy while we can.

Three years when by like a fucking blur we were fighting back and forth with GTG and the Ouroboros motherfuckers. But we out class them from the jump. They were not strong enough to take us down. Plus, we were ready for their ass I have to say were too smart for them as well. We were making money hand over fist as usual BSN at the top of our game knocking shit out the frame.

MAN THIS WAR SHIT IS A BITCH

Monday July first, 2009. The 4th of July came early for us. I had all my peoples doing what we always do stay organized and make our move swift and silent. Then we got hit and it surprise us like a motherfucker. They hit four of our spots all at the same time South West Philly killing five of our peoples and taking all the money and product too. One of them was Damon Gee's cousin her name is Jamila she just bagged up dope at the spot. She was 19 years old.
In North Philly killing six people doing the same thing taking all the drugs and money. Also, West Philly killing four people getting money and drugs. East Falls projects killing eight people, but they did not get the money only the drugs.
But that's 23 people in one fucking day a hurt piece with biscuits & gravy. I got the call before I could wash my face and get dressed from Damon Gee. I said to him,
"I'll have Fly- Ty to help him out."
"Okay, sound good to me also get another man with me to watch my back."
"Okay I'll get Chrome. I'll call him right now where you want him to meet you?"
"Tell him to meet me at the car wash at 6th & Girard."
"Okay I will. Are you sure you got this do you need anything else?"
"No. I got this Almasi you just keep your eyes open somebody is talking."
"Yeah I know but who doe?"
"I don't know but whoever it is when I find them there going to wish they were never alive when I'm done with them. They killed my little cousin Jamila she was just 19 years old. She was just making a little money for school I told her I did not want her working in there, but she said she could handle it and I believed her."
"I'm so sorry to hear about your little cousin Damon but whoever it was I'm going to make them pay very dearly!"
"And so, will I sis Moja! (One)"
"Moja!" Soon as I hang up my phone rings again making me jump. Its Fat Lou-Lou,

"Yo! I'm outside your door we need to talk right now!" I hang up I quickly put on my house coat and when into my dresser getting my pistol cocking it back sticking in my pocket of my house coat. I run up in the living room where Poochie and Goliath to get the door and make sure its Fat Lou-Lou if you see anything funny blast their ass! Poochie and Goliath whipping out their guns peeking out the peep hole opening the door really slow.
Fat Lou-Lou running inside. Fat Lou-Lou all excited running up to me and yelled, "Tulipat hit Kubwa (We got hit big time!)"
"Nini! (What!)"
"Yeah Tano usafirshaji (Five Shipments!) Yeah over 12,000 keys each!"
"Shit!" Jagger came in the door and I looked at him and said, "Did you hear what happen"
"Yeah, they hit five of our spots and these niggas tried to kill me on the way here that's why I'm so late!
"Yeah and these motherfuckers hit five of our big shipments. That means somebody is talking and they know when and where our shit is coming in."
"So, it someone who works for us right?"
"Yeah, but who?"
"I'm getting dressed and find the fuck out something. I'll call EL Braero and make sure if there cool!
And get your crew together Flip Diddy and his boys this shit is going to get really bloody and crazy!" I get washed and dressed soon as I get my guns and I grab an extra one. In this war here I'm taking out everybody moving on me. I'm thinking I'm ready for any sneaky ass motherfuckers and they stick it right in my ass with a cold iron pole too. I go in Little Boom's room getting him up to get wash and dressed he's 12 now. After he was done, I tell him to wait for Auntie in the living room. He nods his head yes and he walks quickly to the living room pouting but he knows I'll whip that ass if he said one fucking word.
Then I went in the back room where Auntie is sleeping in late just like I do on Mondays. I knocked hard and came in and she's in the bed with this dude I don't know. They both was jumping up in the middle of fucking. I backed up closing the door back Yelling, "I'm sorry!" Then I stand near the door and asked, "who the fuck is that Auntie?"

"It's Reggie my friend I told you about him you said it was cool!"
"You know what Aunt-Tee I forgot I'm really sorry wit all this shit going on! Look I'm sorry Reggie I did not mean to embarrass y'all!" Aunt-Tee said, "you can come in now!"
I open the door and said, "look, I'm sorry I just forgot and why y'all niggas did not lock the fucking door!"
Aunt-Tee hits Reggie in the head with her pillow and said, "this nigga when he went to the bathroom!"
"You got one in here?"
"I told him that!" Reggie said, "I didn't know and where is it at?" We both pointing at it on the right-hand side. Reggie said, "damn La'Wanda, this place is so fucking big that's the place I knew where the bathroom is at, so I went to that one down the hall I really had to go, too."
"Okay look Aunt-Tee, it's a lot going on. I'm going to need you to go to the other condo with my sister Robin. I'll have someone to take y'all there. I'll have someone around the clock watching your back. I still want you to get your shit I gave you okay."
"Okay I still have it and I know what to do."
"Okay good. I will get my sister up and I want y'all to listen to Fat Lou-Lou he's going to hold y'all down!"
"I will baby!" I hug her and said, "I see y'all tonight I got to go!
"If you need money you know what card to use, right?"
"Yeah, I got that too." I tell her that Little Boom is in the living room waiting for them. I go down the hall and get my sister Robin knocking on the door really hard. I walked in she's knocked the fuck out sleep. I shake her really hard and said, "hey get up baby." She looked up at me and said, "okay, but where are we going?"
"You are going to my other condo."
"You have another condo?"
"Yeah, I do and you're going to love it."
She jumps up all excited and said, "oh yeah, I want to see this!"
"Yeah get dressed I have to go to work Aunt La'Wanda is going to take you there all right give me a hug. I have to go!"
"Okay I'm see you later on right when you come from work. You promise?"
"Yeah you know that girl give me some!" She bumps fist with me smiling. I walk out of my sister's bedroom.

I roll up in the living room with everybody waiting on me saying okay Lou-Lou I need you to take my son Little Boom my sister Robin and Aunt-Tee to my other condo.
"You stay there until I send someone to relieve you okay." "Sure, and can I get the strap yard while Black Leroy is out of town?"
"Yeah it's all yours. And if he doesn't come back?"
"Why you know something?"
"Go talk to Julio Fagot ass once he came to the yard shit went sideways."
"Who said for him to be working down there?"
"Fat Hanky the old head he said to keep that shit on the low."
"You want to know something nigga come here give me a fucking hug over here nigga!" I'd hugged him and said,
"look come here." I take him into my bedroom I go into my stash under my bed handing him four stacks. His eyes got wide, "is this for me?"
"Yes, you just made me figure that shit out! I looked him right in his eyes I really trust you Lou-Lou you been down for a long time and I'll make sure you run the yard from here on out with a fucking raise! Here!" I hand him a leather bag and continued, "put your loot in there! This is a bitch bag, Almasi I'm not that way." With his eyes getting wide.
"So, nigga that's a lot of money motherfucker! Just take the bag nigga come on!" We both started laughing about it. We walked out of my bedroom to my living room I said to everyone, "look before we go, Lou-Lou here will be running the strap yard from here on out. He will pick his own crew." I bump fist with him and smiled, "okay, let's get the fuck out of here. I have some calls to make in the truck! Jagger ride with me. Poochie you drive his whip to the spot following us, all right?"
"Sure thing, Almasi!" We all quickly go out of the door. Soon as Goliath open the door for me, I get in my truck with Jagger sitting in the back. We drive off hitting the expressway I turned to Jagger and said, "I know whose doing this shit. I just figure this shit out and just who is doing it!" "Who?"
"Fat Hanky!"
"What you're crazy he's an old head."
"Yeah, but he asked for Julio, nigga to work down at the strap yard on the low."

"So what?"
"You did not know about him fucking with Shamika back at one my first crack spots and he know we took care of Shamika and Tamika!"
"Damn, I did not know that shit. Wow!"
"Who else would know all of our shipment routes and all of our new spots too!"
"You're right but nobody is going to believe that shit doe!" "I'll call everybody that I trust to come up to the spot so I can tell them what the fuck is going on."
It took us about an hour to get there I called Dun-Dun, Mookie, Tony Smokes, Black Duke, Crazy Monk, Rah-Killer, Booby Hill, Ty-Kim,Fly-Ty, Puerto Rican Joe, Nugee, Tanya, Gino Gats and Damon Gee.
I put Tanya, Gino Gats, Black Duke, Puerto Rican Joe, Poochie and Goliath on post two-man teams. It took everybody a couple hours to get to the spot so were all talking, eating and getting our smoke on while I think of something to set this motherfucker up. I tell everybody about who is at the head of this new war. Most of them who got there is getting jumpy waiting to hear what I had to tell them we were only waiting on Fly Ty and Damon Gee. It took them a while to get there but they did come. I got some more bad news they hit three more shipments from D.C., B-More and Maine where we make the most money from the heroin. Selling it to the other gangs that's cool with us but double our money drop.
Right from the door getting rich off that shit all the crackers in Maine are hooked on dope. They told me when they got there, and they killed four more of our peoples and Buckshot is dead In D.C. Along with Brenton. They heard they chopped off All their heads and had them all laying on the roof of their cars each one of them Damon Gee handing me his phone. I can see the picture of them with their heads severed off. Once I see that shit, I just hand him back his phone shaking my head now I'm really pissed off. I feel bad because I sent them to D.C. To help them niggas out.

The only good news I got today is that Ayden with half of Rah-Killers crew Billy Blunts, Crowbar Carl, Lace Lawless and Mickey Molly is holding it down in B-More killing all of the niggas that tried to attack them and they got nothing from them. Now everybody is here I looked up at everyone while where in this big back room of the condo round white table.

"Look now that were all here, I know who is fucking with us and they been under our nose the whole time.

Damon Gee asked, "okay, so who is it because I would love to fucking know I been asking everybody about who it was." "Look Fat Lou-Lou ran to my crib telling me about that our shipment got hit. And then he told me everything started going sideways once Faggot ass Julio started working at the strap yard."

Damon Gee said, "I did not know he was working there? Nobody did and if I know that shit, I would have shot that motherfucker on the spot!"

Crazy Monk said, "why would y'all do that. What's up wit him?"

Dun-Dun said, "I tell you why because Shamika use to fuck wit Julio at the crack spot. I used to work there so I know they was fucking."

Mookie said, "I did not know that shit!"

Dun-Dun said, "Yeah, but she stopped fucking wit him once she knew he was messing with some of the homos up in the jails."

"What?"

Rah-Killer said, "did everybody know that he's gay?"

"No, he been keeping it on the low."

Rah-Killer said, "see me I don't care who knows I'm gay but wit dudes its looks really bad being gay and a gangster."

All of us started laughing.

Damon Gee said, "you know y'all just might have something there let's find that bitch made nigga and make him set Fat Hanky up."

I looked up at him and said, "yeah, I like it. I said, yeah let do that?" Everybody started nodding their head yes in agreement.

"Dun-Dun and I know how to find his Fagot ass!"

"How?"

"Were going to holla at his brother he knows just where that nigga is at!"

Rah-Killer said, "so why should he tell us where his fucking brother is at?"

I said, "because he hates that motherfucker because he raped and killed his baby mother and he got away with it!"
Fly-Ty said, "damn I didn't know that shit?"
Tony Smokes also said, "damn I didn't know that neither." "what the fuck are brothers for!"
We all started laughing. Booby Hill chimed in, "wow the shit you find out about people is about a motherfucker!"
Ty-Kim said, "who the hell is his brother?"
Crazy Monk answered, "his name is Emilio and I know where he lives at too. I knew their peoples from around the way I'll take care of it."
"Good take somebody with you just in case. And all of us have to lay low until we make our move on these motherfuckers! And I'm need for y'all to go talk to that nigga Emilio, tonight."
"I'm on it right now." He waves to Tony Smokes for him to come with him saying after I get with him. I'll hit you back and let you know how I made out. They both got up from the table and they quickly rolled out the door.
We talked for a little while then I told everybody to keep their eyes open, we will meet up at our warehouse in Nice town tomorrow. Nobody knows about that place but all of our inside crew niggas. So, I bump fist with everybody and said, "be careful out there I don't want to get any more bad news!"
I waved at Goliath and Poochie so we can get the hell out of there. I called Tanya and Gino Gats over to me and said, "y'all can come to my other condo." They both nodded their heads, yeah, I roll out the door with Poochie and Goliath. We jumped in my whip hitting the expressway were driving along for a while when two trucks started following us. Goliath yelled, "we have company, boss lady!" Poochie reached up under the seat of the Benz wagon cocking back his machine gun.
Goliath getting his Glock out of the side of the door and I reached over to the other seat getting my Bravo company machine gun and my Mossberg 12-gauge shotgun. Soon as one of the trucks sped up shooting at us, I can see the sparks from the bullets bouncing off our truck. I stick my shotgun in the special hole I had made for my truck soon as they drove up closer. I'd pumped back my shotgun Boom! Hitting the back-side window, I can see all glass and blood flying and I can hear them yelling.

"Yeah, I hit that motherfucker right in his face."
I can see the other nigga back there holding his dead homeboy with no fucking face. I pumped my shot gun back again took aim Boom! This nigga holding his dead homeboy ducked down low and he kept popping back up shooting at us.
Poochie quickly stuck his machine gun in the other special hole on his side lighting up the truck other truck on his side. Kapacka! Takca! Tat! Tat! Kapackatatak! He hit the man in the back and front seat along with the driver the truck started swaying from side to side. As Goliath sped up a little more and the truck that Poochie put more holes in then fucking swiss cheese. The truck still swaying back and forth and go to the far-left crashing into the other truck Kaboom! When I looked back, I see the two trucks on the highway with flames shooting up to the sky almost. I'm thinking this shit is all over.
When I see another truck coming up on us really quick going around the two trucks on fire in the middle of the road.
Goliath yelled out, "it's one more cock sucker coming up on our left. Don't worry boss lady I got this shit."
He said to Poochie, hand me that box of Pineapples over there."
Poochie face is real puzzled I say to Poochie,
"Yo, that's an old school name for hand grenades. Dawg!"
"Oh shit, why he just didn't say that?" He reaches into the glove box hitting the button open up the stash trap compartment in the truck. It pops up and he quickly hands it to Goliath sitting them on his lap. Still driving the truck, he rolls the window down halfway. Putting the truck on automatic to keep going straight while the truck with the gunmen is shooting at us.
Goliath yelled at Poochie, "get to working that other hole back there with the boss lady Jagger told us about!" Poochie quickly jumped in the back with me. He stuck his machine gun not too far from my custom-made slot I had put in my truck. Goliath yelling at both of us and said, "okay get those choppers working back there y'all come on!"
We both started shooting at the truck still coming blasting right back at us. But our truck is bullet proof so there not doing shit to us.

But were ripping their truck to fucking shreds. They slow down just a little, but Goliath started tossing those hand grenades at their ass. After he tossed the fourth one, he rolled up the window and started speeding up like he was a stock car racer in the Daytona International Speedway. Kaboom! Boom!

Boom!

When I looked back, I stop shooting seeing the truck blow up like a fucking angry volcano to the third power. My heart is racing faster then a Ferrari speeding on the autobahn.

I got a rush from that shit when we got back to my other condo soon as I came in the door Robin came running up to along with my son Little Boom. I started kissing both of them at the same time. They just don't know how glad I am to see them both and be in one fucking piece.

Auntie is sitting in the kitchen with her friend Reggie drinking coffee. I said, "damn that coffee sure do smell good Auntie."

"I'll make you some have a seat. What about your boys?"

"Yeah. I waved at Goliath and Poochie standing by the door. Come in here boys and have some coffee with us. They both started smiling walking into the kitchen.

"Have a seat brothers your family now relax right." Auntie makes me some with a big cup, then Goliath and Poochie. I pulled out my pack of Newport's offering them one they both took one. I said, "we can go out on the deck and get lit.

Poochie said, "no disrespect boss lady but what just happen to us. I think I need something a little stronger?" We all started laughing. I think so too homey I got you okay"

"It on the deck at the bar, brother." We all began giggling then I said to both of them I really appreciate you guys. They both started smiling then Tanya and Gino Gats came in and they sat down with us drinking coffee.

We started chopping it up with one another like family do having fun. Some of us went out on my deck and made some drinks getting our puff on once I brought out a pound of weed, I had in my stash. We partied to the wee hours of the morning really enjoying ourselves.

Making My Next Move

The next day I got up a little later but when I did get up, I knew I had a lot of shit to do. So, I got washed and dressed soon as I was done, I started checking all my guns, I'm ready. I go make some coffee by myself but Poochie and Goliath are on post. I'm drinking my coffee and said to myself, damn, I have some really good men here I don't have to tell them to get on post there already doing their job. Jagger came by to check on me he came and sat with me drinking coffee telling him what we have to do next and get our spots back up and running. I got the call I been waiting for its Crazy Monk he said, **"Mimi na ndugu yake** (right now)
(I'm with his brother right now)". I'm at the Nice Town warehouse, **"Mimi Niko njiani**(I'm on my way)" I turned to Jagger and said, "come on Crazy Monk is with Emillio Julio's brother at the Nice town warehouse right now."
"Okay let's go I'll follow y'all right as we ready to go here come Tanya saying can I go?"
"Yeah, come on." We all roll out the door Goliath is driving, Poochie is riding shotgun, me and Tanya in the back seat with Jagger following us in his BMW to the spot. It took us a half hour to get there soon as we get up in the spot. Emillio is sitting at the desk with his feet up.
Crazy Monk said, "this is Emillio and he said he will help us, but He wants some money and he could not only get us his brother he can get Fat Hanky as well." I pulled up a chair and said, "okay keep talking, and we will see about the loot."
"No money first and then I'll tell you where Fat Hanky is at right now!"
"Okay how much money are you talking about?"
"30 large."
"Okay wait there Tanya come with me and give me a hand wit this loot." I go in the back room I reach up in the doorway hitting the button and the sheet rock wall slides to the side and it's a safe there. I hit the combination super quick and it pops open I grab three stacks handing it to Tanya standing there.

"I know some James Bond shit, right?"
"I know that shit is fucking lit. I hit the button back and the wall slides back, and I said, "see nobody would know it's there you know what I'm saying. When you run this spot, I'll give you the combination."
"Me?"
"Yeah, you nigga in one month. I'm moving shit back up in here now that were getting hit. You're going to run this shit for me. So put your big girl panties on!"
We both started laughing I hand her the three stacks of bills. We walk back in the room I point for Tanya to set the money on top of the desk that nigga sat up looking at the money soon as he goes to reach at the money. I put my hand on top of the money looking him right in his face. "Now here is the money start talking and if your lying to me you know I'm going to find you and kill you! You do know, that right?"
"Look you have to know this I don't bullshit about nothing I do, okay. I hate them motherfuckers I need the money so I can get back on my feet."
"Okay then where is Fat Hanky at right now?"
"He's in I-Hop with his mistress."
"What is his mistress name?"
"Ruth why?"
"Are you sure?"
"Yeah, I'm sure there going to be there for a while you can catch them there right now if you want."
"Okay you wait here the money is yours, okay nothing is going to happen to you stay here with Tanya after we go pick them up you can go all right."
"Sure, I'm good with that see I know what I'm talking about right?"
"Yeah you do just wait here Tanya keep an eye on him he can roll when I call you."
"Okay, I got it!"
"Come on y'all Jagger ride with me I have something to tell you! Poochie stay here with them Goliath come and drive me to the I-Hop it's not far from here." Soon as we get in my whip, I say to Jagger see now I know who his partner with this shit is!"
"Who his mistress?"

"Yeah to tell you the truth she just might be running the whole show."

"You don't know who she is man!"

"Well tell me then?"

"She's Trevor Tee wife!"

"Get the fuck out of here one of the old heads who run shit." "Yes, that's who she is!"

"She's running this shit not Fat Ass Hanky he's just her muscle."

It took us 20 minutes to get there we park in the big parking lot I tell him to park close. I said to Jagger, "you know what Fat Hanky looks like right?"

"Yes, I do."

"I want you to go in there and see if he's sitting with a slim light skin woman and come back." If he sees me, he knows the Jig is up he don't know you. "Okay, he gets out of my whip walking inside of the I-Hop he goes in a few minutes he comes back.

"Yeah, he's in there with a light skin woman and a thick brown skin chick too."

"Okay, I get out and get my bag from the back of my truck. I pulled out this big floppy hat and a yellow Sun dress. I slip it on. I go in the bottom of my bag getting my pistol and I get the silencer. I screw it on really swift. "Check this out y'all listen up your rolling with Jagger and Goliath when we go to get them into the truck you ride up and get us okay you got it?"

"Yeah I got it!" 10 minutes later I see them coming out okay let's go! I jumped out walking toward them with my floppy hat and sunglasses walking up to them Jagger right by my side. I see the three of them ready to walk to their car soon as I got close, I see its Ruth, Fat Hanky and Neeie. Poooouuffff!

I shot Neeie right in the middle of her head. She falls to the ground near a parked car Jagger walks up sticks his gun into Hanky side whispering, "don't you fucking move or your dead!" I put my pistol into Ruth back and said, "I should kill your ass right here bitch!" Goliath drove up with the quickness. I pushed her with my gun and said, "get the fuck in the truck!" Jagger has Fat Hanky grabbing him from the back of his neck pushing him into the truck from the other side and getting in with him.

We got both of them in the truck swift and Goliath took off out the parking lot then making a Sharpe left getting out of fucking dodge. On the way there I'm holding my gun on Ruth ass I called Tanya and tell her to let that dude roll with the loot. And for her and Poochie meet us outside in the dock area to help us out and I hang up. It only took us about 15 minutes to get to the warehouse Poochie and Tanya is waiting there as Goliath parks closer to the big steel doors of the dock area. I got out first holding my gun on Ruth and said, "come the fuck on and get out the truck you no good bitch!" She gets out bragging, "you know you dead you know, that right?"

"Yeah whatever, bitch!" Kook! I cracked her right in the head. "Now say something else, bitch!" Jagger pulled Fat Hanky out the truck and said, "come on you fat motherfucker!" Poochie stepped up grabbing Fat Hanky by his arm and hitting him in the head and chest really hard pulling him inside the door. Tanya came pulling Ruth with me inside and I close the big steel doors behind myself and locked the doors. I said, "

"take them to the back room on the left!" We get them in this big room in the corner on the right-hand side it's another little room inside with an iron door. We toss both of them inside of the dark dusty ass room and I closed the door and lock it. We walked out to the other side of the warehouse where the desk and chairs are at. Jagger whispered, "what is she talking about your dead?"

"I'll tell you in a minute putting my finger up to my lips."

We go in the other room and I sit at the desk lighting up a cigarette pulling out my phone calling up the troops telling them everything has moved up and the shit is about to hit the fan. Before everybody came, I told Tanya, Goliath and Poochie to step out of the room while I holla at Jagger for a minute. They just nodded their heads went outside the room and closed the door. I looked up at Jagger and said, "that girl I killed outside of I- Hop was Nokey Blaze wife Zelda sister Neeie."

"What?"

"Yeah so shit is going to get real fucked up for real. Yeah but she went rogue doe."

"Yeah I know that but that's his wife family there going to want my head from the door."

"So, what's going to happen then? I already know what they're going to do there going to tell you to kill me and you take over."
"Well I'm not going to do that I'm with you to the end for real Almasi."
"Thanks Dawg but they will get Philly to take me out if you say no and kill you too."
"This bitch was fucking up there money too, doe."
"Yeah, I know but that's their family that's the way they do things."
"Well that's fucked up and I'm rolling with you. I don't care how those motherfuckers do things that bitch fucked up it not your fault."
Two hours later everybody showed up at the Nice town warehouse I get Goliath, Tanya and Poochie to get more chairs from out the closets to set them up for what just might be my last sit down. But while they were doing that, I took Ruth downstairs in the basement started torturing Ruth ass because I know she's the weak link. I know the Fat man would not tell me shit and I was right I got a lot out of that bitch. I did not kill her yet, but I know she wish she was dead. I still have her down there in the dark not knowing when she is going to die.

THE SIT DOWN

Everybody I ask to come came but Gill I don't know what somebody told him, but he did not show up. I had Willie Wack-Wack and Nails Nathen track down Julio and bring him to the warehouse we put him with Fat Hanky in the back room. Sitting at the table is Dun-Dun, Rah-Killer, Nugee, Gino Gats, Mookie, Tony Smokes, Crazy Monk, Damon Gee, Booby Hill, Fly Ty, Puerto Rican Joe, Black Duke, Goliath. Ty-Kim, Chrome, Willie Wack-Wack, Nails Nathen, Fat Lou-Lou and Gavin. Taz Money Tanya and Poppy Low is on post by the doors. I looked up at everybody banging on the table I started talking loud "look this just might be the last time I talk to y'all at this **Meza**(Table)." Everybody started groaning loud and looking up at me in shock. I stand up and said, "hold up let me tell y'all what's going on first! As you know we have been getting hit hard left and right like a motherfucker! Plus, a lot of us are getting killed, I found out who was doing this shit thanks to Fat Lou-Lou! He helped me figure out who was behind this shit and its Fat Hanky one of Nokey Blaze's right-hand men!"

Everybody at the table started gasping making loud noises as I wave my hand for everybody to calm down. I'm yelling at the top of my lungs saying.

I'm not done, and he had a lot of help. I know she is the one running the whole thing is Ruth Trevor Tee's wife and she's fucking Fat Hanky putting this whole thing together to fuck me up at the head of the **Meza**(Table)and I have proof!"

Rah-Killer stood up and said, "so if you have proof why are you saying this might be the last time, you're going to be at the head of the table over here were all with you, Ma!"

"Listen up when I made my move to get them so I can have them in front of y'all to prove it I shot and killed Neeie is Nokey Blaze's wife Zelda sister. So, they just might kill me to cover all this shit up and put one of y'all at the head of the BSN that's why I said that!"

Chrome stood up and said, "so where are they at? I want to hear it from them, and I can tell if there lying or not then I'll let you know where I stand now that's fair right?"

"Yes, it is Chrome" I pointed to Tanya and Taz Money and Poppy Low standing by the door on post.
"Tanya go bring them motherfuckers up in here." Ruth is in the basement and you know where the Fat Man is at don't kill them. She just nodded her head rolling out the door with them. Damon Gee stood up and said, "I don't know about y'all but I'm with you and they can't cover this shit up because everything you said make sense. I'm with you to the end fuck that!" Everybody stands up and started clapping. A few minutes past and Taz Money, Poppy Low is dragging the two men in front of us Fat Hanky and Julio. Then Tanya came in with Ruth all beat the fuck up they close the door behind themselves. I made all of them stand near the table where we all are sitting at.
Chrome stood up walking over to them pulling out his gun and said, "so what do you have to tell me, fat man?" He looked Chrome in his face and yelled, "I'm not telling y'all shit!" Chrome putting his gun to his head ready to shoot him. When Damon Gee jumped up and yelled, "hold up Chrome man let me ask him something first!" Chrome stood back and said, "all right **Ndugu** (Brother!)" He lowers his pistol still standing there. Damon Gee got in his face said, "did the death of your son Dylon have something to do with you turning on Nokey Blaze?"
"No! I don't know what you're talking about!" Damon Gee looks over to Fly Ty. Fly Ty stood up walking over to him and said, "you're a lying ass motherfucker you were talking shit to everybody that Nokey Blaze did not let you get back at them niggas that killed your son! When Nokey Blaze had him as his bodyguard you blamed Nokey nigga for that shit!" Fat Hanky face got all twisted up not saying anything. Fly Ty nodded his head at Chrome and he quickly put the gun to his head Boom! His large frame hit the floor with the blood gushing out of his head laying on the floor twitching.
Chrome said, "yo Almasi that's enough proof for me right there I'm with you!" Then Fly Ty putting his gun up to Julio head and said, "so you got anything to tell us?"
Julio yelled, "I just went along with them after I heard that y'all had Shamika and Tamika killed for nothing!" Damon Gee said, "did you know your girl was working with the FBI?"
Julio answered, "no they did not tell me that!"

Fly Ty yelled, “everybody in this room knows they were working with the FBI but you ass hole!” Boom! Fly Ty blows his brains out he falls to the floor sideway with his brain fragments hanging out of his skull looking like pink peanuts. Fly Ty step around the blood on the floor and he came up grabbing Ruth pulling her away from the other two bodies on the floor. Fly Ty pulls her closer to everybody sitting at the table and said, “okay you know what’s up what do you have to say?”

Ruth screamed, “I don’t give a fuck just kill me! I told that bitch everything she wanted to know ask her! Fat Hanky Killed Black Leroy not me when he got wise about our plan so go ahead and kill me!” Fly Ty looked up at me. I just said, “don’t kill her let her go!”
“Why she should die like the rest of them Almasi!”
“Your right but we don’t have to do it she’s good as dead all ready.”
“I already killed that bitch and she don’t even know it yet!” “Why you say that?”
“Because she was fucking Fat Hanky and the dumb motherfucker didn’t have a code on his phone Trevor Tee is going to kill her himself.”
“But you don’t know that?
“Yes, I do. I have Fat Hanky’s phone and I just sent Trevor Tee all those fuck videos. Fat ass was making with her trust me she’s dead.”
Ruth yelled, “kill me! Kill me now! No, you have to kill me like you did the rest of them you have to!” Fly Ty let her go and said, “you’re right that’s why she wants us to kill her!” Everybody is laughing loud, “Yo Taz take her home get her the fuck out of here. Poppy you go with him and make sure she gets home too.” Everyone is laughing knowing Trevor Tee is one sick ass motherfucker thinking of all kinds of shit to kill people.

Ruth yelled, "No! You have to kill me. You said it yourself I double crossed y'all you have to kill me!" Taz Money and Poppy Low grabbing her by her arms pulling her with them while we were all still laughing. They took her to the front door with Trevor Tee waiting for her to come home because I called him letting him know I was dropping her off to him. Well after that everybody was still down with me being at the head of the **Meza**(Table). Yes, Nokey Blaze wanted to kill me after he heard about me killing his wife Zelda sister Neeie. But after Trevor Tee told him all the foul shit his wife Ruth was doing along with Neeie showing him all the videos I sent him they were talking a whole lot shit about what they were doing.

Plus, all the sex acts put the shit over the top a lot shit she doesn't do with him really pissed him off like licking up the crack of his ass and cum in her face laughing and lapping it up off her lips saying how much she loved it. Trevor Tee killed Ruth ass real slow slicing her ass up with a razor and burning her in a tub of Acid. Trevor Tee told Nokey Blaze that he killed his wife and his sister Neeie were all in the wrong fucking us over. So Nokey Blaze just dropped it and we got shit back on track and making more money then ever. Spider never came back after all these years. I talk to him here and there on the phone, but I never see him or X. They got the fuck out the game and that's what I'm thinking about doing too.

PAY BACK ON THAT ASS

It's the winter of 2010. February, I got Damon Gee by himself about getting some pay back on those Ouroboros ass holes for their role in working with Fat Hanky and Ruth for fucking with us. Damon Gee had some peoples that are close to these low life motherfuckers and I called up Top-Cat from the Black Demons Mcs to help us with some of this get back like he promised me. We had to wait a whole fucking year to get these assholes back. But to me it was too long but Damon said to me it going to be worth it. Damon Gee found out they have what they call a big mandatory meeting and there having it at this abandon warehouse at front & Tioga.

It's a super cold Friday night and the Black Demons MC's were all in the place to be just like Tee-Cee said he would be. I brought in the big guns for this shit I also called in the 3rd street Mob to make sure this shit goes down. The Demon MC's all were coming from the right side and the 3rd street Mob on the left. Then it was the BSN who had the front and the back to cover it all and it was on my word to move in. I just lift my arm and point as we have this place surrounded its midnight and time to fuck some shit up for real. We hit them like a big tree getting hit by a bolt of fucking lighting. We all hit them all at the same time it was a fucking thing of beauty. We smashed the front door with two trucks and the rest of us jumping out our trucks with machine guns and gats Kaboom! The doors caved in like it was a toothpick with the impact from the two cargo trucks we bum rush their ass.

They didn't know what the fuck hit them. Rataa tat tat tat Brrraaatttt! All you hear is machine gun fire and the loud roar of the motorcycles riding inside shooting and mowing motherfuckers down. People yelling and screaming to their deaths.

A lot of them ran out of there and got away in the darkness like little fish. Were there to kill most of the big dogs the so-called Shot callers. But Me, Dun-Dun and Tony Smokes is shooting them five and six at a time. I have to say I have not seen so much blood flying in the air it was like being on an ancient battlefield seeing so many people dying all at the same time. Rah-Killer eyes are wide with blood on her face and a smile with her crazy ass killing people with her crew enjoying every person she shot down. I can see Top-Cat, his son Dream, Jo-Jo Outlaw, Gee-Gee Thug and Doctor Jerry smoking motherfuckers left and right lighting motherfuckers up all you see is muzzle flash and shells flying everywhere. Then I looked up seeing EL Braero and his crew getting busy as well Pete, Butter, Wokey and Vegas it was like letting wild animals lose like a pack of wolfs ripping their prey apart. And blood spraying all over the place. Most of the Ouroboros gave up dropping their guns and machine guns.

Knowing they were overwhelmed, but they did try to put up a good fight. I stepped up after they gave up and I started lining them motherfuckers up Damon Gee came up pointing at all the leaders and the top dog Rey Johnny Rey meaning king in Spanish. I came up to him looking him in the face and said, "oh king Johnny, right?" He stands there with a smirk on his face blowing out smoke from the cold air breathing real hard his eyes getting wide. Top-Cat walked up handing me a machete from off his bike he did not want to get on his knees Dun-Dun and Crazy Monk came over pushing him down on the ground making him stay there holding him down. I swung back really good and Swissssss! Chopping his head clean the fuck of with the blood slashing up on the rest of his men. They all jumped and was freaked out from the blood. I love to see that look in a motherfucker's eyes. I hand the machete to Jagger to do the other three niggas and he stepped up to the plate as Dun- Dun, Mookie, Crazy Monk, Tony Smokes, Goliath and Poochie helped him out chopping of three of their heads and everybody took pictures just like they did our peoples and we got the fuck out there I shook hands with Top-Cat and the others but I gave Dream a big hug with his fine black ass. We all got ghost.

GETTING OUT OF THIS BULL SHIT

June 2018, I'm still writing down shit for my book and I'm just about done but I'm at the year 2012. Time blaze past so fast and so much things change in 2012 when Little Boom was 15 years old. His father got double life for killing his own father Mister Irving and his road Dawg Hugo over that ho bitch Wanda White aka Black Orchid. He then killed her too because she was fucking all his friends, Hugo and his whole crew behind his back. That crazy ass nigga has the fucking nerve to ask me to come see him and put some money on his books. That nigga must have been eating that funky ass bitch pussy too much and the syphilis is eating his fucking brains out or something. Well you get what your hand calls for he wanted that nasty ass bitch now he's going to die behind bars fuck him.

I have a good man by my side his name is Jaylan Black aka Jay Black. I met him 2007, he owns five Hummer and Jeep dealerships. Yeah, I know how he got his money. I can't say shit he knows what I do too. He makes the best traps for whips in the world. That's just how we met when he made some traps for my new whips and making them bullet proof. When I ask for that his eyes lit the fuck up like the Ben Franklin bridge at night laughing his ass off. We hit it off from the door with a wild off the hook romance he was like a breath of fresh air in my life. He was just what I needed too. He took me everywhere and even out of the country to all of the islands and the whole nine. And were still together to this very day

I hear a loud female voice calling my name," Sharonda Miller the warden wants to see you!"

I see the guard this dike bitch who love feeling me up. I put my pen down and I take all my papers from my book putting it back into my large yellow envelope real swift. I put it with my other things in my cell nice and neat. I walk up to the bars of the cell so I can cuff up I stick my wrists in the bar slot. She said really loud, "that will not be necessary, Miller!" When she pulled me out grabbing my arm really hard and walked me down the hall to the elevator there already have another guard bitch holding the door as we get on. The door closes and I looked at both these dike bitches.

I asked, "what the fuck is going on here?" They just looked at one another with the fat bitch who said,
"you're going to find out when you get in the wardens office! When the elevator stops, they both grabbing me on each one of my arms walking up the hall everybody is looking at me, but all the inmates are fucking smiling. I see photographers down the other end of the hallway taking pictures with the guards holding them back.
My mine is real fucked up not knowing what is about to happen. They get up to the door knocking on the door and I hear this voice that said, "come in please!" They pull me inside really fast when I walk in there is my lawyer. James Campbell stands up smiling and asked,
"how are you doing, Sharonda?" He never calls me by my government name this is fucking weird.
"I'm good what the fuck is going on here Jimmy?" He said have a seat please and we will explain it to you dear. I sit down saying to myself where is the fucking warden at. Then sitting right in front of me is this light skin black woman about 40 something with a blue pants suit on the stick up her ass corporate bitch look.
She spoke, "hello Sharonda, my name is Patricia Green I'm the new warden here I need to talk to you about getting out of here?"
"What?"
"Yes, you heard what I said what do you think about you getting out of here?"
"What is this some kind of fucking joke or something?"
"Is she smoking that shit too?"
"No this is real but it all up to you maybe your attorney can explain it to you?"
"Look this is what's going on here they want you to sign this release not to sue them with all the chain of events that happen. He slides the papers towards me.
"Hold up now what chain of events?"
My lawyer picks up the paper and he hand it to me the headlines read drugs & sex scandal rocks the justice system.
I take the paper from his hand I read some of it. And the warden came up taking the paper from my hand nice and slow saying I need for you to sign these papers please and you can go home you can read the rest of it outside of this place."
"So, if I sign this right now, I can get out of here right now?"

"Well not right now but you can leave later on tonight."
"Oh, so you have to release me in the middle of the fucking night."
"We don't look at it like that you're still getting out of here no matter how you look at it then doing life and no trial."
My Lawyer said, "just sign it Sharonda. Your son said he misses you."
"Okay give me a pen, Jimmy!" He hands me the pen I looked it over and I sign it and asked, "when are you going to let me out? We will let you know but it will be today okay."
Jimmy whispered in my ear, "there waiting for the press to go way that's all."
"Okay what I'm going to do about a ride back home?"
"Well there going to let me know when they're going to let you go and I'll pick up your son Little Boom and your fiancé Jaylan. I'll have them waiting for you." I just blew out some air and said, "all right."
I stood up and the new warden Patricia Green put her hand out and said," I'm glad we can see eye to eye on this matter." At first, I was going to leave her ass hanging but I shook her hand because I want to get the fuck out of here. Jimmy stood up and smiled at me nodding his head whispering to me, "you did the right thing." I just smirked as the warden yelled, "Guard!" The two dike twins came in the room with their hard grills grabbing me by both my arms as there taking me back to my cell. I'm walking down the long hallway to the elevator.
I can hear all this banging and all the inmates smiling at me and some of them are cheering. When we get on the elevator to go back up the fat dark skin dike said to me, "your one lucky ass bitch. I don't know what your friends did to get you out this shit but it's going to be a real shit storm with all those cases motherfuckers got up in here!" At first, I did not know what the fuck she was talking about. I'm thinking to myself" Then it hit me I only seen the judge and the pussy ass prosecutor face flashed and slashed up on the front page of the daily news. Damn, Damon Gee is a fucking genius!

The elevator stopped right before we were going to step off, I said to that fat ass ugly dike bitch, "you better be nice to me or you just might lose your fucking job too, bitch!" She grips me up and the light skin dike bitch yelled, "don't lose your fucking job over this serial killer bitch! Let her go come on Sandy! Let her go!" She let me go with her face all twisted up. I said to her, "well Sandy you're going to feel real fucking stupid tomorrow in the unemployment line you fat bitch!"

I started laughing as they walk me back to my cell and I keep hearing the banging and cheering they open my cell and the light skin dike bitch said to me, "she didn't mean it can you let that shit slide please?"

I looked at her and I said, "nigga, please!"

"Did any of y'all give me a fucking break while I was here?" I walked away from her getting my shit together to get the fuck out of there! Shit I'm dancing jumping up and down really happy there going to free a bitch! Two hours later I'm lying on my bed waiting to jet. Then I hear someone whispering to me from the front of my cell I looked up and it this light skin dike bitch again. "What the fuck you want?" She put her finger up to her lips for me to be quiet and she hands me a cell phone threw the bars. I took it and I walked toward the back of my cell and asked, "who is this?" "It's your boy Damon Gee, sis!"

"Yo, what the fuck did you do?"

"You know me girl I worked my Voo-Doo on these motherfuckers. I had all of those Armenian hookers setting up the judge, Warden and the freak ass prosecutor and I had all of it on video doing the nasty and doing cocaine in big piles Scarface style going buck wild. Plus, I have more of them helping us sell our coke and guns we got them by the short ones. That is what made them let you go because this shit been going on for a long time now." "Damn nigga you did your fucking thing!" Thank you, you're a real friend baby boy!"

"I know I'll see you at the spot when you get out and give that girl a break for me, she's working with us now, okay."

"Okay, now that you ask me to and thanks again my nigga **Moja!**(One)"

"Moja!" I walked back toward the front of the cell handing the girl the phone back and I asked, "what's your name?"

"My name is Tiffany."

"Okay Tiffany I'm going to let that shit slide for you, all right?"
"Sure thing, thanks Almasi." I'd winked my eye at her she walked off disappearing in the darkness. I lay back down on my cot and I fell asleep. Next thing I know I hear my cell opening I'm half sleep and its four guards two men and two women. The tall white man I never seen before said, "okay Miller get up and get your things now!" He hands me a plastic container to put my things in I get up getting all my things moving really quickly putting my shit in it. I get everything in there and he asked, "you done?"
I answered, "yes sir."
"Okay let's go so were walking and I don't know what time it is the place is quiet and dark while were walking down the long ass hall. To me it seems like a fucking hour while were walking down the hall to the elevator. We get on taking me down I'm looking at all of them all their faces are stone cold like there pissed off or something. They take me to processing but the funny thing about it nobody is in there just one woman behind the counter. The tall white guard hands me my papers and he point for me to put my things on top of the counter they don't even look in the container. The black woman behind the counter hands me my clothes I came in there with and a clear trash bag for me to put my things in. She points saying change over there. I walked to my right in the big locker room when I put my black blouse and black jeans on then I put my black Reeboks on and my watch two gold chains and one of them say Glock Mommy with diamonds all on the front of it.

I put on my Bamboo earrings on last I came out I had a pep in my fucking step too they point me towards the counter with the woman who said, "sign here and you can go." I pick up the pen on a chain and I never sign something so fucking fast. The tall white man along with the guard walked me to the door to let me out and he said to me good luck. I just looked at him not saying shit all I can see is the fucking front door with the glass looking out towards the dark parking lot. Soon as I walked out, I looked both ways all I can see is the yellow Dall lights and a big empty parking lot with one truck.

I see two people jump out and I looked it my son Little Boom and my man Jay Black. I ran towards them across the street with my trash bag in my hand. Shit I jumped into his arms jumping up and down, kissing my son and then my man with a very long kiss with tears running down my eyes. Then I see Jimmy walking up to me who said, "I'm so glad to see you on this side Almasi." I hugged him and said, "thanks for everything Jimmy!"

"No, you need to thank Damon Gee he's the one who got you the hell out of there I don't know what he did but he did it!"

"I know I talk to him."

Little Boom said, "come on mom lets go home!"

"You don't have to tell me twice. Fuck that!" I jumped in the back holding on to my trash bag with Jay Black closing the door fast and kissing him again. We're talking the whole way home it takes us about an hour to get home. Soon as Little Boom open the door everybody yelled, "welcome home!" Auntie came running up kissing and hugging me long with Dun-Dun with Tawni, Chrome and his girl Pam, Jagger and his lady Ta-Lisa, Rah-Killer, Goliath, Poochie, Mookie and his wife La-Neesa, Tony Smokes with his girlfriend Nashawn, Crazy Monk and his woman Danielle, Booby Hill, Puerto Rican Joe, Nugee, Gino Gats and Tanya, Black Duke and his girl Tya and EL Barero and his wife Maria.

I'm looking around for Damon Gee while each one of them is talking to me hugging me and saying there glad I'm home. Then the door opens and I'm thinking it him but its Mitchum another one of my lawyers who away bailing our peoples out when they get into some shit. He hugs me and said, "I'm so glad your home, girl!"

After an hour or so walking in the door is Damon Gee with his wife Keisha, they both came up hugging me. I asked, "what took you so fucking long, nigga?" He points at Keisha and said, "talk to her she takes so fucking long getting dressed don't look at me!" She hit him playfully laughing.

"I got a surprise for you, sis."

Yeah, what is it you done did a enough already. You're going to love this shit come here." He walks to the front door and he opens it real fast. I looked and its Xavier with his wife Tachell. "Oh, shit nigga where the fuck you been at?" I hugged him.

He said, "so what's up Shorty, you all right?"

"I'm good now, nigga. I was thinking I never see none of y'all. I hugged his wife, "how are you doing, baby nice to see you too."
"Damn, X man have you heard from Spider?"
"Yeah here and there but he's good doe. I'm just glad you're out."
Walking up is my man Jay Black. I said, "I want you to meet my man Jay Black he shakes hands with X and his wife saying, "nice to meet you I heard so much about y'all let's all get a drink?" I waved to Poochie to put my clear trash bag with my book up in the bedroom for me as I hugged him. We all walked to my big Bar on the right-hand side of my condo I waved over to my body bag crew to drink with us. They have Taz Money working the bar he comes over hugging me saying welcome home boss lady! Then he makes all of our drinks Dun-Dun came up and yelled, "everybody be quiet Almasi has something to say!" I stand in front of all of them and said, "I want to thank each and every one of y'all that was holding it down while I was away, and this toast is to my family. **Upendo Mmoja**(One Love)!"
Everybody is cheering were all had a good time until the sun came up and when everybody started going home. I went and spend time with my man. After we got busy later on that afternoon, I got that clear trash bag with my house coat on and I went out on the deck and open up my grill and I tossed that book I was writing inside of it. I got some lighter fluid spraying it. I set that shit on fire. Wassssshhhhh!
I stood there watching it burn smiling my ass off. Jay Black came walking out on the deck and said," what are you doing baby, cooking?"
"No baby just making a new start for you and me that's all."

Mwisho Kwa Sasa (The End for Now)

DEDICATIONS

Just like all of my novels I thank God for all my blessing for doing what I love to do and putting people in my life to help me achieve a level of excellences working hard on my craft. Thank you, lord, for keeping my mind body and soul right every day.

I like to dedicate this book to my younger brother Karrien Ail Williams aka Big Boo. He passed away on December 10th, 2018. He was my brother and a very good friend as well he was a hell of a father and a great music producer and a basketball referee working with the youth on top of being a great storyteller, he should have been a stand-up comedian. Because he was a very funny guy, he would make you laugh he love to laugh and have fun all the time. I talked to him when I put out my first book Dark Secrets, he knew about me wanting to be a filmmaker and writer. He said to me if I wanted to make movies, he told me by writing a good book is the way to make the movies I wanted to make. I have to say this just will be the book they will make out of a movie I know you will be smiling down on me from heaven when they do make a movie out of my books. I love you and I miss your smile and long conversation about making are own books, music and movies.

I like to thank my wife Margaret for all of her encouragement with my work on my books and screenplays she read them first letting me know if she like them or not. And telling me how much I have improved from the first time she started reading some of my work. I thank God every day for putting you in my life thank you Boo-Boo. You're my best friend and confidant in my journey in this crazy world of book publishing.

To Rasheeda wherever you are, I thank you from my first book to now I could never forget you for putting that spark under my ass of putting my stories out for the world read thank you.

To Deborah Watkins the writer thanks you so much for introducing me to your editor Tamyara Brown. I would not have got so much work done and improving in my writing and publishing. I wish you well and much success with your writing career thank you so very much.

To Tamyara Brown words are not enough for all your hard work you have done for me and continue to do for me. Thank you for all of your advice and counsel with my writing career coming from a great writer and graphic artists like your self Sis. It's a great honor having someone like you in my life now we're family. Thank you from the bottom of my heart.

ABOUT THE AUTHOR

Dartanya A, Williams was born and raised on the south side of Philadelphia. Raised by his mother Catherine and his three brothers. Birthed into a family of great storytellers Dartanya he inherited the gift and continued the tradition by writing novels. Dartanya rise from being a gang member to a hardworking citizen. A strange twist of fate, Dartanya suffered an accident on the job getting hit by a car not able to walk for months. He had to learn how to walk again during that period he turned tragedy into triumph completing eight novels and hundreds of short stories about the dark gritty street tales that range from odyssey to wild fantasy roller coaster rides. Adventurous journeys in other worlds to deep introspective tender novels about relationships new love, lost love in this sometime happy and unforgiving metropolis we all live, work and play. Throughout it all embarking on his literary journey. Dartanya is blessed with the knowledge of knowing his purpose.

Books by Dartanya A. Williams Sr.

www.dartanyaawilliamssr.com

Tee-shirts

Designed by Dartanya A. Williams

Available Now.

(Large sizes)

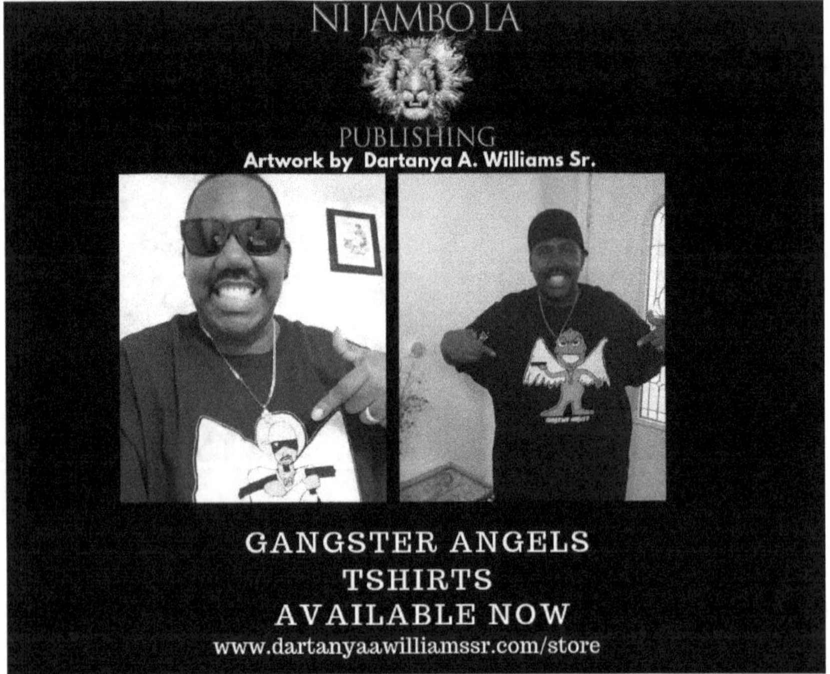

Follow me on Facebook

https://www.facebook.com/Dartanya-A-Williams-SR-Authors-Page

Follow Me on Twitter

https://twitter.com/DartanyaSr

Follow Me on Instagram

https://www.instagram.com/dartanyasr/

Subscribe to my Blog and Newsletter

https://mailchi.mp/899ecbfa8b71/what-is-cool-278395